Special Operations

RH Wood

Copyright ©2002 ©2020 RH Wood
All rights reserved.
ISBN: 9798679949744

Other Titles from RH Wood:

Special Operations
Axis Revisited
Innocence Lost
Silicon Dreams
Plain Sight
Lightning Crashes
The Fourth Estate
Technocracy
Empires
Birthright
Holding Out for Heaven
Thirty Days at Zeta
To Walk with Gods
The Captains

Novellas:

Les Champs-Elysees
L'argent, le Meurtre, et le Football
Pour L'amour et le Football
Partie Finale à Paris

Author's Note:

    This is the first novel I wrote, mainly out of sheer boredom. It was 1995 and I'd been hospitalized for a week for a suspected heart attack (it wasn't). The TV channels in the hospital were shit so I had my wife bring me a five-subject notebook so I could scribble down my ideas for a plot and the characters to populate it. I didn't know how to type at the time and taught myself on a Brother word processor (remember them?) I bought when I got out of the hospital. It was originally published in November of 2002 after I finally got the story to where I wanted it. I'd assumed it was a one-off, just to prove I could author a book (I like trying new things just to see if I can), never planning to write a series of close to two dozen more that would follow between then and now. My life has changed incredibly since that week in the hospital twenty-five years ago, mostly in ways I never thought it would.

    I don't really know why I decided to look this manuscript over now, so many years after it was published, probably fifteen years since the last time I'd read it. I've generally ignored my early stuff once it was published. My writing style has changed over the years and maybe I didn't want to look back and realize how lousy my writing was at the beginning – it still isn't anywhere near great literature, but I found my groove. Reading it now, I'm pretty impressed with myself because it's better than I thought it was, being it was my first effort and the most I'd written previously were book reports for school. Maybe it was because after not writing anything for the past two years since my wife died suddenly (June 2018), I wanted to get a feel for my mindset when I began this adventure to get back in the swing of storytelling again. Maybe because underneath it all, my books are love letters to her (she was the inspiration for the Connie character, if you weren't aware) and it was the first of them. Who knows but I have a new appreciation for it.

That said, when this book was originally published, there was no Amazon (at least not the way it is today), no Kindle, no such thing as an e-book. Since it's fallen out of print with my original publisher and I've done a bit of editing since I blew the dust off it again, I thought of putting out this second edition. I didn't change the story any, just edited a few words and phrases that have become archaic over the past quarter-century and cleaned up some of the grammar. It'll also be less expensive and available in many more formats than just a paper version. I never entertained thoughts of becoming famous or actually making a living off writing, just doing it to entertain friends. If I can make it cheaper to read and have the ability to entertain more people, I'm a happy camper. So, I give you the second edition of my first effort, *Special Operations*, and I hope you enjoy it.

~ Rich Wood
Lawton, Oklahoma
August 2020

***

As always, for Karen and the Little Blue Dog.

~ Rich Wood, Long Island, New York 2002

***

In memory of:

Karen Brickman
1961 – 2018

The Little Blue Dog (Shayna Mädel)
1998 – 2010

***

"Sometimes I sleep, sometimes it's not for days,
The people I meet always go their separate ways,
Sometimes you tell the day,
By the bottle that you drink,
And times when you're all alone, all you do is think,

I'm a cowboy, on a steel horse I ride,
I'm wanted, dead or alive,
Wanted, dead or alive,
Oh, and I ride ..."

~ Bon Jovi

Prologue
Georgetown, D.C.
May 1995

"Jesus Christ," he said as he sat straight up from a sound sleep. The sweat ran from him even though the house was not overly warm. Richard Edward Johnson rose from his bed, careful not to wake his wife, and walked into his den. He walked directly to the bar and poured himself two fingers' worth of Jack Daniel's, which he knocked back in one shot.

It was a nightmare; it always was when he woke up this way. Checking the clock, it said three fifteen and he knew there would be no going back to sleep. He went to the shower instead, washing the sweat away along with the visions of death and destruction that woke him.

It wasn't as if this were new to him, he'd had nightmares for over a decade, but in the last few months, they'd gotten worse, more vivid, more real, and in color. *I need help*, he thought as he toweled himself dry.

But it wasn't as easy as that for the cause of the disturbing dreams was not public knowledge; in fact, very few knew the circumstances of his mental distress. He dressed in the den, again in consideration for his wife, and the coffee was finished when he was. He mixed a mugful with milk and sugar and began his search for the car keys and his briefcase.

"Nightmares again?" His wife asked from the bedroom door.

Johnson went to her, kissing her lips lightly. "Nothing to worry about, baby," he assured her.

"They've gotten worse since ..."

"I know," he said. "But I'll get a handle on them. Have you seen my car keys?"

"You should talk to someone, Rick," she insisted.

"Would you like to make a suggestion as to *whom* I should talk to?" He growled at her.

"The company shrink?"

"And what am I supposed to tell him? I sure as hell can't tell him what went on two months ago," Johnson shot back. "I've had these episodes before and I've dealt with them. My car keys?"

"The table next to the front door," she said, kissing him again. "Will you be home at a reasonable hour tonight since you're going in so early?"

"I'll try, baby," he said. "I love you."

"I love you too," she said, returning to bed as he walked out the door.

The Crown Victoria started without hesitation and he placed the mug in its assigned holder in the door. Backing out of the driveway, he thought about the vivid, disturbing dream, the killing, the blood and gore, and the tragic loss of innocent life. What happened two months ago was just the culmination of events set in motion over a decade before.

"If I'd known then," he said to no one. Thirty-five year old Richard Johnson thought about a time when he was a brash twenty two year old Special Forces troop who believed he had the world by the balls. "But no one knew, no one *could* have known back then. Hindsight's twenty-twenty." He shrugged as he made the right on K Street. In a minute, his destination was in sight. Looming in the distance, the Rotunda of the White House gleaming in the dark sky was breathtaking. "Hell, why did I have to steal that car in the first place?"

Bay Shore, Long Island, New York
20 February 1980

"So, this is it," seventeen year old Rick Johnson said to his father.

"What did you expect, Richard?" The elder asked. "Had I not arranged this with the judge, you'd have a juvenile arrest record."

"Damn it, pop, did you have to sign me up for six years?"

"It is small price to avoid six months in juvenile hall," elder Johnson growled.

"It isn't six years of *your* life," younger fumed.

"I fought in two wars, Richard. Those were *seven* years of my life and I spent them ducking bullets." Richard Johnson Senior shook his head. "Put in your time and learn some responsibility, son," he said resignedly. "They will turn you into a man if you'll allow it."

"I *am* a man, pop."

"You're a punk kid," father shot back. "And six months in prison would have made you a bigger one by the time you got out." There was a knock on the window of the car by a man in uniform.

"Are you ready, Rick?" Tech Sergeant Eddie Otero said.

"I'll be right there, Ed," Rick said with a shrug. "I'll never forgive you for doing this," he said to his father.

"I'd wager you'll thank me for it once you get out of basic training," his father smiled.

"Whatever," Rick sighed and opened the door, but his father grabbed his arm and pulled him into a hug.

"Never forget that your mother and I love you, son," he whispered as he held his only child tightly.

"I won't," Rick said, pulling away and getting out of the car.

"And, Richard?"

"Yeah, pop?"

"Don't volunteer for *anything*."

"What's that supposed to mean?"

"You'll see soon enough, son," he said and drove away.

"Welcome to the U.S. Air Force, Rick," Eddie Otero said.

"Yeah, thanks," Johnson muttered as he boarded the bus that would take him to the Armed Forces Processing Center at Fort Hamilton in Brooklyn. "*What* made me steal that car?" He shook his head as the bus rolled away.

Part One:

Causes

July 1983

Chapter One

The White House, Washington, D.C.

4 July 1983

"They are waiting for you, Mr. President," Secretary of Defense Caspar Weinberger said as he entered the Oval Office.

"Just a minute, Cap," President of the United States Ronald Reagan replied. He turned back to the window, watching the crowd on the Mall as the Fourth of July festivities continued. The Washington monument was backlit by wave after wave of fireworks, the cheers by the enthusiastic masses heard even through the bulletproof windows. He waited a minute longer before turning his attention to SECDEF.

The two men then headed out, down the hall to the elevator, which took them to the basement of the White House. The Situation Room was a short walk from there, where the National Security Council waited. All rose when the President arrived.

"What is the word from Geneva?" Reagan asked of Secretary of State James Baker.

"The talks have broken down, sir," Baker said. "The North Koreans left the table an hour ago and are heading back to Pyong Yang.

"Is the team ready to go?"

"Yes, Mr. President," Weinberger said.

"Very well, send them in and keep me informed."

USS *Tarawa*, (LHA-1), the Sea of Japan

U.S. Air Force Major Nathan Beu flipped the master power switch and began the engine start sequence. The right-side engine spun up before the fuel was ignited, the whine of the turbine getting louder. Behind him, in the cargo bay of the MH-53J Pave Low II, twelve commandos of Alpha Flight, 23rd Special Tactics Squadron gave their weapons and equipment one final check.

They'd practiced this drill before, but this was no drill. It was the real thing and the consequences of failure would be dire. Beu, along with his aircrew and commandos were part of the Air Force's 1st Special Operations Wing and this would be their coming of age.

Major Beu was not thrilled with the idea, born of the failed raid into Iranian territory several years back; the ill-conceived attempt to rescue the American hostages, but he'd volunteered for this duty, along with all the others inside the big black chopper.

Air Force 1st Special Operations was the flying service's answer to the Green Berets and Navy SEALs, the commandos trained the same way as their Army and Navy counterparts. None of the military branches wanted this, but it had been pushed through at the behest of Congress and the President and rammed down the throats of the Joint Chiefs of Staff.

The idea of an Air Force commando unit was redundant at best, a waste at worst, and this would be their first chance to prove themselves. Beu, a Vietnam veteran of the search and rescue fraternity believed that was what the Air Force did best, finding downed airmen and retrieving them from enemy territory. Covert offensive action, he believed, was best left to the Army, Navy, and Marine Corps, but none had asked for his opinion; fighters and bombers were one thing, ground troops another. The fact he was operating off a Marine amphibious ship was another, but that was a completely different argument. He'd already complained to everyone he could, but they said it was imperative this was a joint mission.

"A joint mission, my ass," he muttered. The only involvement and the little commitment on behalf of the Navy and Marine Corps was the fact they were allowing him and the Air Force contingent to take up deck and berthing space on their barge.

"This is Cowboy-261, requesting departure clearance," he said.

"The deck is clear, vector east to zero-nine-zero, Cowboy," the Air Boss aboard *Tarawa* replied.

Beu pulled up on the collective and the big black bird went light, lifting off the deck of the amphibious assault ship. He turned east once he cleared the ship and then dropped to wave top level, a hundred miles out he turned north. The American Navy and the Japanese were conducting training exercises off the Korean coast and that would provide cover for the insertion of the commandos.

North Korean ships could be seen on his radar and, should he be spotted, the Communists would target the Pave Low for he was about to cross over into their airspace. This first commando mission conducted by U.S. Air Force ground troops would come to an abrupt end should he be spotted before he returned to friendlier skies.

"Five minutes until feet dry," Beu said for the benefit of his crew and passengers. In five minutes, they would be over land, over the northern part of the Korean Peninsula where discovery would be construed as an act of war.

Osan, South Korea

The young woman waited as she always did when he was gone, her mind most definitely not on her job. Nineteen-year-old Song Yung Shu wiped off the bar listlessly, her thoughts fixed on the man she loved, though she knew not where he was or what his mission demanded of him. It had been this way for two years, and she'd learned to live with it, though she didn't like it at all.

"Get to work," Song Mai Kim, her mother and owner of the Pink Lady hissed at her. "There are thirsty people in here," the older woman said.

Yung Shu looked to where her mother pointed, to the table around which sat seven Air Force troops who'd arrived a few minutes before. She picked up the tray and began to walk over, passing by her mother who gave her an evil look.

"Don't worry about him," her mother said. "He will be fine."

"And suppose he is hurt or killed, mother," Yung Shu replied. "Will they tell me? Do they even care that he and I are in love? Do *you*?"

"He is tough and strong, but most of all he is smart, and nothing will happen. He said that it was a training mission, didn't he," Mai Kim said in her hard tone.

"It's *always* a training mission, mother," Yung Shu spat. "For two years all they have done is train and practice. One day it will be for real, with real bullets, and he could be killed. What will I do if he is dead?"

"The same thing that I did when your father died," Mai Kim said. "You will carry on, just as I had to. Hopefully, nothing will happen to him."

"I don't want to spend the rest of my life in this bar, mother. I don't want a future waiting on American GIs as they ogle the girls. I want a life with Rick in the U.S., where we can have children and give them opportunities that you or I never had." Yung Shu did not expect the slap on her cheek.

"This place has given you a *life*, Yung Shu," the older woman admonished. "Without the Pink Lady, you would be picking through the dump for your daily bread. Your father died making this place what it is. Have some *respect* for him."

"He died too young, and so will *you*."

"Do you actually think that Rick will *marry* you? He is an American and once his tour is finished, he will leave, just like all the others have for the past thirty years. Don't you see, my daughter, they come here, use us to quench their lust and then leave; many leaving behind children that become outcasts in our society."

"Rick is not like that," Yung Shu protested. "He loves me, and I love him."

"I don't doubt that, but Rick's destiny is not his own. He has to go where the Air Force sends him and you should be realistic about it. Enjoy the time you have with him, my dear. He will not be in your life forever."

"He will marry me and take me out of here, just you wait."

"I hope you are right, Yung Shu," Mai Kim said before returning to her office. "I hope you are right."

Nam Po, North Korea

They took cover as the chopper lifted off, each searching the area for signs of North Korean Peoples' Army troops. After ten minutes of intense silence, the black clad commandos felt confident that they had not been spotted. Using hand signals, 2nd Lieutenant Robert Jenkins called them over. They assembled around a large boulder where Jenkins spread out a laminated map of the local area.

"Campbell and Guthrie," Jenkins said. "You're on point."

"Yes, sir," both said in a southern drawl before moving off into the brush, their silenced Heckler and Koch MP-5 submachine guns at the ready.

Jenkins looked to Senior Airman Richard Johnson and Airman First Class Jerome Emory, the flight's explosives experts. "Do you two have your shit together?"

"Yes, sir," Emory, one of the two African American members of Alpha Flight answered for them while Johnson made one last check of his gear. He carried twenty pounds of the Czech-made Semtex in addition to several types of detonators.

"Johnson?" Jenkins asked.

"Yeah, almost done," the New Yorker replied.

"Change that attitude, Airman," Jenkins warned.

"Do *you* want to play with this shit, Lieutenant?" Johnson held up the bag full of plastic explosive.

"Easy, Rick," Chief Master Sergeant Alvin Corlies said. Corlies was the veteran of the group, enlisting during the Vietnam War and staying in after three tours. His assignment to 23rd was his last before being eligible to retire and had been seriously considering opting for an early out. Jenkins was young, this being his first command after graduating the Air Force Academy, and Corlies spent most of the time ironing out differences between the lieutenant and the enlisted men, between Jenkins and Johnson in particular. "Get going, son."

"Right, Chief," Johnson replied before he and Emory disappeared into the night.

"I'm going to hang that son of a bitch one day, Chief," Jenkins promised.

"He's young, sir," Corlies soothed. "He'll settle down."

"He's crazy and if he screws up, I'm going to be on him like stink on shit."

"You have to be a little nuts to do what he does," Corlies replied before setting off after his men. Jenkins and the rest of the team followed.

Osan Air Base, South Korea

"Alpha Flight is on the ground, sir," 2nd Lieutenant Alan Holmgren said to the colonel that stood at his left shoulder. "Confidence is high."

"Keep an eye on them, Lieutenant," Colonel Williams said. "If you see anything spooky, I want you to send the chopper for them."

"Yes, sir." Holmgren was the intelligence officer for 23rd STS and received real-time satellite imagery of Alpha Flight as they prosecuted their mission. He was tasked with observing the NKPA troops that were massed near A-Flight's target, Foundry #5, just outside Nam Po.

There was a division size unit stationed there, moved from Pyong Yang when the anti-proliferation talks in Geneva began, just in case the talks broke down. The CIA believed that the North Koreans expected a covert assault on the foundry, known to be producing parts for the nuclear breeder reactor program being developed in Songwon.

Construction had begun on the reactor designed to produce weapons grade plutonium for a secret nuclear missile program, located near Yong Hung. It was believed that the North Koreans were operating with the consent of the Chinese and the help of the Soviet Union. Until a few days ago, A-Flight's mission was just a contingency, in case the talks in Geneva that had been progressing smoothly took a turn for the worst. Today, word that come from Washington that the North Koreans had abruptly left the talks and that the mission would go forward as planned.

Holmgren checked the monitors once again for evidence that A-Flight had been spotted, but his thoughts, like the young girl in the topless bar on the other side of town, were elsewhere. He too had reason to worry about a lover who was heading into harm's way, and he too knew that the Air Force cared not of his worry. Unlike the girl though, Holmgren could not go to friends or family for comfort, for his love for Airman First Class Roger Hoffman went completely against Air Force regulation.

They'd kept the secret since they met at Fairchild Air Force Base three years before, a chance meeting between the two closeted homosexuals blossoming into a full-fledged love affair. It was fate that brought them together during survival training and found them assigned to the same unit afterward. Fate had also brought them here, to South Korea, Holmgren counting his blessings that that he was able to keep an eye on Roger via satellite as A-Flight groped through the darkness toward the target.

They'd also made plans for the long term, Roger to leave the military in a year when his enlistment expired. Although Holmgren planned to make the Air Force a career, once Roger was out, they could finally live together with much less fear of discovery. In addition to their homosexuality, the military also frowned on officers and enlisted fraternizing during their off-duty hours. Until Roger was out, they were subject to prosecution on both counts. Holmgren turned his attention back to the monitor, his hand drifting to the screen. He placed his palm over the twelve figures that shone bright blue in the satellite's infrared camera.

"Be careful, Roger," he said softly.

Chapter Two
Nam Po, North Korea
5 July 1983

"Four and Five in position, sir," Johnson whispered into the throat-mounted microphone.

"Rog, Four," Jenkins replied and turned to Corlies, who was scanning the area with his night vision goggles. They'd hiked through the night, arriving at the foundry just before sunrise and setting up a perimeter around the factory.

"All's quiet," the chief said.

"Good." Jenkins allowed himself a sigh of relief. It had been dicey for a while, an NKPA patrol coming within a few feet of his command post several hours earlier. Sergeant John Reasoner was close enough to one of the Koreans to be pissed on as the man relieved himself in the darkness while Reasoner crouched at the base of a tree. "Everyone get comfortable," Jenkins said into his microphone. "We hit them tonight."

***

KGB Colonel Yevgeniy Kosarev knocked back the shot of vodka as he sat across from his aide, Lieutenant Marko Zhukov, contemplating the awful tasting sausage that passed for breakfast at the hotel where they stayed.

"Isn't is a bit early for that, my friend," Zhukov said as he made a face. The thought of drinking vodka at eight in the morning made his stomach heave.

"If you lived in this shithole as long as I have, you would drink your breakfast also," Kosarev growled. The tall, prematurely gray, bear of a man considered the younger Zhukov and shook his head. "Put in for a transfer, Marko. It would be a shame to bring Mira here after you are married."

"Is that why Katherine is still in Moscow, Yevgeniy?" Zhukov asked the older man sarcastically. "Or do you have a little slant-eyed thing here?"

"Katherine lives well in the *Rodina*, in a style that she does not want to give up," Kosarev explained. "And I have Alexa to think about. I do not want my daughter growing up surrounded by these yellow barbarians."

"Ah, the beautiful Alexa. Aren't you afraid that she might fall for one of the young *apparatchiks* that are coming to power in Moscow? How old is she now, Yevgeniy?"

"Nineteen, and all the young men fear her mother," Kosarev laughed. "Should they come calling, she would send them home with a shoe in their butts."

"Ah, now I know why you volunteer for this duty, my old friend, you fear her too."

"It is possible, Marko, but I miss her as well. I miss Alexa most of all." The man got wistful. "She has become a woman while I have been gone."

"Then why are you here? You have enough pull in the Kremlin to get any assignment you want; you could walk in there and demand to be appointed Chairman of the Komitet. Why have you stayed *here* for fifteen years?"

"Unfinished business," Kosarev said, taking a bite of the sausage and making a sour face as he swallowed it.

"*Anyone* can do this job, Yevgeniy," Zhukov countered. "Your talents would be more useful in Moskva; your career would soar."

"I don't care about my career. I care about what that little worm will do with the technology we sold him," Kosarev snapped.

"Major Park?"

"Of *course*." Kosarev stabbed at another piece of meat. "Do you think he will be satisfied with just *having* nuclear capability? The schizophrenic fool will not be content until he is able to *use* it."

"You worry too much, my friend. He would not use it against *us*," Zhukov replied. "It is the South Koreans and the Americans that have to worry about Major Park."

"Regardless of how we feel about the American government and their allies, there are still millions of innocent lives that will be destroyed if he does. War is war, Marko, but Park cannot be trusted to use them defensively. The fools in the Kremlin do not want to believe it, but I know the man."

"He is years away from deployment, Yevgeniy, maybe a decade. Do you plan to stay here that long?"

"As long as I have to, Marko."

***

"Have you confirmed the reports, Lan?" Major Kim Sun Park of North Korean Internal Security asked.

"No, sir," Captain Lan Chen Deng replied, certain this would anger his diminutive commanding officer. Park failed to disappoint.

"There are a thousand troops surrounding this factory and none of them managed to spot an American helicopter? What kind of outfit are you running?" Park stood suddenly and came from behind his desk. The much taller Lan took one step back.

"We only have the word of an elderly dirt farmer, sir, hardly a reliable witness," Lan said, hoping his boss would be satisfied.

"What about the Soviet engineers? They are quartered out there; have they seen anything?"

"No, sir, but they are not the most reliable either. When they are off duty, they drink themselves into a stupor. They would not know if a helicopter landed on top of their dormitory." Lan backed up even more, trying to position himself for a fast getaway should Park become violent. The captain could easily subdue the man, but the burly bodyguard dressed in civilian clothes was much more formidable. With a word from Park, the man known only as Cho would not hesitate to put a bullet into Lan's brain.

"There are Americans here, Lan, and I want you to find them. I do not care what it takes, even if it calls for requesting more troops. You will find them and bring them to me," Park ordered.

"But Major Park . . ."

"Do I detect insubordination in your voice, Captain?" Park gave him a look that said he was only seconds from death.

"No, sir."

"I didn't think so." Park returned to his chair. "Do not come back to this office until you are able to inform me of your success."

"Yes, sir." Lan bowed and left hurriedly.

"Make sure he does his job, Cho," Park said after Lan departed. The man merely nodded and left to carry out his orders.

***

Dusk was falling on the hillsides around Foundry #5, the lengthening shadows allowing the commandos to leave their hiding places and stretch their legs. Work had gone on during the daylight hours at a furious pace, trucks rolling in and loading up with pipe before leaving on their way to Yong Hung.

The patrols were sparse and kept to the dirt roads that circled the perimeter of the plant. There had been a few scares when one of the patrols would stop and scan the hills with high-powered binoculars, but the Americans had avoided detection thanks to their skill at camouflage. Emory and Johnson came closest to being discovered, their hooch a mere hundred yards from the factory's main gate, but luck was on their side and the patrol passed them by.

Jenkins, under Corlies' oversight, had spread the small band out, surrounding the facility in an attempt to monitor the Korean troop movements. As the darkening spread, he moved his men closer; close enough for the building to be within range of their submachine guns. About half the team had now taken positions within the perimeter of the barbed wire fence surrounding the factory.

"It's time, sir. Johnson and Emory have to move now if we want to meet the chopper tonight," Corlies said as he checked his watch.

"It's still twilight, Chief; they could be spotted."

"It's either now or we wait another night. It'll take them a while to plant the charges in the right place. It's your call, sir, but I advise sending them now. From the way their patrols are moving, it appears that they have an inkling we are here."

Jenkins thought for a moment before nodding in agreement. "Give them the word."

***

Johnson slid out of the scrub on his belly, his submachine gun cradled in his arms and the bag of explosives on his back. There was extraordinarily little cover between the fence and the building, aside from the staging area for the trucks. Emory waited at the edge of a small copse of scrub pine, his weapon trained to give Johnson cover should he be spotted. Once Johnson found a reasonably safe spot under one of the trucks, he motioned to Emory to follow.

The process took them twenty minutes, crossing the hundred-yard stretch and working their way to the loading docks. They waited another fifteen while the day shift workers left for the day and the night shift came on duty. When all settled into their routines, the two commandos pressed on.

Again, Johnson went first, slipping inside the open bay doors, left that way to combat the oppressive heat given off by the smelting process. Dropping his pack behind a machine, he gave the signal for Emory to follow, both squatting down behind it.

"Timers," Johnson said as he handed Emory five of them. "Set them for twenty minutes."

"Twenty minutes," Emory parroted, telling Johnson that he heard and understood. Johnson then gave him ten of the one-pound blocks of Semtex.

"Fuse them two in parallel," Johnson said. Two blocks would be detonated by one timer, due to the heavy construction of the machinery used in the foundry. Both men sweated buckets as the hundred plus degree heat assaulted them. Inside their black jumpsuits and under their Kevlar helmets, the heat seemed to be magnified fivefold. "Put them there, there, and there," Johnson pointed to indicate where the explosive bundles should be placed. "Put them close to the floor on the supports. When they go, it should be enough to bring the smelters down. I'll take the ones on the other side, so give me a couple minutes to get over there."

"You got it, New York," Emory said, giving him a toothy grin. Both were fired up, their adrenaline coursing at light speed through their veins. Both loved to blow things up and this was the first time that they could do it for real. Johnson gave him thumbs up and returned the grin before setting off along the wall.

As he neared his destination, he froze in fear when a group of engineers approached him, their attention to the clipboard one of them held, only paying cursory mind to where they were going. Johnson ducked behind an equipment cart before being spotted, waiting as they passed, moving toward Emory's location. *Shit, that was close*, he thought. Although he was, by definition, an adrenaline junkie, that was too close for comfort.

Richard Johnson had always been one from the time he'd been a teenager, boosting cars and going for joyrides, ditching them just before the local police caught him. The last episode was the reason he was in the Air Force in the first place, a juvenile court judge making military service a requirement of his probation. Looking back at it, he realized that he'd let himself be caught; a cry for help from a young man who'd known that a life in jail would certainly follow if he continued on that path. The Air Force had given him a place where he could achieve the release he sought and a sense of honor and duty that his parents had tried desperately to instill on the unruly teen. It also carried an unexpected benefit in the form of the beautiful girl called Song Yung Shu.

He shook his head to clear the picture of her from his mind's eye and bring his attention to the task at hand. Still having to traverse another fifty feet, plant his explosives, and then make his way back out of the building, he did *not* need the distraction; something Yung Shu did very well.

Johnson poked his head from around the cart, checking for others that might sound an alarm. The coast clear, he moved on, stopping for a second to watch the huge bucket dump a load of molten steel into a crucible with a shower of sparks. The sight and the intense heat required to turn steel into a red liquid awed him. He pressed on, reaching his destination in another ninety seconds.

Looking back, he caught a glimpse of Emory as he slithered to the other smelter before disappearing behind it. Johnson opened the bag and took out the Semtex, making five small bundles before attaching the timers. Leaving one behind after setting it, he moved on quickly, positioning the deadly parcels in the appropriate places to do the most damage. The charges planted, he retraced his route back to the equipment cart, the halfway point between himself and where Emory waited patiently for his return. As he peeked around the side to see if the coast was clear, he was startled by a sound behind him. Johnson turned quickly to see an engineer come around the cart from the other side.

"Who are you?" The Caucasian man asked in Russian. Johnson's answer came in the form of his Ka-Bar slamming into the man's chest. Blood spurted from the wound, showering Johnson with the sticky red fluid. He removed the bloody knife and jammed it back into the man, this time into his neck, severing the spinal cord. The man dropped in a heap and Johnson took off at a run.

There was no time for stealth as the timers wound down. There were shouts behind him and bullets spat from several rifles, zipping past his head. Emory had his H&K raised and returned fire, dropping Rick's pursuers, but they had already sounded the alarm.

Johnson spun and fired off a fusillade in the direction of another group of soldiers, sending them scrambling for cover. Emory was already out the bay door by the time Johnson reached it, again firing to slow the defenders.

"We got trouble, Lieutenant," Johnson screamed as soon as he was out of the building, his radio's performance no longer affected by the concrete and steel structure. He did not need to elaborate as searchlights on the roof pierced the night with their sodium beams.

Bullets flew from both sides as the commandos opened up on the security people who found cover wherever they could. A dozen fell in the doorways as the men of A-Flight laid down withering fire. SRA Gibbs and A1C Hoffman returned fire with the fifty caliber M2, Hoffman feeding the bandoliers into the breach as Gibbs kept the trigger buried. Several of the red-hot slugs hit trucks parked nearby, causing their fuel tanks to explode in a shower of burning diesel and deadly metal shrapnel. A squad of NKPA was doused with the flaming liquid, setting them afire. They writhed on the ground, trying to extinguish themselves before they were immolated, but to no avail.

"Pull back," Jenkins ordered from his command post, but the words were unnecessary. The commandos continued the horrible fire as the two explosives people ran across the open yard to the cover of the trees. Johnson and Emory arrived, out of breath but unharmed.

"What the fuck did you do, Johnson?" Jenkins was furious.

"I was spotted, and I had to kill one of them," he replied. "We gotta get out of here. The place is going to blow in about ten minutes."

"You were supposed to do this *quietly*," Jenkins continued.

Johnson just shrugged. "Shit happens," he said by way of explanation.

"We have to go, sir," Chief Corlies insisted. "We have four miles to go to meet the chopper and it'll be here in an hour."

"Your ass is in a sling when we get back, Johnson," Jenkins warned. "This isn't the end of it."

"We'll see," Johnson spat. He shouldered his weapon and set off in the direction of the landing zone.

***

"We have the Americans, sir," Captain Lan said as he reached Park's office. "They are on the run, but we will catch up with them soon enough."

"What happened downstairs?" Park asked.

"Two of them were spotted inside the foundry when they killed one of the Russian engineers," Lan informed him.

"Ready my helicopter; we will follow them from the air," the little man said. Park's Chinese made helicopter waited on the roof, the engine running by the time the three men got there, lifting off as soon as they were aboard.

***

"Do they have air support?" Corlies asked Airman Nick Mason over the radio. Mason's six-foot seven-inch body was perched on a rocky outcropping above them as he scanned the area with NVGs.

"I see a small chopper up, but that's it," Mason replied. "It doesn't look armed."

"They may have infra-red; we have to keep moving." Corlies turned to Jenkins. "What about troops?"

"They're coming out of the place like ants, they'll be up here any minute," Mason said, just as a shot caromed off the rocks at his feet.

"Let's go," Corlies said and one by one, the commandos disappeared into the woods.

Osan Air Base, South Korea

"Acquiring satellite," the overhead imagery specialist said as she typed commands to the computer. "Online now."

"Oh my *God*," Holmgren gasped as the monitor came to life. The infrared cameras showed several hundred NKPA troops streaming out of the dormitories near Foundry #5, not far behind the men of A-Flight.

"Where's the chopper?" Colonel Williams asked.

"About forty minutes out," another of the intelligence people said.

"It's going to be close," Williams said, mainly to himself.

"Can we get them any more help?" Holmgren asked, trying to keep his emotions in check. Roger was down there, probably trading fire with the NKPA as they closed in on the small band.

"They're on their own until the Pave Low gets there," Williams advised.

"You can't do that," Holmgren shrieked as he stood to face the senior officer. "We have to get them some air support."

"At *ease*, Lieutenant," the colonel admonished. "We can't start a war and we will if we send a bunch of fighter planes across the border. There are a million NKPA troops waiting on the other side. Sit down and man your post or you will be relieved."

"Yes, sir," Holmgren said as he took his seat. He forced himself to look at the monitor as one of the commandos was hit.

Nam Po, North Korea

"Hoffman's down," Johnson called over his radio as the man fell next to him. He bent to his mate, tearing open Hoffman's shirt, revealing the carnage that was once his chest. Roger struggled for every breath as the life began to slip out of him. "Hold on, Rog."

On either side of him, the others fired relentlessly into the approaching Korean line. Grenades exploded nearby as the Koreans lobbed them in non-stop. The noise of the grenades was diminished by a succession of louder explosions, ten of them in rapid fire when the charges in the factory blew. It sounded as if Hell had been unleashed but Johnson ignored everything, opening his med kit, and packing Hoffman's chest with bandages.

"Hold on, Roger, we're almost home," he said to the dying man. Hoffman grabbed his arm.

"Leave me, Rick, I'm dead anyway," he said between gasps.

"Bullshit." Johnson finished packing the wound and hoisted Hoffman onto his shoulders in a fireman's carry. He felt Hoffman's blood saturate his uniform as he ran though the brush, branches whipping his face.

More fire erupted from the Korean lines when they spotted him, bullets ricocheting around him. He felt a few more rounds hit Hoffman and then heard the last breath escape his body before it went limp.

***

Beu pushed the engines to full power when he saw the conflagration in the distance. Tracer rounds pierced the night below, telling him that the commandos were under fire and fighting for their lives. Smaller explosions erupted as grenades were exchanged between the NKPA and A-Flight.

"We got another chopper in the air, Major," Sergeant Hermann Wood, the door gunner, said. "It doesn't look friendly."

"Concentrate your fire on the ground troops," Beu said as he dipped the nose toward the LZ.

"I can't see where our guys are," Wood replied.

"It doesn't matter, spray everything on the low ground."

Wood and his counterpart on the other side of the aircraft did as the pilot ordered, firing off a terrible barrage that split the night with tracers. Seconds later, the chopper began taking sporadic fire from the Korean ground troops in a vain effort to shoot it down.

***

They fired blindly now; a perimeter of sorts was established on a promontory and the American commandos made their best attempt to keep the Koreans to the low ground. Chief Corlies activated an infrared beacon and tossed it into the clearing behind them, a marker for the Pave Low crew indicating the LZ. Jenkins was giving Corlies cover when a rocket-propelled grenade blew only feet away, shredding both men with ruthless efficiency.

"Chopper's here," John Reasoner informed his men, as he was now in command, and began to work his way the last few yards to the LZ. "Let's *go!*"

At Reasoner's words, their perimeter tightened as the chopper flared for a landing. One by one, the commandos fell back, still firing into the Korean forces. The Pave Low's gunners joined, the merciless twenty-millimeter fire cutting down soldiers and trees alike without discrimination.

"We ain't gonna make it, Rog," Johnson said to the corpse on his back as he emptied another clip into a group of NKPA that seemed to materialize in front of him. He walked backward, praying that he didn't trip over anything as he reloaded.

"We're pinned down," he heard over his radio, the voice was that of A1C Jack George. Johnson spotted him, along with Nick Mason, about twenty yards from the LZ, crouched behind a group of rocks that seemed far too small to conceal the two men.

"Move it, Jack," Johnson ordered as he leapt from behind cover, lobbing two grenades at the attackers. He stood fifteen yards in front of the chopper, firing like a madman at anything that moved. He continued to back up slowly as George and Mason headed toward the back of the chopper and its relative safety.

***

"Crazy bastard," Beu muttered as he watched the commando standing in the open, sweeping his machine gun back and forth until his clip emptied. "Give him some cover," he demanded. The door gunners added their fire to Johnson's, pushing the Korean troops back. He saw Johnson drop the MP-5 and take up with his pistol.

***

"Get *in* here, Rick," John Reasoner screamed into the mike. Those left alive were already aboard. Johnson turned and broke into a run, heading for the big black bird that had gone light and was hovering a yard off the ground.

He felt a white-hot pain in his left thigh and knew that he'd been hit. His leg didn't want to work, but he forced himself on, the pain causing his head to swim.

"*Leave* him, Rick," Reasoner implored, jumping out of the chopper, and running to the wounded man.

"*No*," Johnson screamed back as he limped toward the helicopter. Reasoner met him by the left sponson, helping with the load. Another shot creased Johnson's back as many arms reached for him, pulling him inside onto the cargo deck.

Hoffman's body was laid on the deck as the chopper's crew chief and Reasoner cut the jumpsuit off Johnson's leg. Blood squirted from the wound to cover the two men. "Shit," Reasoner muttered. "Get over here, Nick," he said as the helicopter leapt into the sky as ground fire continued to assault the belly of the Pave Low.

***

"*Shoot* them, you fool!" Park thrust an AK-47 into Lan's hands as Cho slid the door open. The pilot swung the unarmed helicopter sidewise to the Pave Low as it tried to gain altitude, its engines screaming. Lan opened up with the Kalashnikov, peppering the right side of the Pave Low to no effect.

***

"We're taking fire from that chopper, Major," Wood said as he ducked away from the open door, a shot ricocheting off the frame.

"Take them down, Woodsy," Beu ordered and the sergeant complied, training his gun on the helicopter less than half the size of the one in which he rode. He raked back and forth across the engines until smoke poured from the small craft, and then watched it spin wildly toward the ground.

In the rear of the Pave Low, Reasoner and Mason packed Johnson's thigh wound with a bandage, Reasoner ordering the big man to squeeze it closed to stop the flow of blood. Johnson screamed as Mason applied pressure at the limits of his strength.

"Roger," Johnson groaned through the pain.

"He's gone, Rick," Reasoner said looking over at the corpse that lay feet away. "You're a crazy bastard, you know."

"Anytime, anyplace," Johnson replied with a grimace, reciting the motto of Air Force Special Operations. "How many, John?" He asked, watching Reasoner's eyes become moist.

"Jenkins and the Chief," he said. "Everyone else is okay."

"We have to go back." Johnson tried to sit up, but Mason pushed him back down. "We can't leave them there."

"There wasn't enough of them left *to* get," Reasoner said, wiping a tear from his cheek. "The NKPA lobbed a grenade into their position."

"Fuck." Johnson slammed his fist onto the deck, spraying them with the blood that had pooled there, his mixed with what had drained from Hoffman's corpse. The crew chief arrived with a syringe. "What's that?"

"Don't worry about it, just relax," the sergeant said as he jabbed Rick's other thigh. The morphine worked quickly, and Johnson's head began to swim, the pain that wracked his body began to subside.

"John," Johnson said feeling as if he was losing consciousness. "If I don't make it . . ."

"You'll make it, New York."

"If I don't make it," he continued. "Tell Yung Shu that I love her."

"I will, but you'll make it; *right*, Nick?" Reasoner looked to Mason, who still had his hands clamped on Johnson's thigh, squeezing for all he was worth.

"As long as I don't let go you will," Mason said with a laugh, earning a dirty look from the young sergeant. "What's it worth to you, Rick?"

"Shut *up*, asshole," Reasoner growled, but that was Mason's way. "You'll be fine."

"If you let go," Johnson said with dry mouth. "I'll kick your big ugly ass all the way back to Florida before I die." Seconds later, his head fell to the side as the veil of unconsciousness draped over him.

Osan Air Base, South Korea

"Three dead, one wounded, Mr. President," Colonel Williams said into the phone. "The chopper should be landing shortly, sir."

"Was the mission a success?" The former actor asked. President Reagan made the call personally.

"Yes, Mr. President," Williams replied. "But we had to leave two of the dead behind."

"Can we be connected to it?" Reagan had been shooting questions at him since he picked up the phone.

"No, Mr. President, they carried no identification."

"Good job, Colonel," POTUS said. "Give them my thanks and congratulations."

"Yes, sir." The phone went dead then.

"Do we have ID on the casualties, sir?" Holmgren asked, approaching the colonel's station. He was ashen; his emotions in torment after watching the firefight unfold on the satellite link.

"Not yet," Williams said. "We'll know as soon as the chopper lands."

"Are they going to *Tarawa*?"

"No, they're coming straight here." Williams looked up at him. "Are you all right, Lieutenant?"

"Yes, sir, sorry." Holmgren turned to go back to his station.

"Lieutenant?"

"Yes, sir?"

"Is this the first time you've watched one of these?" Williams made a sweeping gesture encompassing the Intel facility.

"Yes, sir," Holmgren said, swallowing the bile that had formed in his throat when he saw the first of the commandos go down. Williams considered him for a second.

"Why don't you go home, Lieutenant," he said. "Be back here at oh nine hundred."

"Thank you, sir, but I'd rather . . ."

"Go *home*, Lieutenant; that's an order. You won't do me much good here in your condition anyway."

"Yes, sir," Holmgren said, coming to attention.

He left the building quickly, but instead of heading to the barracks, he got in his car and drove to the Base Operations building. The sound of sirens caught his attention as he parked; an ambulance sped by him, entering the flightline area via the gate at the end of the parking lot. Holmgren ran to the gate but was stopped by an Air Force Security Police sergeant.

"Do you have a line badge, Lieutenant?" The well-armed security man asked.

"No, I left it at the barracks."

"This area is temporarily restricted, sir," the sergeant explained. "I can't let you in unless you have authorization. Sorry."

"I'm with squadron intel, Sergeant, I have to meet the chopper that's inbound." Holmgren tried to bluff his way in but could see right away that the sky cop wasn't buying it.

"Sorry, sir," the sergeant said, bringing the M-16 from his shoulder just in case Holmgren was willing to push the issue. "You can wait for the chopper inside Base Ops." He pointed to the building. Holmgren realized that it was futile to argue with the man and any more would get him thrown in confinement.

"All right, thank you, Sergeant."

"You're welcome, sir."

Holmgren walked away, toward the building, when he heard the thump-thump of rotor blades in the distance. He looked to the west as the ghostly image of the Pave Low materialized out of the night. It flared, setting down twenty yards from the flashing strobes of the ambulance. Instead of heading to Base Ops, he walked to the fence as the two paramedics from the ambulance boarded the helicopter via the rear cargo ramp.

They emerged within seconds with one of the commandos on a gurney, followed by seven more of the black clad men, two of which carried a body bag. He studied the faces, what he could see of them from a hundred yards in the darkness, his heart threatening to pound out of his chest and the tears beginning. Roger was not among those who walked out under their own power.

The siren on the ambulance began to wail as it pulled away, back though the gate toward the base hospital. *He's hurt*, Holmgren thought, watching the ambulance grow smaller as it sped into the night. He ran to the car and left with a squeal of the tires.

***

Across town, Yung Shu sat straight up in the bed that she shared with the man she loved. The dream had been horrible and in color, each gory detail playing before her eyes during REM sleep. Perspiration flowed from every pore and her breath came in gasps as she tried to squelch the overwhelming feeling of dread. She felt, to the core of her being that something had happened to Rick, just as the dream foreshadowed.

A glance at the clock informed her that dawn was still five hours off and she laid her head back onto the sodden pillow. Her heart raced as she considered the possibilities, whether he was hurt or killed, his body lying somewhere to be picked over by the scavengers, be they of the swimming or flying kind.

"Please come back to me," she whispered to the darkness.

Chapter Three
Nam Po, North Korea
6 July 1983

"You are an incompetent *fool*," Kim Sun Park hissed as he hobbled onto the ward. Lan lay in his bed, a cast from his hips to his ankles, keeping his shattered legs immobile. Kim had fared better, suffering only compression injuries to his back from the crash landing of his helicopter. Miraculously, his bodyguard Cho emerged from the wreck unscathed. Lan opened his eyes. "Your incompetence has set us back years."

"I did not know …" Lan protested, becoming silent when Park raised his pistol.

"That is no excuse," Park said, firing one shot into the man's forehead. The body convulsed and then lay still.

"What is going on here," the doctor said as Park turned from the bed.

"You do not have to waste your time with this one anymore," Park told him as he limped from the ward.

Osan Air Base, South Korea

"How is he, Doc?" Reasoner asked when the doctor appeared. The commandos had come straight here after their mission debrief, not bothering to get cleaned up. The seven remaining men had taken over the waiting room, sprawling across the chairs and on the floor in an effort to get some much-needed sleep while they waited for news of their mate. The doctor regarded them all for a few seconds before speaking.

"He'll be fine, just a little lame for a while," Dr. Everett said. "The bullet grazed his femoral artery. Which one of you is Mason?"

Nick stood and walked over to the man, towering over him. His bloody clothes stank of sweat and gore, causing Everett to attempt holding his breath.

"I am," Mason said. "What of it?" His tone was combative, the adrenaline hangover having a deleterious effect on his disposition, which wasn't pleasant on a good day.

"He owes you his life, son," Everett said as he backed up a step. "Had you not done what you did, he would have bled to death before he arrived."

Mason only shrugged. "Part of the job, Doc," he said. "You know, anytime, anyplace."

"Can we see him?" Reasoner asked. The others were in various states of consciousness, aroused by Everett's appearance.

"Maybe in a few hours," Everett replied. "We have him sedated and he lost a lot of blood. Are you in charge of this bunch?"

"Yes, sir."

"Why don't you all get some rest, I'll call you if there's any change. If you don't hear from me, be back around noon," Everett said. "I don't need you guys hanging around when the morning rush starts." Everett could just imagine the reaction of the wives and children that would arrive for appointments when they saw the gore covered commandos.

"Yes, sir," Reasoner said, turning to the others. "You heard the man." They rose in a chorus of groans and mumbled curses, none of them happy about having to leave their comrade.

"I'd recommend an attitude change as well, Sergeant Reasoner," Everett added. "This is still a *military* hospital."

"My apologies, Doctor."

The Pink Lady

"Go away, we're not open yet," Song Mai Kim said as she opened the front door a crack. "I get a broom!" She retrieved it from behind the door.

"I don't want to come in, ma'am," SRA Campbell said. "I was wondering if Yung Shu was around."

"She already has a boyfriend; he'll kick your ass if he knows you bother my daughter. Go away or I hit you with broom." She shook the implement at him. Campbell backed up a step.

"No, ma'am, you don't understand, I'm Rick's friend," Campbell said, holding up his hands in a gesture of surrender. "There's been an accident." He watched the older woman's face fall.

"Come in." She swung the door open. "Quick, before others think we're open." Mai Kim dragged him inside and shut the door quickly. "Yung Shu," she called up the stairs.

"Yes, mother?" Yung Shu emerged at the second-floor landing. "Hi, Chuck," she said, looking past him for any sign of Rick. She ran the rest of the way down.

"Hi, Yung Shu," Campbell said, trying to sound lighthearted. He failed miserably. Her eyes welled with tears by the time she reached them. Her mother drew her close.

"Where's Rick?"

"He'll be okay," Campbell said. "There was an accident." The news did not stop the sobs from making their way to the surface.

"How ... how bad?" Yung Shu was doing her best to keep her composure.

"A leg injury, he's at the base hospital now," Campbell said. "They have him sedated but he's out of danger."

"What happened," she asked, taking the tissue from her mother, and dabbing at her emerald green eyes.

Campbell shook his head. "Sorry, but that's classified," he told her. "I shouldn't really be telling you this, but we all figured you should know. Rick said to tell you that he loves you and he'll see you as soon as he can."

"When will he be home?" Yung Shu felt a little better.

"I don't know yet, none of us have seen him since we got back. He was in surgery most of the night," the Arkansan explained.

"Can …" another wave of sobs came. "Can I see him?"

"I'm going back there now. I'll know more later this afternoon. We just didn't want you to worry." Campbell turned to leave, but she stopped him, putting her arms around him, and hugging tightly.

"Tell him that I love him, Chuck. Tell him …" and she started to cry again.

"I will, Yung Shu. I will."

Nam Po, North Korea

"Your cooperation would have been most welcome yesterday, Comrade Kosarev," Park said. He'd left the hospital with the help of Cho and came back to his office. There were difficult questions from Pyong Yang waiting to be answered. He'd summoned the Russian as soon as he arrived.

"What help could I have given, Major Park?" Kosarev shrugged. "I am not privy to the Americans' plans."

"And your ships in the Sea of Japan did not spot the Americans when they crossed into North Korean territory," Park spat. "I find that very hard to believe."

"Believe what you will, Major," Kosarev said. "I am not kept informed of naval operations. The raid was as much of a surprise to me as it was to you. If anything, your argument is with Moscow."

"I expect that you will relay my displeasure to your superiors, Comrade."

"As you wish," Kosarev shrugged again. "But our Chinese comrades are better equipped to detect the American incursions than we are. Perhaps you might discuss the matter with them."

"I already have, and they are as uncooperative as you are."

"Major Park," the large Russian said. "My duty in North Korea is to facilitate your entry into the nuclear community, not augment your surveillance measures. Territorial defense is *your* purview, sir."

"Without North Korea, your intelligence operation in the South would be greatly reduced. I suggest you inform Moscow of *that*."

"I will relay your concerns, Major. Will that be all?"

"For now, Comrade Kosarev." The Russian nodded and left the office. Once again, he prided himself on his self-control, for it took extreme strength of will for Kosarev not to shoot the man out of hand.

Little monster, he thought as he got in his car and drove away from the wrecked facility, thankful the Americans had been so thorough in their task.

Osan Air Base, South Korea

Johnson opened his eyes, disoriented and dry mouthed. It took a few seconds for the memories to come flooding back and he thanked the stars that he was still alive. Trying to raise himself into a sitting position, a sharp, shooting pain knocked him back down. *Shit that hurts*, he thought.

"You're awake," the pretty nurse said as she came over. "How are you feeling?"

"Like shit," he said.

"I see that your disposition has survived," she observed.

"When can I get out of here?" He pushed himself up again, this time gritting his teeth and fighting against the pain.

"Not for a while, Airman." She came over to him, straightening the pillow. "Be careful when you do that. We don't want to rip out the sutures, do we?"

"*We?* I don't see you lying here," he growled. She looked him over, deciding not to get into a verbal sparring match with the young man.

"Do you need anything else before I make rounds?"

"Yeah, a hot blonde and a bottle of Jack Daniel's."

She laughed at him. "You couldn't handle either of them in your condition."

"You wouldn't want to test that, would you?" He gave her a sly grin. She smiled back at him, brushing her blonde bangs from her forehead.

"We wouldn't want to kill you," she replied, looking him over. He was muscular and handsome in a rugged way, and even in his current predicament, he projected self-confidence. "But I'd think about it after you're released. How about some water instead?"

"It'll have to do." He took the cup and drank slowly, stopping when he saw her come to attention.

"Good morning, Colonel," she said.

"At ease, Lieutenant," Colonel William 'Stonewall' Bryant said as he entered the private room. "How's my boy?" Bryant was the commander of 23rd STS, a veteran of Vietnam with thirty years of service under his belt.

"He'll be better in no time, sir," she said before leaving. She gave Johnson another smile as she left the room.

"Good morning, sir," Johnson said.

"How are you feeling, son?"

"I've been better, Colonel, but I'm ready for action."

Bryant laughed. "I'll bet you are," he said proudly. "But you'll have to let the docs poke and prod you for a few more days at least."

"I'd do better at home, sir."

Bryant laughed again. "If I had a little sweetie like yours waiting for me, I'd feel the same way. We got word to her that you were okay," Bryant told him.

Johnson let out a sigh of relief. "Thank you, sir. I didn't want her to worry. I'd like to see her if I could."

"I'll arrange something," Bryant promised. "Are you up for a visitor?"

"I'm talking to *you*, sir."

"You don't have a choice about that," the colonel chuckled. He rose and opened the door, making a hand signal to someone in the hall. A tall, lanky man appeared wearing dress blues with silver aviator wings above the ribbons on his left breast. "This is Major Beu," Bryant said. "He's the chopper pilot who pulled you out." Beu walked over and offered a hand, which Johnson shook.

"Pleased to meet you, Major."

"Sorry to bother you, Airman," Beu said, his voice proclaiming that he could only have been born in Texas. "But I just wanted to meet the crazy fool who had the balls to stand up in front of a platoon of NKPA infantry."

"Shit, sir, if I would have known there was so damn many of them, I would have beat *you* back to Osan on foot." Both officers laughed.

"Somehow, I don't believe it," Beu said, then turning to Bryant. "May I speak with Airman Johnson privately, sir?"

"I don't see why not," Bryant nodded. "I'll check on you later, son."

"Thank you, sir." Beu and Johnson waited until the door closed.

"I hear that you're a bourbon man, Johnson," the chopper pilot said.

"Yes, sir," he replied as Beu pulled a chair over to his bedside.

"Whoa, boy, stop right there. The name's Nate, my daddy was a *sir*."

"Nate it is, I'm Rick." They shook hands once more to certify it before Beu produced a silver flask from his pocket. He opened the top and handed it to Johnson.

"I like bourbon too," Beu said as Johnson took a swig. "Figured you'd need a belt after what you've been through."

"Greatly appreciated," he said, letting the alcohol swish around his mouth before swallowing. Johnson regarded the helicopter pilot. He had a square face, with an even more squared off jaw, with streaks of gray in his black hair. Rick figured him to be in his early thirties. "Thanks." He returned the flask and Beu took a swallow.

"I put you in for the Silver Star this morning," Beu said. "Would have been the Medal of Honor, but we're not at war."

"Can you stop it," Johnson said, taking the flask back. "I'm no hero."

"Bullshit, I haven't seen anything like you did since Nam. I'm not stopping shit. If they give it to you, wear the fucking thing proudly because you deserve it. None of your flight would have made it out had you not done what you did, let alone bring your friend's body out," Beu said.

"Any of them would have done the same," Johnson shrugged.

"But *you* were the one who did." Beu stood, dropping the flask back in his pocket. "Get some rest, I'll be back to check on you."

"Why?"

"What do you mean?"

"Why the interest?" Johnson asked.

"Let's just say that I pick my friends carefully and you seem like someone I'd want for a friend."

"They have regs against that, officer-boy," Johnson joked.

"I've fractured my share of regulations in the past and I don't plan on stopping now. I'm old school, Rick, not one of those by-the-book maggots that pass for officers nowadays. Take care of yourself."

"You too and thanks." Johnson watched him go, trying to figure out the man that just left. *And they thought I was crazy*, he thought as the alcohol made him drift back to sleep.

***

Holmgren's stomach heaved once more as he threw up into the toilet. He had no idea how he made it through the debrief, let alone back to his room afterward. Roger was dead; the names of the casualties had been made official a few hours after A-Flight returned, and Holmgren felt that his world had died along with his lover. He'd alternated between tears and sickness since returning from the meeting with the Intel staff and was seriously contemplating suicide. He rose from his knees, stopping at the sink to splash water in his face. Looking in the mirror, he saw a face that he didn't recognize, didn't want to recognize, for his life was over.

Not able to grieve openly, never share with anyone his feelings for the man he'd given his heart to, and none would show any sympathy toward him. Nor could he share the grief of Roger's family, for they knew nothing of his orientation, believing that their son was heterosexual, waiting for the day that he would introduce them to a woman whom he'd planned to share his life with and produce children to carry on the family name.

None of that mattered anymore, and to Alan, life didn't matter anymore. He had nothing to live for, save the work that he enjoyed, and even that would not make up for the horrible sense of loss that had overtaken him.

Holmgren, just as Roger, could not even look to his own family for comfort, for they too knew nothing of their relationship, they too under the illusion that he was heterosexual, and also waited for him to introduce them to a love with whom he would share his life in married bliss.

I want to die, he thought as he headed out of the bathroom. He went to his dresser, taking out the picture that was taken in Taegu, the picture that he never dared display. He and Roger had spent a day there, meeting another gay couple, Americans on vacation in South Korea, and they had taken the picture, sending it to him after it was developed.

He fell on the bed, the picture pressed to his chest, and the tears began again, the cycle that would have him sprinting for the bathroom in a few minutes, his now empty stomach still trying to rid itself of something that was no longer there.

***

Johnson felt lips pressing lightly against his and thought that he was having a very realistic dream. Upon opening his eyes, he knew that this was real. He reached up and drew her to him, disregarding the pain as her barely hundred pounds pressed on him.

"Hi, baby," he whispered. "I love you." She did not answer, but he saw her eyes moisten. "Don't cry, Yung Shu, I'm fine," he said, running his fingers through her long coal black hair.

"I love you too," she said, a tear falling from her cheek as she kissed him again. "Mother sends her best. She wanted to come along, but I don't think that the Air Force is ready for her."

Rick laughed loudly. "I'd have to agree with you. I don't think *I'm* used to her and you and I have been living together for two years."

"I don't think that is a good idea," the nurse said when she came in the room, seeing Yung Shu draped over him. "If his sutures open, he'll have to go back to surgery."

"Nag, nag, nag," Johnson told the blonde lieutenant as Yung Shu got back on her feet.

"He seems to be feeling well enough," Yung Shu joked with the nurse. "When can he come home?"

"That's up to the doctor," she replied. "It all depends on how well Airman Johnson listens."

"Then he'll be here *forever*," Yung Shu sighed.

"I don't think that we could stand him that long, Miss," the nurse said as she left the room.

"What happened to you," Yung Shu asked looking at his leg that was covered in a soft cast.

"The chopper had a bumpy ride, that's all," he told her. It was the official line that would be fed to the families of the dead, a training accident involving the crash of a helicopter. It was what he would have to tell Yung Shu also, and here was not the place to tell her that three of his unit died, and how close *he* actually came to death.

"You're lying to me, Richard," she said, still smiling. She knew him too well, knew when he was not being truthful or bending the truth to save her from worry. She forgave him because he did it out of love for her. He shrugged.

"You know the drill, babe. All that matters is that I'll be fine, and I'll be home soon."

"I know the drill." She crossed her arms on her chest. "That doesn't mean I have to like it."

"That's part of being in love with a GI," he said. "You'd better get used to it."

"I'll *never* get used to it, but if it's the price I have to pay, then I'm willing."

He reached up and took her hand in his. "Are you *sure*, baby?"

"I've been sure for two years, Rick. I love you and that's all that matters."

The nurse came back into the room. "You'll have to leave now, Miss," she said. "The doctor wants to examine him."

"Trust me, you won't show her anything she hasn't seen before," Rick said.

"Remember what she said about listening, Rick," Yung Shu admonished. "I will see you soon. Mother is alone at the bar and she will need my help for the evening rush."

"I'll be home soon, baby," Rick said, drawing her back down to him. He kissed her before releasing her. "I love you, Yung Shu."

"I love you too, Rick."

"I see why you want to get out of here so quickly," the nurse said when she left.

"I'm going to marry that girl one day, Lieutenant," he said.

Panmunjom, North Korea

Kosarev looked past the barbed wire fence that separated the country of North Korea from the Demilitarized Zone, the sense of history he felt was heady. Thirty years before, on this spot, an armistice was signed to end the war between the Koreas. It was here, straddling the 38th Parallel that the fighting stopped, although the war of sorts went on. It was a dirty, secret war that still claimed its share of lives every year.

Both sides fought it, the North Koreans sending spies through tunnels under the DMZ into the south, the South Koreans and Americans sending troops to the north to foil the plans of the Communists. It was an undeclared war, neither side admitting that they were participants, but both playing the game where the stakes were life and death.

Kosarev also played the game, and he did it well. He played it on behalf of his homeland, Mother Russia, the largest and most powerful state within the Soviet Union, but he also played for personal reasons. His deputy Marko was right, Kosarev had power, more than enough to get his choice of assignments, but there was a very important reason for staying in the Far East. While he was certain his beloved wife capable of chasing off any of young Alexa's suitors, there was something in Moscow Katherine had no control over.

The winds of change were blowing across the Union, a draft now, but they would begin to howl soon. Those in the West would not notice for years yet, maybe even a decade or two, but Yevgeniy Kosarev could smell what was carried on the gentle breeze. Communism had already begun down the path to failure and there was little chance of return.

It will come, he thought. *Maybe not in my lifetime, but it will come.* He knew it when he was recalled to Moscow a year before to receive the news. The Soviets were selling intermediate-range nuclear missiles to their comrades in North Korea in an effort to raise hard currency, namely American dollars and German marks. He thought it was a joke at first, when Chairman Andropov advised him of the facts of the deal, learning soon enough that Andropov was deadly serious.

"The ruble is next to worthless, Comrade Kosarev," Andropov said at the time. *"The Koreans are willing to pay us in hard currency; American dollars, Yevgeniy."*

"Do we need the money that badly, Comrade Chairman?" Kosarev had asked him. *"I have documented their treachery in my reports*

over the years. They cannot be trusted to adopt the same doctrine we share with the Americans. If it is advantageous to them, they will use them in a first strike scenario."

"Against whom?" Andropov shrugged. "The South Koreans? The Japanese? The Chinese? Who cares?"

"Against the Soviet Union, Comrade Chairman," Kosarev said.

"Nyet," Andropov shot back. "You will see to it."

"But why, sir. Why must we proliferate nuclear weapons to East Asia?"

"Because the Union needs the capital, damn it," Andropov leaned close to him. "Fuck your mother, Yevgeniy, we are almost bankrupt," he hissed.

And Kosarev returned, his official title was chief liaison officer to the North Korean rocket program, in addition to his actual job as the KGB's *rezident* in Pyong Yang. *This is insane*, he thought as he made his way back to the car. He looked at the North Korean border troops with disdain when he drove though the checkpoint and then he thought about another place just like this, a half a world away. *It's just like Berlin.* Just like every place where the two ideologies rubbed against each other. It was that way in the Caribbean too, in the water on either side of the Florida Straits.

The whole damn world is insane, Kosarev thought, driving on into the Korean twilight. And then he thought of the other fact he'd learned. *She's going to die.* Katherine came to him that night, after he'd spoken with Chairman Andropov, and her news unsettled him far more than the knowledge of the North Koreans acquiring offensive nuclear weapons. Cancer would take the life of the woman he'd loved more than any other, save his beautiful daughter, and he was helpless to stop it.

And he'd come back to the Far East, though he knew he probably would not see her alive again, for there was something to be accomplished that could only be done here. The Union was bankrupt, and his wife was dying, and he'd be damned if his daughter would be caught in the middle. It had taken a year to set up, but now everything was in place. *Almost everything,* he thought as the car bucked down the bumpy dirt road.

Osan Air Base, South Korea

"What are you doing out of bed?" The night nurse asked when she caught him halfway across the room.

"I have to take a leak," Johnson growled. "And I *ain't* pissing in that can."

"If you tear out the sutures . . ."

"I'm not tearing *anything,* Lieutenant, but I'm going to piss like a man." She followed him into the bathroom. "I *know* how to do this by myself," he barked.

"I'm not leaving until you're back in bed."

"Suit yourself," he said and relieved himself. "By the way, I'd like you to tell the person in charge that I'm ready to go home."

"The flight surgeon will make that determination," she informed him.

"I'm fine."

"No, you're not. You suffered two gunshot wounds not twenty-four hours ago. You're *not* fine." She took his arm and got him back to bed. "Do you need anything?"

"Nothing you'd be willing to provide," he grinned.

"You're an arrogant bastard, aren't you?" She hissed as she made for the door.

"I *can* be, darling," he laughed as she left. It was then when he heard a sound outside the window. It slid upward, a black-clad figure climbing into the room, followed by another.

"You ready to leave, boy?" Chuck Campbell grinned.

"I was ready an hour after I got here," Johnson replied, getting himself to his feet once more. Guthrie handed him a set of BDUs and then went to the door to check for any of the medical staff.

"Sweet looking nurse," Guthrie observed when he saw her at the nurses' station.

"Pain in the ass bitch," Johnson muttered as he finished dressing.

"Can you get out the window, crip, or do you need me to help you?" Campbell asked him.

"I can do it, asshole," Rick shot back.

"I got your asshole," Campbell shot back as he slid out the window. Johnson followed, a small grunt escaping from his lips when he rappelled to the ground. Guthrie followed and pulled the ropes free from the roof. "Did you say something, Rick?"

"No," Johnson barked. "What did you do for wheels?"

"Over there," Guthrie pointed to the Ford F-350 with Air Force markings.

"Where'd you get that?" Johnson was impressed.

"There's two supply weenies at the NCO club trying to figure out where they left it," Campbell said as they climbed in. "Let's get out of here before they call the APs."

The young men were quiet as Campbell drove sanely within the confines of the base. Johnson reached over, fished a pack of Marlboros from Guthrie's shirt pocket, and smiled when he found a joint inside. Lighting it, he took a deep hit and passed it on to Guthrie.

"Just take liberties with my shit," Guthrie said as Johnson bummed a cigarette as well before giving the pack back.

"Eat me," Rick grumbled as Campbell passed the joint back.

"How's the leg," Guthrie inquired.

"Don't feel a thing," Johnson lied while he passed the joint to its original owner. The leg was on fire and the flesh wound on his back burned almost as badly every time Campbell hit a bump with the big pickup.

"You're a lying sack of shit," Campbell replied. "Watch this Jake," he said to Guthrie as he aimed for a pothole. The truck bounced through it and Johnson grimaced. "Look at that face, the boy's hurting like a motherfucker."

"I repeat," Johnson said, his eyes burning into Campbell. "*As*shole!"

"It sure ain't changed his disposition worth a shit," Guthrie observed.

"I could have gotten this ration of shit from those fucking nurses and they're a hell of lot prettier than you two ugly fuckers." They were quiet again as the road darkened, away from the base. The reality was sinking in and neither of them cared to admit the emotions they all were feeling. Johnson was the first to say something. "Are they really gone?"

"Yeah," Campbell replied as he gazed over the steering wheel into the darkness.

"The Chief, Roger, and the ell-tee," Guthrie recited the names of the dead. "Chief was gonna retire in a couple months." He shook his head sadly.

"Poor bastard," Johnson agreed. "He lived through Viet Nam only to be killed during peacetime."

"What about Roger's suck-boy?" Campbell asked the inevitable question.

"Who cares?" Guthrie spat, "fucking queers."

"Rog was your friend, he was my friend," Johnson said. Though what he said was true, the two southerners were less tolerant than their colleague from New York. "They had a relationship, two years' worth. This guy, what's his name, is in the same position Yung Shu would be if I were killed."

"So, what do you propose we do?" Campbell asked. "Rog said that this guy didn't know that we knew about him. All of us going to see him would blow his cover. Pardon the use of the word blow," he added with a grin.

"I'll go see him," Johnson volunteered. "I'll have Yung Shu take me over to the BOQ in a day or two."

"You're saying that this guy was the wife?" Guthrie looked at him suspiciously.

"Something like that," Johnson nodded.

"How do *you* know so much about them?" Guthrie persisted.

"I'm from New York, where the majority of people are open-minded and tolerant of others' differences," Johnson barked back.

"Is that the same New York where somebody can be stabbed in the street and no one comes to help?" Campbell asked with the ever-present grin.

"We only do that to ignorant rednecks, especially height-challenged ones like our friend here," Johnson laughed. Nothing irked Guthrie more than a remark about his five-foot seven-inch stature.

"Fuck you, carpetbagger," Guthrie hissed.

The road began to brighten as they entered the town of Osan, and Campbell kicked the speed back under the limit. The Korean cops took a dim view of American military turning their streets into a speedway. The fact that the truck was almost certainly reported stolen by now made Campbell doubly cautious. Within minutes, he pulled up to a place that resembled a luxury hotel. Instead of a dapper bellhop waiting out front, a glaring marquee announced they were parked in front of the Pink Lady. Another, only slightly less glaring sign proclaimed 'Live Nude Girls' danced within. "Get out," Campbell ordered. "I gotta ditch the truck."

Guthrie and Johnson climbed out, heading for the broad wooden steps as the truck took off with a squeal of the tires. Campbell would leave it a few blocks away with the keys under the mat. One of the locals would report the truck to the Air Police who would come with someone from the motor pool to pick it up. As of yet, none had made the connection to Campbell.

The rock and roll music became louder as the two airmen approached, assaulting them with its volume when Guthrie opened the door. "Ladies first," he said to Johnson.

"Beauties before beasts," Johnson corrected and stepped through the door. His eyes roamed the dimly lit club, trying to see through the haze of cigarette smoke and strobe lights.

"Mama-san got a new girl," Guthrie observed, his gaze resting on the Pakistani beauty dancing on a table. "Let's sit over here." Johnson nodded, not caring who was dancing before him, and followed Guthrie to a pair of seats.

"Hey, boys," one of the waitresses said. "Are you having the usual?"

"Yeah," Guthrie said absently while stuffing a dollar bill into the waistband of the Pakistani girl's G-string.

"I'll tell Yung Shu you're here," she said to Rick before he could ask.

"Thanks, Lin Yii," he replied with a smile. The waitress wasn't gone thirty seconds when he felt Yung Shu's arms come around him. He turned and guided her onto his lap, putting her weight on the undamaged leg. "I love you," he whispered before kissing her passionately.

"I have to get back to work," she breathed as he bit her neck. "If you think you're hurt now, wait until mother sees us like this while I'm supposed to be working." She turned when she felt a nudge. "Hi, Jake," she grinned at Guthrie. "Where's Chuck?"

Guthrie made a show of checking his watch. "Any second now," he looked to the front door. Campbell burst through with a flourish.

"Hey, y'all," he shouted. "Did ya miss me?" Assorted pretzels, chips, and other debris were tossed at him.

"Sit down and quit making an ass of yourself," Guthrie ordered. Campbell conceded with a stupid grin, tossing some of the litter back at the assailants.

"Hey, boy," the voice of Hermann Wood penetrated Johnson's reality. "You impressed the shit out of Nate Beu."

"Hey, Woodsy." Johnson shook his hand. Wood was a fellow New Yorker as well as being the crew chief for Cowboy-261. "What's his deal, anyway? Officer-boy should play with his own kind."

"Ah, Beu doesn't give a shit about rank," Wood waved the question away. "Done a couple tours in Nam, doesn't care about the brass on your shoulders, just about your character."

"Rick is a character," Yung Shu said. "What did Rick do to impress this officer?"

"Ah, sorry, sweet thing, that's classified," Wood shrugged.

"I had to try," she smiled at Rick, kissing him again. "I have to get back to work. I'll be back after my shift." She stood and turned to leave, but then turned back. "What are you doing home so soon?"

"Yeah, how did you get the flight surgeon to release you at this time of night?" Wood seconded the question. Johnson smiled and Wood shook his head. Yung Shu went back to the bar. "They're gonna have your ass one day, Rick."

"Anytime, anyplace," Johnson said with a shrug, repeating the motto of Air Force Special Operations Command. The doors opened again, and a tall officer stepped into the club. "Speak of the Devil." Nate Beu made eye contact and walked over.

"Ten-hut," Campbell said and all at the table came to attention.

"Siddown," Beu growled. "We aren't on base."

"Thanks for the lift, Major," Guthrie said.

"Don't thank me," Beu said as he poured himself a shot of Jack Daniel's. "Thank this idiot." He jerked a thumb in Johnson's direction. "He's the silly bastard that slowed the NKPA down so you could be extracted." Beu knocked the liquor back and looked up at the Pakistani girl. Pulling a dollar out of his flight suit, Beu folded it lengthwise down the long axis and stood it up on the table. "Watch this," he said. "I was in here last night and saw her do it." The girl danced over and squatted over the erect dollar, pulling her flimsy G-sting aside to expose herself. With her private parts, she picked up the bill and stood, prancing around as if it were a paper penis, shaking it at the GIs who all begged her to do it again. "Cool, huh?"

"Talented," Johnson agreed, tossing back a shot.

"They let you out of the hospital?" Beu asked.

"Nah, Chuck and Jake came to get me," Johnson said conspiratorially. "I'd have killed myself if I had to stay there another day."

"The nurses?" Beu gave a knowing smile.

"Meddlesome busybodies," Johnson muttered. "The night nurse wouldn't let me take a leak without making sure I got to the bathroom and back in one piece. She wanted me to piss in this fucking bottle."

The doors opened once again, this time a squad of blue bereted Air Force Security Police entered. The officer in charge scanned the club, his eyes coming to rest on the men of 23rd.

"Don't look now," Beu said. "But I think the flight surgeon has other plans for your evening."

***

Kosarev was unnerved when he saw the white and blue cars pull up in front of the strip club; to be discovered here would create an international incident at the least. He watched the police enter and then leave a few minutes later with three men in custody. Another followed them out, staying behind as the police drove away with their charges.

"You keep bad company, Major Beu," Kosarev whispered as he hunched down behind the wheel. "But I am not interested in your choice of friends," the KGB colonel added.

Chapter Four
Osan Air Base, South Korea
7 July 1983

"Can *one* of you idiots care to tell me why the base commander, the flight surgeon, and the Services Squadron commander are all standing in line, waiting to assault my nether regions with a non-lubricated blunt instrument?" Colonel Bryant stared at them as they remained at attention.

"For three clowns who never shut up, you pick a great time to be at a loss for words," Bryant went on. "This fucking asshole," he pointed to Johnson, "is supposed to be in a bed at the base hospital."

"I couldn't stay in that hospital any longer, Colonel," Johnson said.

"You'll do what they tell you, Airman, unless you managed to get your medical degree in the past two years," Stonewall Bryant barked at him. "And you two morons," he turned his attention to Guthrie and Campbell. "How long did you think you could get away with your grand theft auto ring?"

"You *knew*, sir?" Campbell said.

"I must look pretty stupid to you," Bryant growled. "The motor pool is getting tired of sending a man into town to pick up a vehicle every time you need a set of wheels, the Air Police too. Guess what, the auto thefts pick up every time we rotate in and, coincidentally, go down when we rotate out. Jesus fucking Christ, did you have to be so *blatant* about it?"

"We didn't think they'd notice, Colonel," Guthrie offered.

"Didn't think they'd *notice*?" Bryant got in his face. "You ditched all the cars a block away from Johnson's place, you moron." Bryant turned back to Johnson. "That leg hurts, doesn't it?"

"I've started to feel it, sir."

"Yeah, I'll bet you have," Bryant replied. Johnson was waiting for Bryant to motion him to a chair. He didn't and Johnson remained at attention. His thigh was on fire. "The Security Police commander wants all of you in confinement." That statement caused worried looks to cross their faces. "The Services commander does too. Unfortunately for them, I need all the able-bodied people I have so I made a deal." Bryant smiled. "*You two* ignorant assholes are assigned to the motor pool for the next week," he said to Campbell and Guthrie. "You are to do every shit job the First Sergeant has for you." Bryant turned to Johnson. "*You* are going home and are restricted to the premises. You will not be allowed back on base until you are fit for duty. If I catch you on base, you'll spend the remainder of your convalescent time in Corrective Custody. Have I made myself perfectly *clear*?"

"Yes, sir," they all said in chorus.

"Good, get out of here before I change my mind," Bryant ordered.

"Could have been worse," Campbell said when they were in the outer office.

"Old Stonewall is okay," Johnson agreed.

"They're gonna fuck our asses at the motor pool," Guthrie observed. "They're gonna have us cleaning the shop floor with toothbrushes."

"You could be in the stockade, shithead," Johnson said.

"You're one to talk, New York, you're gonna be spending a week at home with your babe," Guthrie shot back.

"Ladies, please," Campbell said, looking as if his sensibilities were being offended. "Working in the motor pool might have its advantages."

"Do you think they will let *either* of you near a car?" Johnson asked him.

"I just need some time to feel out the situation," Campbell said with a grin. As they stepped though the outer door, a white Mitsubishi van pulled up to the curb, squealing to a stop. "Hi, Yung Shu," he said when the girl came around the side.

"What are you doing here, baby?" Johnson asked her just before she kissed him.

"Colonel Bryant called and told me to pick you up. He said you were to stay home for a week. It'll be so much fun." She gave him a devilish grin.

"Lucky bastard," Guthrie muttered.

"Can we watch?" Campbell asked.

"The Colonel also told me to drop the two of you at the motor pool," she said.

"Do you work for him?" Guthrie growled.

"No, but he knows you guys listen to me," Yung Shu replied, giggling. "He also told my mother to restrict your alcohol at the club until further notice."

Guthrie threw up his hands. "This is getting *way* out of hand."

"Mother has to comply, Jake," she patted his shoulder. "She can't take the chance of having the place declared off limits. We'd go out of business."

"We'll have to go to the NCO Club on base. We're actually gonna have to *pay* for drinks," Guthrie was dazed with the realization.

"It'll just be for a little while," Johnson soothed his friend.

"Why are you idiots *still* here?" Colonel Bryant's voice bellowed from the second-floor window.

"Just leaving, sir," Campbell smiled and threw up a mock salute. They piled into the van and Yung Shu took off.

***

"Shit, Major, she took a beating," Hermann Wood said as he and Beu looked over Cowboy-261. The sheet metal and hydraulic techs were working on the damage collected during the incident in the North. There were a few thirty-caliber divots in the door bulkhead at Wood's gun position.

"Hell, Woodsy, that's nothing," Beu laughed. "I got a Navy pilot out of a hot LZ near I Trang, shot the shit out of my chopper, but I got her home. Had to crash it to get it on the ground."

"You going to the memorial service, sir?" Wood asked him.

"I'll be there," Beu nodded. "Did you ever find out what happened to Johnson after the AP's took him last night?"

"Ah," Wood waved it away. "Old Stonewall probably reamed them all a half inch oversize and turned them loose. It depends how much shit he got from the APs and the pencil pusher over at Services."

"He lives there?"

"At the Pink Lady?"

Beu nodded. "Yeah."

"Sure does," Wood nodded. "Ever meet his girl?"

"Nope."

"Hot little number," Wood said. "If her mother let her dance, they'd double the profits. The girl works the bar and the mother owns the place."

"Are she and Johnson serious?"

"As a heart attack," Wood replied. "Been together two years and Johnson doesn't even look at other women. A million guys have tried to put the make on her, when Rick's not around of course, but she's turned them all down."

"Seems awful young to be getting that serious," Beu observed.

"Johnson isn't a confirmed bachelor like you, Major," Wood laughed.

"Damn right," Beu smiled. "I can't have a woman telling me what to do all the time."

***

Kosarev laid the field glasses on the seat of the car and made some notes. He was parked outside the perimeter fence, but the high-power lenses allowed him to see into the open hangar where the damaged Pave Low was being repaired. "So, you were at Nam Po the other night, Major Beu. You were the one who shot that little bastard out of the sky," Kosarev laughed. "My only regret is that you didn't kill him, but you Americans don't work that way, do you," he laughed again. "You should have killed him when you had the chance."

***

"Give me another," Holmgren slurred as he pushed the empty glass back to the bartender.

"It isn't even noon yet, Lieutenant," the sergeant observed.

"I didn't ask for commentary, Sarge, just give me another scotch," Holmgren demanded.

"Yes, sir," he poured and placed it back in front of the young lieutenant.

Holmgren considered the glass, lifting it and gazing at the light filtering through the amber liquid. He'd come to the Officer's Club for breakfast and then moved to the bar in an attempt to feel better. Contemplating his fourth in the past hour, he realized his motivation had changed. He was drinking so he didn't feel anything at all.

The Pink Lady, Osan, South Korea

They'd been in his apartment on the sixth floor since they arrived, their lovemaking tender and sensuous. Yung Shu had taken care not to aggravate his wounds, positioning herself to pleasure him without pain, but the throbbing in Johnson's leg and back were forgotten as he returned the pleasure. It was always like this with them, time, space, and pain had no meaning when they were in each other's arms. It was the reason for the incessant banging at his door that finally penetrated their blissful encounter.

"What," Johnson barked at the door. Mama-san took that as an invitation to enter. "Shit."

"*Mother,*" Yung Shu cried.

"Oh," Mama-san gasped and covered her eyes.

Rick slid under the sheets along with Yung Shu, the mood most definitely gone. "What is it, Mama-san?"

"John Reasoner here," Mama-san said, still covering her eyes. "Some of the others too. Say he need to talk to you."

"Tell him I'll be right down," Rick said.

"Yes, Rick," she smiled sheepishly. "Sorry to bother you." Her gaze turned to her daughter. "You on shift in ten minutes. You don't be late," she shook a finger at the girl.

"Yes, mother," Yung Shu's cheeks were still red. "Oh *God*," she groaned when her mother left. "I'm so embarrassed."

"I'm sure your mother hasn't seen anything new," Rick chuckled.

"She's never seen *me* like that. How would you feel if you had a daughter and caught her on her hands and knees in her boyfriend's bed?"

"It would probably involve gunfire," he grinned.

"You'd better hope mother doesn't come back with her broom," she giggled as she went to run him a shower.

***

Johnson's thigh was burning again by the time he made it down to the lobby. It wasn't difficult to spot Reasoner in his pressed and starched BDUs, looking as always, as if he just stepped out of a recruiting poster. Reasoner was Johnson's age and had been in the service just as long, but he'd already made buck sergeant where Johnson had just sowed on senior airman stripes. "Brown nosing maggot," Johnson muttered as he approached the Californian.

"What did you think you were doing," was Reasoner's greeting.

"Why, I'm fine, John," Johnson said facetiously. "Thanks for asking."

"Damn it, Rick, we're the new guys on the block over here," Reasoner ignored Johnson's attitude. "There are twelve other squadrons sharing this patch and we have to get along with them. Your disregard for any authority on this base save Colonel Bryant will hamper our ability to operate here."

"Don't worry, John, I'm restricted here for the next week."

"And what about later Rick?"

"As they say in AA, 'one day at a time'," Johnson grinned. "Look, I took a ton of shit from the old man this morning, I don't need it from *you*," Johnson barked. "Did you come out here just to break my balls?"

"No," Reasoner looked away. "I came to ask what we're doing about Roger's . . . you know. I talked to Jake and Chuck this morning and they said you'd handle it."

"I will."

"What about the memorial service?"

"I'll be there," Johnson told him.

"Hey, boy," the massive form of Nick Mason appeared out of the haze. "You gonna live?"

"Yeah, Nick," Johnson nodded. "Thanks to you."

"Ah, I had nothing better to do at the time." Mason waved and went off in search of a dancer willing to put up with him.

"Have you talked to the Chief's wife?" Johnson asked Reasoner.

"Yeah," Reasoner took a sip of his beer. "Don't ask." His eyes met Johnson's. "Chief was John Jr.'s godfather, you know."

"Yeah, how's Ang doing?"

"Wrecked, I called her after we found out you were okay. She got to Tammy Corlies' with the notification detail and the base chaplain," Reasoner explained. He and Corlies were the only married members of A-Flight and their wives were close.

"You gonna take some leave to be with her?"

"No," Reasoner shook his head slightly. "We'll be back in Florida in a couple weeks."

"Jesus Christ," Rick muttered.

"What?"

"Bryant would give you emergency leave," Johnson said. "Go home to your wife, A-Flight is on stand down anyway. We'll be playing with our dicks until B-Flight rotates in."

"I'm the senior NCO now, Rick," Reasoner lectured. "I have responsibilities."

"You're a fucking buck sergeant," Johnson hissed. "Do you think you'll remain senior NCO when we get back to Florida? Our fucking CO and senior NCO are dead; we'll get new ones once we get back to the States. Don't delude yourself into believing you'll be in command of this motley bunch for long and don't make your wife go through this alone. Tammy Corlies needs someone strong now too and you're the one who's closest to them."

"And that puts you in charge as soon as I'm gone," Reasoner spat.

"Fuck me, John, I don't *want* to be in charge and old Stonewall thinks I'm a few clicks off as it is," Johnson said. "Just ask him to let you go back a few weeks early. I'm confined here and Campbell and Guthrie are paying penance in the motor pool. The squadron First Sergeant can take care of anything that might come up administratively."

"But how will it look?"

"Your career will remain intact, damn it, go home to your wife and kid and help Tammy Corlies get through this."

"I know you all laugh at me, but some of us want to make this a career," Reasoner said defiantly. "I plan to put in my twenty. I'm not here to escape jail time, you psycho."

"This psycho got all your butts out alive, didn't he?" Johnson stood. "Or are you pissed off that they're giving a psycho the Silver Star? It must irk you that they're wasting it on someone who doesn't give a shit. Is that why you really came out here, John, to talk me out of accepting it?" Reasoner looked away. "For your information, I already tried when Beu informed me he put in the paperwork. He won't take it back and he told me to wear it proudly. You know what, I will."

"*I'm* not fighting," Rick said. "I'm going upstairs and then to bed. Go back to Florida, John, you and I will settle this when the rest of us get back there."

"Bet on it," Reasoner hissed and headed for the door.

"Oh, John," Johnson said, and Reasoner stopped. "Don't go telling Ang and Tammy it was my fault. There's no need for the families to get involved, regardless of *our* differences."

"Agreed," Reasoner nodded and left the club.

Johnson turned back to Emory. "So what do you really think, Jerry? *Was* it my fault?"

"Don't be an idiot, Rick," Emory waved the question off. "We did what we had to do in order to complete the mission. The fact we lost three of our own is bad, but they all knew the risks. The Chief lived through three tours in Nam and if he thought you were out of line, he would have counseled you. Fuck what Reasoner says, we did what needed to be done."

"I have to see the IG day after tomorrow," Johnson informed him.

"It's just after-action bullshit," Emory said nonchalantly. "Those desk weenies in the Inspector General's office get to live vicariously through us for a couple days while they look for discrepancies in our reports."

"I gotta go see Roger's . . . you know."

"You're as redneck as Guthrie and Campbell, New York," Emory laughed. "You can't even say the word and you claim you're open minded. Do you refer to me as 'one of the coloreds' when I'm not around?"

"No, you're just a crazy nigger. I'm gonna lay in bed and put my leg up," Johnson muttered, and Emory laughed again.

"Do you want me to go with you to pay condolences?" Emory offered.

"Nah, one of us going is enough. Thanks anyway," Johnson waved and hobbled up the steps.

"I thought I could talk some sense into you," Reasoner rose as well. "You could tell Bryant to stop it."

"Why, for the good of the unit? Is it because I have no regard for any authority outside of SOCOM? Because I'm setting a bad example for the younger guys?"

"Yes," Reasoner shot back. "If they see you rewarded for your cowboy style it will only encourage them. Your devil may care attitude caused us to take casualties we probably wouldn't have, had you done it by the book."

"You weren't the one inside the foundry, motherfucker," Johnson took a step toward Reasoner. "I had to make a command decision and I did, end of story. Don't you lay their lives at my feet and if you accuse me of that again, we'll discuss it out back." Johnson jerked his thumb in the general direction of the back door.

"You're in no condition . . ."

"You want to try me, John?" Rick took another step, his face now an inch from Reasoner's. "You might actually kick my ass with me in this condition."

"Hello, gentlemen," Jerome Emory gave them a toothy grin as he stepped between them. "You two aren't going to do what I think you're going to do, *are* you? That would not be too bright since you're already in Stonewall's doghouse, Rick."

"Do *you* think I'm responsible for Roger, the Chief, and the ell-tee, Jerry?" Johnson asked him through clenched teeth.

Emory looked up at Reasoner. "You're not going down that road, are you, John? Rick didn't fire that RPG on their position, a People's Army infantryman did."

"What happened in the foundry?"

"You know it, it was all in the report," Emory said. "A group of Soviet engineers spotted us, and we had to fight our way out, the rest is history. Leave it alone and let's get on with it. The memorial service is tomorrow, how will it look if we're fighting amongst ourselves?"

***

Kosarev watched the injured airman ascend the steps, certain now that he was part of the raid into North Korea along with Beu. The Russian rubbed his temples as the rock and roll music blared around him. *Infernal noise*, he thought as he nursed his vodka. He wanted to leave; this was not his sort of place, a symbol of the decadent West. He laughed then, knowing the United States and its minions would be the eventual winners of the Cold War.

Vietnam would be seen as the one and only Communist victory in the fifty year, low-intensity conflict. *And we almost lost there too*, Kosarev mused. The Americans did not know how close they came to winning, the unrest in the States at the time turning public opinion against the war. *A united America would have been unstoppable*.

"Another vodka, mister?" The waitress asked him, breaking the trance.

"Yes, please," Kosarev nodded and she drifted away toward the bar. "The Union is dead," he said softly and that surprised him. It was the first time he'd said it aloud. "But it will take another twenty years for it to fall down." His attention was drawn to the front door where Nathan Beu appeared along with a man wearing sergeant stripes.

***

"Hey, Rick," Hermann Wood yelled, and Johnson turned round.

"Hey, boys," Johnson smiled. He stopped as Yung Shu came down the stairs and then took her hand before descending.

"Hi, Woodsy," she said, casting an appraising look at Beu. "A fly boy," Yung Shu noticed the wings on Beu's uniform. "Are you the officer who is so impressed with my man?"

"Yes, ma'am," Beu drawled. "Nate Beu," he held out a hand.

"And I suppose it was your helicopter that experienced . . . *technical* problems?" She asked, taking it.

"Yes, ma'am," Beu looked to Johnson.

"You'd better get to work, babe, before your mother blows a gasket," Johnson urged her on.

"Nice to meet you, Major Beu," she said, giving him a sly look. "We'll talk later." She kissed Rick and headed off to the bar.

"What is she, an intelligence agent or something?" Beu asked him.

"Just nosy," Johnson shrugged. "It bugs her that our missions are classified."

"Women," Beu groaned.

"There's no Mrs. Beu?" Johnson asked and Wood laughed.

"I haven't got that drunk yet," Beu smiled. "Can I buy you one?"

"Why not," Johnson shrugged again, still annoyed at having his lovemaking session interrupted by John Reasoner's bullshit. Johnson led them to a vacant table, noticing the man dressed in civilian clothes that averted his eyes. "He seems out of place here." Johnson indicated the civilian with his chin.

"Probably a tech rep," Beu offered. The civilian was forgotten when they sat, Lin Yii arriving seconds later.

"Hey, Rick, Woodsy, who's your friend," she indicated Beu.

"Nate Beu, ma'am," Beu stood and took her hand, kissing it lightly.

"You a pilot?"

"You bet, darling," he smiled. "You wanna go for a ride?"

"I get off in two hours," Lin Yii said in a sultry voice.

"Yes, you will," Beu replied.

"What'll you have?" She asked.

"In addition to you?"

"Yes," she giggled.

"Wild Turkey," he told her. "And a glass."

"The usual guys?" She asked Johnson and Wood without taking her eyes from Beu.

"You bet," Johnson said for both of them and she hurried off.

"You gotta tell me how you do that," Wood said to Beu.

"It's a gift," Beu bragged and leaned back in the chair.

"Officers, go figure," Johnson muttered.

"So?" Beu asked. "What kind of trouble are you in?"

"Minor," Johnson waved it away. "Stonewall's cool."

"That he is," Beu agreed. "Flew with him at 9th SAR on one tour in Nam. Biggest set of brass ones I ever saw."

***

Kosarev left a hundred won on the table and departed with haste. The airman named Johnson had noticed him and that was not good. Beu had also seen him and that was worse. The saving grace was the three airmen would probably not remember anything tomorrow at the rate they were putting away the bourbon. While Kosarev had liberal opinions regarding alcohol, it amazed him how much the chopper pilot and his friends consumed and were still able to perform at their peak. As he turned onto the highway toward Inch On, Kosarev considered what he was planning to do. He would be operating unofficially and alone, and Beu's new friends could add a deadly complication.

Osan Air Base, South Korea

"I look dead already," Holmgren slurred at the mirror, his face an inch from the glass. "I should just get it over with." The fact that his suicide might lead to questions about his motive, Holmgren resolved to wait a few months to commit the act. Whether he had to live those months in an alcoholic haze to bear them mattered not, only that the secret remains so.

Roger swore to him that their relationship would remain clandestine, Holmgren knew of the closeness among the men of A-Flight. It would not surprise him if at least a few of them were aware of the situation. Holmgren's suicide would surely bring them forward to the investigating authorities. "I won't do that to Roger's memory, I won't do that to mine," he said to his reflection.

He would be remembered not as an outstanding officer, but for his homosexuality and that only, and that was totally unacceptable to him. "And I have to know how Roger died." It was something he was adamant about. Before his own life came to an end, he would learn the facts of how his lover died.

The Pink Lady

"Hey, Nate," Johnson said as he worked a key off the fob.

Beu shifted Lin Yii on his lap so he could see Johnson. "Yeah?"

"Catch," Johnson tossed him the key.

"What's this?"

"Fifth floor," Rick explained. "I fixed it up into a guest wing of sorts. You can't bring her back to the BOQ and you can't nail her in your car, can you?"

"I appreciate it, thanks," Beu dropped the key into the pocket of his flight suit.

"Hey," Johnson protested when Yung Shu slapped his shoulder.

"That's awful of you to presume she will sleep with him," she said.

"Is Ol' Nate gonna get lucky tonight, Lin Yii?" Johnson asked her.

"You bet, GI," she smiled drunkenly.

"See," Johnson shrugged. "I call 'em as I see 'em."

"Come on, it's time for bed," Yung Shu urged. "You're starting to get obnoxious. Say goodnight to your friends."

"Yes, dear," Johnson grinned stupidly. "Goodnight friends." He waved drunkenly and followed her upstairs.

Nam Po, North Korea

"Where have you been, Yevgeniy?" Marko Zhukov said, out of breath. "He's been asking for you."

"Who, that insane midget?" Kosarev said disgustedly.

"Yes, he wants you to contact him as soon as you get in."

"He can wait until morning," Kosarev bellowed. "I'm tired."

"Where were you?"

"Taking care of some business, it is of no concern," Kosarev waved it away. "Have they come to any decisions regarding the reconstruction of the foundry?"

"That is probably what he wants to talk to you about," Zhukov said as he tried to keep up with Kosarev. "He wouldn't tell me what was on his mind."

"That is fine, it can wait until morning as well. I will have to leave again for a few days in the near future," Kosarev explained. "Moscow is sending me on an inspection tour to Vladivostok."

"The engineers are afraid, Yevgeniy," Zhukov admitted. "Two of our people were killed at the foundry and the rest are afraid there will be more attacks once it is rebuilt."

"Tell them they can be safe in Siberia," Kosarev growled. "Or they can go home with their nine ounces." Nine ounces of lead through their brains in other words, an old Russian saying. "The foundry will be rebuilt, and they will do their part to assist our North Korean comrades in their efforts to join the nuclear fraternity." He felt the bile rise in his throat as he parroted the Party line. "We need the money," Kosarev added before closing the door to his room.

The Pink Lady

"Are you all right," Yung Shu asked in the darkness.

"Yeah, why wouldn't I be," Johnson replied.

"Because three of your friends are dead and you seem to be taking it very well," she said. "Is there something you want to talk about?"

"I wish I could, baby."

"That is just so ridiculous." Yung Shu was exasperated.

"Probably, but that's the way it is," Rick said. "Will you go with me tomorrow?"

"To the memorial service?"

"Yes, I'd like it if you were there, Yung Shu. Roger was your friend too and you knew the Chief. I'd like you with me, baby."

"Of course, I'll go with you," she smiled to herself and took his hand. It was a turning point in their relationship, something she'd never thought he'd do. He kept up the image of strength, arrogance, and bravado that all of the commandos of A-Flight shared, but every so often, he would reveal the sensitive man hiding just below the surface. He was hurting now and his request that she join him at the service was his way of asking for her support in this tough time. Yung Shu was also surprised as she caressed his cheek, feeling the wetness there. She'd never seen him cry, she'd never *see* it, but the dampness on her fingertips told her that he'd lowered another wall. He'd let her take another step closer to the real man that was Richard Johnson. It was his way of telling her how much he loved her, how much he trusted her not to break his heart, and how much more of himself he wanted to give to her.

It was then, lying in the darkness, as Johnson's breathing got more regular, that her mother's words came back to her. *His destiny is not his own.* And it was then she made up her mind to assure that a part of him would be with her always.

Chapter Five
Osan Air Base, South Korea
8 July 1983

There was a crowd in front of the base chapel on the hot summer day that was July 8th, and every pair of eyes in it turned to the young airman in dress blues and the Korean girl walking toward them. He was handsome and walked with the same swagger the rest of those with the black berets did. The girl was beautiful, her coal black hair blowing in the hot breeze, and while every other woman there wore black or Air Force Blue, Song Yung Shu did more than mere justice to the white cocktail dress.

"White?" Reasoner whispered when Johnson stopped at his side.

"White is the color of mourning in Korea," Rick hissed. "Pass the word to the rest of the Ugly Americans. I don't want the Pink Lady picketed by the Wives Club because they're not up on local custom."

"Can do," Reasoner nodded as Chaplain Corrigan appeared at the chapel door. "Rick," Reasoner grabbed his arm as they walked up the steps. "About yesterday . . . I came off a little strong."

"Look, man," Johnson said. "I know we're never going to be best pals, but I respect you and I respect your principles. Let's work this out when we get back to Florida."

"Agreed," Reasoner said. "I'm leaving tomorrow," he added. "I talked to Angie last night and then I asked Bryant for emergency leave."

"Good for you," Johnson gave him a small smile and placed a hand on his shoulder. "I'm sorry, John, really I am. I know how close you and the Chief were. If there's anything I can do . . ."

"That means a lot, Rick, thanks," Reasoner offered a hand and Johnson took it.

***

Holmgren sat in the back, his head pounding. He'd never consumed as much alcohol in one day as he'd done the day before and the hangover was threatening to split his skull. And then he saw them, seven of them in the black berets, one accompanied by a local girl.

Alan did not know why, but he felt his face flush with anger, and it was directed at Roger's comrades, the men he'd considered brothers. *It was their responsibility*, he thought and then pushed his emotions away. The airman with female accompaniment was injured, Holmgren could tell by the slight limp. He had debated asking one of them for the details, the things that weren't written in the after-action reports but decided against it. He knew how they looked at him, how they would see him for Roger had explained that at the beginning.

He fit in the categories the combat troops classified as weenies. There were admin weenies, legal weenies, maintenance weenies, and Intel weenies, the category in which Holmgren fell. They saw weenies deserving of less respect than the men who'd dodged bullets for a living and they would tell him nothing. Should he confess his relationship to Roger in attempt to inspire their cooperation, they would categorize him another way, as a fucking queer deserving of even less respect than a weenie. The most he could expect from them was cool indifference, the least, ridicule and taunting and most likely the end of Holmgren's career.

***

Johnson spotted Beu, Wood, and the rest of the crew of Cowboy-261 in a pew a few rows back and nods were exchanged. Colonel Bryant slid in the pew next to the chopper crew, nodding to Johnson as well. Chaplain Corrigan took his place before the altar and the muted conversation ceased. Almost ten thousand miles away, an identical service was taking place at Hurlburt Field, just north of Pensacola, Florida the home of 1st Special Operations Wing.

"It is always sad when a member of the U.S. military is lost in the line of duty," Corrigan, the Protestant minister, began. "But a few days ago, we lost three of our own and that makes it even more difficult for us to bear. Today we say goodbye to a young officer and an airman, each beginning their careers and a twenty-year chief, on his last assignment before retirement. And today we remember Al Corlies, a veteran of the Vietnam Conflict and a mentor to the young men in his unit, Bob Jenkins, a young officer fresh from the Academy with his first command, and Roger Hoffman a man who'd distinguished himself many times in his short career. Even though we are at peace, these brave men must be prepared for war. Though it is tragic, training accidents do happen . . ."

Blah, blah, blah, Johnson thought as he sat trance-like. Not a religious man, he didn't like being inside houses of worship. He had his own ideas of how life and the universe worked and interacted, and it didn't depend on his faith in some almighty being. He didn't believe in a heaven or an afterlife and could never get a grip on the idea of some guy sitting somewhere with a scorecard, keeping a tally of Johnson's rights and wrongs. If he were mistaken about that, he'd know soon enough, and he was willing to take responsibility for his transgressions. *If they send me to Hell, I'll cut Lucifer's balls off and feed them to him.* It was then he spotted Holmgren.

Of course you'd be here, Johnson thought, as he regarded the young lieutenant, not much older than he. He tried to picture Holmgren and Roger together, enjoying the same things he and Yung Shu did when they went out. *It must have been terrible for them.* Johnson tried to imagine maintaining a relationship while having to keep it hidden from all but the most trusted of associates. *You poor bastards.*

Corrigan's service droned on, just a background as Johnson's mind went other places, namely to the woman sitting demurely next to him. Yung Shu had come to be his life, living for the regular rotations from Hurlburt to Osan. He felt alive here, anywhere with her and though he would visit his parents in New York on every leave, he felt as if he were only going through the motions when he was away from the green-eyed beauty.

I love her, Rick thought. She did things to him, good things, and he never wanted the feelings to end. He felt it more now because this rotation was coming to an end. In less than two weeks, he would be on his way back to Florida, two weeks on Long Island with his mom and dad, and then two and a half dreary months before he would see her again. They would write weekly, but it wasn't the same, not being able to touch her, smell her, and of course not being able to make love to her. *I have to marry her*, he thought for the thousandth time, but this time with determination. *I want to be with you forever*, Johnson said silently as he gazed upon her.

Yung Shu sensed it and turned toward him. "What?" She whispered.

"Nothing," he grinned.

"With that stupid grin on your face, I would say that it is anything *but* nothing." Yung Shu gave him the smile that was his alone.

"I love you," he whispered in her ear.

"Hold that thought until we get home," she said and gave his hand a squeeze.

Vladivostok, Soviet Union

"Papa," she breathed and ran to him.

"How is my love?" He said as he took her in his arms and spun her around.

"It was a long ride on the train, but I would go twice as far to see you," the young woman said as she kissed his cheek.

"The ride will be longer still, Alexa dear," Kosarev said sadly.

"I don't understand, papa," the nineteen year old said as she shook her head, her strawberry blonde curls bouncing around her shoulders. "I have to go back to school in a few weeks."

"You are not going back to Moscow, my sweet. It is no longer safe for you there," Kosarev told her, his steel blue eyes becoming moist.

"But mama ..." And she read her father's eyes. "There is something wrong, isn't there, papa?"

"Your mother has been diagnosed with pancreatic cancer; Alexa dear. The prognosis is terminal, a few months at most," the bear of a man let a tear run down his cheek.

"And you're leaving her in Moscow *alone*? How can you let mama die alone?" Alexa's tears came freely.

"Your mother knows the reasons I must remain here."

"What reason could possibly justify . . ."

"When you are older you will understand, my sweet," Kosarev said. "This involves much more than a single family."

"You sound like those Party apparatchiks back home, papa," she hissed.

"The Party is dying, Alexa," Kosarev insisted. "The Soviet Union is dying, and it will not be long before things become intolerable in Moscow. My position puts your life in danger, my dear, and we are both here at your mother's insistence. We want what is best for you and that cannot happen in Moscow, it cannot happen in Russia."

"You're sending me away?"

"For your protection, my dear," he insisted. "When the Union falls, you will be valuable to my rivals in the Komitet. I will not see you kidnapped and used to guarantee my loyalty. I will not see you used, period."

"Where am I to go, papa?" Her head hung; the enormity of what she was told beginning to sink in. She would never see her mother again, never have the chance, and it was doubtful that her father would be in her life as well.

"I am making the final arrangements now," he said and took her to him. And they cried.

Osan Air Base, South Korea

"Sorry to bother you, Lieutenant," Johnson said when Holmgren opened the door. It looked as if he were packing. "My name is Richard Johnson, and this is Song Yung Shu. We were friends of Roger's, may we come in?"

"Yes . . . please," Holmgren said tentatively. "I'm taking a few days leave." He was agitated, not expecting a visit from those in Roger's unit. Depending on what Johnson knew, this call could mean the end of his career. He bade them to the couch and shut the door quickly. "You . . . you knew?"

"Yes, sir," Johnson replied with a nod. "I'm sure he told you that we consider each other brothers. Roger told us about his sexual orientation, none of us had a problem with it."

"He told you about me too?"

"Only a few of us know about you," Johnson told him. "The rest of the guys think Roger practiced abstinence. I'm here to convey our condolences and to tell you that he died honorably."

"How?" Holmgren's voice was choked.

"He was hit as we were bugging out," Rick explained. "He knew he was dead when I got to him. His chest was wrecked, and I did what I could before carrying him out. He died on the way to the chopper." He turned to Yung Shu, her eyes wide. "This stays here, baby," he warned her. "But Lieutenant Holmgren has a right to know and so do you." He looked back to Holmgren. "I did my best, sir, but I couldn't save him. I brought his body out so he'd be buried on American soil; Lieutenant Jenkins and Chief Corlies will never come home."

"I saw it happen," Holmgren said absently. "I was monitoring the satellite transmission and I saw one of you go down. I didn't think . . . I didn't think it was Roger."

"If there's anything I can do, sir, just let me know," Johnson offered.

"There isn't much to do, is there?" Holmgren looked up at him. "Unless I want to destroy my career."

"Your secret's safe with us, sir," Rick promised.

"I appreciate that, Airman Johnson," Holmgren nodded.

Johnson stood and Yung Shu followed. "I have to go, sir. I'm restricted to quarters, just allowed on base for the service. I'm sorry for your loss, Lieutenant, we all are." Johnson shook Holmgren's hand and beckoned Yung Shu out the door.

"So, what *really* happened to you?" She asked him when they were in the van.

"I was hit twice getting back to the chopper," he said flatly.

"Where *were* you?"

"In the North," he said. "And I'm not telling you anymore."

"But you had no qualms about telling *him*," Yung Shu hissed.

"He's with squadron Intel, he was monitoring the mission," Johnson explained. "You're a civilian."

"Don't you trust me?"

"More than anyone in the world, baby," Rick replied.

"Then why . . ."

"Suppose you let something slip? The North Koreans have agents everywhere. If they knew we were responsible for what happened at the foundry it would cause big problems, not only for the U.S. but for South Korea as well," Rick said. "You can't tell anyone that you know about this, not even the guys."

"I'll keep your secrets, Rick."

"I never had any doubt, baby," he smiled as she steered the van out the front gate.

The Demilitarized Zone
38th Parallel between North and South Korea

It looked like any of the nondescript huts that leaned against one another outside the fence on the northern side of the DMZ. This one was different however, for it was the northern terminus of one of the many tunnels that ran under the no man's land between the Koreas.

There were three men inside the hut: Major Kim Sun Park, his aide Cho, and another man not officially part of North Korean Internal Security. The man was a freelancer, a Japanese with exceptional skills in this arena, referred to Park by members of the Yakuza years before.

"There will be no tolerance for failure," Park said.

"Have I ever failed you, Major?" The man asked, annoyed with the little man.

"The ones with the black berets. It *has* to be one of them," Park insisted.

"It will be, I assure you," the Japanese said, removing the tin cover of the tunnel.

"Do not bother to return if you are unsuccessful," Park said as the man disappeared into the tunnel. Cho reinstalled the cover and both men walked out to the waiting car.

Kim Po International Airport
Seoul, South Korea

"Give me a screwdriver," John Reasoner said when he sat down at the bar. The bartender gave him a friendly smile and prepared the drink quickly. "What a fucking week," he muttered before taking a healthy swig of the vodka-based concoction. He looked over when he saw the young 2nd Lieutenant sit down. "Heading home?" Reasoner asked.

"No, just taking a couple days leave, Sarge," the other man replied. "You're with 23rd?"

"Yeah, rotating back to the States," Reasoner finished the drink and motioned to the bartender.

"Sorry to hear about your mates," the lieutenant said. "I was at the memorial service this morning."

"Thanks, did you know them?" Reasoner asked.

"I went through the Academy with Bob Jenkins," the lieutenant replied. He ordered a scotch on the rocks while the bartender was making Reasoner's second.

Reasoner offered a hand. "John Reasoner," he said.

The lieutenant took it, shaking it firmly. "Alan Holmgren. I'm with squadron Intel."

"Were you ..." Reasoner's voice trailed off as he checked the bar for signs they were being watched.

"Yes, I was monitoring the sat feed that night," Holmgren replied.

"So, you know what *really* happened," Reasoner asked him. "Not that crap they fed the chaplain, the dependents, and the press."

"It looked hairy to say the least," Holmgren told him. He was certain Reasoner was one of the members of A-Flight not aware of his relationship to Roger Hoffman.

Reasoner gulped down the second drink and wiped the moistness from his eyes. "It didn't have to be," he said.

"What do you mean?" Holmgren asked.

"Never mind, Lieutenant, I shouldn't run off at the mouth." Reasoner waved it away, accepting a third drink from the bartender.

"I'll get that one," Holmgren said and threw some bills on the bar.

"Thanks," Reasoner nodded and took a sip.

"We both know how to keep secrets, Sarge," Holmgren pressed.

"It was supposed to be clean and neat," Reasoner said. "But one of our explosives guys is a real cowboy. He decided it would be fun to kill a few Communists before leaving the foundry. There was a battalion of NKPA infantry providing security for the place and bodies dropping all over the place aroused their attention."

"Did you tell them that during the debrief?" Holmgren asked, trying to hide his surprise.

"Nope, didn't have proof. If I did, he'd be in custody right now," Reasoner shrugged. "But we lost radio contact with them when they went inside, all that steel and concrete, and I'm sure you didn't see anything on the sat."

"No, the ambient heat in the building didn't allow us to use infrared," Holmgren said.

"Then his story stands."

"What's his story?"

"That they were spotted by a group of Russian engineers and one of them sounded an alarm," Reasoner replied.

"It sounds reasonable," Holmgren offered.

"Yeah, but you don't know Johnson the way I do," Reasoner chuckled.

"That's his name?"

"Yeah, but forget I told you, Lieutenant. Stonewall Bryant likes him, and the old man will cut your nuts off if he hears rumors to that effect," Reasoner warned.

"Consider it forgotten," Holmgren made gesture of surrender.

Reasoner looked at his watch. "I've gotta catch my flight. It's been good talking to you, Lieutenant."

"Same here, have a safe trip home." Holmgren watched him go, his mind spinning. *Was that why Johnson came to see me? Was it to ease his guilty conscience?* He finished his drink when he heard his commuter flight to Taegu being called. *I have to know more*, he thought as he grabbed his bag.

The Pink Lady

"Hey," Beu said when he spotted Johnson and Yung Shu enter. "What took you so long?"

"Had to take care of something on the way," Johnson informed him. Yung Shu went straight upstairs to change. He looked around to see most of his comrades were there as well. "Did you bring the chaplain over here too?"

"I don't think this is his kind of place," Beu laughed as Lin Yii arrived with a shot and a beer for both of them.

"Hi, Nate," she said dreamily, ignoring Johnson.

"What am I, wood?" Johnson asked.

"Don't take the gunner's name in vain," Hermann Wood proclaimed as he came over.

"Yeah hi, Rick," Lin Yii said before leaving.

"I wanted to thank you for letting me use your spare room," Beu said, fishing the key out of his pocket.

"Hold on to it," Johnson said before tossing back his shot of Jack Daniel's. "I might not always be nearby when you need it."

"You're okay for an enlisted guy," Beu kidded.

"Just don't tell anyone you have it," Johnson warned. "The property value will go down if they know an officer stays here and the Mama-san will shove her broomstick up your ass."

"She's wicked with that thing," Beu agreed, having seen the little woman chase an inebriated Marine out a little under an hour before. "She chased a Recon Marine out of here with his tail between his legs a little while ago. By the way, why hasn't she killed you yet for sleeping with her daughter? How old is she anyway?"

"Yung Shu's nineteen," Johnson replied with a conspiratorial smile. "The Mama-san I have no idea about, but she loves me. I broke up a robbery my first day here and she took a shine to me."

"The Mama-san or Yung Shu?"

"Both, officer-boy," Johnson grinned.

"Did you go see the IG yet?" Wood asked Johnson.

"Tomorrow, I can't wait," his voice dripping with sarcasm. "Fucking pencil pushers are going to second guess everything we did, easy to do from the relative safety of an American base a couple hundred miles away from the action." Johnson took a healthy gulp of his beer.

"It's not that bad," Beu said. "The bird colonel running the show, a guy named Forrester, was a forward air controller in Nam. He knows what happens on the ground."

"I hope so," Johnson shrugged and contemplated his empty shot glass.

"Is there a problem?"

"I've got a rep, Nate," Johnson looked up at him as Lin Yii refilled his glass. "Some of the lifers in the squadron consider me a cowboy and I'm sure they made the IG aware of that."

Beu laughed heartily. "Do you know how many times they've called me that?"

"Yeah, but you're an officer *and* one of the best chopper pilots from what I hear. I'm just an enlisted weenie in a bad economy. They can get rid of me and there'll be a hundred guys standing in line for my job," Johnson said.

"From what I hear, you don't plan to stay in anyhow," Beu said.

"Yeah, but I don't want to get thrown out halfway through my hitch. I try to finish what I start. I don't need to go looking for a civilian job with a dishonorable discharge and maybe some time in CC on my record."

"They *won't* throw you in jail," Beu insisted. "You worry too much."

"If they throw me out, I won't be able to come back here either," Johnson said.

"Why would you want to? This place is an armpit," Beu countered. Johnson just gave him a dirty look. "The girl?" Johnson nodded. "Have you fallen that hard?" Johnson nodded again. "Aren't you a bit young to be thinking of commitment?"

"I'm twenty-two."

"I'm gonna be *thirty*-two and it's the farthest thing from my mind."

"It was until I met Yung Shu," Johnson admitted with a grin.

"So, marry her," Beu said.

"I'm planning on it," Johnson knocked back the other shot. "I'm going to make the arrangements the next time we rotate in."

"Why don't you do a civil thing now before we leave?"

"And deprive the Mama-san of making the wedding plans? Remember the broomstick?" Johnson smiled. "Besides, Yung Shu has the right to feel like a princess on her wedding day. Lord knows, working here isn't conducive to that feeling."

"You're a hopeless romantic, aren't you, boy?"

"Hey, what can I tell you?" Johnson shrugged. "I'll remind you of this conversation when you find the love of your life."

"Until the Air Force issues me a wife, I'll be a bachelor," Beu declared.

"That's a good thing," Lin Yii said as she passed, once again looking at Beu longingly.

"You made some impression," Johnson said conspiratorially.

"Ah, it's a gift," Beu said, leaning back and downing his shot of Wild Turkey. "Once you've had Beu, nothing else compares," he grinned.

"Pardon me while I puke," Johnson joked. "Are all chopper pilots such good bullshit artists?"

"It's another gift of mine," Beu told him.

"Don't get him going," Wood warned. "His ego is as big as yours, Rick."

"Mine's bigger," Johnson said with a smile.

Taegu, South Korea

Holmgren changed out of his uniform into jeans and a polo shirt on the plane, arriving at Taegu appearing as just another tourist. There were American military personnel here but not in the concentration they were farther to the north. Most of the white faces here belonged to tourists, mainly European, and that worked well for Holmgren should he be spotted arriving at his destination.

The destination was a hotel that he and Roger frequented; a place not so inclined to scrutinize the identity of its patrons. He signed in under a false name and went directly to his room, depositing his bags and departing. Holmgren's next stop was to a place that did not appear on any of the tourist maps. It was down a few blocks and then down an alley, an establishment that bore no markings to denote it from any of the other buildings that backed on to the alley.

Stepping through the door was as if he'd stepped into another world. The lighting was garish and dance music pounded from the speakers, strobes flashing in time to the music. Holmgren made is way to the bar and was noticed by the bare-chested young man immediately. "Hi, Alan," he said.

"Hi, Quanh," Holmgren replied without emotion. "Scotch neat, please."

"Where's Roger," Quanh asked as he placed the drink on the bar.

"Roger died last week," Holmgren said, his voice quavering.

Quanh's face revealed shock and sadness, knowing the American couple since they became regular customers almost two years before. "Good god, how?"

"A helicopter accident," Holmgren told him, wiping a sleeve across his eyes. "It's why I'm here; I had to get away from the base for a while, everything reminds me of him."

"What are you going to do?"

"I haven't thought that far," Holmgren admitted. "I don't think I've been sober since."

"Have you talked to anyone?"

"Who am I going to talk to, Quanh? My career is the only thing I have left," Holmgren said as he shook his head sadly.

"Are you staying in the usual place?"

"Yes, the *Tongdaegu-jang Yogwan*," Holmgren replied as he tossed back his drink.

"I'll stop by tomorrow," Quanh offered. "We can talk then."

"If you want," Holmgren shrugged.

"You shouldn't be alone at a time like this, Alan," Quanh insisted. "I'll be by in the morning and we'll do something, get your mind on something else."

"Thanks, you've always been a good friend, Quanh," Holmgren smiled sadly.

"You and Roger have been good to me. I'm happy to be a friend when you need one so badly."

"I'll see you tomorrow."

The Pink Lady

Yung Shu stared at the package of tablets in her hand as she stood before the toilet in the midst of the biggest decision of her young life. With a nod of determination, she began pushing them all out of the bubble wrap, watching each drop into the water with a splash.

"This is the right thing," she said aloud as the last of the pills was discharged. She moved tentatively to flush, but another nod steeled her resolve and she pulled the lever, her mother's words echoing in her mind once more. *His destiny is not his own.*

"Are you up here, baby?" Rick's voice penetrated the door.

"In the bathroom," she called back to him. "I'll be right there." Yung Shu checked to see if all the pills had disappeared before opening the door.

Johnson's eyes grew wide when he saw her naked form emerge. "I thought you were coming down."

"I had other ideas," she said in a sultry voice smiling as she began to remove his shirt.

"I see that," he chuckled when she started on his pants after letting the shirt drop to the floor. Pulling his pants around his ankles, she reached for him; slowly stroking his manhood to attention while playing her tongue over his abdomen, working steadily lower, finally taking him in her mouth. Johnson let out a groan and she felt him becoming even more aroused.

"Not yet," she whispered.

"What about my boots?"

"I can't wait that long," she breathed as she stood, putting her arms around him. Rick picked her off the ground and slid her onto him, eliciting small cries as he impaled her on his erection. "Oh yes, Rick," she whispered as his rhythm became faster. Yung Shu felt like his toy as he held her, furiously slamming her into him until she felt her climax coming.

"Oh shit," he groaned as he exploded inside her, his pleasure arriving in concert with hers. Yung Shu wrapped her legs around him as he stood there, holding her as she quivered in violent orgasm.

"I love you, Rick," she breathed in his ear.

"I love you too, baby, more than anyone and anything."

Vladivostok, Soviet Union

"Kamchatka? What is there, papa?" Alexa Kosarev asked.

"Friends," he replied. "They will see to your safety until the final details are in place."

"When will that be?"

"Soon, very soon, my sweet," he caressed her cheek.

"Where will I go then?"

"It is best you don't know until the time comes," Kosarev said. "You will be safer that way."

"But I don't want to leave. I want to stay with you and mama."

"Please understand, Alexa dear," he soothed. "I would not do this were it not absolutely necessary. Do you think I could bear to do this if it weren't imperative?"

"No, papa," she said as the tears came again. "But is there no other way?"

"None," he shook his head as he took her to him. "If giving my life so you could stay in Russia were an option, I gladly would take it." Father's tears fell along with his daughters once again, both knowing that this would probably be the last bit of time they would spend together.

Chapter Six
Osan Air Base, South Korea
9 July 1983

"Hey, boy," Nate Beu said as Johnson approached the steps of the headquarters building.

"What are you doing here?" Rick asked him.

"Just offering moral support," he replied, taking a bite from an apple. "Your boy, Campbell, is inside."

"Fucking bullshit," Johnson muttered.

"Don't go in there with that attitude, Rick," Beu warned. "Old Forrester won't put up with it."

"This is unnecessary," Johnson declared. "They watched it all on a sat feed."

"It's standard operating procedure, especially when the operation involved loss of life," Beu explained. "Just answer their questions."

"Why do I have the feeling I'm going to need a lawyer before this is over?"

"Just go and get it over with," Beu urged, taking another bite of the fruit.

"Yeah, yeah," Johnson waved and entered the building, making his way up to the second-floor conference room. Campbell was just leaving.

"Hey, New York," he said.

"How bad was it?"

Campbell looked at his watch. "It took a little over a half hour, not bad."

"I'll be the judge of that," Johnson nodded and knocked on the door twice before entering. "Airman Johnson reports as ordered," he said as he came to attention in front of the five men seated at the long table.

"Sit down, Airman," Colonel Jack Forrester said. "As you may know, we are not here to assign blame, just to get all the relevant facts of the mission."

"Yes, sir," Johnson said. He looked over the panel, recognizing Captain Vaughan from the intelligence section. Vaughan would be an ally; at the least, he would understand the situation. The other three he had his doubts about. Two wore Senior Missileman badges, a major and a captain, and the third, a lieutenant who seemed to be an admin officer. *Great,* Johnson said to himself. *Two SAC weenies and a titless WAF, shoot me now*

"Would you please give us your version of what happened once you entered Foundry Number Five, Airman?" Forrester asked him.

"I'll give you the truth, sir. That's the *only* version."

"There is no need to get defensive, Airman," the SAC major said.

"I think there is, sir," Johnson shrugged. "I have a problem with being judged by a couple of pencil necks who've spent most of their careers locked in a hole in the ground waiting for doomsday and another who probably couldn't find the business end of an M-16 if you paid him." He saw Vaughan stifle a laugh.

"I'd recommend a readjustment of that attitude, Airman Johnson," Forrester warned. "You could leave here in the custody of the security police."

"Sorry, sir," Johnson said, not meaning it.

"This is not a trial, Airman," the SAC major continued. "Please give your account or a trial *will* be convened, and you will be court martialed for failure to follow a direct order."

"Yes, sir," Johnson nodded and proceeded to recite the chain of events that led to the deaths of three of his comrades. When he was finished, he looked up at the five of them defiantly.

"I'd say you left a few things out, Airman Johnson," Forrester said.

"I don't believe so, sir," Johnson shot back.

Forrester considered him for a few seconds before checking the papers before him, making a show of finding the correct one.

"According to Major Beu, the helicopter pilot who extracted you, you displayed incredible heroism and disregard for your own safety, allowing the rest of your team to reach the safety of the helicopter. In addition, you risked your life in order to bring the body of your fallen comrade home."

"Major Beu impresses easily," Johnson said nonchalantly. "Any of the other guys would have done the same, sir."

"No he *doesn't*, Airman," Forrester growled. "I've known him for a decade, and you are the first person he's recommended for a decoration."

"I will have to express my gratitude," Johnson said facetiously.

"While I am impressed by your heroism, Airman Johnson," the SAC captain said. "I can't help but wonder if things could have been done a bit less dramatically."

"Are you accusing me of something, Captain?" Johnson snarled at him.

"We have heard you have a reputation, Airman," the captain shot back. "Rumor has it you have a flair for . . . taking the *initiative*."

"Isn't that what the Air Force wants, sir, men who can think on their feet?"

"Not when their actions put the lives of the team at risk and jeopardize the success of the mission."

"The mission *was* a success, Captain," Johnson said.

"But three Air Force personnel are dead."

"Don't you think I wouldn't trade my life to bring the three of them back? But that's what happens in combat, sir; sometimes people die. Captain Vaughan understands that, and I'd wager Colonel Forrester does too." The SAC weenie didn't reply. "Have *you* ever had a thousand infantry troops chasing you through a forest at a run? Have *you* ever dodged enemy fire, Captain?" The captain averted his eyes and shook his head. "Well then don't judge until you *have*. Everything came apart and we did our best to ensure the success of the mission."

"*How* did it come apart, Airman?" Colonel Forrester asked.

"I'm not blaming anyone, mind you, but Intel said there would only be a skeleton crew on the night shift. If that were a skeleton crew, I'd hate to see how many were on the day shift, sir," Johnson told him. "That's not counting the contingent of Russian engineers that were present. One of them spotted me and sounded an alarm after I placed the charges. Airman 1st Class Emory and I had to shoot our way out. After that it all went to hell."

"Why didn't you abort when you saw how many people were in there?" The admin weenie finally spoke up.

"And then what, Lieutenant?" Johnson asked him.

"What do you mean, Airman?"

"I might be on the bottom of the food chain around here, but I know the reasons we were there," Johnson said. "We were there to send a message to the North Koreans. Either they return to the talks in Geneva or we'll systematically take out their infrastructure. The President needed us to be successful and he needed us to do it now, not in a week or a month. We gave him the leverage to force the Koreans back to the table."

"That wasn't your call, Airman," the admin lieutenant fired back.

"Yes, it *was*, sir," Johnson shot back. "Just as the satellite couldn't see inside the foundry, our radios didn't work worth a damn either. I couldn't raise Lieutenant Jenkins, hell, I couldn't raise Emory and he was inside with me. It *was* my call and I made it, period. If I have to hang for it, then I'll hang alone."

"You just might, Airman," the lieutenant said.

"So be it," Johnson spat as he turned to Forrester. "Do I need a lawyer, sir?"

"No, Airman Johnson," Forrester said. "It seems Major Beu's account of your heroism has made it to the attention of the President. It wouldn't do to convene a court martial in light of that, don't you think?"

"I don't hide behind *anyone's* skirts, Colonel Forrester, not even the President's," Johnson said boldly. "If you feel I've done something wrong then put me on trial. I'll stand behind my decisions and you can take your best shot."

"You've got a set, that's for sure," Forrester chuckled, drawing dirty looks from all but Vaughan who smiled.

"Solid brass, Colonel. You and I both put our pants on one leg at a time."

"That we do, Airman," Forrester said with a nod. "Thank you for your time." Johnson came to attention. "You're dismissed, Johnson."

"Thank you, sir," Rick said and did an about face, heading for the door.

"One more thing, Johnson," Forrester said, and Rick stopped.

"Yes, sir?"

"Good work out there, son. Major Beu was right about you."

"I'll take that as a compliment, sir."

"You'd better," Forrester traded a smile with Johnson. "Good luck."

"Thank you, Colonel." Rick gave him a nod and left the room, nearly bumping into Stonewall Bryant. "Sorry, sir; got my head up my ass."

"I just came by to see how you were doing," Bryant said. "Major Beu said you were inside."

"It went okay, Colonel," Johnson told him. "Thanks for the support."

"I came by for something else too," Bryant said. "Just got word from Washington, your commendation went through. There'll be a ceremony tomorrow at the base theater."

"Couldn't you just hand me the damn thing in your office, sir?"

"No," Bryant said without explanation. "Is Forrester in there?"

"Yes, sir."

"Be at the base theater at 0900 and leave your girlfriend at home, clearances and all," Bryant ordered.

"I understand, sir, and thanks again," Johnson said as Bryant went into the conference room. He went in the opposite direction, down the stairs and back outside. Beu pulled up to the curb in a government Chevrolet just as Rick was about to cross the street.

"Need a ride, big boy?"

"I was gonna call Yung Shu," Johnson replied.

"I'll take you. I need a drink anyway and I think a little celebration is in order," Beu said.

"You heard?"

"Yeah, ran into Bryant a little while ago."

"They're doing a thing at the theater at 0900 tomorrow," Johnson muttered. "I hate these dog and pony shows."

"It's good for morale, Rick," Beu explained. "Three of our people are dead and everyone else is walking around in a funk over it. Having someone in our wing being given one of the highest honors in the military might just be the thing to snap them out of it."

"You say so, pal," Johnson shrugged. "*My* morale would be better if I wasn't put on display for them all to ogle."

"You're too young to be so grouchy," Beu observed as he drove through the main gate.

Taegu, South Korea

"So, tell me what happened," Quanh said as he sipped his Mimosa.

"It was a training accident," Holmgren replied. Though it was ten thirty in the morning, scotch was his beverage of choice as they waited for their meals to come.

"That sounds like the bullshit they feed the press," Quanh noted.

"Then call it a live fire exercise," Holmgren hissed. "And somebody fucked up."

"Do they know who?"

"Sure," Holmgren said disgustedly. "One of the guys who was there told me."

"So, they're going to put him in jail, right?"

"They don't have any evidence, no eyewitnesses, nothing," Holmgren shrugged. "They can't touch him. Besides, his commanding officer likes him, so it'll all get swept under the rug."

"Can't you do anything?" Quanh asked as the waiter brought their meals.

"Not without firsthand corroboration," Holmgren said. "I feel so helpless, so violated. Roger was my life, Quanh." He wiped away a tear. "Would you believe he came to see me?"

"Who, the one who screwed up?"

"Yes, to offer his condolences," Holmgren nodded. "He came with his girlfriend."

"He knew about you and Roger?" Quanh was astonished.

"Yes, they're all close. They depend on each other to stay alive when they're in combat and they consider each other brothers," Holmgren explained. "I'm sure the one who told me about the screw up didn't know about Roger and me or he wouldn't have said anything."

"Why did he talk to you as it is?"

"We're part of the same outfit but I'm with the intelligence section. He knew I had clearance and was aware of the particulars." Holmgren looked over at the young man. "Why are we talking about this anyway? I thought we were trying to get my mind off it?"

"You have to talk about it," Quanh lectured. "You can't keep it all bottled up inside."

"I'm going to get him one day," Holmgren promised. "I'm going to make him pay for what he did to me."

"That's not a healthy attitude," Quanh said.

"What attitude am I *supposed* to have? Am I supposed to just shrug it off? I have a *right* to be angry."

"Yes, you do," Quanh replied. "But no good can come in the pursuit of vengeance."

"We'll see about that."

Quanh's hand went to Holmgren's, patting it softly. "Promise me you won't do anything until you have time to think this out." Holmgren just stared, looking past Quanh to a spot a million miles away. "Please, Alan, promise me."

"I promise," Holmgren said, returning to this world. "I'm just frustrated."

"Let's get out of here," Quanh said as he tossed two hundred won on the table to cover the meal. "We have to get your mind on something else."

The Pink Lady

"They're giving your boy a medal tomorrow," Beu told Yung Shu when she stopped at their table.

"Yeah, thanks to this clown," Rick indicated Beu.

"For your actions during the helicopter accident?" Yung Shu gave them both a knowing smile.

"She knows?" Beu asked him.

"A little," Johnson grinned. "She tortured it out of me."

Beu smiled as well. "You should be proud of him, darlin'."

"I am," she replied. "As long as he doesn't get himself killed. Medals are nice, but I'd rather have him less decorated and alive."

"Amen to that," Beu said with a nod. "Can we get a round?"

"Sure," Yung Shu said. "I'll be back in a minute." Not long after she departed, the five other members of A-Flight entered along with Hermann Wood.

"I hear it's time to celebrate," Campbell said.

"*I* should be the one getting the medal," Mason kidded. "Without me, your ass would be fertilizer right now."

"And I'm eternally grateful," Johnson said.

"So, you're buying the drinks?" Mason asked him.

"Since when do you pay for drinks here?"

"True," Mason agreed.

Yung Shu arrived with a tray full of beers and several bottles of bourbon. "Here you go, boys."

"Thanks, baby," Johnson pulled her close and kissed her. "When is your shift over?"

She looked at her watch. "Two hours, as soon as Lin Yii gets here," she said. "And then you're all mine." Yung Shu gave them the stern look she'd inherited from her mother. "We're going to celebrate *privately*."

"Are you *sure* you don't have a sister, Yung Shu?" Guthrie asked her.

"I'm one of a kind," she said proudly.

"I've said it before and I'll say it again," Campbell said. "You're one lucky bastard, Rick."

"I know." He kissed Yung Shu once more before she left to see to the other patrons. "And she's all mine."

***

Is drinking their only recreation? Kosarev watched them all entering the club, knowing it would be another late night of partying. *They drink more than a Russian.* The KGB colonel had seen how they celebrated firsthand and decided that another surveillance was unnecessary. They would be inside until the wee hours of the morning and there was no point in sitting in his car for hours. He put it in gear and took off, leaving Osan and heading north to Inch On. Once on the coast, Kosarev would meet his contact, a fisherman who would take him to his destination on the coast of North Korea. The next time he crossed into the South would be when he put his plan into irrevocable motion.

***

Holmgren looked over at the young Korean man who slept peacefully next to him and railed at himself. *It's too soon*, he thought, yet the sex was astonishing. Quanh had done things that Roger and he never had. Holmgren cursed himself for enjoying the feeling and wanting more. He leaned over and brushed his lips against Quanh's, waking him.

"Hi," Quanh said. "I'm sorry if I came on a little strong, but I've wanted you for a long time."

"I hope you still do," Holmgren said as he reached under the sheet, finding what he sought.

"Yes, I do," Quanh smiled as Holmgren's lips, fingers, and tongue aroused him.

***

"Oh yeah," Rick moaned as he climaxed. He lay on his back as Yung Shu rode him without abandon, collapsing on top of him when his orgasm subsided.

"I love you," she whispered in his ear.

"I love you too, baby," Rick replied, his breathing returning to normal. "Can you get the day off day after tomorrow? Tell your mother I'll owe her a favor."

"I'll ask her in the morning," she said as she decoupled from him and lay at his side. "What do you have planned?"

"It's a surprise," he grinned.

"Tell me," she nudged him.

"Nope, then it wouldn't be a surprise." He shook his head.

"So I'll have to wait for *two* days?"

"I think it'll be worth it," Rick declared. "At least, I hope you think so."

"We'll see, won't we?" Yung Shu gave him a sly smile.

***

He looked down on the base from the thickly wooded hillside, his Honda dirt bike leaning against a tree and covered with branches.

He'd arrived earlier in the afternoon after meeting a contact in Osan. Provided with a rifle equipped with a long range scope and the motorcycle along with a supply of food and water, he found this spot from which he could survey the entire base and flightline concealed from the prying eyes of the Air Force Security Police. Not that he was worried about his being discovered, the SPs weren't much concerned about what happened outside their perimeter fence. They were more interested in those speeding on base than their perimeter security and that worked out well for the man atop the hill. He got himself comfortable and settled in to wait.

Nam Po, North Korea

"I am starting to believe that you are not giving our predicament your full attention, Comrade Kosarev," Major Park hissed. "Your unexplained absences are most disturbing."

"And to you my absences will remain unexplained," Kosarev growled. "The business of the Soviet Union is none of your concern, Major Park."

"What do you plan to do about this unexpected contingency?" Park demanded.

"The security, or lack thereof, at your facilities do not concern me," Kosarev informed him. "Just as the loss of two of our engineers does not trouble you. My people are here at your request and your arrangements for their safety are a dismal failure."

"They are paid well enough for the risks they take," Park shot back.

"After the fiasco at your foundry, they don't care about the money, Major Park. They want to leave, and I don't blame them. They are worried that another attack will come when the facility reopens. Before they go back to work, the Soviet Union will need some guarantees."

"They will go back to work when I tell them to," Park insisted. "The Soviet Union has been paid handsomely for their expertise and you will honor your commitments."

"If my people are scared, they will not work, regardless of how I motivate them," Kosarev replied. "When operations are restarted, you will be expected to provide adequate security for my people or there will be no commitment. They are not Korean, Comrade Park, and you may not use them at your whim. Your people's lives might have little value to you, but these are some of the best and brightest the Soviet Union have to offer, and I will not have their lives wasted. If you want our continued cooperation, you *will* provide adequate security."

"My superiors will hear of your insolence, Kosarev," Park promised.

"And mine have already been informed of *yours*," the Russian shot back. "You might be the big fish in this pond, but you will not be permitted to dictate terms to the Soviet Union."

"Do not threaten me," Park warned.

"Do not test the determination of the Kremlin, Major Park. Without us, North Korea will continue to be the Third World toilet of Asia. Your Chinese brothers have given up on you and we will do the same if you do not learn your place." Kosarev turned and left the office then, his anger at the little maniac threatening to overwhelm his common sense.

I would be doing the world a favor if I killed him, Kosarev thought. *But we need his money*, he added to himself disgustedly.

Kosarev was proud, a Hero of the Soviet Union five times over, first recognized as such at the battle of Leningrad as a conscript tank gunner, facing down the German blitz, and later for his part in protecting Moscow from the Nazi menace during the Great Patriotic War. He was proud of himself and proud of his country, not necessarily the Communist system, but he would gladly give his life to protect Mother Russia. Having to associate with these Korean barbarians, let alone help them gain admittance into the nuclear community, galled him.

He felt it a mistake, not only because Kim Sun Park was a madman, but also the government of North Korea itself was close to dysfunctional. Corruption and patronage abounded, not that the Soviets were much better, but a nuclear doctrine had been established, an understanding of sorts between the Soviets and Americans. Neither side believed the other would launch a nuclear first strike and the weapons had been classified as defensive armament, only to be used if the other side fired first. Kosarev was certain the Americans would never attack and was just as certain the Soviet leadership felt the same way.

He did not believe the North Koreans would show the same restraint, nor would they hesitate to sell the knowledge acquired from the Soviets to other, even less responsible parties. As he made his way to his car, Kosarev was determined to assure the Koreans would never enter the nuclear fraternity. *At least, not so long as I am here.* His superiors would be surprised to learn it was he who'd allowed the location of the foundry to be discovered by the Americans, and he would do it again once the facility was rebuilt at another location.

"Hopefully, Park will be dead by then," he said aloud as he drove to his hotel.

Taegu, South Korea

"I have to go to work," Quanh said as he rose. Holmgren remained in bed. "I'm sorry we didn't do anything today the way I promised."

"Do you call that nothing?" Holmgren said of the sex they shared. They'd remained in bed all day, each taking turns pleasuring the other. "You did take my mind off my problems."

"I feel like I was treading on Roger's grave," Quanh replied as he buttoned his pants.

"That's my problem, not yours," Holmgren assured him. "Were I not willing …"

"I know, but I feel as if I seduced you."

"So, what if you did," Holmgren shrugged. "I am an officer in the United States Air Force. I doubt you could have talked me into anything I wasn't willing to do."

"If you say so," Quanh leaned over to kiss him. "Will I see you again before you go back?"

"I hope so," Holmgren said. "I'll be here until tomorrow. Why don't you come back when you get off work?"

"I'll do that," Quanh promised and kissed him once more before leaving the room. He took the elevator downstairs and then made a left heading directly to the Tondaegu train station. He took a seat in the waiting area just as the train to Seoul was pulling in and it wasn't long before a man sat down next to him.

"This had better be important," the man said to Quanh, disgusted that he'd been summoned to this shithole city from Seoul.

"I have one for you," Quanh told him, wilting under his glare. "An American Air Force intelligence officer."

"Where is he?"

"At the *Tongdaegu-jang Yogwan*," Quanh told him. "In room 212," he added. "I'm going back there in a few hours."

"Very well, I will alert our team," the man informed him and reached into his pocket, surreptitiously handing Quanh an envelope. "This had better be worthwhile."

"It is," Quanh nodded. "I am almost certain he has knowledge of the raid last week."

"*We* will determine if what he knows is useful," the man growled before getting up and leaving the station.

Quanh left via another exit, feeling suddenly dirty. Yes, he'd sold out other Americans who'd kept their sexual preferences hidden, but he'd always considered Alan and Roger friends. The financial benefit was too powerful to pass up however and Quanh needed the money to supplement the meager salary he earned tending bar. His heroin addiction demanded a steady cash flow and North Korean Internal Security was always willing to pay handsomely.

Chapter Seven
Osan Air Base, South Korea
10 July 1983

"While on a classified mission, Senior Airman Richard Johnson risked his life to save the lives of his unit and return the body of Airman 1st Class Roger Hoffman to friendly territory," Colonel Bryant told the assemblage. "On behalf of the President of the United States, the U.S. Air Force, and 1st Special Operations Wing, it gives me great pleasure to present Airman Johnson with the Silver Star." Bryant turned to Johnson and pinned the medal to the left breast of his dress uniform.

"Thank you, sir," Johnson said as he saluted.

"No, thank you, son," Bryant replied while returning the salute and then offering a hand. The forty people present in the theater began a hearty applause as Johnson shook it. "See, that wasn't so bad," Bryant whispered.

"Speak for yourself, sir," Johnson smiled. "This ain't my cup of tea."

"Well, you'd better like it for the next few minutes," Bryant ordered. "I expect you to go down there and accept their congratulations or I'll kick your ass."

"I read you five by five, Colonel," Johnson grinned as he stepped off the stage.

"As if you didn't have a big enough ego," Ron Gibbs said as he shook Johnson's hand.

"There'll be no living with him now," Emory added.

"Ah, can it, will ya?" Johnson muttered.

"Good job, Rick," Beu said, also offering congratulations.

"Thank you I think, Major Beu," Rick smiled. "Do you see the crap I'll have to put up with from here on?"

"Suffer," Beu kidded.

"Johnson," the voice of Colonel Bryant could be heard.

"Yes, sir?"

"Reasoner's replacement from B-Flight will be arriving at Kim Po in an hour," Bryant said. "Go get him."

"Me?"

"Is there a *problem*," Bryant raised an eyebrow.

"No, sir, no problem," Johnson replied. "I think the old man is messing with me," he whispered to Beu.

"You're his golden boy for the time being," Beu explained. "Who better to pick up the senior NCO from B-Flight? I'm sure Stonewall expects you to let it slip about the medal. It might motivate the B-Flight boys a little when they get here."

"The guy's name is Garza," Bryant called to Johnson from the door. "He's coming in on the Korean Air Flight from San Francisco."

"Yes, sir," Johnson sighed and turned back to Beu. "I gotta go and change. I hate wearing Class A."

"Don't dawdle," he warned with a wink. "Yung Shu can wait until you get back with Garza." Beu gave a chuckle.

"Don't be smart, officer-boy," Johnson muttered. "It's not you."

Beu gave Johnson a ride to the motor pool where he signed out a government Ford and headed off base. He thought about his new friend, the officer who seemed slightly off kilter. *Takes one to know one*, Rick thought. Johnson thought Beu one of the better officers he'd ever met, in a league with Stonewall Bryant and probably even Colonel Forrester from the Inspector General's office. They were men of character, not among those who'd derived their power from rank alone. They had their power because they had the respect of the troops; they'd been there and come out alive, just as he had, just as the survivors of A-Flight's last mission had. Johnson admitted he would follow any one of them into Hell because he knew they would lead him back out again. "And we'd cut the Devils balls off on the way," he laughed. He liked that saying and he felt genuinely capable of accomplishing the task. He had to or he wouldn't be good at what he did.

Nam Po, North Korea

"There you are," Marko Zhukov burst into Kosarev's office.

"What do you want, Marko?" Kosarev said tiredly.

"We have been recalled," he said excitedly. "Chairman Andropov gave the order himself." Zhukov thrust the communiqué from the embassy in Pyong Yang at him.

"What does that windbag want now," Kosarev looked at the paper and then laid it aside.

"Do you think Major Park caused some trouble for us?" Zhukov said nervously.

"It would have the same effect as a flea biting a dog's ass," Kosarev muttered. "An irritation, nothing more."

"You have been out here too long, my friend," Zhukov replied. "That tone would not be tolerated at the Kremlin."

"They will tolerate what I give them, Marko. The Chairman owes me much and he knows it," Kosarev explained. "It is I who has kept the Chinese out of his backside as they looked longingly to Siberia for its natural resources and he is *quite* aware of that. Were it not for my support when his predecessor died, he would be fertilizing a *collektiv* rather than occupying the Kremlin."

"But you cannot dictate to him," Zhukov exclaimed. "I do not want to live out my days in Lubyanka."

"We're not going to prison," Kosarev waved it away. "He probably wants the facts of the attack this week."

"Will you tell him the Americans were behind it?"

"We have no evidence of that," the KGB colonel said. "All we know is someone sabotaged the facility, engaged and evaded the inept security force, and killed two of our engineers in the process."

"Who else could it have been, Yevgeniy?"

"The South Koreans, the Japanese, the British just to name a few, Marko. I am only concerned no one will pay for the lives of *our* people. I don't give a damn about the Koreans or their facility."

"Major Park expects us to help them rebuild."

"If he has hard currency, we will help him," Kosarev replied. "Make the arrangements for our return, Marko, I will deal with Park."

Zhukov nodded and left, and Kosarev turned to the window. *The wind is about to change direction,*" he thought.

He doubted Andropov even cared about Major Park and his ranting; this recall was something else. *Andropov is worried. He is consolidating his power base,* Kosarev thought as he watched the bulldozers clearing the wreckage of the foundry. *He wants me to watch his back.* And it was then Kosarev knew why he was being recalled. *A power struggle is about to begin.* He was certain of that and he was all the more certain he made the right choice with regard to his beautiful daughter. Kosarev checked his watch. *She should be in Kamchatka by now.* The plan would have to be put in motion before he returned to Moscow and there was one more thing to do here as well. *Time will be tight,* he thought as he returned to his paperwork.

Kim Po International Airport, Seoul, South Korea

"You Garza?" Johnson asked the tech sergeant in Class A although he didn't have to. The black beret signified him as a member of 23rd Special Tactics Squadron and the nametag displayed the correct moniker. "Johnson," he offered a hand and Garza shook it.

"You're the guy who got the Star, aren't you?" Garza asked him.

"Yeah," Johnson muttered. "Through here." He led the way to the baggage claim.

"How bad was it?" Garza inquired.

"It went to shit quick," Johnson told him. "Were you at the memorial service at Hurlburt?"

"Yeah," Garza nodded. He was an inch or two shorter than Johnson and his face was round, giving him the appearance of a bobble-head doll.

"They bought it on the way back to the LZ," Rick said. "It looked like the forest was on fire and then the place blew like we opened up the gates of Hell. There were rounds in the air as thick as mosquitoes in a Florida swamp. A couple of them had RPGs, you know, that Russian made crap." Garza nodded again and spotted his bags. "Thankfully, about a quarter of them were duds or we all would have been cut down. Did you know any of them?"

"I knew Al Corlies," Garza replied. "Went to the seminar he gave at the NCO Academy last year. We shot the shit over a few beers after the class. He seemed like a straight up guy."

"He was up for retirement in a couple months," Johnson shook his head as he led the way out of the terminal. "The poor bastard," he added. "He lived through Nam only to buy it here. Over here," he pointed to the blue Ford in the parking lot. "You ever been here?"

"Nope, we worked in and out of the Philippines at last year's SPECFOREX," Garza replied when he was seated, and Johnson had the air conditioner going.

"Seoul is cool if you like cities and crowds, the rest of the place is the inside of a dog's asshole," Johnson said. "Although there are one or two bright spots. There are some nice places but Taegu sucks, so do Osan and Puson. They got a nice beach at Inch On and a park they made as a memorial to MacArthur. If you drink, get what you can before midnight if you're in town or you'll have to come back to the base. They got some sort of morality law. If you do drugs, be careful of the Korean cops, you'd rather get busted by the APs."

"Is there a drug problem here?"

"I don't ask, and I don't care," Johnson shrugged. "I'm just giving you the information they won't give you at the in-processing briefing. You married?"

"Yeah, wife is back in San Antonio with her mother. I'm a Marine Corps retread, got out a few years back and I missed it. There were no openings in Force Recon when I came back so I talked to the Air Force. I figured I might teach you Wingnuts a few things."

"You might learn something yourself, jarhead," Johnson laughed.

"Stranger shit's happened," Garza smiled. "As I said, the wife's back in Texas. Do you know any good places off base?"

"One or two," Johnson said with a sly smile. "One in particular. It's one of the bright spots."

Osan Air Base, South Korea

"So, what's the problem?" Beu asked Wood as the engines spooled back down.

"Shit, Major, I don't know, just a vibration, but not really, right up here over the door," Wood said as he tapped the sheet metal with his knuckle. "The ringing at high engine rpm is going to make me nuts."

"None of the other guys hear it," Beu grumbled.

"They're not at one with the machine the way I am," Wood told him seriously. As crew chief and door gunner of Cowboy-261, he knew the aircraft better than Beu did. "There's a hydraulic line running through here, Major." He pointed to the bulkhead. "If a hold-down bracket is cracked, the vibration will wear a thin spot in the line. I wouldn't have wanted to lose a hydraulic pack last week when we got the boys out of Nam Po."

"You think the maintenance crew missed something," Beu asked.

"Maybe," Wood shrugged. "We should get someone from sheet metal shop to come out and open this up."

"Put in the order," Beu said.

"Why don't you run it up once more, Major," Wood asked him. "Let me see if I can find it so we don't have to ground her."

"Once more and then I'm going to the Pink Lady," Beu barked. "If you can't find it this time, I'm outta here, Woodsy."

"If I don't find it this time, I'm going with you, Major."

***

One of the big choppers on the flightline was running its engines and the man peered through the scope on his rifle. He'd debated putting one silenced shot into the engine, putting the helicopter out of commission for a while, but that was not the reason he was here.

He was here to send a message to the people who'd attacked the North Korean factory in Nam Po. The message would say that Major Park knew who'd perpetrated the crime and that he would be waiting for them should they return. He trained the scope on the officer and enlisted man standing by the door. They were aircrew though he could have killed them both with ease. He remembered Park's words. *The ones with the black berets*, Park had said and that's whom he'd wait for.

***

"You're done already?" Johnson looked up when Garza approached the car. He'd opted to stay there because the air conditioner in the new Ford worked better than the one in the admin building.

"I missed the daily briefing; I'll get it tomorrow. Did I hear one of the Pave Lows running up?" Garza asked.

"Yeah, wanna head over to the flightline? If it's who I think it is, I can introduce you to the pilot who got us out," Johnson said. "Crew chief's a straight up guy too." He started the car and headed over to the gate that allowed access from the public roads to the flightline.

"Sounds good," Garza nodded.

Johnson followed the road as a flight of four F-16 Fighting Falcons from the 51st Tactical Fighter Wing taxied by on the right. The car was buffeted by their wash, but Johnson maintained control with little effort. The helicopter parking area was ahead, where six of the big Pave Lows sat between several UH-1H Hueys of Vietnam fame and a dozen HH-47s with the Marine Corps transport squadron attached to the base.

"There it is." Garza pointed to the chopper with the main rotor spinning.

"What's the tail number?"

"80-261," Garza replied.

"That's him," Johnson said and steered in that direction.

***

"There it is," Wood said. "Hold that rpm, Major."

"Rog," Beu said from the pilot's seat.

Wood pulled an empty ammo box over and stood on it. Armed with a screwdriver, he felt behind the lip of the bulkhead, lightly resting the tip on the sheet metal. He felt the vibration through the handle and moved it farther down the blind track. "Son of a bitch," Wood muttered. "I got it, Major. Would you look at that? It's a seven-point-six-two-millimeter shell casing." He fished the spent brass from the track and headed to the flight deck as the blue Crown Victoria pulled up in front of the helicopter.

"Johnson's here," Beu said. "That must be Garza," he added as the two men stepped out of the car. "Stonewall sent Rick to get him."

"Looks Mexican," Wood said as he flipped the shell casing to Beu who caught it. "Probably from *your* neighborhood." Beu gave him a dirty look and Wood smiled. "The sheet metal boys missed it," he said of the bullet. "It probably ricocheted up in there. I *knew* I heard something."

"You got the ears of a dog, Woodsy," Beu said, dropping the shell in the pocket of his flight suit.

"Anybody home?" Johnson said as he arrived at the flight deck.

"Hey, Rick," Wood said.

"Hermann Wood, Felipe Garza," Johnson said as they shook hands. "This is Major Beu, one hell of a pilot and not a bad guy for an officer."

"Call me Phil," Garza said.

***

The man was searching for targets in the opposite direction when movement caught his eye. The blue car pulled up in front of the helo and it didn't give him pause, assuming it to contain maintenance people. The aircraft had been running engines for close to an hour but hadn't left, so he assumed they were testing one system or another. His full attention turned back there when he saw the two men exit the car and walk up the steps into the chopper. "The ones with the black berets," he said in his native Japanese, sighting in on the side door of the large craft. "They have to come out sooner or later."

***

"I'm taking Phil over to the Pink Lady," Johnson told them. "Are you coming?"

"In a few," Beu said. "While Woodsy has me out here, I might as well run through the maintenance forms. I'm flying in two days with a squad of Marines and I want to see if there's anything I should worry about. We found a few things they missed when they put her back together."

"Yeah, you gotta worry about the Jarheads licking the windows," Rick laughed.

"See you there," Garza said and followed Johnson out.

***

He steadied the rifle on the blanket. Keeping his breathing under control, he sighted up on the first one, the one wearing tiger-stripe camouflage. Then he went to the other, just appearing in the door of the helicopter, dressed in the more formal blue uniform. And then back to the first as he stepped around the back of the car. He took careful aim, his finger beginning to exert pressure on the trigger.

***

"Shit," Johnson said as he bent over to pick up the keys he dropped as he pulled them out of his pocket. "I can't hold onto my keys and I ain't even drunk yet." And the driver side window shattered above him, showering him with glass.

"Whoa," he heard Garza say from the other side of the car.

"Get *down*," Johnson called as he reached for his forty-five, flipping the safety off as he brought it up.

"Wha ..." and Rick heard Garza fall.

And it clicked in his mind. *Sniper*, he thought and directed his eyes upward toward the hills. He worked his way around the back of the car as the rear tire was flattened by another shot. This time Johnson saw the muzzle flash. Garza was prone a few feet away and Johnson went to him, another shot caroming off the Pave Low reminded him to keep down.

He rolled the man over to find an entrance wound between his eyes. Johnson dragged him to the chopper as Wood appeared at the door. "Get down, Woodsy, there's a sniper in the hills." They got Garza's body inside and Johnson headed for the flight deck, tapping Beu on the shoulder. "We got a sniper up there, Nate. Garza's dead." A shot bounced off the Lexan windscreen.

"Shit," Beu said.

"Will this can fly?" Johnson asked him.

"Damn straight," Beu replied.

"I saw a muzzle flash," Johnson said. "Let's get him."

"Roger that," Beu agreed, flipping on the radio. "Osan tower, this is Cowboy-261. We have come under fire on the flightline from a sniper to the north. I have ground troops aboard and have a location on the sniper. Request emergency departure clearance to neutralize."

"Roger 261, you are clear for immediate departure, local airspace will be closed, and the security police have been contacted," the controller said. "You are free to operate in the local area."

"Rog, tower," Beu said and firewalled the throttles and the chopper lifted skyward. "Go see Woodsy," he said to Johnson. A helmet was tossed at him when he got to the cargo deck and then Wood fed a bandolier of twenty millimeter into his door gun.

"I'm on the right, Major," Wood told Beu.

"Rog."

"Do you see him?" Johnson asked.

"Five o'clock, in that grove of trees," Wood said.

"I got him," Beu replied and the chopper swung hard right over the base housing area at a hundred feet. "He's running."

**

He ran for the motorcycle, never imagining the helicopter would come after him. As he looked skyward, there was no doubt the pilot had spotted him. The big black helicopter swung sharply and came over from his left. His only chance was to get to the motorcycle before they gunned him down. The man pulled the branches away just as he heard the whine of the twenty-millimeter cannon spitting out shells at a hellish rate. Dust and rocks were thrown up as the door gunner walked the deadly fire toward him. He hopped on the bike and kicked at the starter.

**

"He's running," Wood called to Beu as the motorcycle fired just as he was about to rake it and its driver with cannon fire. The sniper took off in a cloud of dust.

"I see him," Beu said and dipped the nose in pursuit.

"You got a rifle in here, Woodsy," Johnson asked as he holstered his pistol.

"Under the seat," Wood yelled over the wind noise. "Should have a clip in her." Johnson found the M-16 forthwith and chambered a round.

"He just went over the top of the ridge, Woodsy," Beu called to him. "He's heading for the border."

"I got him, Major," Wood replied as Johnson found a length of rope in the rear of the cargo bay. He hooked it into the D-ring in the deck as Wood opened up on the motorcycle. Garza's body was strapped across three of the web seats.

"How do you open the rear door?" Johnson called to Wood.

"On the left," he pointed with one hand as he swung the gun around with the other. "Both switches," Wood added. Johnson did as he was told and the rear cargo deck swung down, adding more velocity to the wind swirling through the empty bay. Wood took aim and opened up on the bike once more.

***

His face was stung as debris from Pave Low's rotor wash pelted him. The gunner was refining his aim, the shells walking closer to the bike every time he rode through a clearing. The pilot was good, keeping the chopper above the trees while still staying low enough to see through them. He felt as if he were about to twist the throttle off the handlebars trying to squeeze every ounce of power out of the small two-stroke engine.

***

"I got his ass now," Wood said when he saw the large clearing in the distance. The rider would have to cross it and Beu could give him a stable platform from which to fire. The trees thinned and Wood walked the shells toward the rear of the bike. "See you in Hell, motherfucker," he said as the first rounds struck the rear wheel.

***

He was thrown from the bike when the rear tire and wheel disintegrated. He watched for a second when the hot slugs ignited the gas tank and then took off at a run. A hundred yards from the tree line and safety, he sprinted for all he was worth, zigzagging to avoid the small arms fire from the helicopter.

***

"Hey, keep this thing *steady*," Johnson yelled as he lay prone on the open cargo deck, directing fire at the running figure.
"I'm doing the best I can," Beu said. He was low and the chopper was being tossed by its own rotor wash. Beu swung the aircraft around so Wood could have a shot with the more powerful twenty-millimeter.

***

His lungs felt as if they were about to explode and his heart about to pound itself out of his chest by the time, he reached the rocky outcropping. He stopped for a second, but two small caliber shots hit the rock above his head, he kept moving, finding an outcrop that would give him shelter. The helicopter flared into a hover above his position.

***

"Rope away," Johnson said as he kicked it out the back of the Pave Low.
"Where are you going, Rick?" Beu called on the radio.
"I'm gonna get him. Take Garza back and bring friends," Johnson said. "We'll never get him from up here and the DMZ is just over the next ridge. I want to take him before he gets to a tunnel and

we don't need you drifting over the border. You don't need a SAM up your ass." A surface to air missile was a viable threat should Beu cross over the DMZ and the Pave Low would be a sitting duck. "I'm outta here," Johnson told them as he disappeared over the edge of the deck, rappelling the twenty feet to the ground. Quickly finding cover, he waited until Beu dipped the nose and spun off to the south. The sounds of nature came back a minute later and Johnson stopped to listen. Hearing something scrabbling over a rock, he set off in that direction.

***

He let himself relax a bit when the helicopter returned to the base, stopping long enough to catch his breath and take a sip from his canteen. *I thought I was dead*, he said to himself as he pulled the compass from his pocket. Having the bike blown out from under him was the closest he'd come to losing his life in this business and that shook him.

Checking his bearings, he estimated the mouth of the tunnel to be about a half-mile away to the northeast and he scoped out a path that would take him there in the shortest possible time. He was certain the helicopter, maybe more than one, would return with troops. The tunnel was his only means of survival, for he could not escape a squad of the black berets for long. They would hunt him down like a wild animal and they would kill him slowly out here in the hills. He'd killed at least one of theirs and they would exact payment in the most prolonged and painful manner.

***

"Fucking guy's a mountain goat," Johnson muttered as he pulled himself up over a crag. He'd caught a glimpse of the wiry Japanese just after he hit the ground and was struggling to keep up. There was no time for him to stop and set up a long shot, the guy was moving too fast and the field of fire was cluttered with gnarly pines. At a hundred yards, the M-16 was no sniper rifle. The light bullet was too prone to deflection by the wind or a twig to be accurate at that distance and there was not enough open area to lead the target. Rick struggled on.

"This turned out to be an interesting day," he said to no one when he got to the top of the outcrop and pulled himself to his feet. "I get a medal, I get to see another one of my guys get blown away, and I might not live until dinnertime; fucking wonderful." He broke into a run down the trail.

***

The sniper thought he'd heard someone following but could not be sure and didn't want to slow down to find out. It was close now and once inside the cool, cramped darkness he would be safe, making his way under the DMZ and back to North Korean soil over the next two hours. Major Park would be pleased, and he would be alive. Had he not killed the man, he would not have bothered returning to the North, even if it meant his death at the hands of the Americans. He pushed on.

***

"I don't believe this fucking guy," Johnson gasped as he tried to make up time on the footpath. "I gotta quit smoking." Rick could run a respectable mile and do ten miles without flinching, but he'd been gaining in altitude since he set off on this jaunt, having to hoist himself over boulders and natural formations. "He can't keep this up forever." Rick looked southward, hoping to see a chopper or two but the sky was clear. "Hurry the fuck up, Nate," he said as he ran.

The Pink Lady

Yung Shu noticed something wrong when she heard beepers going off among the clientele. The off-duty Air Police got their calls first and then some of the Recon Marines. Air Force Special Ops was next and the guys from A-Flight waved to her as they left. Three of the Intelligence specialists departed soon after.

"What happened?" Her mother asked as she came down the stairs. "Place half-empty."

"The combat crews and the Marines all were recalled," Yung Shu said. "There's something going on at the base. A-Flight left too."

"Rick's friends?"

"Yes, mother."

"Good, we might make a profit tonight," she threw up her hands and went to the bar to motivate the waitresses to sell more drinks to the diminished crowd.

"And Rick could get hurt," Yung Shu said softly. She knew he'd be in the middle of whatever was happening, he was just that way and she had yet to figure out whether trouble sought him out or vice versa. He'd come close only a week before and most other men would still be in the hospital, but not the man she loved. "He loves it too much."

Fifteen miles north of Osan Air Base, on the 38th Parallel

"I *hate* this fucking shit," Rick cursed as he came over a rise and stumbled. Catching his balance, he stopped and listened, trying to hear something over his breathing and heartbeat. "Why did I have to steal that car? I could have gone to college and been an officer. I'd be flying a big fucking chopper with big fucking guns on it instead of chasing through the fucking woods after some fucking marathon runner. I'd rather set my hair on fire." He was about to resume his run when he heard a branch break.

***

There is someone following me, the Japanese thought and turned quickly. The slight incline and sandy soil caused him to lose his balance and instinctively grab for a branch. It snapped with a crack. *I'm dead.* He raised his pistol.

***

Rick saw movement just below the path in the trees and dove for cover as a shot splintered the rock. "Shit, Jesus Christ, I *hate* this fucking shit," he cursed and got off two bursts in the general direction of the shooter. "You little motherfucker," he added for the Japanese. "You make me chase your skinny ass all the way up here and then you shoot at me too?" Rick fired off another burst to keep him down and moved closer. "Where is that fucking helicopter?"

***

He smiled when he realized where he was. He would have to leave a gift at the temple when he returned to Japan for the gods had smiled on him. Twenty yards away was the camouflaged entrance of the tunnel. He saw the American for a second before the man disappeared again in the undergrowth. *He is closer, too close*, the man thought and closed on the mouth of the tunnel. He saw Johnson move again and fired a shot in that direction.

***

"Shit, *that* was fucking close," Johnson muttered as leaves fell in front of his face, sliced from the branch a foot over his head. "Scrawny little prick." Rick squeezed off a few shots and waited, peeking up to look for his target. "I'm gonna shave your ass and make you walk backwards." Not seeing the man, Rick moved on until he heard rustling ten yards ahead. He ducked down, crawled toward sound, and prayed it wasn't some kind of wild animal taking a dump. Now was not the time to be run up a tree.

His fears were allayed when he saw his quarry removing the last of the branches that covered the mouth of the tunnel and disappear inside. "Now I *really* hate this shit." He approached the tunnel slowly, peeking into the entrance that was barely wider than his shoulders and shorter than he was tall. He would have to hunch over to avoid hitting his head. "Jesus-fucking-Christ, this is *so* gonna suck," Rick said as he took off the helmet and laid it on the rock above the opening. He removed a smoke grenade from his pocket and pulled the pin, laying it next to the helmet. "Any time now would be nice, Nate," Johnson said to the sky before he ducked into the black pit.

Aboard Cowboy-261

"Can you drunken clowns shoot straight?" Beu asked Campbell.

"You betcha, Major," Campbell gave him a cockeyed salute and grinned.

"That's comforting," Beu grunted.

"Just get us there, Major," Campbell said.

"We gotta find Johnson first," Beu said. "Are they ready back there, Woodsy?" He asked over the radio.

"Yes, sir," Wood replied. "But the target's gonna smell them coming, if you know what I mean."

"You idiots better sober up by the time we get back or we're all screwed," Beu warned them. Beu had returned to the flightline at Osan just as Campbell and the A-Flight guys were arriving. They offloaded Garza to the Air Police and left with Beu before anyone could ask any questions. Beu's bird had priority right now until they could scramble another crew. When they lifted off three minutes after he touched down, Beu saw two more Pave Lows spooling up. "I don't want them to think I'm flying drunk and some of your stink might wear off."

"I see smoke," Campbell pointed out the windscreen, ignoring Beu's remark.

"Time for you to go," Beu said, jerking a thumb over his shoulder.

"You got it, Major, thanks."

"Anytime, anyplace." Beu gave Campbell the thumbs-up.

"Anytime, anyplace," Campbell replied.

"Ropes away," Wood yelled as Campbell made his way to the rear door.

Under the 38th Parallel

This is stupid, Johnson thought but he kept going. The tunnel became narrower and Rick could hear the man in the distance. *Maybe twenty feet*, he figured but it was almost pitch black, Rick could barely see his hand in front of his face. The hand that carried the pistol, he'd abandoned the M-16 just inside the mouth of the tunnel. Its length made any forward speed in the confines of the tunnel prohibitive. He stopped and listened, and he could hear the man breathing. *Closer than I thought. I could probably reach around the corner and touch him.* Johnson brought the pistol up.

***

He is tenacious, the Japanese thought. *And he is right behind me.* Sweat poured off him, the adrenaline screamed at his muscles to produce, but they'd just about given up and he felt suddenly cold. His sweating stopped and his skin became clammy, and he knew he had pushed himself to the limit. The physical and mental exertion had taken its toll and he had to rest, or he would collapse. But he couldn't, not until the chase was over, it had to end soon. The tunnel widened a bit up ahead and he walked quickly, finding a natural alcove, and pressing himself inside it.

***

Shit, he stopped. There were none of the telltale noises coming from ahead of him and he knew what was happening. His quarry was desperate and was preparing to stand and fight. *You may have been faster, but I have more stamina,* Rick thought and smiled. *This is where it ends for one of us.* He was focused now, as if every pore, every hair on his body listened for the slightest sound, a noise, a breath, anything that would foreshadow his opponent's position.

The next few seconds would be a time of reckoning, two tired, exhausted predators realizing that the battle had to be fought now, or not at all. His senses on a razor's edge, he double-checked the safety on his Model 1911 Colt .45 caliber automatic, assuring it was off and crouched down to a squat. He stayed low, against the wall at his left, pistol ready as he inched forward. *You should be just about . . .*

***

Keep walking, the Japanese willed Johnson forward, and he'd rehearsed it in his mind. He would stand and fire chest high and keep firing until his pistol was empty, every shot in the center of mass. In the confines of the tunnel, at least two would hit squarely, maybe more for the man was only a few steps away. His body coiled, he waited as long as he could before springing into action. *Now.* And as he stood, he felt a hand grab his leg and he fired.

***

. . . here, Johnson felt the cuff of a trouser and then an ankle. His finger instinctively squeezed the trigger and all hell broke loose.

On the surface

"Don't tell me he went in alone," Campbell muttered. They'd found Rick's helmet and rifle just inside the mouth of the tunnel.

"Talk to me, Airman Campbell," Beu said over the radio. Cowboy-261 circled just overhead and two more MH-53s approached from the south, no doubt loaded with Marines and Security Police.

"Rick must have followed him into the tunnel, Major," Campbell replied.

"Crazy bastard," Beu said aloud.

"We're going in," Campbell said.

"Negative," Beu told him. "You are to wait until the Marine commander is on the ground. He's a bird colonel, Chuck, and he'll have your ass if you cop your usual attitude. I'm sure some of his people were at the Pink Lady when you were, and they know you've been drinking. Don't give him any shit."

"You got it, Major, we'll wait," Campbell promised, not liking it in the least. They should be the ones to go in after one of their own, not the jarheads. But they shouldn't have been under arms in their condition and all of them were armed to the teeth. They shouldn't have been here at all. Campbell was certain none of the Marines that were rappelling from the two Pave Lows were at the Pink Lady a mere twenty minutes before. And then they heard the shots, fifteen to twenty of them their echoes reverberating out of the tunnel like a giant wind instrument. "What the fuck?"

"Fuck the jarheads," Guthrie said. "Let's go."

"I'll go," Campbell said. "Stay here with the guys and deal with the Marines."

"At ease, Airman," a voice boomed at him from the trail. They turned to see a Marine colonel followed by a squad of Force Recon. "I'm Colonel Strickland, Force Recon, and this is *my* party now."

"It's *our* boy in there," Mason growled.

"Could somebody give me a hand with this asshole," they all turned toward the tunnel as Johnson stuck his head out. "What are you all doing out here, having a fucking party?" Johnson crawled out, dragging the dead Japanese by the collar. "What the fuck did you call the Marines for, Chuck?"

"I *didn't*," Campbell said as he helped Johnson with the load.

"What the fuck is going on down there?" Campbell heard Beu's voice in his ear.

"Rick got him, Major," Campbell replied.

"We won't need your help after all, Colonel," Johnson said to the Marine officer. "I'm gonna have Cowboy close this thing up permanently." He pointed to the tunnel and then looked to Campbell. "Ask Beu if he has any rockets on that can." Campbell spoke into the mike for a second and nodded affirmative. "Let's get out of here then," Johnson said and turned back to the Marine. "Unless you boys feel like hanging around when it all goes to Hell."

"Watch the attitude, Airman," Strickland warned. "You aren't the prima donnas you think you are."

"You know, Colonel," Johnson walked over to the officer and was about to say more but thought better of it. "Yes, you're right, sir, let's *all* get out of here so Major Beu can blow this place to shit."

"Are you in charge of this bunch, Johnson," Strickland asked him.

"For now, yes. Colonel Bryant is the CO. This asshole just killed our senior NCO." Rick pointed to the Japanese whose body was being carried between Mason, George, Gibbs, and Emory.

Strickland walked with him up to the path and then the Air Force personnel mixed with the Marines for the walk back to the high ground where the choppers could pick them up. "You're the guy who got the Star this morning," he said.

"Yes, sir. It looks like word has gotten everywhere. Even the Marines know about it," Rick muttered.

"Word travels quickly in our circles. We heard you were up north."

"Wish I could tell you, sir," Johnson shrugged.

"What in hell made you go in that hole alone?" Strickland asked, indicating the tunnel with his thumb.

"I was pissed that the little bastard made me run all the way and then had the nerve to shoot at me instead of making for the tunnel. Besides, he killed our senior NCO and nearly killed me on the flightline. I take that kinda personal, Colonel. He was a Marine, you know."

"Who?"

"Our senior NCO, Garza, he was a retread, left Force Recon for a while and then came back. You didn't have any openings, so he came over to us," Johnson explained. "He's got a wife in San Antonio. Don't know if he had any kids, he just got here today to replace our senior NCO who was killed when . . . when I earned the Star."

"By rights I should put you in for another one," Strickland said.

"Don't you *dare*, sir. I've gotten nothing but grief over this one," Johnson shook his head. "If you want to do something for me, just forget about it. Why don't you see what the Corps can do for Garza's old lady? It would be nice if you could do a joint thing with the Air Force."

"Will do, Airman," Strickland nodded as they reached the crest of the promontory.

Two of the Pave Lows swung off to the east, loitering as Beu brought –261 around to come in with the sun at his back. The chopper came in low and he sighted up on the tunnel entrance, firing two anti-tank missiles at the target. The ground below their feet shook when they hit, sending tons of soil and rock into and over the opening.

It was over quickly, the noise and dust dissipating as nature went back to its routine. The first chopper flared for a landing and the withdrawal began. It took no time at all and three minutes later, the helicopters were on their way back to base.

Beu reached out a hand when Johnson got to the flight deck. "Good work, boy," he said when Johnson shook it.

"What the hell took you so long?" Johnson said, half serious.

"I set the world record for getting there and back, son," Beu shot back. "Who told you to run so fast?"

"The little bastard was quick, Nate," Johnson said with a chuckle. "I thought I lost him a couple times, but I finally ran him to ground. He might have been fast, but I could have followed him for another hour at that pace. He didn't have any more, so he had to stand and fight. I surprised the shit out of him, and he fired over me. I got about ten good ones in his abdomen and chest."

"Crazy bastard," Beu laughed. "You wouldn't have gotten me to go in that hole."

"I didn't think about it, pal," Johnson said as Beu banked hard right and then left as he lined –261 up on the runway approach. "Do you have to fly so fucking fast?" Rick growled as the ground came up quickly.

"Pussy," Beu muttered as he followed the runway centerline at ten feet of altitude.

Chapter Eight
The Pink Lady, Osan, South Korea
11 July 1983

Beu pulled up in front of the club just past midnight and Johnson got out. They'd been at debriefings since their return to the base earlier in the afternoon. "Are you coming in for a quick one?"

"Not tonight, I have to get some sleep," Beu waved the suggestion away. "Say hi to Yung Shu."

"Later, pal," Johnson said and shut the door. Beu pulled away and made a U-turn, blowing the horn once as he disappeared into the night. Rick walked up the steps and reached for the door, but it opened from the other side. Yung Shu appeared and put her arms around him, hugging him to her.

"What happened?"

"We went on alert, baby," he said as he kissed her. "I got stuck on base."

"Everybody left at once, I was so worried," she said, holding him tightly.

"I'm fine, baby, just really tired," he said as they walked inside, one arm draped over her shoulder. Lin Yii came over with a shot and a beer for him.

"Where's Nate?" She asked while Rick downed the shot and took the beer.

"Home in bed, darling," he told her. "The same place I'm going."

"What really happened today, Rick?" Yung Shu pressed as they walked up the stairs.

"There was a sniper in the hills outside the base," he replied, not wanting to get into a verbal parry with her. He was too tired; he'd tell her anything she wanted to know. "He killed the guy I picked up from the airport before we got him." Rick gulped the beer down as he walked.

"Is that a general 'we' or a specific one, meaning *you* got him?"

"I shouldn't have told you that much," Rick said tiredly. "Please, Yung Shu, it's been a shitty day since they pinned that fucking medal on me this morning."

"How long can you continue this, Rick? How long can you put yourself through this? You should be resting your body after all it went through last week," she admonished. "Look at you, you're exhausted. I love you and I can't watch you kill yourself."

"I'll be fine. There'll be time to rest when I get to Florida," he said. "I just need a little sleep and I'll be ready to go by nine. You got the day off, right?"

"Yes, I did, but you don't have to . . ."

"I *want* to, Yung Shu. I want to spend the day with you more than anything else in the world," he declared.

"But we don't have to go . . ."

"Just wake me up by eight if I'm still sleeping," he interrupted with a smile and a kiss. "I'm gonna take a shower and get into bed." He kissed her once more before heading into the bathroom. Yung Shu went to the bedroom, took off her clothes, and got into bed.

You'll get sleep, my darling, she thought as she pulled the sheet up around her neck. *But you will love me first.*

Osan Air Base

Holmgren made it back to his room with just enough time to shower and change for work. *I cut it too close,* he thought but the sex with Quanh was addictive and he stayed in Taegu longer than he'd planned to. *It was worth it.* He smiled and then felt instantly guilty, feeling as if he was unfaithful to the person he loved.

"But he's not coming back," he said aloud of Roger Hoffman. "And nothing I do will bring him back." He finished knotting his tie. "But someone *will* face justice for it." And he felt his anger rise, anger at the man who knew his most cherished secret, the man who was beside Roger when he fell, and the man who'd come here to exorcise his guilt by offering condolences.

Alan was certain he would remember that face forever, and the face of his beautiful girlfriend, sitting obsequiously by his side. *He had the nerve to bring her here.* He didn't know if that made him angrier. *If it weren't for the girl and her people, we wouldn't be here to begin with.* And his rationalization made her culpable as well, a symbol of the people who lived in this God-forsaken place. *How many Americans have died for these people?*

And he thought about Quanh, and the parallel between the boy and Johnson's girl, both toys used by Americans to make their stay here just a bit more palatable. *I will use you, Quanh, just as Johnson uses her, and I will leave just as quickly when my tour here is over. They are all savages.* He put on his jacket and stepped out the door.

The Pink Lady

Rick woke on his own to the smell of coffee brewing and checked the alarm clock, 7:30. He felt good, a slight throbbing of the bullet wound on his thigh and a bump on his head, which he received in the tunnel, were the only aches and a few aspirin would cure that. He expected to feel worse and rose quickly, following the aroma and finding Yung Shu in the kitchen, humming softly to herself as she peeled some vegetables. She looked up at him and smiled warmly.

"I expected I'd have to shake you to get you up," she said. "Are you okay?"

"Fine and I'll be better when I make a cup of coffee," he said and kissed her cheek.

"Sit," she took the mug from him. "I'll make it."

"I'm not an invalid, Yung Shu," he said after allowing her to guide him to a chair. "I feel great," he declared as he reached for the aspirin bottle on the table.

"So much so that you have to take three aspirin?"

"The good parts still work, or have you forgotten last night?" He grinned.

"I want *all* of you to work properly," she replied. "Not just your manhood."

"Don't worry, baby," he took the cup from her and washed the pills down. "I'm a tough guy." He made a muscle and grinned.

"You're silly," she kissed him. "What should I wear today?"

"A bathing suit," Rick told her. "We're going to the beach at Inch On."

"When do you want to leave?"

"As soon as possible," he rose, taking his coffee into the bedroom where he found a pair of cut off shorts and a T-shirt emblazoned with the 'anytime, anyplace' slogan.

Yung Shu joined him, rummaging through the closet for a bathing suit forgotten since they went to Inch On last summer. She tossed him the keys to the van, though she preferred to drive. Rick would sit in the passenger seat and offer unsolicited driving advice in the form of grunts and winces, so allowing him was the lesser evil though she thought him too aggressive. "You should have told me earlier; I would have packed something to eat."

"It's all taken care of," he grinned as he pulled his hi-tops on. "We gotta stop at Old Wong's on the way out."

"You'd better hope he remembered," Yung Shu laughed. "You know how forgetful he can be."

"I stopped by last night before I came home. I told him that if he forgot, I would tell everyone what he uses for meat in his spicy beef," Rick gave her a conspiratorial grin. "None of the GIs would eat there if they knew."

"No one has *ever* died from Wong's cooking," Yung Shu said defiantly.

"Did you ever notice there are no stray dogs or cats anywhere near his place?"

"Oh stop," she swatted at him. "Let's go." Yung Shu pulled him by the arm out of the apartment and down the stairs. He waved at a couple of Marines whom he'd met up in the hills yesterday as they crossed the main floor, calling out to two more as she fairly dragged him out the door. If she let Rick get into a conversation, it would be another hour getting him out the door.

"I bet those guys have been partying all night," he told her.

"Recon Marines?"

"Yeah, gung-ho bunch they are," he agreed. "Their CO is a tough bird too."

"Like Colonel Bryant?"

"Better disposition."

"That's not saying much," she said. Yung Shu liked Bryant, but he had a gruff manner and she'd noticed it had begun to rub off on Rick. "Is that what you'll turn into, a grouchy old soldier?"

"Not as long as I'm with you, baby," Rick said as he started the van. "I'll be a happy man until the day I die."

"Try not to make that day come prematurely, my love," she told him as they drove away.

Taegu, South Korea

"Did you get it?" Quanh asked the man eagerly.

"Yes," he said curtly for he was the one operating the concealed camera in Quanh's apartment as the two men had their fun. It nauseated him to be near the young man. "Here." He gave Quanh the envelope of bills. "You are to keep in contact with this one while he is in Korea," the man ordered. "My superiors are most interested in him."

"As long as they continue to pay," Quanh shrugged. "Why do they want him so badly?"

"It is none of your business, just do as you're told," the man admonished. "I will be in touch." He walked off, leaving Quanh in the bus station.

Of course you're interested, Quanh thought. *He's a squadron intelligence officer for a combat unit.* The North Koreans would probably confront Holmgren with the tape they'd made of the two men having sex and that saddened him a bit. Alan was a nice guy who didn't deserve this, but that was the way things went. Life wasn't fair. Quanh needed to feed his habit and the North Koreans needed intelligence.

It was an acceptable partnership, one of need for him, one of convenience for the North. Quanh's only hope that his addiction would kill him before he outlived his usefulness to the North Koreans. He was under no illusions that he was as much a pawn as Holmgren was. The only difference was that at twenty years of age, Quanh knew he would not live until his thirtieth birthday, regardless of how clean a life he lived. They told him it was a thing called Acquired Immune Deficiency Syndrome at the clinic in Puson, a result of unprotected gay sex, a new disease they thought originated in the darkness of the African jungle and for which there was no cure. The outward physical signs had yet to manifest themselves, but it would come soon, and he would know the end was near. *Sorry, Alan, but you have the chance to live a long and healthy life. I need to live now.*

MacArthur Park, Inch On, South Korea

"Here," Yung Shu handed Rick a towel as he emerged from the lake. Drying his upper body and face, he flopped down on the blanket next to her. "Did you have a good swim?"

"You bet, baby, you should go in," he said, accepting the beer from her.

"Later, do you want some lunch?" She unwrapped a sandwich for him. Neither of them knew what was on it, the lettuce was recognizable but anything else Wong put on the brown bread was anyone's guess.

"In a second," Rick took another sip of his beer and fumbled around in his bag. He found what he was looking for, palming the small black box before she could see it.

"What do you have?" Yung Shu asked him.

"In a second," he insisted with a grin, finishing the beer. Rick turned to her, his eyes meeting hers, which burned with an emerald fire. "You know we're going back to Florida next week," he began.

"Don't remind me," she crossed her arms on her chest. "The next three months will be hell for me."

"For me too, baby," he agreed. "That's why I want them to be the last time we are separated." Rick looked at the box in his hand and handed it to her. "I want you to marry me, Yung Shu," he said as she opened it with a gasp. "I don't want to be away from you anymore. As soon as I get back, we'll make the arrangements and we'll be married before the next rotation is over. You'll come back to the States with me, or wherever the hell they send me, it doesn't matter, and we'll start a family. Maybe when your mother decides to retire, she can come live with us too. Will you marry me, please, Yung Shu?" He took the ring from the box and waited.

"I'll marry you, Rick. I want to be your wife and the mother of your children." She kissed him then and he slid the ring on her finger. Yung Shu looked at it for a second before putting her hand in his and following him into the lake. They made love in a secluded place in knee-deep water, quietly, passionately, oblivious to everything outside their little world.

Osan Air Base, South Korea

"Aw, Jesus Christ, Woodsy," Beu growled. "I was looking forward to this."

"Sorry, Major, but that shell casing we dug out yesterday must have done some damage to the hydraulic line after all," Wood shrugged. "You could have been a little easier on her instead of trying to impress Johnson with your mastery of the third dimension."

"So now I'm *grounded*?" Beu threw up his hands.

"At least until tomorrow, sir," Wood said. "Maybe the day after."

"Shit, this would have been my last run before we went back to Florida, a squad of Recon Marines in exercises with the Army guys," Beu grumbled.

"You can still take this for a hell of a check ride when it's fixed," Wood offered.

"It's not the same."

"You're starting to act like an officer again," Wood warned with a smile.

"Get your shit together and I'll take you to the Pink Lady. The first round is on me since I'm not flying tomorrow," Beu returned the smile.

"That's the Major Beu I know and love," Wood said and hustled to get his tools together.

Nam Po, North Korea

"You cannot just *leave*," Major Park was incensed.

"I do not make those decisions," Kosarev said. "I have been recalled to Moscow. Any communications from now on should be placed through our embassy in Pyong Yang."

"And what of our foundry?" Park hissed. "Our infrastructure cannot handle the demand for the specialized castings and forgings made here."

"I suggest you rebuild," Kosarev laughed. "Far away from here and try to do it a little more quietly so someone doesn't blow it up on you again."

"What about the engineers?"

"They will become available again when they have a place to work," the Russian explained. "For now they will remain on the embassy grounds in Pyong Yang where Soviet forces can assure their safety."

"I will find them office and lab space," Park said. "When will you return?"

"That is up to Chairman Andropov," Kosarev shrugged. "I have been summoned by the Chairman himself and I do not put demands on his time. I will return when *he* deems fit to do so."

"This has put us years behind schedule, Colonel Kosarev. My superiors will hear of Moscow's refusal to cooperate," Park hissed.

"Do what you must, I will be leaving tonight," Kosarev did not wait for a reply. He was tired of being threatened by the little man and glad he would not have to see him again for a while. He also thought of his dear Katherine. He would not return to Asia until she was gone, he'd made up his mind then that he would be with her until the end, regardless of mission *or* Mother Russia.

Kosarev got in his car and headed into town, taking a circuitous route to determine if he were being followed. Satisfied there was no tail, he parked in front of the restaurant, one of three in this remote town. It was the only one outside the hotel where he would eat, but he was not here only for nourishment. The waiter came over and took his drink order, the reservation had been made for two and his dinner guest came over nervously.

His name was Soon Yat Oh, an engineer Kosarev met when construction on the foundry was begun a few years before. He'd intimated to Kosarev on several occasions he was amicable to barter information for Western currency and this afternoon Kosarev would take him up on his offer.

"Good afternoon, Yat," Kosarev said. "Sit please." He beckoned the Korean to the chair. "Moscow has finally moved on your . . . request." Kosarev passed a small black book to Soon who read the first entry and smiled. "The Bank of Switzerland, you may verify it with them if you wish."

"I will, Comrade Kosarev," Soon put the book in his pocket.

"There will be semi-annual deposits of the same amount so long as your reports remain regular and useful," Kosarev said. "This is no game, Yat," he warned. "Do not let me find you are playing both sides of the fence."

"No, comrade," Soon said, looking away. The Russian terrified him, but Major Park scared him more. Soon Yat Oh wasn't afraid of any personal harm the major would inflict but of the harm he was doing to North Korea. He would work with the Russians to save Korea. He smiled at the irony of it, but there was precedent. It was the Russians, along with the Chinese, who'd wrested Korea from the Japanese grip during the Second World War.

"What is it, Yat?" Kosarev expected more from him, but the man just sat there and stared at his plate.

"When it is time, I want you to assure me safe passage to the West. I will be loyal to you, Comrade Kosarev, but I want assurances for the protection of my family."

"I demand your loyalty," Kosarev insisted. "But you must earn mine. *I* will make the determination if you are worth saving."

"Then that is what I will do. I will earn my money and your loyalty and when the time comes, I will demand it from *you*," Soon Yat Oh said as their drinks came. The waiter took their dinner orders and lingered until a glare from the Russian chased him.

"As long as we understand each other," Kosarev said. "I will be leaving for Moscow tonight." He pushed a card across the table to Yat. "That is a direct line to my office there. Should that insane dwarf do anything stupid, I expect a call immediately."

"Yes, Comrade Kosarev," Soon said. "When will you return?"

"I am unsure, but if I don't, someone will make contact with you," Kosarev told him. "I will not leave you without a control officer." The waiter came again with their dinner orders, Kosarev regarding his after the man left. "I can't wait to eat real food again," he muttered as Soon dug in heartily. Kosarev realized this would be the best meal the man would eat in a year and shook his head sadly.

The Pink Lady, Osan, South Korea

"Where's Rick?" Beu asked Lin Yii when he and Wood were seated.

"Out with Yung Shu somewhere," she replied. "Where have *you* been, fly boy?"

"Out flying around, darling," Beu smiled, pulling her onto his lap.

"Mama's working the bar," she giggled as he bit her neck playfully. "She's going to get the broom."

"When do you get off?" He asked her.

"In a little while, when Yung Shu gets here," Lin Yii explained as she stood and straightened her outfit, a pair of silk shorts that barely covered her butt a color of orange that could only be called flaming and a matching halter top. "I'll see you later."

The door opened and Wood looked up to see Rick and Yung Shu arrive. "Hey, boy," he called. Johnson waved but didn't come over.

"I love you, Yung Shu," Rick whispered, taking her hands in his. "Are you sure about this?"

"I said yes, didn't I?" she smiled. "I have to go to work."

"I don't want to let you go. This will be the longest three months of my life."

"We will have the rest of our lives together, Rick, unless you get mother angry by keeping me here," she kissed him again. "Go see your friends, I have to change."

"Okay," he kissed her once more and set off to Beu's table.

"What are you grinning about?" The pilot asked him.

"I proposed today, and she said yes," Rick smiled.

"No shit?" Wood and Beu said as one.

"No shit, boys," Rick said. "I bought the ring before we went into Nam Po. I was going to ask her when we rotated back in, but after that . . ." he shrugged.

"I hope you know what you're doing, boy," Beu said.

"Just wait, Major," Johnson said with a smile. "One day the right one will come along and bite you in the ass."

"Never," Beu shook his head. "They're gonna bury me with my boots on and my balls attached."

Johnson looked at him as if he were crazy. "What are you doing here tonight anyway? I thought you were driving a bunch of Marines around tomorrow."

"Don't ask," Wood said. "He hasn't stopped bitching since I found that leaking hydraulic line today."

"Need I remind you that you're both enlisted men," Beu kidded.

"Yeah, be glad we let you hang around with us," Johnson told him as Lin Yii brought his beer and Jack Daniel's.

"I can't believe you proposed," she said to Rick.

"Why?"

"You guys don't do things like that," Lin Yii declared. "You just use us and leave."

"I didn't plan to fall in love when I came here," Johnson shrugged. "But shit happens."

"Fucking romantic," Beu chuckled.

"So I shouldn't wait for *you* to propose, should I, fly boy?" She said to Beu.

"Nobody's gonna lasso me," he said with determination.

Osan Air Base, South Korea

"Who was the guy who finally got him?" Holmgren asked as the briefing continued.

"Johnson, A-Flight from 23rd," Colonel Williams said.

"Followed the sniper down into the hole without backup, killed the guy in the dark," Marine Colonel Strickland added. "We're gonna have to run patrols up in the hills," he said to the Security Police commander. "It looked as if this guy was up there for a couple days and could have lasted another week."

"Did we close down the tunnel?" Holmgren asked after the churning in his gut stopped. Johnson was a cowboy and his carelessness was what got Roger killed. He put that away for now as the Marine regarded him.

"Of *course*, Lieutenant," Strickland barked. "Did you think we'd leave it open so the North Koreans can come over and kill us at will?"

"No, sir," Holmgren replied sheepishly. "I was just thinking we might have wanted to use it for *our* purposes."

"Too dangerous," Williams from squadron Intel said. "We'd have no idea where it comes out. There could be a squad of NKPA waiting for us and they'll surely yell and scream that we're making incursions across the DMZ. It's best the tunnel is out of commission."

"Did we get an ID on the sniper," Colonel Forrester asked Strickland. The IG's office was represented as well as they always were at these things.

"He's Japanese," Williams replied. "The Agency says he's affiliated with a group based in Osaka called Aum Shinrikyo. They follow this blind monk or something. They've been linked to bombings in the Tokyo subway system."

"So why was he here taking shots at *my* people," Stonewall Bryant said. It was nice the intelligence weenies and the Sky Cops knew who the guy was, but Bryant wanted to know if there would be any others to follow. "It seems to me this guy would do better shooting at the Tokyo MPD."

"We don't know," Williams said with a shrug.

"So what are we supposed to do, walk around with helmets and flak jackets?" Bryant barked at him.

"I'd suggest leaving the berets at home and wearing ball caps," Williams offered.

"Do you think the North Koreans ran this guy too?" Holmgren asked him. "They might be taking revenge for our action last week."

"That's a reach," Bryant said. "My men are …"

"At least *one* of them is a hotshot, Colonel. Do you think one of them might have revealed something to the North Koreans at that time?" Holmgren spat back.

"Anything's possible, Lieutenant," Bryant grumbled. "Why don't you find out instead of sitting here and casting blame? I've had to write four letters home in the past week, you know."

"We're depending on the CIA for resources here," Colonel Williams said coming to Holmgren's rescue. "And they don't have the assets in Pyong Yang to be effective."

"So what, all of the SOCOM people have to *hide*?" Bryant was nonplussed. "I say we go get them, let them know they can't get away with this."

"Don't hold your breath, Stonewall," Strickland, the Marine, said. "Your guys aren't up to strength anyway."

"B-Flight's in next week," Bryant said.

"They won't do it. I doubt they'd let the Marines do it," Strickland replied. "What if they're trying to provoke us into action? Could you imagine the results if some of our people were killed during the operation? It could start a war with the Chinese or the Russians; Washington wouldn't go for it and this *definitely* has to go through the Pentagon."

"So, light a fire under those pencil pushers," Bryant shot back.

"It's already done," Forrester told him. "Until further notice, all of the SOCOM troops will wear ball caps and green fatigues, no more berets and no more tiger-stripe. Until we're sure of whom we're dealing with, I don't want your people to be obvious."

"Fine," Bryant muttered. Though he and Forrester were good friends, what the IG said was law until countermanded by the Pentagon. He would discuss it with Forrester over a couple of beers later, but there would be no more argument in this setting.

"You know your guys shouldn't be wearing those uniforms anyway, Stonewall," Forrester went on. "They haven't been regulation since Vietnam. The Secretary of the Air Force made mention of it when I talked to him this morning."

"It's a matter of pride and unit cohesion," Bryant shot back. "They're one of the few ground combat units in the Air Force and they want to set themselves apart from the others."

"I *understand*, Colonel Bryant," Forrester growled. "I've looked the other way since this experiment began. Jesus, Bill, give a little on this. Do you want to write *more* letters?"

"Fine," Bryant threw up his arms and left.

"And you wonder why his men are that way," Holmgren muttered.

"That's enough, Lieutenant," Forrester said. "If your career is half as distinguished as Stonewall Bryant's you can consider yourself damn lucky. There is a reason all his men would follow him into Hell and back."

The Pink Lady

Johnson sat in his sixth-floor window as the hot breeze blew past him, throwing the curtains aside as it swirled through the bedroom. He thought about love, not caring what the wind did to his room, and whether he even knew what it was. He'd been in love once, when he was a teenager, to a German girl he'd known since childhood. Rick used to spend summers there with his mother's sister and family, and Sabine was the daughter of one of his mother's childhood friends. They'd lost touch once he'd entered the Air Force and she was all but forgotten since Rick found Yung Shu. His first love was now not much more than a warm and fuzzy memory.

Will we fall out of love, he asked himself and the noisy street below. Johnson didn't think so, so long as he kept feeling about her the way he did now. He wanted to be with her all the time, to share every small thing with her, from a beautiful sunrise to a day at the beach, and the time spent apart left him feeling incomplete. Yung Shu was a bright, happy, incredibly beautiful girl and he could not picture himself without her.

"Shit, I have to tell mom," he said aloud, realizing only now the enormity of what he'd done this morning. His mother had no idea of his love for the Korean girl and this would be a bombshell when he dropped it on her. Not only was he in love with a woman who *wasn't* Sabine – his mother still pushed him in that direction – but he was also going to marry her before the year was over. "She's gonna have a heart attack," Rick said and smiled. His mother had threatened him with that since he was a small child and had never followed through. "She just might this time," he chuckled.

He called her an old artillery horse and did so with every bit of love and respect he carried within him, but she was just that, a tough old German. And he could hear her saying 'I'm not old', in her clipped accent, which she swore she didn't have. "I don't have an accent," he heard her say as if she were standing next to him and he smiled warmly. Maria Johnson was in her mid-sixties and still walked two miles to the grocery store and back twice a week, taking the bus only during inclement weather. All the neighbors were amazed at her manicured gardens and the energy with which she lived her life. "You're a tough old broad, ma," he said absently. "Please don't be too mad at me."

Rick thought about calling and warming her up to it before he arrived on his native Long Island but decided against it quickly. "I've gotta do it in person. She'd be even more pissed if I called her and then let her stew over it for a week." Johnson shook his head. "She's gonna kill me."

"Who's going to kill you, love?" Yung Shu said from the door.

"My mom," he smiled. "She's gonna love you once she meets you, but the old broad is gonna kill me for springing it on her this suddenly." Johnson clutched his heart and mimicked his mother's accent. "You're going to give me a heart attack one day, Richie."

"*Richie?*" She giggled.

"If you think that's bad, my dad's name is Richard. It was *Little* Richie until I was fifteen and my mother called me that in front of my friends. I nearly flipped out and mom agreed to just Richie, but the damage was done. I heard it every day in school for the rest of the year. Rick came the next year," he explained, able to laugh about it now.

"An effort to compensate with the macho name?"

"I guess," he shrugged.

"Your mother sounds like fun," Yung Shu observed.

"She's a pisser," Rick grinned. "She'll try anything as long as it's entertaining. One day, I'll tell you about how she rode a skateboard for the first time a couple years back. She's a piece of work. The old lady was a mountain climber when she was young and bicycled across Europe. Shit, the stories I've heard about her, I could go on all night."

"Tell them to me another time, I have to go back to work," she said as she rose, but he took her hand.

"I love you, Yung Shu," he said.

"I love you too, Rick," she leaned over and kissed him. He tried to pull her on top of him, but she got away giggling. "Hold that thought until my shift is over," she said before running out the door as he gave chase.

"This is too good," he muttered as he found his place in the window. Regardless of the consequences dealing with his mother, he could think of no way he could be happier.

Chapter Nine
Osan Air Base, South Korea
12 July 1983

Holmgren was hung over for the seventh straight day as he made his way to the chow hall on the first floor of the Bachelor Officer's Quarters. He was fuzzy and listless and didn't feel much like eating but opted for the bacon and eggs with toast to counteract the nausea from too much scotch and not enough food.

"Somebody kill me," he muttered as he found a seat, setting the tray down heavily.

"You okay, Alan?" Captain Biff Kutscher asked him when he sat down. Kutscher was Colonel Williams' executive officer and technically Holmgren's boss.

"Yeah, just a tough week, that's all. I was in on the Nam Po thing and I guess it bothered me more than it should have," Holmgren replied as he pushed his eggs around, opting for the bacon and toast.

"I remember the first time I watched one of those," Kutscher mused. "The Iran thing in '80; nasty business watching that chopper go down with our boys on it. I couldn't sleep for a month," he admitted.

"What did you do?"

"Saw the base shrink," he shrugged. "I was drinking a lot too." Kutscher looked up at him. "You?"

"Don't ask, Biff."

"You went through the Academy with Jenkins, didn't you?"

"Yeah," Holmgren sighed and sipped his coffee and the acid in his gut began to churn.

"Go see the shrink, Alan. I'll talk with Colonel Williams and get you some leave if you want."

"I just took a couple days and hit the beach at Inch On," Holmgren lied. There was no reason for him to be in Taegu; nobody went to Taegu unless they were passing through. "It didn't do any good."

"I just gave you the day off," Kutscher told him. "Go to the hospital and see the doc."

"I don't know . . ."

"I'll make it an order, man," Kutscher warned. "*Go.*"

"Can I finish my coffee first?" Holmgren mustered a smile.

"Don't be ashamed to get help for something like this. That's what hurt many of the guys who came back fucked up from Nam. They didn't get help and their problems got worse," Kutscher said softly. "I know how much your career means to you. Don't screw it up by crawling inside a bottle."

"I'll go, I'll go," Holmgren surrendered.

The Pink Lady

He woke when she stirred, and he hugged her to him. "Good morning, my love," she said as she kissed his cheek.

"Hi, baby," Rick replied, still sated from what they'd done to each other before falling asleep. While their sex was generally passionate, this was the most intense since they'd been together. "Stay here, I'll make coffee."

"All right," she said, pulling the sheet over her. The hot wind continued to blow from the north, picking up moisture from the East China Sea and then bringing sauna-like conditions to Seoul and its environs. "I'll let you."

Johnson went into the kitchen and began rummaging, wondering when he would be doing this on Sunday mornings in their own house back in the Good Ole' U.S. of A. It was a dream that did not seem much closer to reality, yet he'd taken the first step yesterday. He could imagine a couple kids running through the room as he prepared coffee for his wife, resting now because she had to deal with the little anklebiters all week. *We'd have beautiful children*, he thought as he heated the water. *As long as they took after their mother*, he added with a grin.

Yung Shu was beautiful and though he was handsome, he had to work at it. Rick gained weight easily and had to watch everything he ate, even with the amount of exercise he got on a daily basis. He didn't want his kids to have that burden, having been on the chubby side in school, he'd received his share of jibes, but he overcame that with his athleticism. *Let's hope they get Yung Shu's genes*, he smiled again.

"Are you going to work today?" Yung Shu asked him when he returned. Normally he'd be up and out by now.

"Colonel Bryant told me to come by the orderly room around noon," Johnson shrugged. "He'll probably have me doing paperwork until we rotate home."

"At least you won't be getting shot at or flying around with your crazy friends," she said, accepting her cup. "That's my only concern with marrying you, Rick. I dread the day one of your friends comes by to tell me you're dead, and not just me, it's our children too. Do they deserve to lose their father somewhere, God *knows* where? I don't know if I could take it as well as that officer we went to see."

"I won't be in a combat unit forever, baby," Rick soothed. "I don't plan to grovel in the mud until I retire."

"But . . ."

"Look, baby," he said, getting back into bed with her. "I don't exactly love what I do," Rick admitted. "But I'm damn good at it and my country needs me to do it. I'll do it as long as they want me to. You knew this from day one, Yung Shu."

"I know, I know." She patted his hand. "But I am allowed to worry. I care about you, Rick and though you say you don't like it, you love the rush. You crave the excitement of combat just as an addict craves opium. I saw it in your eyes the other night; it was as if your blood was on fire with it. You scared me then, my love."

"I would *never* . . ."

Her fingertips went to his lips to silence him. "I do not fear for myself; I know that in your arms is the safest place for me. What I am unsure of is whether you can control that need should you no longer be able to do what you do."

"It's not like I'm a crazed . . ."

"I shouldn't have brought it up," she waved it away. "I do not think you are insane, nor do I think you are psychotic. I'm just worried that you might not be prepared to leave the life if it happens."

"I'll leave SOCOM one day, when I'm tired of it," he said.

"My mother said something to me not long ago," Yung Shu told him. "She said that your destiny was not your own. Suppose the Air Force has other plans for you?"

"Like what?"

"I don't know, Rick, but living and working here, I've heard many GIs tell stories about the military's . . . *enlightened* personnel decisions. Suppose they make you a file clerk somewhere?"

"A *file clerk?*" Johnson laughed. "I doubt they'd lock me in an office."

"Listen to you," she said. "You said *lock* you in an office. Even the thought of your having to work inside, on a regular schedule, doing the same thing every day reminds you of prison. What if that actually happens? What if some pencil pusher, as you call them, decides you would be better off filing reports than groveling in the mud?"

"I'd twist his skinny pencil . . ."

"Neck?" She asked as she saw that fire ignite in his eyes. "What *would* you do, my love? You can't just quit, could you?"

He stared at her for a minute, for he had never considered the possibility seriously. "I don't have any idea what I would do."

"Just keep it in the back of your mind, darling," she said. "And think about how that eventuality might affect you."

Rick got up, taking his coffee to the window and a filterless Camel off the dresser. He cared not if passersby observed his nudity. *That's what they get for looking into sixth floor windows,* he thought as he caught a man staring up at him from the sidewalk. Johnson remained, debating what Yung Shu had just told him while he lit the smoke.

That's why I volunteered for this bullshit, Rick said to himself. He was a grease monkey in a local garage for the few months after he'd been arrested and before he'd enlisted, and the recruiter talked him into an open mechanical field, 42XXX, the Air Force called it. Then during basic training, he volunteered for Pararescue School and once there, volunteered again for the new Air Force Combat Control units. Johnson wanted to be on the sharp end and now that he'd tasted the rush, he didn't want anything to do with the mundane.

Yeah, I could see me rebuilding jet engines all day. I'd put a bullet in my head. And then he understood why Yung Shu showed such concern. *I'd be a crazy man,* he thought. And he looked back to her.

"What?" Yung Shu looked at him strangely.

"I see what you mean," he said. "I could see where I could become . . . difficult."

"For want of a better term," she giggled. "Look, Rick, I don't expect you to have an epiphany right here, today, or this week, but I want you to think about it. Once we're married, something like that will affect us both *and* our children."

"I hope they look like you," he declared.

"Who?"

"Our children. I hope they are as beautiful as you are, Yung Shu," he said, flicking the cigarette out the window and crawling into bed on top of her. "When are you going to stop the pills," he breathed in her ear as he bit her neck lightly.

"When we're married," she replied, putting her coffee down on the nightstand. "But it's never too early to start practicing." Yung Shu pulled him onto her, not wanting to tell him it had been a week since she'd taken her birth control.

Osan Air Base

"They'll be done in a couple hours, Major," Wood said as they stood on the flightline, watching the hydraulic people run a new line though the bulkhead. "How long did you stay at the Pink Lady last night?"

"We turned in early," Beu grinned.

"Are you falling for the natives, like Rick?"

"Nah," Beu waved it away. "But Lin Yii is a hot little number and as long as she's willing, so am I."

"It doesn't hurt that Rick fixed up his guest wing," Wood laughed. "I've slept off many a drunk there."

"Do you think we'll get her for a check ride this afternoon?" Beu indicating the black helicopter as the hot wind blew the dust in tiny cyclones across the unpaved areas of the field.

"The maintenance super says so," Wood shrugged. "You okay to fly?"

"I told you, we turned in early and I slept the rest of the night . . . you know, afterward." Beu looked at his watch. "It's fourteen hours since I had my last drink. By the time we fly it'll be almost twenty."

"Minimal crew?"

"Just you and me, Woodsy," Beu replied. "I don't want too many witnesses," he laughed. Beu's check rides were lively, to say the least, and he didn't trust any of the others on the crew far enough to keep the degree of liveliness a secret.

"Why don't you grab something to eat, Major? I'll call you when she's ready," Wood offered. "There's no point in your hanging around, making these poor enlisted folks nervous."

"I guess you're right," Beu shrugged. "I'm sure there's a ton of paperwork I should be doing. I'll be over at squadron headquarters, you'll probably find me there later too," he grumbled. "Call me as *soon* as they're done."

***

Kosarev pulled the car onto the base and headed toward the flightline, not entering but driving next to it. The car was an American Chrysler Grand Fury, painted gray with an officer's ID sticker on the front bumper and received nary a cursory look from the SP at the gate as he was waved in. He'd rather not have tested this cover just yet, but Marines and Air Police now patrolled his vantage point in the hills.

Something must have happened, he thought as he watched three of the big Pave Lows lift off and swing north. Kosarev knew nothing of the assassin sent by Major Park to exact revenge from the Americans. While the American security troops exhibited their usual laxity when it came to motor vehicle traffic on base, the patrols in the hills told the Russian that security had been breached somewhere up there. *It was just a matter of time.* And then he saw the man he was looking for, walking across the flightline toward the Ops building.

"Ah, Major," Kosarev said under his breath as he drove along the fence. "Yours must be the craft undergoing repairs or you would be flying today."

Kosarev had done his research and he knew that Beu had logged more flying hours than any other in 20th Special Operations Squadron, the flying unit based out of Hurlburt Field in Florida. They flew the Pave Low II, Special Operations variant of the CH-53 Jolly Green Giant of Vietnam fame and those were two of the requirements of Kosarev's operation. The last two was that Kosarev himself had the nerve to pull it off and Beu was willing to break the oath he took fifteen years before.

Beu's record appeared in Kosarev's mind, joining the Air Force after two years at Arizona State University and accepted into flight school with a rotary wing preference. Awarded the Distinguished Flying Cross twice for his exploits during the Vietnam War, saving downed airmen from capture in a Search and Rescue unit, he volunteered for spec-ops duty in '81 and transferred to 20th after training on the updated –53s. He'd been there since, distinguishing himself most recently in Nam Po, pulling his comrades out of a deadly and hopeless situation. At 20th Special Operations, Beu was the senior pilot, The Man, to Kosarev also, for Beu was the chap he had to trust with his daughter's life.

I have passed the point of no return, he thought, driving back out the main gate and into Osan proper. Kosarev had less than forty-eight hours to act or more than a year of planning would go to waste. He had to meet a contact that worked for North Korean Army Intelligence and also for the Soviets in South Korea. Once Kosarev was in possession of the information the contact would bring him, the timing would be critical. Alexa could not stay in Kamchatka much longer and he could not stay here. He'd delayed his departure as long as possible and Chairman Andropov would become suspicious soon. He had to return to Moscow. *And Katherine has little time left.* The tone of her last letter told him as much, regardless of how upbeat she tried to make the narrative. Were it not for his daughter's safety, he would have been back there already. *You will not die alone, my love.*

***

"Airman Johnson," Beu said as he passed Johnson, poking him in the ribs.

"Major," Johnson grunted.

"Who pissed in your Wheaties?" Beu asked him.

"Look at me," Rick hissed. "What am I doing?"

"Paperwork," Beu replied.

"You got it, sir, hence my bad mood," Johnson said as he stuffed some paper into a file and then stuffed the file in a drawer.

"Don't bother the help, Nate," Stonewall Bryant called from the door of his office.

"He thinks he's funny in that cruel way of his," Johnson whispered. "He is taking great joy in seeing me behind a desk. Watch it or he'll put you on a shit detail too. I saw the Marines take off and you're still here and now he knows it."

"Shit," Beu muttered. "I should have hung on the flightline with Woodsy."

"*Major* Beu," came from Colonel Bryant's place of work.

"Good luck, old man," Johnson snickered as Beu headed into Bryant's office.

"What's with the Colonel today?" Campbell asked when he saw Beu leave.

"We lost four guys in the past week and we're rotating home in a couple days," Johnson explained. "The guy's got too much shit to do in too short a time."

"A little less lip, a little more filing," Bryant's voice echoed through the Orderly Room.

"Shit," Campbell muttered. "You'd think the old fart's ears would be going by now. Hey, heard you proposed to Yung Shu. Are you sure you know what you're doing?"

"Of *course,* I know what I'm doing, asshole."

"You know the story, Rick, a lot of the locals will tell a guy they love him, so he'll marry her and take her back to the States, to that big Base Exchange in the sky. Then she divorces him once she has her citizenship."

"Not Yung Shu," Johnson said without hesitation. "And you know what? I don't care. I love her and she's willing to marry me, and that's *all* I care about."

"You say so," Campbell shrugged. "She a right pretty girl, are you sure you're not …"

"*No,*" Johnson hissed.

"Hey," Bryant appeared around the corner. "If I want to listen to a fucking soap opera, I'll turn on the TV. Now you two idiots get back to work or I'll loan you out to a sewage detail."

"Yes, sir," they came to attention. Bryant turned away and then turned back to Johnson. "Campbell's an asshole," he whispered. "Yung Shu is a nice girl, pretty too. Good luck to you, boy."

"Thank you, sir," Johnson replied, giving Campbell a grin.

"You're welcome. Get back to *work,*" Bryant growled before stalking back to his sanctum.

"See, even Stonewall thinks you're an asshole," Johnson taunted.

"That's *Colonel Bryant* to you, boy," Bryant said from afar.

"Fucking ears on that guy," Campbell muttered.

"To *you* too, Campbell," he added.

"Gentlemen," Guthrie came up behind them.

"What are we doing tonight?" Campbell asked him.

"I'm taking that new admin sergeant to the movies," Guthrie said proudly.

"The tall one?" Johnson asked and Guthrie nodded with a grin.

"Damn, she's as tall as me," Campbell said. "What the hell does she want with a little shit like you?"

"I can get into places you can't," Guthrie snickered.

"What are *you* doing?" Campbell asked Johnson.

"We're going back to Florida soon," Rick said. "What do *you* think I'm doing?" *Young Shu and I are gonna fuck each other's brains out*, his mind screamed. *And we're gonna do it every free minute until I leave.*

"Neither of you are any fun," Campbell shot back. He looked at his hand. "Come on, girls," he said to his fingers. "It's just us again tonight."

"Fucking asshole," Guthrie said.

"You two," Bryant appeared again. "Come here." They followed into his office. Beu was parked on the couch in the corner. "Take these," Bryant pointed to a stack of files on his desk. "And get them over to Seventh Air Force." The Headquarters of 7th Air Force was also based at Osan about a mile down the road from the Special Operations detachment.

Johnson looked over to Beu who winked at him before turning back to Bryant. "Yes, sir." Rick went to take half the stack, but Bryant stopped him.

"Make sure *you* sign out the jeep," the colonel warned. "The Services commander doesn't want this idiot behind the wheel of *anything* official." He looked up at Guthrie. "Do you *both* understand me?"

"Yes, sir," Rick said, and Guthrie nodded.

"No stops at the NCO Club or the barracks, just go straight there and back," Bryant added. "If you get into trouble, I'll run both your butts up the flagpole."

"Yes, sir," Rick repeated, and Bryant let him take the load, Guthrie taking the rest. They left quickly. "This should take the rest of the afternoon," Johnson said when they were downstairs, walking across the hangar. Two Hueys were undergoing Phase Inspections and were in various states of disassembly on the floor. Johnson put the file box in the rear of the jeep parked near the doors and Guthrie followed suit. "Wait here," Rick told Guthrie and went to sign out the vehicle.

"Sign here," the sergeant at the window said. Johnson did and received the keys. He looked up on the wall to see Campbell and Guthrie's pictures pinned to the bulletin board. "Who are those guys?" He asked the sergeant.

"We're not allowed to sign vehicles out to them," he explained.

"I see," Johnson nodded. "Thanks, Sarge." He was laughing by the time he got back to Guthrie.

"What's so damn funny?"

"They got you and Chuck on a wanted poster in there. Public Enemies Number One and Two," and Rick laughed louder.

"Let me drive," Guthrie demanded.

"No," Johnson shook his head. "Get in and shut up." He threw the vehicle in gear and drove away, squealing the tires.

***

"Hey, asshole," Holmgren shouted as he stepped into the hangar to be almost run over by a jeep. The driver didn't stop, and Holmgren resumed his walk turning back to see the jeep disappear down the perimeter road, he bumped into someone.

"Are you all right, Lieutenant?" Nathan Beu asked him.

"Yes, sorry, Major," Holmgren said and walked on, taking the steps up to the Orderly Room. He looked inside tentatively, checking to see if Johnson was nearby and was relieved to see him absent. *Good*,

Holmgren thought and walked to the desk occupied by Colonel Bryant's admin specialist. "For Colonel Bryant," he said waving the sealed envelope.

"I'll take it," the staff sergeant said.

"It's classified," Holmgren told him.

"Is that the guy from Intel?" Bryant's voice came from his office.

"Yes, sir," the sergeant called back.

"Send him in."

Holmgren walked back to see Bryant behind his desk. "Second Lieutenant Holmgren reports as ordered, sir." He handed over the envelope and Bryant scanned it for a second.

Bryant stood, casually flipping the material in his desk before going to Holmgren's side, leaving the younger man at attention. "The next time you criticize my people in front of the IG, boy, you'd better prepare to have my boot in your ass," he said through clenched teeth.

"Excuse me, sir?"

"You know what I mean, Lieutenant. I won't be second-guessed by some green, wet behind the ears Intel weenie. You sit there and watch the sat feed in the safety of friendly surroundings, my guys were *there,* and they handled themselves the best . . . the *only* way possible," Bryant growled at him. "You've been on my boys since Nam Po and Johnson especially. The kid has a promising career and I won't have you fuck it up by speculation and conjecture. I don't care if you're an Academy ring knocker, Holmgren. If you get in *my* way, Hell will seem like a ski vacation. Got me, boy?"

"Yes, sir."

"Now get out of my office. You're dismissed."

"Yes, sir," Holmgren turned on his heel and marched out, leaving quickly not making eye contact with the sergeant who'd heard everything. *Old dinosaur,* Holmgren thought when he was down in the hangar. In his opinion, there were too many like Bryant in the Air Force, old officers in search of glory after blowing it in Vietnam. *Things will be different once that crowd retires.*

There would be a paradigm change in the U.S. Air Force and the armed forces in general in the next decade. Holmgren saw it firsthand in the technology that was available to the intelligence community with the advent of high-speed computers, now able to observe operations in real time. "The old ones can't keep up," he said aloud, walking across the hangar floor. *We don't have to outgun the Soviets anymore, we can outthink them,* he thought as he stepped through the door into the afternoon sun.

***

Kosarev gained easy access to the base once more, hurriedly driving over to the flightline. This time, however, he pulled up to the checkpoint, showing his falsified line badge to the AP. He also gave the cop his false ID verifying he was a tech rep for Fluid Dynamics out of their Zurich plant.

"What's your business, Mr. Osterhaus," the AP asked, looking over the Swiss passport.

"One of your Pave Lows was having hydraulic problems. It almost went down the other day with a squad of Marines on board," Kosarev replied. "I was the closest tech rep in the area, so they sent me over. I'm here to meet Major Beu with 20th Special Operations."

"The Pave Low area is just past the Huey squadron," the cop pointed down the interior road. "There's a maintenance crew at –261 so that's probably where you'll need to be."

"Thank you, Airman," Kosarev said and drove through the gate, keeping to the fifteen-mph speed limit. While his ID passed casual scrutiny, actual verification with the Department of Defense and Fluid Dynamics would reveal him for what he was, and he would soon be residing in a federal prison somewhere in the U.S. The step-van was just pulling off the flightline when Kosarev turned down the row of helicopters. Passing the van, he read the 51st FMS/Hydraulics sign on the side and hoped the situation at the helicopter was as he'd expected. Beu and maybe one or two others should be the only ones there. If any more troops were there, Kosarev's situation would be untenable. His hope lay in his ability to speak with Beu one on one, man to man and ask his help. Another maintenance crew or a few of the commandos that were Beu's friends would be too many for him to incapacitate. He let out an audible sigh when he saw the main rotor begin turning and no other vehicles could be seen. He parked near some ground equipment and got out of the car.

***

"Who's that guy?" Wood asked Beu who looked out the windscreen.

"I've seen him somewhere before," the pilot replied. "I think someone said he was a tech-rep or something."

"Well, he's coming aboard," Wood said.

"Then he's gonna have a fun ride," Beu declared. "Tell me when he's in."

"Is Major Beu aboard?" Kosarev asked Wood when he stuck his head in the hatch.

"Up front," Wood said. "Get in or get out."

Kosarev climbed in, towering over Wood who pulled the hatch shut. "I am Conrad Osterhaus of Fluid Dynamics." He offered a hand and a smile.

"Wood, I'm the crew chief. We didn't hear anything about a tech-rep." He yanked Kosarev's line badge from the lapel of his jacket, comparing the picture to the man who stood before him.

"You have hydraulic problems, right?" Kosarev said. "They flew me here from Okinawa to look your bird over."

"We're just about to do that, Mr. Osterhaus," Wood told him. "Let's go, Major," he said over the radio to Beu and the chopper went light, lifting off and following the taxiway toward the main runway. He handed Kosarev's line badge back to him. "I suggest you grab a seat," Wood warned, pointing to the web seats. "It'll get bumpy once we get out of local control." He smiled devilishly but made no attempt to sit himself.

Kosarev heard Beu apply power and the Pave Low accelerated following the runway at twenty feet of altitude until he cleared the threshold. The black chopper then shot skyward, forcing the Russian to hold onto the adjoining seat. "Does he always fly like this?"

"Yup," Wood replied with a grin. "You guys make good stuff. It took a stray shell casing to nick the line and it held up through two hours of hard flying before it popped."

"I will relay that to my superiors," Kosarev said as his stomach did a flip. He reached in his pocket and produced a syringe, jamming it into Wood's leg.

"What the . . ." Wood fell unconscious to the cargo deck. The syringe went back into Kosarev's pocket and a pistol was produced before he made his way up to the flight deck.

***

"Hey, is that what's-his-face?" Guthrie asked Johnson as Cowboy-261 lifted off on the other side of the fence.

"Yup, looks like Beu got off easy with old Stonewall," Johnson agreed. "They probably got that can fixed and he and Woodsy are out joyriding."

"Hey, pull over on the perimeter road," Guthrie said, pointing to the dirt track that led off to the right.

"What for?"

"Let's take the long way back," Guthrie insisted as he produced a joint and lit it. "I want to puff one up."

"Go for it," Johnson said, taking the joint from him, as the jeep ambled up the small rise. "They say they're gonna start doing random piss tests soon," Rick added. "We're gonna have to give this shit up."

"Ah, let them throw me out," Guthrie shrugged. "Fucking Air Force ain't all it's cracked up to be."

"What would you do?"

"Go back to my band," Guthrie said. "I was the best front man in Memphis."

"Yeah, in a wedding band," Johnson said.

"It's steady income, my carpetbagger friend, and it's what I love to do." Guthrie took the joint back. "You should think about getting out of this nasty business too."

"You volunteered for this, Jake," Johnson shot back.

"I've made a couple mistakes. I figured we'd *play* soldier; never thought we'd actually *do* it. Playing games with the jarheads and the grunts is one thing; a division of NKPA infantry trying to kill us is another. I got a son back home, remember?" Guthrie was divorced, two year old Jason the only upside of the marriage. "I'd like to see him grow up. You got nobody, Rick, nobody who depends on you for guidance and parenting. Wait until you and Yung Shu have kids, you'll look at things differently."

"Maybe, but just remember it takes thirty days to get this shit out of your bloodstream," Johnson said.

"Whatever," Guthrie shrugged. "Just watch the road."

***

"What's wrong, Woodsy?" Beu called on the radio but heard no reply. "What's going on back there?" Again, no reply and Beu put the ship on autopilot. Unlimbering his belts, he turned out of the seat only to stare into the business end of a ten-millimeter Makarov pistol.

"Please stay seated, Major Beu," Kosarev said. "The *last* thing I want to do is kill you."

"You're no tech-rep, Mr. Osterhaus," Beu shot back. "Did you kill Woodsy?"

"No, he will sleep for a while though," Kosarev chuckled. "And he will have a headache when he awakens."

"Who are you?"

"I am Colonel Yevgeniy Kosarev of the KGB," he said proudly.

"I'm not flying this across the border," Beu said. "I'll crash this bitch before I let you take it."

"I do not want your helicopter, Major," Kosarev said, lowering the pistol but not putting it away. "I will need your services for a while though."

"No way, pal," Beu shook his head. "I won't betray my country. I'll splatter us all over the DMZ." He rested his hand on the stick, a mere movement would disengage the autopilot and another push would send the Pave Low into a nosedive.

"I am not asking this in an official capacity," Kosarev admitted. "I am asking this as a father whose wife is dying." He wormed himself into the copilot's seat and laid the pistol on the instrument panel. Kosarev rubbed his eyes before looking up at Beu. "There will be changes in the Soviet Union, Major Beu. It has begun already but you will not see it for a decade, maybe longer. I am in a position of relative power, what would be comparable to a CIA station chief, and have influence at the Kremlin. My wife will be gone shortly, maybe within a month, but there is the matter of my daughter." Kosarev rubbed a tear away before continuing.

"There will be a power struggle within the next few years," he declared. "And if I survive, my daughter would be a pawn to influence my loyalties. I will not have her kidnapped or the object in a political marriage. She deserves more than that, more than she can get in the Soviet Union. I want her to enjoy the freedoms of the West, to be able to live a normal life anonymously, free from the intrigue in Moscow."

"So, what do you think *I* can do?" Beu shrugged.

"A pilot with your level of competence, in such a spectacular machine as this one, would be able to bring her to South Korea," Kosarev smiled.

"Oh boy," Beu shook his head. "No way. How would I know if she really was your daughter?"

"You would be able to tell immediately," Kosarev said matter of factly.

"She looks like *you*?" Beu imagined the stereotypical Russian *babushka*.

"My daughter is *beautiful*," Kosarev said and his steel-blue eyes flickered to life.

"Whatever, I can't do this," Beu said. "Look, you can kill me, or I can take you back and we can say this thing never happened, but I can't just . . ."

"You *have* to," Kosarev insisted but the gun remained on the instrument panel. "There is no other way. I have been recalled to Moscow and this has been a year in the planning. I will not kill you." He put the pistol in his pocket. "I had hoped we could overcome our national differences and cooperate as two *men* would, honestly and with honor. The pistol was only to make you listen to me. You may return to your base."

Beu checked his position and realized he had gone farther north and east than he'd wanted to. He looked over at Kosarev. "Where is she?"

"Kamchatka," Kosarev said sadly and Beu laughed.

"How did you expect me to get there and back? I can't carry that much fuel in this thing."

"I have arranged to have you refueled," Kosarev replied, a smile creasing his face. "You are thinking about it, no?"

"I can't justify . . . and what about Woodsy?"

"He will be asleep for the duration of our mission. You can tell him he hit his head when you ran into turbulence, but the way you fly, it is a dangerous proposition on a clear day." Kosarev smiled again and Beu returned it.

"Where would I refuel?" Beu asked him as Cowboy-261 went feet wet over the Sea of Japan.

"PVO Vladivostok," Kosarev said without emotion.

"You want me to land this thing at a *Soviet* air defense base? You're kidding, right?"

"I guarantee you safe and unhindered passage," Kosarev replied firmly.

Beu adjusted the autopilot and altered course a little more north-northeast. "I'm supposed to take the word of a KGB colonel?"

"*Nyet*," Kosarev growled. "You are to take the word of a man who fought against the Nazis in Leningrad and Moscow, through the cold of winter and the mud of spring. You are to take the word of a father who has to know his daughter safe before he can go home and comfort his wife in her last days. I am not a Communist, Major Beu, but I am a Russian and Communism is an unpleasant fact for now. I am a proud Russian man who is asking a proud American man to help me save my daughter from an uncertain future. It will be dark when we return, and she and I will leave you as soon as we land. You will never hear from me again, but you will have my eternal debt and gratitude. This is a promise I make from one man of honor to another," Kosarev finished.

"It'll either be a good story at my retirement party, my court martial, or my funeral," Beu said as he took over from the autopilot and shut off the transponder. Dropping the chopper to wave top level, Beu turned it nearly due north.

Osan Air Base

"Sir," the senior controller said to his commanding officer. "We lost Cowboy-261."

"Lost?"

"Drifted out of our radar coverage, sir," the NCO said. "He was heading east, about five miles this side of the DMZ."

"Any radio communications?"

"No, sir," the controller told him. "We tried to raise him several times over the last hour, but we figured they were on the fritz. He's on a check ride, you know."

"Shit," the captain who ran Osan's tower during the night shift muttered. "Get something in the air over his last known position. See if he went down somewhere. I have to make some calls."

Chapter Ten
Aboard Cowboy-261 at PVO Vladivostok, Soviet Union
13 July 1983

"Thank you, Vladivostok Tower," Beu said as he added throttle. It had been tense when he approached, but just as the KGB colonel advised, he and his helicopter were unharmed. Four armored infantry vehicles surrounded the chopper and fuel truck and the replenishment was conducted without incident. "You've got some juice, old boy," he said to Kosarev when PVO Vladivostok was miles behind them. "Tell me something."

"If it is not classified," Kosarev nodded affirmative.

"Don't the Soviets have pilots and helicopters? Why did you get *me* into this?"

"Few helicopter pilots have your talent and capability, and *no* Soviet pilot has a helicopter like this," the Russian said. "I would not trust anyone but the best with Alexa's safety."

"More likely, you didn't want any Soviet personnel knowing your daughter was defecting," Beu laughed.

"That too," Kosarev smiled.

Osan Air Base

"Shit," Johnson said when he arrived on base. His beeper had gone off at the most inopportune time, as usual, and he came directly to the Orderly Room. Some of the others were there, Guthrie, Campbell, Mason, Gibbs, and Emory. Jack George arrived a minute after Bryant briefed them on the disappearance of Cowboy-261. "Guthrie and I saw him take off late in the afternoon."

"They say he was heading east until he dropped off radar and was just getting ready to go feet wet over the Sea of Japan," Bryant went on. "He was holding a steady speed and course."

"Do we have any ships out there, sir?" Johnson asked Bryant.

"It's awful close to North Korea," Bryant said. "And *they* have ships in the area too. We don't want this to turn into a skirmish between the North Koreans and us. This is a rescue mission and the Navy is doing what it can."

"What can *we* do, Colonel?" Johnson indicated his men.

"Get ready to go if they need you," Bryant said, regarding Johnson for a second. "Come with me, Airman," and he led the young man into his office. "I want sergeant's stripes on your uniforms tomorrow."

"Sir?"

"You're the highest-ranking member of A-Flight and they need an NCO. With Reasoner back home, *I* need to have an NCO there and you deserve the endorsement. Consider it a below the zone promotion and it will go on your record as such. You've impressed me over the past week and a half, Sergeant Johnson, and I feel you're more than ready for the responsibility."

"Thank you, sir, and thanks for your support with Yung Shu."

"Don't tell anybody," Bryant growled through a sly smile.

"I won't, sir," Johnson returned it. "I'll keep up your reputation."

"And *what* reputation is that, Sergeant?" Bryant's face was an inch from Johnson's.

"That you're an old hardass, sir."

"Good answer, Sarge," Bryant laughed and clapped him on the back. "Prepare your men for a rescue operation. If they're alive, I want you guys getting them out."

"Yes, sir," Johnson came to attention and saluted.

The Kamchatka Peninsula, Soviet Union

The wispy snow was flung from the willowy pines surrounding the clearing when Beu pulled the Pave Low into a hover, fifty feet off the ground. "I've gotta turn on the landing lights," Beu said and got a nod from Kosarev. The blowing flakes became a blizzard before them in the reflected glare. "You could have picked a more hospitable place."

"It had to be remote," Kosarev said as the chopper settled to earth. A figure clad in a parka ran from the tree line to the rear of the helicopter.

"Do you know how to open the hatch?" Beu asked Kosarev.

"Yes, we stole the technical information for this helicopter two years ago," Kosarev smiled and went back to the cargo area.

"Figures," Beu shrugged. Looking over his shoulder, he got a wave from Kosarev and brought the power up, the Pave Low responding to his commands. They were airborne seconds later. It took him about five minutes to set a return course to Osan and engage the autopilot once he was safely out of Soviet territory, over water and headed south. He unbuckled his restraints and rose, squeezing between the avionics racks back to the cargo deck. He arrived just to see the two figures end an embrace.

"Alexa, my dear," Kosarev said. "This is Major Nathan Beu of the United States Air Force." The shorter of the two turned to face him, pulling back the hood of the parka to release a mane of strawberry blonde hair. Her face was full, and her figure was hourglass, a sensual voluptuousness that held his gaze longer than he'd expected. "This is my daughter, Alexa," he said to Beu. Her eyes were bright, the same steel blue of her father's and they twinkled as they appraised the American.

"It is a pleasure, Major, and my thanks," she said.

"It's *my* pleasure, ma'am," Beu stammered, surprised at his reaction to the beautiful young woman. He'd never had a problem communicating with women before. He became suddenly nervous and would have sworn a cold sweat broke out on his forehead. "I have to see to my machine," he said and returned to the flight deck. *What in Hell is wrong with me?*

Other things came to the forefront of his consciousness when he sat down, namely, what he was going to tell them when he got back to Osan and how he was going to get Kosarev and his daughter off the chopper without being spotted. *What in Hell is wrong with me?* He asked himself a second time for a completely different reason. *By the letter of the law, I'm guilty of treason.* And then he realized that by *any* measure of the law he was guilty as hell.

Beu was certain Alexa Kosarev was who she said she was. If she was a spy, so be it, but she had those blue eyes, the same as her father. *And she's beautiful,* Beu added in his mind before going back to the subject of his career the question of whether jail time was in his future. *I have to get them off the chopper before the rescue people get to me.* Rescue people. His thought process said that the only way he could get away with taking this joyride is if he pleaded equipment failure. *They'll never believe me.* He'd come in without lights and a radio, completely dark and claim total electrical failure. He'd have to fry the data recorders too. *This will never work.*

But it had to work; he'd let the man talk him into it. *Damn it; why?* And he knew because it was the reason he'd joined the Air Force at the height of Vietnam, and it was the reason he and Rick Johnson got along so well. It was the adventure, the adrenaline rush that they all craved, all the ones who stayed, the ones who didn't *need* that shot of natural speed in their veins quit soon enough. Beu was conspiring with a KGB officer to help his daughter defect to the West, probably the first American pilot to fly in and out of Soviet airspace unchallenged and unescorted, and he was heading home to face court martial and imprisonment if his story wasn't believable enough. And he felt that surge, the heating of the blood as his body produced the drug he yearned for.

Osan Air Base

"Where are we going?" Campbell asked Johnson when the chopper went light.

Rick gave the crew chief the thumbs-up and turned to the taller man. "We're gonna search off the coast a bit," Johnson informed him. "I want everybody at a window with a pair of binocs as soon as we go feet wet. The last transponder signal was a mile offshore over the Sea of Japan."

"Man, I don't want to go in the water," Campbell grumbled.

"Be glad it's summer," Johnson shot back. "We could be doing this in a Manchurian windstorm at twenty below with twenty-foot swells."

"True," Campbell motioned to Mason, the hand signal telling him to get into his wetsuit. Campbell scored lowest in his class on the water portion of the Pararescue final and avoided water duty when possible. If anything was found, one or more of them would have to go into the water to help the survivors and Campbell pulled rank to assure he wouldn't be the first off the chopper. All they knew was that Beu and Wood were the only two aboard Cowboy-261. "What do you think happened, Rick?"

"Who knows?" Johnson shrugged. "It must not have been good if they went down. Woodsy can handle most anything mechanical and Beu can fly the shit out of a helo."

"They could have drifted over North Korean waters," Campbell offered. "It's not hard to do this far north and their navy has patrols out all the time. If they were shot down …"

"Let's not speculate, okay?" Johnson growled. "They'll be all right. I refuse to lose any *more* of my friends this week."

Aboard Cowboy-261, approaching the South Korean coast

"Are you all right?" She asked and he froze.

Beu forced himself to speak. "I'm trying to think my way out of the trouble your father has got me into."

"You are not a man who lets other people make trouble for him, Major," Alexa Kosareva said plainly.

"You think you know me?" He turned then and the beauty of her Slavic features struck him, as they had the first time he'd seen her.

"I know the type of man my father would trust with my safety," she said. "You are a man of honor who knows when to do the right thing."

"It helped that he pointed a gun at me," Beu turned away.

"I am certain he just used it to get your attention. My father has never shot an honorable man," Alexa replied as if it were just that simple.

"That's nice," Beu shook his head.

"Do you not think I hear things, Comrade Major?" She hissed at him. "My schoolmates never let me forget my father is a KGB colonel and a *rezident*."

"I would think he'd want to keep that a secret," Beu looked back at her. "Would you like to sit down?" He indicated the copilot's chair.

"Thank you," she smiled at him brightly.

"Where's the old man?"

"He is taking a nap next to your friend," Alexa informed him.

"Shit, I forgot about Woodsy," Beu muttered. "What will I tell *him*? Jesus Christ, *why* did I do this?"

"To save me from the horrible Communists," she giggled, and he smiled back. "Moscow is a strange place, Major. The school I went to is for the children of high-level Party members. My friends' parents knew who I was and invariably spoke about my father around their children, usually the ones who came on the wrong side of the KGB."

"It's like getting on the wrong side of the IRS," Beu chuckled.

"But my father is also a Hero of the Fifth Order, Major Beu. He has sacrificed much for the good of Mother Russia. He is not just a spy but also a warrior, another who has proven himself in battle defending the country he loves. He is man like you, Comrade Major."

"I'll take that as a compliment," Beu said. "Please call me Nate."

"Very well," she replied. "And it *was* a compliment. I know what you are risking doing this."

"What are you going to do once we land?" He asked her.

"I do not know. I assume father has something set up in the United States or Canada. He said the less I knew the safer I would be."

"Do you know anyone over there?"

"No," she said sadly. "But I make friends easily. I will fit in wherever I go."

"I'm sure of it," Beu said. "Is your father going too?"

"He cannot," a tear ran down Alexa's cheek. "If he came with me, we would never be safe. They would hunt him down and bring him back or kill him. He will go back to Moscow, to be with mother until . . ."

"I know, I'm sorry," Beu handed her a Kleenex. "He told me about your mother on the way out to get you."

"Do you have a wife, Nathan?" Alexa asked him after drying her tears.

"Never met a woman who could corral me, ma'am," he said proudly but not as confidently as he had in the past, as he had until today when he met Alexa Kosareva, and then he chided himself for even considering it.

"Have you ever met a *Russian* woman?" She regarded him slyly.

"Not until today," he replied with a smile. *Not until today.* And the screen on his Multi-Function Display turned into what looked like a laser show. "Shit, they're looking for us." The screen showed search radar, on various bands from different sources, filling the ether with emissions designed to locate and report the position of the missing helicopter. "Shit," Beu punched the control panel and tore his attention away from the young woman, pushing the Pave Low to the waves.

"What is wrong?" Alexa asked.

"They've got ships, planes, and everything else out looking for me. I'll never get out of this," he told her.

His words sounded down, but the grin that crossed his face told her otherwise. He was up, sharp, and sure. Alexa thought that he was firmly in control of the situation. "Can you avoid them, Nathan?"

"Yeah, their radar probably, but not visually," he said. "We're gonna have to act the part. Wake your father up. The ride's gonna get bumpy from here on out."

Aboard Cowboy-377

"I got 'em," SRA Gibbs called out. "Four o'clock low, maybe a half mile out," he said, his eyes pressed to the binoculars and they in turn pressed to the window. "He's flying, not well but he's flying."

"How in the hell did you do that?" Johnson came over and took the binocs from Gibbs. The Pave Low was out there, flying erratically as hell, but flying. −261 was dark, no running lights, no interior lights, portending of a massive electrical failure. The pilot of −377 swung into a descending right-hand turn and came up behind. "Can you raise him?" Rick asked the crew chief.

"Nah," the tech sergeant waved. "They're trying but nothing yet. They got a *Spruance*-class destroyer on an intercept course to try and give Beu a place to land if he needs it."

"How far out are we?"

"Seventy-five miles," the crew chief replied. "If he can make it feet dry it would be a lot safer."

"Can he ditch it?"

"I wouldn't," the crew chief shook his head. "I'll bet one of these big bitches sinks like a fucking rock."

"Shit," Johnson muttered and went to look out the forward hatch.

Aboard Cowboy-261

"Shit," Beu barked, the acrid smoke still filled the flight deck from his little wiring experiment. "I think I torched something I didn't want to." Everything was dead but thankfully, the engines were still running. The instrument panel was a dark void before him.

"What happened?" Kosarev came forward.

"I did a little more than I wanted to," Beu shrugged. "I'm gonna have to fly this by the seat of my pants so you'd better get strapped in. I doubt I'll make it to the base, and we have an escort as it is." He caught a glimpse of –377 on his radar before his self-inflicted electrical failure. "Make sure Woodsy is secure too."

"He is," Kosarev nodded. "My car is still at the base."

"Give me the keys," Beu said. "I'll bring it later." He handed Kosarev the key to the fifth floor of the Pink Lady.

"What is this?"

"There's a soccer field around the corner from the Pink Lady," Beu instructed. "I'm gonna set it down there so you and Alexa be ready to go when I land. You can be sure the other helo will follow me down so get away fast. Go directly to the Pink Lady, the key will open the fifth-floor apartment. Wait there for me and I'll bring the car when I get done answering questions."

"*If* you get done answering questions," Kosarev extended a hand. "You have done more than I dared hope for, and I thank you."

"Give me twelve hours," Beu shook his hand. "If I'm not there, assume the worst and take off."

"Da," Kosarev nodded. "*Spasibo*," he added as he turned.

"Hey," Beu called back. "Where is she going?"

"New York eventually," Kosarev said.

"She doesn't have any friends there."

"And where do *you* suggest?" Kosarev cast him a wary eye.

"Florida, Fort Walton Beach ideally," Beu replied.

Kosarev turned on him. "If you think I'll give you my daughter as payment for ... I'll kill you with my bare hands."

"No," Beu held up his hands. "I'll keep an eye on her, but I wouldn't ... don't misunderstand ..."

"Another minute and you would have me sold into slavery, would you, papa?" Alexa said from behind, causing them both to turn. "Don't you think *I* would like a say in my future?"

"Yes, Alexa darling, but I only ..." Kosarev gave up. "What do *you* want to do, my dear?"

Beu saw now what Kosarev meant when he said Beu would know she was his daughter. Alexa handled him well. *Her mother must be a pistol*, he thought and smiled. "And what are *you* laughing at, Comrade Major?" She turned on him. "Do you want me to come to Florida to be your whore?"

"I ... I didn't mean ... it's *your* life," Beu surrendered as well.

"That's right and I'll think about my options," she gave Beu a wink as she turned back to the cargo deck.

Kosarev rolled his eyes. "She is just like her mother." And then the eyes hardened. "And never forget *I* am her father, Major Beu. If she shows poor judgment and decides she likes you, do not think distance or the military will be enough to protect you if you hurt her."

"Whatever happens, be assured I will treat her with respect, Colonel Kosarev," Beu promised, wondering just what this man got him into.

Aboard Cowboy-377

"Where in Hell is he going?" Johnson asked the crew chief.

"Pilot says they think he's trying for Osan," he replied. "You guys ready? We'll follow him in and we're ten minutes from the field."

"Yeah, just don't set us on top of him if he goes in hard," Johnson said. "He's probably almost out of fuel and there will be enough fumes in those tanks to start an explosion."

"You got it, Sarge," the copilot gave him the thumbs up and Johnson grinned.

It was the first time he'd been called that by one of his peers. "Looks like he's heading for the field," Johnson said when he got back to his men. "If he can keep it flying."

"Where's he been?" Jack George asked.

"Who knows, but we'll be first on scene," Johnson shrugged. "Be fucking *careful*."

"He's going down," the crew chief yelled to them. "Hold on."

Aboard Cowboy-261

"Get ready," Beu called to them. "The landing's gonna be a little rough." He flared the craft as he came in over the grandstands and the generator went, killing power to the engines. –261 went tail heavy but Beu managed to right her and auto rotate to a hard but safe landing. He was out of his seat after he killed master power and into the back of the chopper, but the Russians were gone. The sound of rotor blades made him look skyward to see –377 flare into the stadium, the cargo door dropping open as the wheels touched the ground.

"Come on, Woodsy," Beu said as he hoisted the man onto his shoulders. He had only taken ten steps from the craft when familiar faces surrounded him.

"You all right, Major?" Johnson said as Mason and Campbell took Wood from Beu.

"Fucking serious electrical casualty," Beu said as they got him away from the chopper. They began assessing Wood's condition and Beu sat down next to them. "Autopilot wouldn't disengage, and I was going at full speed out to sea for a couple hours, and then everything went dead."

"What happened to him?" Johnson asked.

"When the electrical system torched, the bottom dropped out and we lost about two hundred feet in a matter of seconds. When I called back to him to see if he was all right, he didn't answer. I set it down on some little island out there to check on him and I found him down on the cargo deck. I figure he hit his head on something and treated him as such," Beu explained.

"Good man," Johnson patted his shoulder and turned to Campbell.

"We figure he has a wicked concussion," Campbell said. "Good thing he had his flight helmet on, or he'd be dead."

"Get him aboard –377 and to the hospital. I'll wait here for the cavalry with Major Beu," Johnson said as sirens could be heard in the distance.

"Are you sure you're okay, Major?" Campbell asked once more.

"I'm fine," Beu said. "Just get Woodsy to the hospital."

"You got it, sir." Campbell and the rest departed with Wood on a litter as the first of the cars with flashing lights entered the stadium.

"I'll bet the locals are pissed about the grass," Johnson kidded him. The manicured soccer field now had one huge divot ripped out and several smaller ones, courtesy of the Pave Low and its hard landing.

"The Air Force is gonna be pissed about the chopper," Beu chuckled. Fortunately, there wasn't much damage to it, a good part of the electrical system was fried, but physically she was intact. A thorough inspection of the landing gear was definitely in order, however.

"I'll buy you a drink when we're done with this," Johnson offered.

"I'll buy you two if I get out of it with my career intact," Beu countered.

"As long as you're here with your ass intact. Haven't we lost enough friends for a while, Nate?"

"Amen, pal."

The Pink Lady

They sat in the darkness, neither making a sound, Kosarev listening by the door. "What is wrong, papa?" Alexa whispered.

"We should leave," he said. "It is not safe here, especially if the old woman finds us."

"He said to wait twelve hours," she insisted.

"Why, do you want to go to Florida with *him*?" Father spat.

"It is warmer than Moscow, all year round," daughter shot back. "And I have always wanted to go to Disney World," she giggled.

"And you are infatuated by a man who is older and leads a dangerous lifestyle, Alexa darling."

"He might not *have* a lifestyle," she offered. "He risked everything for us."

"I did not force him," Kosarev declared.

"But you knew of him, of how he would probably react when you asked him for help, you knew the right things to say in order to convince him."

"There is nothing I can do to help him," Kosarev shrugged. "But he is a smart man, I am certain he will formulate a believable alibi."

"I wonder if he can live with himself," Alexa mused.

"He is a strong and principled man as well," Kosarev said. "And he is certain he was doing the right thing."

"So why do you not want me to get closer to him?"

"I do not want you close to *any* man, my beautiful daughter," and he hugged her to him. "You will always be my Little Alexa."

"Oh stop, papa," she hissed. "So, what is so bad about the Major?"

"He is a womanizer, dear," Kosarev told her. "I am certain he is sleeping with one of the little sluts that work in this place."

"I wonder if I could get a job here," she jibed him.

"Alexa," he raised his index finger as he always did when he scolded her.

"I am kidding, papa, and I am a *woman*. I am grateful you have done this for me, and I am grateful to Major Beu, but I am in a free country now and I can make my own decisions."

"So, you will go to Florida?"

"I haven't decided yet," she kissed his cheek.

"Do not leave yourself vulnerable, Alexa," he warned. "I have done surveillance on these men for a year, Beu and his commando friends. They are wild, dangerous creatures that drink too much and bring arrogance to the extreme.

"It sounds like someone else I know," she hugged him. "I will be fine, papa, regardless of where I live. I am sure that you will be keeping watch over me as well," and her eyes became moist. "Tell mama ... tell her I'm sorry I couldn't say goodbye."

"She knew it had to be like this and I will always be here for you, my darling."

Osan Air Base

"*What* island, Nate?" Colonel Bryant asked.

"I *don't know* what island, shit I didn't even know where I was, let alone what they call a piece of rock the size of a football field," Beu shot back. "My only concern was getting the auto disengaged and checking on my crew chief. I got him immobilized and checked his vitals and then went about seeing what it would take to get the thing flying. Most of my electronics were out but I had manual flight control. Rather than wait around somewhere in the dark, my first thought was getting Woodsy to a hospital."

"What if you would have had to ditch at sea?" Bryant barked. "What would you have done with him then?"

"I figured I could make it back, sir, at least back far enough to attract someone's attention. I knew you'd be looking for me."

"Jesus Christ, Nate, you had no lights, nothing, do you know how goddamn lucky you are that you didn't run into something or something run into you?"

"Like I said, getting Sergeant Wood to medical care was my first concern. He had a head injury, the severity of which I didn't know, and I made the call," Beu crossed his arms on his chest.

"Your new butt buddy outside used those words at the IG inquiry into the Nam Po operation," Bryant said.

"Johnson?"

"What are you doing hanging out with the enlisted guys, Nate?" Bryant took on a fatherly tone. "You know it's just a matter of time until some greenhorn fresh out of the Academy calls you on it. Do you *really* need the hassle?"

"What did *you* do when they called you on it, sir?" Beu shot back. "Besides, it's better than hanging out with fighter pilots."

"Take it from someone who's been through the hassle. It's seldom worth it, not with a career as promising as yours," Bryant lectured. "You'll have your own squadron one day, Nate, maybe a base, maybe a place at the Office of the Secretary or the Joint Chiefs of Staff. When you get that far, breach of fraternization regs can stop an appointment cold."

"Just like wrecking a forty-million-dollar helicopter?"

"We'll see about that, son. There will be an investigation, you know," Stonewall Bryant told him. Beu nodded. "Is there anything I should know now? If something happened, it's better to come clean than to hide it."

"It's the way I told you, sir, and I'll tell it to the crash board the same way," Beu said firmly as if he believed it.

Bryant nodded. "Why don't you take off and take Johnson with you? I'll call you when the board wants your ass."

"Thank you, sir. I'll need a lift out to the flightline to get my car. I left it there yesterday," Beu said, remembering the last piece of evidence that would undo his story.

"Tell Johnson to take you and tell the Mama-san to put the first round on my tab," Bryant said. "You guys earned it."

"Thank you, sir," Beu stood and came to attention.

"Get some rest, Nate," the old colonel said. "You look like shit." Beu left the office and tapped Johnson on the leg as he read an *Airman* magazine, beckoning him to follow.

"You're *done*?" Rick said when he caught up.

"For now," he said. "Take me out to the flight line to get my car."

"*Your* car?"

Beu stopped and turned to him. "Promise me right now that you won't ask any questions."

"What are you talking about?"

"You'll see soon enough. Promise me, Rick; word of honor," Beu insisted.

"Okay, I promise," Johnson surrendered.

"Good, sign out the jeep and take me out to the spot." They walked down the stairs in silence and Rick signed out one of the squadron jeeps.

"Can I ask you how you're feeling?" Johnson said. Beu's eyes were focused out on the flightline as they approached 20th Squadron's parking area.

"I'm fine," Beu said. "Where's the car?" It wasn't where Kosarev left it.

"Maybe the motor pool picked it up," Rick offered.

"It was a POV," Beu used the military acronym for personally owned vehicle.

"Maybe the sky cops impounded it for illegal parking?"

"This isn't New York, Rick," Beu muttered. "They'd figure out whose it was and talk to them when they came back for it. They don't tow shit away if it's been parked someplace a couple hours."

"I say it's *happy* hour," Johnson offered. "I don't know about you, but I could use a drink."

"Me too," Beu said. "I guess you can take me to the motor pool to sign out a car."

"Yes, sahib," Johnson put his hands together and bowed his head.

"Shut up and drive," Beu ordered.

"Are you sure you don't want me to drop you at the barracks? You look like shit, Nate," Johnson observed.

"Stonewall said the same thing," Beu said. "I need a drink first and then I'll think about sleep."

"Did something happen last night?"

"I thought you weren't going to ask any questions," Beu growled.

"Man, you're the best chopper pilot I've ever seen," Johnson said as he steered back onto the public roads. "Your chopper just took you on an all-night ride, God knows how far out to sea, and then you crash land it in a soccer stadium fifteen miles from the field. You don't strike me as the type to let your machine get the best of you."

"I brought the bitch back in one piece, *didn't* I?"

"Barely. Who's on the investigation board?" Johnson asked and Beu shrugged. "Well you'd better hope they don't know you or they'd get the same hinky feeling I have."

"You know me for a week and a half, boy," the pilot shot back.

"You've got a good rep among the combat officers," Johnson said, pulling up in front of the motor pool. "And you're a surrogate son to old Stonewall. And I know you well enough that your pleading ignorance is bullshit. What *really* went down out there?"

"Believe what you will," Beu said and got out of the jeep. "But you know the story."

"Fine," Johnson shrugged. "Are you going to the club?"

"Yeah."

"Pick me up at the hangar and give me a ride home," Rick said. "I gotta drop off the jeep."

"Maybe," Beu turned and went inside.

"Officers," Johnson muttered as he set off for his starting point. Johnson debated Beu's reaction to his questions and whether he cared in the slightest. Rick wasn't one to make longtime friends, he had one friend from childhood whom he kept in contact with, but he hadn't been the least bit interested in dealing with any of his schoolmates, none of which had joined the military.

I've changed and they haven't, he thought as he stopped at the security checkpoint to gain access to the flightline. His friends were still doing the same things they did in high school. Rick had tasted combat and killed men in the heat of battle, he'd been all over the world and they were still on Long Island, the common ground was gone. He saw it when he went home on leave to visit his parents, invariably stopping in to see how the old gang was and found them still hanging around the same places, chasing after the same girls they did when they were in school.

Johnson's A-Flight comrades would always be his brothers and he was certain he would never forget their names or their faces, but he knew he would lose touch when some would leave the service and others would be transferred. That didn't bother him either, but what did was how he felt about Beu, feeling a kinship for the man that he didn't think he could with anyone who wasn't family. He drove through the gate, parked inside the hangar, and returned the keys. Beu was waiting outside when he stepped out the door.

"Hurry up," Beu barked and Johnson quickened his pace.

"Just cool your jets," Rick replied when he got in the car. Beu took off before he had the door closed. "They're gonna bust your ass for speeding and it will take that much longer."

"Who appointed you my mother?"

"Never mind." Johnson lit a cigarette and sat back in the seat. "Look, I don't want to know anything, Nate. I just have one question and then I'll lay off. Are you okay? I mean *really* okay?" He tapped his index finger against his temple. "You're my friend, man. Shit, I owe you my life. I know we don't know each other that long but I don't want to see your career go down the tubes. If you ever need someone to talk to, just let me know. That's it, I'm done." Rick turned to the window and stared into the new morning.

"I appreciate it and you don't owe me anything," Beu nodded. "I don't mean to be a prick, but I have to see this through myself."

"I understand, just had to say my thing," Rick shrugged.

"You're all right for an enlisted guy," he joked.

"Damn right I am to put up with an officer for a friend," Johnson smiled. "You're as fickle as a woman." Beu parked across the street from the club and they walked inside, Yung Shu greeting them.

"It's good to see you are all right, Major," she said after giving Rick a kiss.

"Thank you, darling," Beu said making for the stairs.

"I thought you needed a drink?" Johnson called after him.

"I'll be right down," the pilot promised. "I think I left something here the other night." And he continued up the stairs.

"What's wrong?" Yung Shu asked her man as his eyes followed Beu until he was out of sight.

"Something happened to him out there, baby, and he won't tell me. He's different somehow."

***

Beu opened the door tentatively to see the lights on and smell coffee brewing. She came out of the kitchen and smiled at him. "Do you want some coffee, Nathan," Alexa Kosareva said.

"Where is he?"

"Papa?"

"Yes," Beu growled.

"He left," she said. "He will not be back." She turned away and brought a tissue to her eyes. "He said he was going to your base to clean up any loose ends."

"So, he got the car?"

"I would think," she sniffed and turned back to him. "Why did you want me to come to Florida?"

"To help you adjust," he shrugged. "The U.S. is a lot different than what you're used to. I figured if you lived close to someone you know, you might have an easier time fitting in."

"And I might be grateful to you for helping me?" Alexa raised an eyebrow.

"I don't expect anything in return, Ms. Kosareva. As you said, I made my own decisions. I just thought you might need a friend when you're all alone in a strange place. America is a *free* country; you can do and live wherever the hell you want." He turned to leave. "Good luck to you."

"I guess I didn't make the impression on you I thought I did, Comrade Major," she said to his back, causing him to stop.

Beu debated continuing out the door but something inside stopped him. While he found himself actually infatuated with this woman, this girl, and while the directness he found irritating in her father was much different when it came from her. *She's nineteen*, he said to himself, yet he turned back to her. "What does that have to do with anything?"

She picked up the envelope on the table and walked over, handing it to him. "It means I will have to ask someone else to take me to Disney World," Alexa smiled.

Beu opened the envelope and found tickets aboard Korean Air from Kim Po International to San Francisco with a connecting flight to Orlando via American Airlines and then a commuter flight to Pensacola. "I don't understand."

"I have been the object of men's desire since I was sixteen, Nathan, with this body it was inevitable." Alexa spread her arms wide and he couldn't keep his eyes from roaming over her. "I know when one is interested," she giggled as he tried to control his gaze. "And I want you just as badly. I'm not asking for commitment now and if you want to keep it as just friends, I will abide by your wishes, but I want more than that."

"I'm sure your father told you I'm a confirmed bachelor," he said, looking into her eyes.

"He said you were having sex with one of the girls who works here," she replied, holding his gaze.

"He's right," Beu's voice was a whisper.

"You're very honest, Comrade Major," she moved closer.

"I thought you would appreciate honesty," he said.

"I do," she came closer. "Do you want me to come to Florida?" She put her hands on his waist.

"Yes," he said and kissed her.

***

"Where the hell is he?" Johnson said as he sat at the bar. Finishing his beer, he looked up the stairs and saw nothing.

"Maybe he wants to be alone for a while," Yung Shu offered.

"He was alone half the night," Rick shot back. "I'm going to see if he's all right." He hopped off the stool.

"He's a grown man, Rick," she insisted but he was already taking the stairs. "You said he's been through worse in Vietnam."

"Maybe this put him over the edge, who knows," Johnson shrugged. "But I'm not going to let him do anything stupid." Yung Shu just shrugged and followed him up to the fifth floor.

"Do you think he would hurt himself?"

"Who knows," he said. "But he thinks this incident could end his career. From what I know of the man, I don't think he lives for anything else. Do you see why I'm worried?"

"I smell coffee," Yung Shu observed, sniffing at the air.

"What the fuck is going on?" Johnson went directly to the closed kitchen door and flung it open. His jaw dropped when he saw Beu and a young woman in the middle of a passionate kiss.

Yung Shu came up behind and stopped at his side. "Wow," she said.

They parted, Beu turning to look over at Rick and Yung Shu. "Jesus Christ," he muttered. "Close your mouth before you catch a bug," Beu said to Rick whose eyes settled on Alexa.

"Hi," he said, still staring until Yung Shu elbowed him in the ribs.

"This is Alexa ..." Beu began.

"Osterhaus," Alexa cut him off, offering a hand first to Johnson and then to Yung Shu. "I'm with the U.N. in Seoul," she said without hesitation.

"You dog," Johnson said to Beu, grinning until Yung Shu cuffed him in the back of the head.

"You're not American," Yung Shu asked the girl who didn't look much older than she was.

"I'm Swiss," Alexa smiled. "I'm on an internship at the U.N. from the university in Bern."

Johnson turned to ask Beu where he'd been hiding the beautiful young woman, but the officer read his mind. "I told you, no questions."

"But ..."

"*No* questions, man, but I have a feeling you'll be seeing more of her in the future," Beu smiled at Alexa.

"But ..."

"Do you mind if she stays here a couple days until she has to leave?" Beu went on without letting Johnson get in a word.

"But ..."

"I'll show you where everything is," Yung Shu said to Alexa who smiled at Rick and his frustration. "Stay as long as you like."

"Thank you," Alexa said. "It was nice talking to you, Sergeant," she added with a giggle.

"But ..."

"Come on, Rick, I'll buy you a drink," Beu threw an arm over the younger man's shoulder and followed the women out.

"She's hot, pal," Johnson became a bit more literate.

"That she is," the pilot replied.

"Where have ..."

"I'll tell you the story one day. I promise you that, now *shut up* about this," Beu insisted.

"Yes, sir," Johnson gave him a mock salute and led the way to the bar.

Osan Air Base

"Hello?" Holmgren said when he picked up the receiver.

"Hi, Alan, it's Quanh."

"What do you want?" Holmgren became suddenly nervous.

"I have to see you soon," Quanh replied.

"Don't call me here for that," Alan barked.

"No, Alan," Quanh pleaded. "I have information for you."

"What kind of information?"

"Not over the phone," Quanh insisted. "Can you meet me in Seoul?"

"How did you get it?" Holmgren asked.

"I'm a bartender, remember?" Quanh said. "I'll be in Seoul tomorrow night at the *Olympia Hotel* on the Choggyechono. Can you meet me there?"

"I don't know," Holmgren replied.

"I'll only be there overnight tomorrow; I go back the next morning."

"If I'm there, I'm there," Holmgren said, hanging up the phone. He looked around to check for eavesdroppers and found none. *It's coming apart*, he thought. Quanh's calling him here was dangerous. As a member of the military, Holmgren did not enjoy the same rights as a civilian would. Tapping of the public phone was not out of the question for the Air Force Office of Special Investigations in their attempts to root out drug use and solve other crimes. Fortunately,

Quanh mentioned nothing about the hours they spent together or what he had planned for the future. Holmgren would have to insist Quanh never call him here, for whatever reason.

He could destroy my career, and that was all Holmgren had left. It was something he had to protect at all costs for the end of his career would be the end of his life. He would have nothing else to live for. Love was no longer in the cards for him, not with this new disease raising its head. AIDS had them all terrified, homosexual, and heterosexual alike, but it was ravaging the gay community. *Monkey fucking Africans*, he thought as he made his way back to his billet.

It was thought AIDS originated in the jungles of Africa, brought to the U.S. and the rest of the world by a gay flight attendant. Promiscuity and unprotected sex, rampant in the clubs and bathhouses of New York, San Francisco, and the Far East served to spread the epidemic that much faster. *I will have to do more than insist*, Holmgren thought when he got back to his room. There was only one way to assure Quanh never called the base again.

The Sea of Japan, aboard the trawler *Yong Ji*

Kosarev peered into the dusk to see the shore slowly disappear along with the seagulls and terns as the big diesel engine chugged into the breeze. "Goodbye, my dear," he said quietly as the smell of burnt fuel filled his nostrils.

He would be back in Moscow in sixteen hours, provided the imbecile at the wheel of the boat didn't sink her. The *Yong Ji* began life thirty years before as a Russian spy ship named the *Elena*, given to the North Koreans as payment for information on the Chinese activities near Siberia. Kosarev had arranged the trade a few years before and the captain was also on his payroll. He had quite a network built within the North Korean government and it was a shame to leave it in the hands of another.

Marko Zhukov would return to run it and though Kosarev considered him a friend, he knew the man was not the one for the job. *You are an administrator, Marko, and this job requires a field agent.* If Kosarev was correct, he would not be returning to Asia, even after his dear Katherine passed. *Things will change soon*, he thought as he went forward to the pilothouse.

Chapter Eleven
The Pink Lady, Osan, South Korea
14 July 1983

"So, what do you think?" Rick asked her as they lay in the darkness.

"About what," Yung Shu said.

"Nate's new babe."

"I don't know," she said. "She's not very talkative about herself but she goes on about your friend forever."

"The girl better not get her hopes up," Rick chuckled. "He'll have his fun and move on."

"You never know, Rick. Didn't you say that something changed him? Maybe *she* is what changed him," Yung Shu offered. "She's very pretty, and intelligent too."

"The guy's thirty-two, baby," Rick said. "He ain't gonna fall for some young babe he just met."

"Love happens in the strangest places," Yung Shu kissed him. "You should know that better than anyone, my love."

"Lightning doesn't strike twice," Rick laughed.

"Never say never, Rick," she admonished. "No one knows what the spirits have in mind for us."

"You're starting to sound like your mother," he chuckled.

"I'm serious," Yung Shu whispered in his ear. "Did you see the way he looked at her, and you said he was acting strangely since he crashed?"

"I was thinking he hit his head," Johnson replied. "I don't think he fell madly in love with some babe from the Alps."

"Trust my intuition," she told him as he nibbled on her ear.

"What's your intuition telling you now?" He whispered as his erection pressed against her thigh.

"I don't need intuition for that," Yung Shu giggled and let him inside her.

***

"When is your flight?" Beu asked her when she joined him in the kitchen.

"Four o'clock this afternoon," Alexa replied as she put her arms around him. "I expected you to be in my bed last night."

"I was thinking," he said.

"Nothing happens when you *think* about it," she reminded him.

"You've got this all figured out, don't you?" Beu said softly. "You're nineteen, Alexa, I'm thirty-two. Don't you think people would ask questions?"

"Don't people in the southern United States get married at fourteen?" She asked innocently and he laughed.

"We're already moving toward marriage?"

"I just meant that if a fourteen year old can get married, a nineteen year old can keep company with the man of her choice," she said, her hands going to her hips. "Provided he is *willing*, of course," Alexa added for effect.

"I'm *too* willing, that's the problem," he shrugged. "I promised your father that I would always treat you with respect and I intend to honor my promise. Much as I'd love to ... well, you know, most of my relationships are of the short and casual kind." Beu looked at her hungrily. "Before I sleep with you, I want to be sure I can give you what you're looking for and also be able to fulfill the pledge I made to your father."

She came over and kissed him on the lips hungrily. "Papa was right about you," she whispered in his ear.

Sherematyevo Airport, Moscow, Soviet Union

Kosarev stepped off the Aeroflot plane directly into the waiting Zil limousine. It was raining this morning, or night, or whatever it was. Kosarev disliked flying west and trying to figure out the time zones into the past. Marko Zhukov was behind the wheel.

"The Chairman has been calling every few hours since I returned," Zhukov said. "And there was another who was interested in your whereabouts as well."

That was expected. It was what he'd felt blowing in the wind. "Did he leave a name?"

"No."

"Very well," Kosarev nodded. "I need sleep and I need to see my wife."

"The Chairman wanted me to bring you to the Kremlin as soon as you arrived," Zhukov said, praying Kosarev didn't refuse to see Andropov. The Chairman expected the Pyong Yang rezident yesterday and was in no mood to accept Zhukov's report.

"Hear me, Marko," Kosarev raised his index finger. "The old bastard will not live two years."

"Please, Yevgeniy," Zhukov cried. "Don't speak like that here. The Komitet has ears all over."

"You are an old babushka, Marko," Kosarev laughed. "You worry like an old woman twice your age. Go to the Kremlin," he sighed. "Let us see what the windbag wants."

Osan Air Base, Osan, South Korea

"We meet again, Johnson," Colonel Forrester said, offering a hand, which Rick shook warmly.

"It's good to see you again, sir," he replied honestly.

"You seem to always be in the shit when it comes down, don't you?"

"Yes, sir, apparently I'm a shit magnet," Rick smiled. "I *always* get splattered with it."

"What did you see, Rick?"

"Shit, not much, Colonel," Rick shrugged. "My guy Gibbs spotted him, damned if I know how he did that on a near moonless night, and we pulled up behind him. As soon as he was down, we came in a hundred feet away from him to check for casualties. Woodsy was unconscious and Major Beu was carrying him out of the chopper by the time I got there. There was no fire, so we triaged them right there. The Major was okay, and I waited with him until the ground units came. They took Woodsy to the hospital on the rescue chopper."

"I hear he'll be allowed visitors this afternoon," Captain Vaughn said.

"I'm headed over to the hospital as soon as I leave here, sir," Johnson smiled.

"Did Beu tell you anything, son," Forrester asked.

"No, sir, just that he had a major electrical casualty not long after takeoff. I believe him because he was flying dark when we spotted him. I didn't even see interior lights on, and it smelled like burnt wiring in there when we got to him," Rick said truthfully.

"Is that all?"

"Yes, Colonel Forrester."

"Thanks for your time, Rick, and give Sergeant Wood my best."

That was easy, Johnson thought as he came to attention and turned on his heel. He could imagine what Beu would go through, first with the IG and then with the crash board, maybe a court martial after that if they found he was negligent. *Your nuts are in a vise, pal.*

Johnson left the building and walked over to the hospital, a ten-minute exercise that didn't tax him in the least. Two officers and an enlisted man were leaving Wood's room when he got there. "Hey, Woodsy."

"Hey, Rick," Wood's face brightened.

"Who were those guys?"

"Incident investigation," Wood told him. "Been talking to them since I woke up."

"How are you feeling?"

"Fine except for this fucking headache," he rubbed his temple.

"What happened up there?"

"I don't know," Wood shook his head slowly, wincing from the pain when he did. "I don't remember taking off, let alone what happened," he admitted. "I have to go by what Beu told me."

"Do you think he's telling the truth?" Johnson asked him.

"He's never lied to me yet," Wood replied, this time keeping his head still.

"Does he seem different to you?" Rick pressed.

"No, not really considering what he said happened. I just wish I'd been awake to help him out. Are you running your *own* investigation?" Wood looked at him suspiciously. You didn't question friends, not in a business where trust was everything.

"No, man, but we followed you in," Rick explained. "I was the first on the scene and I think he's been a little weird since he put it down in the soccer field. I'm trying to help him, and it seems like he's hiding something. Do you know anything about a girl?"

"Just the barmaid," Wood shrugged and even that movement brought pain to his head.

"He never said anything about a girl who worked with the UN? She's blonde, huge tits, serious ass, name's Alicia . . . Alexa, something like that."

"Nah," Wood said. "But I don't listen to his stories anymore. He could have."

"You're a help," Johnson muttered. "Can I bring you anything? I'll mix a pitcher of screwdrivers or kamikazes if you'd like."

"Can you get that in here?"

"Sure, medics have no idea about security," Rick laughed.

"Kamikazes," Wood grinned. "Maybe I can get rid of this headache."

"I'll be by this afternoon," Rick gave him a wink.

"If it isn't our escape artist," the young blonde lieutenant said as she came through the door, the same who'd had the pleasure of having Johnson as a patient.

"Lieutenant," Johnson smiled at her.

"Are you conspiring to break Sergeant Wood out as well?" She batted her eyes at him.

"Nah," Rick waved in Wood's direction. "Woodsy's a good boy. *I'm* the boy your mother warned you about."

"Of that I'm sure," she giggled. "I seem to remember a request for Jack Daniel's and a hot blonde, Sergeant Johnson."

"Indeed," Johnson said as he regarded her appraisingly.

"You seem to have recovered nicely," she observed as she took a pad out of her lab coat and a pen from the bun in her hair.

"I didn't hurt any of the parts required to enjoy Jack Daniel's and blondes," he grinned.

"Pardon me while I puke," Wood muttered.

"You'll have to leave now, Sergeant Johnson," she said, tearing the top sheet off the pad and handing to him. "We have to do some more tests on your friend."

"I'll see you later, Woodsy," Johnson said as he folded the sheet and put it in a pocket. "You too, Lieutenant," he smiled at her and she returned it. Written on the paper was her number, of course, and Johnson tossed it in the trashcan near the hospital entrance. *It's not the kill, it's the thrill of the chase,* he thought as he stepped into the hot wind.

He enjoyed flirting with women, enjoyed women in general, especially of the officer persuasion. He disarmed them, initially with his arrogance; the mere fact he would attempt flirtation with a superior took them off guard and got them to drop the veneer of military bearing. Though they were officers, they were women after all and they needed the same things as every other woman, primarily to feel desirable. He'd learned, in his early teens, that women found him desirable and he'd learned how to use it to his advantage. It was the rush, the same one he felt in combat, and the paper containing the phone number was the culmination of that. It would go no farther with the pretty lieutenant, for although Johnson might have enjoyed the chase, he was in love with a woman he could never be unfaithful to.

Picking up the van from in front of the headquarters building, he drove off the base before lighting a cigarette and rummaging through the glove box for the list Mama-san gave him. It was her condition for his borrowing the van. He would have to do her shopping.

And I'll probably get everything wrong, he thought as he parked near the market in Osan. And the old woman would bitch at him about it, and he smiled. "She's going to be my mother-in-law," he muttered as he crossed the street.

The Kremlin, Moscow, Soviet Union

"He's worried," Kosarev said when they were back in the car. "The Chairman knows his days are numbered."

"Stop, Yevgeniy," Zhukov warned. "I haven't swept the car for bugs."

"Ah," Kosarev spat. "Take me home." And the rest of the drive was made in silence. He waved to Zhukov as he drove away before going inside. The nurse was in her room when he arrived, and he went directly to the bed. "Hello, my love," he took his wife's hand.

"Is it done?" Katherine Kosareva asked as she squeezed his hand weakly.

"Yes," he nodded and kissed her cheek, saying nothing more in front of the nurse.

"When will you be going back?"

"I am not sure," he lied. "I have meetings to attend here for a while."

"It is good to have you home, Yevgeniy," Katherine said, caressing his cheek.

"I have to go out for a few hours, my love," he said as he kissed her hand. "But I had to see you first. This will not take long."

"I will be waiting," she sighed.

And he left; driving himself for this was nothing to share with his driver, or with Marko Zhukov. It was a gamble, but there were some in Moscow who saw the end of the Communist Party's hold on the lives of the citizens. Unlike Andropov, these men had seen what the West had to offer and had the wisdom to see that Communism could not survive much longer.

The Soviet Union was bankrupt, both fiscally and philosophically. There was so much waste and corruption, and reform was inevitable either by peaceful means of violent revolt within some of the states. It was coming at them like an onrushing freight train and it was up to them to see that the Union did not end in civil war. They would hold it together until reforms could be enacted and then slowly slough off the states that required too much capital to hold on to. It would be years still until they were ready, but they had to begin now.

He turned into the warehouse district, shutting the car off near a concrete and steel structure, the sign denoting a freight warehouse. There were two other cars parked nearby and he pushed the iron door open.

"Welcome, Yevgeniy," the voice of Ivan Popov greeted him. Popov was Kosarev's age, another veteran of the Great Patriotic War and a colonel-general in command of an infantry unit just returned from Afghanistan. Another man stood next to Popov, shorter, stockier, and balding, a noticeable port wine stain on his forehead. "You know Comrade Gorbachev, I presume," Popov said.

"Mikhail and I have worked together in the past," Kosarev eyed Gorbachev warily. He brought political power to the equation and he was a public figure, a minor one now, but that would change.

"The question is," Gorbachev said. "Can we work together for a future?"

The Pink Lady

"I tell you bak choy, not leek," Mama-san bitched at him. "You *idiot*," she added before heading back to the kitchen.

"Hey, they look the same," Johnson called after her.

"No taste same," he heard her yell back. "*Idiot.*"

"Not bad," he shrugged. "I only got one thing wrong."

"Are you ready?" Yung Shu asked him as she came from behind the bar, a thermos of Kamikazes hidden in her overly large handbag.

"Your mother is mad at me," he said, following her out to the van.

"No, she's not," Yung Shu shook her head, her long hair whipping across his face. "She only called you an idiot twice," she smiled.

"*My* mother calls me that too," Johnson observed.

"Maybe they both have you figured out?" Yung Shu offered with a smile.

"So, when you start calling me an idiot, I'll know you have too?"

"I'll never call you an idiot, Rick," she kissed him. "I love you."

As he got behind the wheel, he noticed Beu and Alexa heading out the side door and climbing into a government Chevy. "I wonder what's going on?"

"I think he's taking her to Kim Po," Yung Shu said.

"Have you found out anything else about her?"

"No, just that she's leaving for home today," she replied.

"What does your intuition say?"

"She's hiding something," Yung Shu agreed. "And so is Nate. She doesn't strike me as a malicious person though. Just very private."

"There's something going on that ain't too kosher," he declared.

"But is it any of your business, my love?" She asked him.

"He could be in a lot of trouble."

"And if he needs your help, he will ask for it," Yung Shu admonished. "Now let's go before visiting hours are over."

***

"Is that your friend?" Alexa pointed out the windshield as the white van passed on the main street.

"Yeah," Beu replied. "He's probably going to the base to visit Woodsy." He started the car and made a left off the side street, heading toward the highway that would take them just outside Seoul.

"When will you be coming to Florida?"

"I'm leaving in two days; will you be okay until then?"

"I am *not* a helpless woman, Comrade Major," she hissed.

"And I'd leave the comrade business here," he warned. "That word is synonymous with Communism in the States."

"I understand."

"Are you sure you won't be needing anything until I get there?"

"I will be fine, Nathan, thank you for your concern," she patted his thigh. "If I get bored, I will spend the time shopping." Alexa smiled. While sad she was leaving everything she knew, she'd been to the United States before and was overwhelmed by the variety of stores and businesses catering to women. She would begin her quest to visit all of them very soon. "Maybe I will begin applying to the local colleges as well."

"There are many to choose from in the area," Beu nodded. "How about Disney World next weekend?" And he saw her face light up.

"That would be wonderful. I can't wait to see Mickey." She leaned over and kissed him. "And I can't wait to see you in one of those hats with the ears," Alexa giggled.

"Don't hold your breath," he smiled.

"We'll see," she replied knowingly and Beu remembered Kosarev's words.

She's just like her mother, her father had warned and Beu realized Alexa was used to getting what she wanted. And for the first time, he found that a desirable trait in a woman, in *this* woman.

Seoul, South Korea

The Olympia Hotel was of the same era as the Pink Lady, originally catering to foreign tourists in the late fifties, it had fallen into disrepair and seediness. It was a place where hookers took their johns and where business of the more disreputable kind was done. It was here Holmgren found himself this late afternoon. He stopped at the desk and asked for Quanh, the old man who smelled like opium pointed him up the stairs. "Two-sixteen," he said and went back to watching the baseball game from the States.

Holmgren took the stairs two at a time, trying to be seen by as few people as possible, and found Quanh's room in a hurry. He answered the door wearing only a pair of boxer shorts. "Hi, Alan," he smiled and put his arms around Holmgren's waist.

"I thought you had information for me," Holmgren pushed his way into the room.

"That can wait," Quanh said as he closed the door. He came up behind Holmgren, getting down on his knees and reaching for the buttons of Holmgren's jeans.

"You can't call me at the BOQ," he said as nonchalantly as he could while Quanh pulled his pants down.

"Uh huh," Quanh grunted as he took Holmgren's manhood in his mouth.

Kim Po International Airport, Seoul, South Korea

"What are we doing?" Beu asked her when they stopped at the final security checkpoint. Only ticketed passengers were permitted to move further on.

"What do you mean, Nathan?"

"We've known each other for what, two days. It's as if we're both settled on this relationship or whatever we have. This is crazy," the Texan shook his head.

"You are over thinking this, Major," she said. "I saw the way you looked at me and I am certain I had the same look on my face. This isn't settled by any means, don't flatter yourself, but we both want to see where this goes. If you're honest with yourself, you will see that you do. Do you believe in destiny?"

"You make your own destiny," Beu said.

"Sometimes," she smiled and then reached up and pulled him close. A passionate kiss followed and then she released him, handing her bag to the security officer. "See you in a few days," she waved as they checked her through.

Beu returned it and walked back through the concourse. *Shit, I miss her already*, he thought. *Oh, this is* not *good.*

Seoul

"You can't call me at the BOQ anymore," Holmgren said as he lay in the rumpled bed.

"I didn't say anything," Quanh replied as he stepped out of the shower.

"It doesn't matter, the phone isn't secure." Holmgren got out of bed and didn't bother dressing, going to his bag instead. He removed a towel and toiletries and walked to the bathroom. Quanh had left the shower running and Holmgren stepped inside, placing the folded towel nearby. "Could you do my back?" He asked Quanh who'd returned.

"No problem," he winked, aroused again at the thought. He stepped into the shower as Holmgren reached for the towel. Wrapped within was an extremely sharp dagger with a finish chosen for its inability to hold fingerprints.

It was quickly thought out, but Holmgren was certain of success and the shower played a big part. As Quanh came to him with an erection leading the way, he smiled when Holmgren reached out for it with one hand, grasping it firmly. Quanh let out a moan of ecstasy and leaned back against the wall. The sensation he felt next made his eyes go wide.

Looking down, he saw his severed penis in Holmgren's hand, blood squirting from between his legs and he tried to scream. Holmgren spun him around and then plunged the dagger into Quanh's chest from behind, holding it there as the other man fought to pull it free. Quanh faded quickly from the blood loss and Holmgren laid him in the tub leaving the water running. He moved the body and the severed organs to look as if it were an act of self-mutilation and suicide, taking anything from the room that would indicate another beside Quanh was here. If the forensic people even bothered to check, they would know Quanh had gay sex recently, but Holmgren doubted it would get that far. He was certain Quanh's would not be the first body the cleaning staff found at the *Olympia Hotel*, if there even was a cleaning staff. He dressed quickly and checked the door before leaving, taking the rear exit instead of passing by the stoned old man at the desk. He wasn't too worried about the old man, Holmgren was just another American looking to get laid or for drugs to him, if he even remembered Holmgren at all.

He walked calmly and casually to his car, parked several blocks away, and got in. He sat there for a few minutes, surprised at how composed he actually was. He had just killed a man in horrible fashion, and he felt fine. *And my career is safe*, he thought as he turned the key and drove back toward Osan.

***

"That was unsettling," one of the North Korean Intelligence men said to the other.

"We have more than we'd ever thought we'd get," his partner said, ignoring the other's remark about the gory killing they had just filmed. "All I *thought* we'd obtain is more footage of Holmgren taking it in the ass again. Being labeled a queer is one thing, being convicted on first degree murder charges is quite another."

"I will contact Major Park," his partner said. "What will we do about Quanh's body?"

"Leave it," the other advised as he began packing the cameras away. "Someone will find it sooner or later."

The Pink Lady

"So, is she gone?" Johnson said to Beu as he pulled up a chair.

"Yeah, thanks," Beu handed him the key to the fifth floor. "I won't be needing this anymore."

"She going home?"

Beu thought about that for a minute. "No . . . well, she's going to her new home."

"*Don't* tell me she's going to the States," Johnson shook his head.

"Yes," Beu replied before downing a shot of Wild Turkey. "She is in fact."

"Man, you can't do this to me," Johnson downed a shot of his own.

"This is best for all concerned, Rick. You've gotta promise me you'll keep this quiet. I know you've been talking to Woodsy and I'd like you to drop it. I don't need the crash board or anyone *else* asking questions about my personal life right now," Beu demanded.

"Fine." Johnson sat there and fumed. It only lasted a few seconds because he couldn't hold it in any longer. "But how are you going to explain her? Jesus Christ, Nate, it's like she just fell off the moon the other night and landed here."

"I won't have to explain *anything* if you keep your mouth shut, since you're the only one who knows about her," Beu suggested, downing another shot. "I told you I would tell you one day. You'll just have to wait, that's all."

"I'm not a good waiter."

"Suffer," Beu said with a smile.

"Hi, Nate," Yung Shu said as she came over from the bar, her shift finished. "I'm stealing him from you." She put her arms around Rick. "We only have a few more days and even fewer nights, you know."

"Duty calls," Johnson said with a grin as she cuffed him in the back of the head.

"Don't make it sound so dreadful," she hissed and looked up at Beu. "Will we see you before you leave, Major?"

"Bet on it, darling," he replied with a grin.

"Come on, Rick," she took him by the hand. "Time to do your duty."

Beu watched them up the stairs before he took his seat. *Am I going to be like that*, he asked himself. It seemed certain, to him, that he and Alexa would find something he'd never known before. Pretty women had caught his eye before, but never had they done . . . *What*, he thought.

Infatuation, it was a word he knew but never had any experience with. *Could it be an infatuation*, his brain asked his heart. He felt different. *Did I hit my head?* Johnson would have been happy to know that Beu questioned his own sanity as well. He poured another shot and knocked it back quickly. As if reading his mind, Mama-san appeared with a cold beer.

"Whatsa matter, flyboy?" She asked him in her clipped English. "You look miserable."

"Women problems," Beu replied as he accepted the bottle. "Thanks."

"You got too many women, big boy," she shot back. "I see you trying to make all my girls. You no fool me," she grinned as she pointed to herself. "You too smart to sniff around like old cat. You're a flyboy, college boy, you know what you want for woman and you know what wife will do for career. About time you get squared away."

Beu laughed and looked up at her. "You're pretty smart yourself, mama."

"Nah," she spat. "Come from watching GIs make fools of themselves over women. You no fool, Major Flyboy," Mama-san grinned again, studying his face. "There is one, right? One special one who you like more than the others, right?" She poked him in the shoulder after each 'right'.

"There could be," he admitted.

"Let her see real man you are, not old cat that sniff around my club," she insisted. "If she sees real man you are, she shows you who she really is. That is where it starts. From there you can do anything."

"You're a wise woman, Mama-san."

"Just a bartender," she shrugged.

"A bartender who swings a wicked broom."

"Special broom," she whispered to him. "Has metal rod in middle of handle. Had it made special so it no break on Marine heads."

"I'm gonna miss you, Mama-san," Beu said as he kissed her cheek.

"You okay for officer," she conceded.

"You sound like Rick," Beu chuckled and considered her. "Do you think Rick let Yung Shu see the real man?"

"Yes," Mama-san said with a sad smile. "I hope she not disappointed." She looked him in the eye. "Like Rick, your destiny is not your own."

"What does *that* mean?"

"It means what it means," she said with a shrug and set off for the bar.

Osan Air Base

For the first time in over a week, Holmgren felt good. He sipped his drink, his only drink, slowly and thought about what he'd done a few short hours ago. He thought he should feel more, regret, revulsion, shame, but he felt none of that. He felt as he did before all this began, before last week when he had so much more to live for. *I just committed murder*, he thought but it did not bother him.

"Hi, Alan," Biff Kutscher said as he slid onto the adjoining barstool. "You're looking better."

"Thanks," Holmgren smiled, motioning to the bartender to place Biff's drink on his tab. "I took your advice and it was just what I needed.

"Good deal," Kutscher nodded appreciation as he accepted his drink. "I'm glad when we're out of this toilet," he observed.

"I'm leaving day after tomorrow and not a day too soon," Holmgren said.

"Tonight's my last night," Kutscher informed him. "I can't wait to see Holly and the kids again. When are you gonna find a woman and settle down?"

"When I begin to make enough money to support them," Holmgren said. "Hopefully, I'll have 1st lieutenant's bars in a couple weeks and a little more cash."

"You'll find that you *never* have enough cash when you have kids," Kutscher chuckled as he finished his drink. "I have to pack," he said, hopping off the stool. "See you in the States."

"Take care, Biff," Holmgren waved as Kutscher left the Officer's Club.

"I'll have to do something about that," Holmgren whispered to himself. He was young still, but he would need a wife eventually if he planned to have a long career. He would not have to have her long, five years at most, just long enough to maintain the illusion he was heterosexual. A forty year old officer, never married and seldom dating would certainly elicit whispers. If he ever expected to make it to the colonel and general officer ranks, there could be no whispers, no speculation about his sexuality, not even a shadow of a doubt he was a straight man.

His thoughts went to Quanh, the boy who'd expected anything than what Holmgren did to him, and he smiled. *He would probably have died of AIDS anyhow*, Holmgren thought. And then terror held him in its grip. *Did he have it already?* He tried to recall if any of Quanh's fluids entered his body and saliva was the only thing that came to mind. He felt better although he resolved to be tested at a civilian clinic once he got back to the States.

"That would be ironic," he said softly, finishing his scotch and standing. *Quanh taking his revenge from the grave*, he thought and laughed aloud as he exited the club, walking the three blocks to the BOQ. And then he pondered the subject of revenge.

You made me do this, he thought as Rick Johnson came to mind. *If you had protected Roger, it would never have come to this. Instead, you wanted glory and you let him die. I will exact* my *revenge one day*, he thought as he took the stairs up to his floor. *If Quanh doesn't kill me, I will kill you, Johnson.* And he felt better as he unlocked his door.

***

Just down the hall, Nate Beu was in his room, doing what most of the SOCOM people were doing, packing their gear before the rotation home. He found himself checking the clock frequently as he rummaged for things remembered but their location forgotten. He found himself missing the blonde girl whom he'd known for a few short hours, yet happy she would be waiting when he arrived at home. "You were right, you crazy son of a bitch," he said aloud to Johnson, remembering his friend's words. "Is Alexa the one who'll bite me in ass?" He knew now what Johnson meant, and now how Rick felt toward Yung Shu. *Is this what love feels like?* And he checked the clock again.

The Pink Lady

"Mmmm, I love you, Rick," Yung Shu purred as she lay her head on his chest. He was still inside her and enveloped her in his arms.

"I love you too, baby," and he squeezed her tightly. "I'm going to miss you terribly."

Chapter Twelve
Osan Air Base, Osan, South Korea
15 July 1983

"Hey, man," Johnson said when he caught up to Beu as he left the administration building. He threw up a halfhearted salute.

"You ready to leave?" Beu asked him.

"Yes and no," Rick shrugged. "I hate being in this armpit and can't wait to go home, but I hate being away from Yung Shu and I can't wait to come back. Where are you headed?"

"Gotta turn in the key to my room at the BOQ," Beu replied. "Take a walk?"

"Sure," Rick fell in step with him.

"I had a talk with the Mama-san last night after you and Yung Shu went upstairs," Beu went on. "She's a smart old bird."

"And you wonder why I worry about you?" Johnson stopped. "What's the deal?"

"What does it feel like, Rick?" Beu asked him. "What you and Yung Shu have, how did you know …"

"The blonde honey does that to you, does she?" Rick grinned.

"I don't know," Beu shook his head, resuming his walk. "It's just … man, from the minute I saw her … and the thing is, I know she feels that way about me, or at least she thinks she does."

"So, she *is* going to be waiting when we get back?" Beu only nodded in response. "And this feels right to you?"

"Yeah," Beu said, a smile coming to his face.

"Yeah, it's obvious," Rick laughed. "Now you've got the stupid grin too."

"She's nineteen, Rick."

"No shit?" She struck Johnson as a bit older, but then so did Yung Shu, both strong, self-assured women. "You old dog." He followed Beu into the BOQ and he caught sight of another coming down the stairs. Holmgren turned his eyes to meet Johnson's stare and it wasn't broken until Holmgren was out the front door.

"You know him?" Beu asked.

"He's one of the squadron Intel weenies," Johnson said. "It's nothing," he waved it away as they entered the Charge of Quarters office. Beu did the required paperwork assuring the room was left as it was issued and that he had not copied or duplicated the key in any way. The sergeant at the desk gave him a receipt and bade him good day. "So, are you going to live with her?" Johnson asked when they were outside.

"I hadn't thought about it?"

"The chick ..."

"Alexa," Beu corrected him.

"*Alexa* moves ten thousand miles to be close to you and you're *not* going to live together?" Johnson looked at him strangely.

"I don't know if she wants to," Beu shrugged as they got into the car.

Johnson gave him a sideways look. "You're both doing this on a *whim*?"

"Yeah, I guess."

"What do they teach you in college anyway?" Johnson began looking into Beu's ear.

"What are you looking for?"

"A functioning brain," Rick replied. "Results negative, the boy's in love."

"You're a help."

"Jesus Christ, Nate," Johnson threw up his hands, banging them into the roof. "First you tell me not to ask questions and now you want my help? I don't know anything," he barked. "Where in the hell did she come from, anyway? Her appearance and the incident with you and Woodsy are related, aren't they? What, did you rescue her from somewhere while you were at the mercy of your autopilot?"

Beu considered him for a second. "No comment."

"There was no autopilot problem at all, was there?" Johnson pointed at him.

"No comment." Beu kept driving.

"Where in hell are we going anyway?" Johnson asked finally. He'd just followed Beu, more concerned about getting the story than what he had to do and where he had to go.

"Security Police, gotta turn in my line badge," Beu replied.

"Yeah, me too. Good, at least I'm getting some shit done too," Rick said and then returned to the subject at hand. "You rescued her from somewhere . . ." and then it hit him, Alexa's accent. "You helped her *defect*, didn't you?" And Beu nearly wrecked the car.

"Don't *ever* let that word cross your lips again," he warned.

"I'm done asking questions, pal," Rick raised his hands in surrender. "I don't want to know any more. The subject is closed, and I won't tell a soul. As long as the two of you are happy, it's all academic to me."

"Just say you are right, Rick," Beu offered. "What would you think of me as a man?"

"You're not my type," Johnson laughed.

"Don't be an asshole."

"As long as she isn't some kind of KGB spy and you're in love with her, who am I to argue? She *isn't* some KGB spy, is she, Nate? I mean, you thought this out, right, you know in your heart and mind that she's not a security risk, right?" Johnson asked rapid fire.

Beu considered him for a second after parking the car. "No, she's not."

"Then go for the gusto, pal. It doesn't matter how old she is if that's what you're worried about and as long as she claims to be Swiss you have no problems. I'll keep your secret until they put my dead ass in the ground. I hope you're as happy as I am," Johnson said sincerely.

"I hope I get my head screwed on right," Beu said. "I've been walking around with it up my ass since I met her."

"I won't say it," Johnson laughed. "Ah, what the hell. I *told* you so, Major Beu. I said that one would bite you eventually."

"Are you ever going to let me forget it?"

"In about twenty or thirty years," Johnson smiled.

"Do you think we'll be friends that long?"

"Nah, probably not," Johnson said. "In our line of work, odds are we won't live that long."

***

The bastard acts as if he owns the place, Holmgren thought after seeing Johnson at the BOQ. He knew the pilot by reputation only, another hotshot named Beu. *It figures they'd be friends, two cowboys trying to out-crazy each other.*

Holmgren headed off to his appointments for he too was going back stateside, and out-processing was an unavoidable necessity when leaving any duty station for another. His first stop was to the post office to turn in his mailbox key.

I can't wait to get out of this place, he thought as he crossed the street. He disliked Korea before he had a potential murder charge hanging over his head, now he just counted the hours until he could leave. Holmgren still felt confident he would never face charges or even be suspected, but he would be able to completely relax once he was safely on U.S. soil.

And I will kill Johnson as well. It would take time to arrange, but he had all the time in the world and the resources of the military at his disposal. *And anyone else who stands in my way.*

The Pink Lady

"Tonight is his last, isn't it?" Mama-san asked her daughter.

"Yes, mother," she said sadly.

"He expects to come back?"

"Yes, as always," Yung Shu replied. "He will be back, and we will be married."

"I hope so, my angel," Mai Kim said with a shake of her head.

"I will love him regardless," the girl said and walked away.

Osan Air Base

They finished with the cops and Beu was heading off base. "Buy you a drink before you take me to the airport?"

"Yeah, sure," Johnson nodded. "I'm leaving tomorrow."

"Are you gonna be miserable for three months until you get back here?"

"Indeed," Rick replied absently. "I always am." He looked over at his friend. "But this will be the last time," he added.

"You know," Beu said. "The Mama-san said you and I were alike, that our destinies were not our own."

"Oh, Jesus Christ," Johnson barked. "She thinks she's some old voodoo woman or something."

"They don't practice voodoo here."

"You know what I mean. Mama-san will tell your fortune if it's profitable," Johnson said. "She's so full of shit and gunpowder I'm surprised she doesn't explode."

Beu laughed at that and changed the subject. "What are you doing when you get home?"

"I'm dropping my shit in the barracks and heading out to the airport," Johnson told him.

"Yeah, heading back to New York, where are you from again?"

"Long Island, Suffolk County," Rick replied. "My folks are there. I'll take two weeks with them, catch up with some old friends while I'm there, and then head back to Hurlburt. I might buy a car while I'm up there and drive back, you never know."

"That's a long ass drive," Beu said with a whistle.

"Not if you have the right car," Johnson smiled. "I guess I'll see how you and Alexa are doing when I get back. A couple weeks should be enough to feel each other out."

"Yeah, probably," Beu sighed. "I just wish I knew what was going to happen."

"That's the fun of it, pal," Rick told him. "You never know unless you give it a shot. At least you'll get some good sex while you're figuring things out."

"I wouldn't know."

"You haven't …"

"No, not yet," Beu admitted. "Because of her age and her situation."

"Fucking pilots, always over thinking things," Johnson chuckled. "She's an *adult*, Nate," Johnson tapped his temple with his index finger. "Was *she* willing?"

"She was surprised *I* wasn't," Beu told him as he parked the car behind Mama-san's van.

"Besides, you didn't even bother to wonder how old Lin Yii is. What makes you so altruistic suddenly?"

"She was underage?" Beu was taken aback.

"You didn't seem to care when you were nailing her, what does it matter now, big boy?" Johnson smiled. "You should nail her once more before you turn over your new leaf," he laughed aloud as they crossed the alley.

"Asshole," Beu grunted.

"Yes, but you love me anyway," Rick grinned as they stepped inside. "Hi, baby," he said to Yung Shu. "I have to take flyboy to the airport, so I brought him by for a quick one on the way."

"The highway to Seoul is the other way," she smiled. "But it's good to see you once more, Nate." Yung Shu kissed his cheek.

"Same here, darling," Beu said. "We'll be back before you know it."

"I hope so," she sighed and went to set up their shots with beer.

"I'm sorry to put you out," Beu said. "I should have got someone else to take me."

"That's okay," Rick shrugged. "I'll slow down to thirty at the terminal and kick you out. This way I'll be back that much faster."

"You're funny," Beu said as he offered up his shot glass. "To new friends who will become old friends, God willing."

"Amen to that, pal," Johnson clinked his glass to Beu's and they both tossed them back together. The beers went almost as quickly, and Rick sought out Yung Shu. "I'll be back in a couple hours."

"I'll be waiting," she said as the two men walked out the door.

Moscow, Soviet Union

He laid her hand on her chest and turned away, for none could be permitted to see his pain. "Goodbye, my love," he said and left the room, leaving the medical people to their work. Kosarev walked as if in a fog, fingertips to his lips trying to relive the sensation as he kissed hers for the last time, as she took her last breath. A strong hand on his upper arm steadied him and he looked to his right and saw he was in the grip of Marko Zhukov, his fiancée Mira at his side.

"We came as soon as I heard the news, my friend. I am so sorry," Zhukov said sadly.

"She is finally free of the pain," Kosarev replied. "She is at peace now."

"What about Alexa?"

"She is on a retreat in Kamchatka. I have sent for her," Kosarev said through the fog before his eyes. He knew not where he went, relying on Zhukov for direction. At this moment, he didn't much care, didn't care if Zhukov dropped him face down in the street, and didn't care if a bus ran him over shortly after he fell. He'd lost the love of his life and he didn't care about anything. *But I have to*, he thought. *I have to for Alexa.*

He knew that the timing of Katherine's death and Alexa's escape would be close, seeing her daughter out of the Soviet Union was what kept her alive over the last few months, and once it was done she could let go. He would receive more bad news over the next few days, something absolutely necessary to assure Alexa's safety, but then he would be free to operate. Kosarev the widower, the man who had lost his only child, would be very difficult to influence. "Take me home, Marko," he said. "I need to rest."

Wantagh, Long Island, New York

She was pretty, with a bright, beaming smile and that smile now threatened to crack her face. Constance Wasserman was twenty-three years old yet acted like a little girl as she opened the envelope. The letterhead advised the letter came from the registrar's office at C.W. Post University.

"Mom, dad," she called out from the kitchen. Connie still lived with her parents while pursuing an economics major at Post, until her ambitions changed, and the letter confirmed her major did as well. "I've been accepted to pre-law."

"We're proud of you, honey," her father said. Murray Wasserman pulled her close and kissed her cheek.

"Are you going to stick with this?" Rita Wasserman, Connie's mother asked. "You were dead set on being an accountant."

"I've wanted this ever since I took that job at the law firm last summer, mom," Connie replied. "I wanted to be an accountant because that's what dad and grandpa were. This is what I *really* want to do."

"As long as you stick with it this time," Rita said. "Unless you plan to be a professional student all your life."

"I'm going to be a lawyer, mom. My mind is made up." And in the following months, Connie Wasserman would begin her law courses. She was an ambitious, determined young woman and would complete her degree requirements in a little over two years. Years later, she would look back at this moment as one of the milestones, the first major one of her young life. It would be years until she passed another of such magnitude.

The Pink Lady

Rick made excellent time getting back from the airport and he grabbed Yung Shu as soon as he entered the club, taking her directly upstairs. He was smoking a cigarette after having made love to her for a second time. She rolled over and hugged him.

"Write to me every week," she insisted.

"I will, baby," he assured her. He ran his fingers through her hair in the darkness.

"Rick, I …"

"What's the matter, honey?"

"I can't help thinking that you will never come back," she said, her voice very small.

"I'll be back," he promised. "Don't worry."

"Mother said that God might not want us to be together," Yung Shu offered.

"Yeesh," he muttered.

"I know you think she's a crazy woman but there are some things she knows," she countered. "Have you ever considered the possibility?"

"Change comes slowly in the military, baby," Rick said. "They wouldn't change this rotation so quickly, so suddenly. I'll be back in three months," he said confidently.

"I love you so much, Rick, I don't want to lose you," she held him tightly. "I can't wait to be your wife."

"I love you too, baby, you're the best thing that's ever happened to me."

They made love again that night and once more when they woke up. It was a sad, tearful goodbye at Kim Po, neither wanting to let go of the other, both declaring their love until the final boarding call for Johnson's flight.

Moscow, Soviet Union

The incessant ringing of the telephone woke him. "Da?" Kosarev said, half asleep.

"I … I don't know how to say this, Yevgeniy," the voice belonged to Marko Zhukov.

"Just *say* it, Marko," Kosarev snapped.

"Alexa's flight from Vladivostok … it crashed in bad weather over Siberia," Zhukov stammered. "There are rescue crews on the way … but the weather and the temperature out there . . . I am so sorry, my dear friend."

"Keep me posted," Kosarev said flatly and hung up the phone. *It is the end and it is also the beginning*, he thought. Zhukov's news was the last piece of the puzzle. His daughter would be declared dead in the crash and she would be free to live her life in America, and he would be free to bring change to the place that so resisted it. He picked up the phone again and woke another.

"Da," Gorbachev said when he answered.

"Everything is in place, Mishka," Kosarev declared.

"And it cannot wait until morning, Yevgeniy?"

"Call Ivan and we will meet first thing," Kosarev said.

"First thing," Mikhail Gorbachev said as he hung up.

Part Two:

Mitigations and Extenuations

1983-1991

Chapter Thirteen
Hurlburt Field, Fort Walton Beach, Florida
23 October 1983

Johnson was uncomfortable in his mess dress uniform. Basically, a military tuxedo, the black uniform was the most seldom-used piece of his equipment and he regretted not having it altered before this occasion. Bought when he arrived in Florida after Special Forces school, Rick's daily workouts had the effect of shrinking the damned thing. It was the uniform of the day this sunny morning.

As he stood next to his friend, he thought of Yung Shu alone in Seoul without him. The months spent in Florida seemed to blend into one long, monotonous stretch. All he could think about was his Asian love, waiting tables for a bunch of GIs. He would get angry then, jealous of the soldiers, sailors, airmen, and marines able to gaze upon her while he killed time training under the hot Florida sun.

This brought him back to his uncomfortable mess dress and the event at hand. He looked to his right. Nate stood there, a bit pale and Rick was shaky as well. The bachelor party last night was obviously bad planning, but they had fun. They should have called it for a few days earlier; judging from the way the rest of the men in the wedding party looked.

"Do you have the rings, Sergeant?" Chaplain Corrigan said, his voice snapping Rick's reverie.

"Yes, sir." Rick fished the gold bands from his pocket, giving a smile to Alexa who'd sworn that he would forget them in his present condition. He was honored when Beu asked him to be his best man and he and Wood were the only enlisted in the wedding party. It brought some protest from some of Beu's officer friends, but he silenced them. Today, in front of all gathered, Rick Johnson stood next to Nathan Beu when he wed Alexa Osterhaus a little more than three months after they met. Someday soon, Nate would do the same for him.

***

He watched from the rear of the chapel, in the shadows where he would not be recognized, but Yevgeniy Kosarev would not miss his daughter's wedding. Nathan Beu was a good man and looking at them together, he could see his daughter had a calming effect on the pilot. And Kosarev could see how Alexa looked at him and he knew she loved him.

And that must be good enough for me, he thought as he looked at the groomsmen, he knew them all by reputation, all good, honorable men and he was happy for his only child. *He has chosen to consort with good men*, and that was also a mark in Beu's favor. A tear ran down his cheek when Nathan Beu officially became his son-in-law. Kosarev left the chapel soon after, taking the next flight to Washington and then on to Moscow. Things were moving along well with Gorbachev and Popov and they would soon be ready to make their play.

***

The reception was an unqualified success. The booze flowed like water and Alexa Beu danced with almost every man in the place. Nate and Rick even danced together. That would be brought up at the next aircrew meeting; Beu was certain of that. Stonewall Bryant made a congratulatory speech and even danced himself; that would *not* be brought up at the meeting. Halfway through the reception, the colonel called for quiet.

"I'm sorry to be a party pooper, but an alert order has come down from SOCOM. We're going to have to break up this little shindig," Bryant said. A chorus of good-natured boos answered him. He let everyone vent for a minute before raising his hand.

"I'm sorry, but that's the way it is. Congratulations, Major Beu, but duty calls. All aircrew will report to their quarters; you'll be flying tomorrow and you're going to have to sleep this off. All combat control and recon personnel will report directly to their squadron orderly rooms for a briefing. I expect you *all* to keep your military bearing. *Dismissed*." People stood there for a minute before filing out of the club, wondering what the alert was all about. In forty-eight hours, the whole world would know.

"I don't like this," Johnson said to Beu as they said good night to the guests. "We were heading back to Osan in a couple days. This is going to fuck it all up."

"We'll know in a couple hours," Beu said as he shook hands with Captain Vaughan.

"Ever hear of a place called Grenada?" Vaughan whispered.

"It's some Third World toilet in the Caribbean, isn't it?" Beu asked him.

"Well the Cubans just took some American students hostage and we're gonna get them out," he was smiling. "Besides, they just built a ten thousand foot runway at the airport there. Do you think the President wants the Russkies using it to base bombers?"

"So, we're going to set them free and introduce them to the American Way?" Beu said sarcastically.

"That's about it," Vaughan chuckled. "See you at the briefing."

"This is gonna be good," Rick muttered. "And in five years they'll be yelling Yankee go home. Are we going back to Osan anytime *soon*?"

Vaughan considered him for a second. "I didn't tell you this," he said conspiratorially. "But we probably won't be going back. You'll hear about it soon enough, probably after this Grenada thing is over. Sorry, Rick," he waved to Alexa and Nate before heading out. Johnson felt as if a blunt spear had been rammed through his heart. His breath became ragged and his knees felt like rubber. He turned away.

"Are you all right, pal?" He heard Beu say.

"I'm okay," he said and wandered off to the men's room. Once there he felt urgency, springing the last few steps into the stall, barely making the toilet when he retched. His body convulsed, his guts expelling everything they held, his body turning itself inside out. At least that's what it felt like and he prayed death would take him right there instead of letting him live with this feeling. He retched a last time, though nothing else came up and he leaned his head against the cool porcelain. He began to cry silently for he'd refused to consider this possibility.

This can't be happening, he thought. Johnson had been high as a kite for the last week, with Beu's wedding approaching and his imminent once they got back to Korea, he suddenly felt terribly low. But he had some money saved; he would make some calls when he got back from wherever they were going and see what it would take to get her into the country.

"I can do it," he began to brighten, and he stood, composing himself enough to make it to the sink. He splashed water in his face and rinsed the bile from his mouth, his stomach flipping once more but not forcing him back in the stall. "I have to do it," he said to his reflection. "She's my life."

***

It was past midnight when he got to his room, but he didn't sleep, he couldn't, not with what he'd learned tonight. He had to write, to tell her their plans were on hold indefinitely.

> My love,
>
> I know I'm writing earlier than I normally do, but I was given information today that directly affects both of us. We received a new mission this afternoon; Nate and Alexa's wedding day, how ironic, and I will not be arriving as planned. You will hear about this mission by the time you get this, so you'll understand. Anyway, they're extending B-Flight's stay over there and we're leaving in the morning. I have it on good authority that we probably won't be heading back to Asia at all and there are rumors saying they are going to disband the unit at the end of the year. If they do, I have no idea where they

224

will send me. They still have me until '86 so I am bound to the dictates of the Air Force. I will write as soon as I can. Please don't worry about me as you normally do. Nate and Alexa say hi, so do Woodsy and the guys. By the way, they threw Jake Guthrie out for smoking dope a couple weeks ago. I love you, my darling, and we will be together as soon as I can figure out how. Say hi to your mother.

All my love,

Rick

He went to his bed then, drained emotionally, he'd gone through almost all of them today and sleep came easily.

***

A mere twelve hours later, Johnson and his A-Flight comrades were seated in the belly of a special operations version of the venerable C-130 Hercules, the MC-130 Combat Talon along with C- and D-Flights of 23rd Special Tactics Squadron. A-Flight had been brought back up to strength, Captain Roberts, the new CO, and three others to replace those killed and otherwise discharged were also there, John Reasoner in his glory after sewing on his fourth stripe and named senior NCO.

Rick was quiet as the four Allison turbo prop engines droned on, checking his watch periodically. This mission was something they'd practiced a few times, something he wished they'd practiced a bit more since they'd be doing it for real this time. It was one of those joint things, the Army and Marine Corps charged with rescuing the students at the university here and the Air Force tasked with taking the airport with its brand new ten thousand foot runway.

They would be coming in the front door, the Combat Talon, along with two others landing on the main runway without lights to discharge the troops they carried at the terminal buildings. Normally, stealth was the watchword, a small group of commandos transported into the target area aboard relatively stealthy helicopters. Tonight, the Pave Lows that followed the Combat Talons like baby ducks, relying on the big aircraft for the fuel that extended their range to make the trip, were full of Army Rangers and Marines. The noise of three Talons and two Spectre gunships circling overhead was anything but a stealthy approach.

What the fuck is a Grenada, anyway? Rick wondered as night fell over the Caribbean. He'd never been to any of the islands south of the border, never been *anywhere* south of the border and never had any desire to be. *Too hot, too humid*, he thought memories of Korea came back. The Korean summers were oppressive too but at least they had winters to offset the sweltering humidity. True, there was no spring or autumn there, but he had something that made the temperature extremes worth bearing.

He thought about the letter he'd written and mailed this morning before leaving Hurlburt and how Yung Shu would react to the news. *Probably better than I did*, Johnson thought with a grin. And he thought of Mama-san and her prophetic words and he knew Yung Shu was better prepared for this eventuality than he was. The old woman had been preparing her since they first fell in love. Roberts and Reasoner approaching brought his attention back to the present.

"Ten minutes," Roberts said.

"Rog, Captain," Johnson replied and rose, going over his gear.

"You okay, Rick?" Reasoner asked him.

"Yeah, I'm fine," he said.

"We're waiting on you, Johnson," Roberts said. "So, keep your head in the game."

"Yes, sir," he replied as Roberts walked up to the flight deck.

"It's Yung Shu, isn't it?" Reasoner asked him.

"Do I look that out of it?"

"Yeah," Reasoner nodded. "Don't have your head up your ass when the door goes down or you'll be going back in a body bag."

"Don't worry about me, I'm annoyed enough to kill a division of Cubans," Johnson growled. He looked over to Campbell and Mason who would be going with him into the terminal building to roust whatever Cuban security troops were present there. Intel told them security at the airport was minimal, but that's what they said about Nam Po too and three of them never made it back. "You guys ready?"

"You bet," Campbell said.

"Yeah," Mason replied.

"Five minutes," Roberts said as he came from conferring with the flight crew. He said it over and over again as he walked back through the belly of the plane and the tension level rose measurably. Everyone checked their gear once more and those who found peace in prayer said a final one. And then the deck began to incline as the Talons lost altitude quickly.

The cargo door in the rear began to part when they were two minutes out and was at a level position in thirty seconds. Johnson was amazed to see how low they were, still over water for forty seconds before going feet dry. It seemed they were skimming directly over the rooftops in Port Georges and he could see lights going on in the town as the five aircraft screamed by. And it felt as if the pilot was going to dive it into the ground.

The aircraft flared and the main gear hit the ground a second later, the pilot bleeding off speed to get the big bitch slow enough to make the hard-right turn onto the taxiway. Johnson was on his feet on the cargo deck, Campbell and Mason on either side, the nose of another Talon seemed dangerously close as it followed the aircraft he rode in down the taxiway toward the terminal. And the pilot applied the brakes.

"Go," Roberts yelled, and Rick took off as soon as the –130 came to a stop. He was met with small arms fire almost immediately, shots ringing off the fuselage and splintering the concrete at his feet. Behind him, the others poured out of the plane, taking cover positions behind anything they could and began returning fire. The two Talons that followed them in also had their cargo doors open, three Air Force Security Police armored vehicles exiting from each set off to secure the perimeter of the field.

"This ain't good," Johnson said to Mason and Campbell as they dove for cover near the terminal entrance. "There weren't supposed to be this many of them."

"So, what's new?" Mason asked. "Are we gonna go?"

"Yeah," Johnson said, taking a fragmentation grenade from his web gear. He ran for the door, pulling the pin along the way, and dumped the grenade into the departure lobby. Rick took cover behind a truck as the grenade blew, taking the doors out and anyone standing inside.

He was first to the door; Campbell and Mason at his side a second later. The remnants of four people littered the floor along with most of the acoustic ceiling and its support structure. There were moans coming from behind one of the counters. Johnson peered over, his H&K MP-5 submachine gun ready. The man looked up at him, a nasty wound on his leg.

"Cubano?" Johnson asked. He nodded. "English?"

"Yes," the man said.

"How do I get up on the roof?"

"Go to Hell, Yanqui."

Johnson removed the silenced pistol from its holster and placed it against the Cuban's forehead. "You can either get medical treatment and be sent home or I can kill you now. Ten seconds."

The man considered the options for a second. "The stairwell, second door on the left. There should only be five or six up there."

"Gracias, Amigo," Johnson said before turning to the others. "Take care of him, I'm going upstairs."

"You can't go alone, Rick," Campbell told him.

"Yes, I can." He turned and left them there.

Entering the stairwell, he heard heavy fire coming from above. "They've moved a machine gun up," he muttered. "Shit," he raced up the three floors, two steps at a time. The big machine gun burped again as he got to the roof. "Cocksuckers," he swore as he got to the fire door. Wondering if the door was alarmed, he heard the gun spit again and made up his mind. Rick kicked the release and the door flew open.

Two Cubans on the roof turned to him, their Kalashnikov rifles aimed his way. He saw the muzzle flashes and heard the bullets whiz by him, but none connected, and he cut them both down with his MP-5. Killing two more as they came across the roof at him, he made his way toward the sound of the machine gun emplacement.

Johnson peeked over the roof to see if any friendlies were below and then grabbed two baseball grenades from his webbing. He pulled the pin on one and tossed it, throwing the other two seconds later. He saw they both dropped into the nest before ducking behind cover.

They exploded and he heard the corner of the roof give way, the fractured brick and twisted sheet metal taking the corner I-beams with them. Johnson held on for dear life as he felt the section of the roof he was on begin to sway. "Bright idea, asshole," he muttered to himself. He heard the door fly open and brought his MP-5 up.

"Easy, boy," Campbell said, looking into the business end of the submachine gun. "What the fuck you trying to do, bring the terminal down? We could have called in the gunships for that."

"No time," Rick said. The AC-130 Spectre gunships were busy on the perimeter and their tracers could be seen engaging targets in the Army and Marine sectors.

"You okay?" Campbell asked.

"Fine," Rick said. "There anymore?"

"Our guys are going through the hangars now," Campbell told him. "So far, the only troops were in the terminal and up here."

"We'd better get out of here," Johnson suggested. "The rest of this roof is shaky."

"You just love blowing shit up," Campbell said when they were on their way down.

"Yeah," Rick replied with a grin.

"Hey," Emory yelled up the stairs. "The SPs got the perimeter secured. We have to hold down the fort here until the Army's done. Captain Roberts wants your ass down here, New York."

"Think I'll get reamed sixty over?" Johnson asked Campbell with a smile as they came out of the stairwell into the lobby.

"What did you think you were doing?" Roberts growled as Reasoner came up behind him.

"Neutralizing the resistance," Johnson shot back. "Don't worry, I checked to see that you weren't underneath when I tossed the baseballs."

"We wanted minimal damage to the building," Roberts said.

"There's a Red Horse team standing by in Panama," Johnson said. "They'll rebuild this place in two days." Red Horse was the Air Force Civil Engineers.

"That wasn't the point, Johnson."

"Did you *like* getting shot at with fifty caliber, sir?"

"Stow it, Rick," Reasoner warned.

"I give up," Johnson threw up his hands. "I await your orders, sir," he said to Roberts.

"Come on, Rick," Reasoner said. "Let's go."

"I'd keep off the roof, sir," Johnson called to Roberts as he left. "She's swaying like Little Egypt."

"Come on, god damn it, don't fuck with him," Reasoner dragged him outside. "The brass at Scott is going to crawl up his ass about the roof."

"Jesus Christ," Johnson muttered. There were several explosions outside the perimeter, and they looked up to see a gunship fire off a volley of forty millimeter. "They got it tough out there," he observed.

"Did you hear the news?" Reasoner asked him. "They're gonna disband the unit by the end of the year and reorganize. I hear they're gonna send most of us to the combat control and Pararescue squadrons."

"Yeah, the ones they *want*," Johnson grumbled. "My ass is gonna be shipped off to Thule, Greenland or the Aleutians or something."

"Not with the Star, that'll go a long way when it comes to giving out assignments. They might give you a choice," Reasoner sounded hopeful, but both knew Johnson was right.

He got as far as he did in SOCOM because Stonewall Bryant liked his grit. To most of the other officers, he was a pain in the ass, and they would do their best to get rid of him. "I appreciate that, John. You can be an asshole when you want, but you're all right."

"I never thought I'd hear it, Rick," Reasoner laughed. "You're all right for an asshole too. Come on, you can relieve one of the guys guarding the prisoners."

"Cool," Johnson slung his MP-5 on his shoulder. He still wasn't happy, but he felt better. He didn't like to pull strings, but he would make an appointment to speak with Colonel Bryant. Reasoner was right; the Star should get him *something*.

Chapter Fourteen
Hurlburt Field, Fort Walton Beach, Florida
15 November 1983

"Sergeant Johnson reports as ordered, sir," he said, coming to attention in front of Bryant.

"At ease, Rick," Bryant said. "Close the door and sit."

"Yes, sir." Johnson took the chair across from Bryant, who looked at him for a minute.

"I won't lie to you, son," Bryant began. "There were quite a few slots open with the PJs and combat control."

"But none of them had my name on them, right, sir?"

"Not a one," Bryant shook his head. "But I arranged things so you'll be on the stand down crew. You'll be one of the last to leave the squadron, Rick."

"Where *am* I going when it's over, sir?"

"Fort Worth," Bryant said, and he saw the disappointment on Rick's face. "It was the best I could do. You'll be going to 7th Field Maintenance at Carswell as an aide to the squadron maintenance chief. It was either that or go for cross training into one of the maintenance disciplines, but SAC has personnel shortages and you don't have many friends here where it counts, Rick."

"This sucks, sir," Johnson muttered. "I don't want to be in SAC."

"Look, Rick," Bryant was firm. "You've ruffled too many feathers to stay in SOCOM and you've got a little over two years left in your hitch. In all honesty, you probably won't be considered for reenlistment, even with the Silver Star. That was what got you these orders instead of a trip directly to tech school."

"I never considered the possibility that I wouldn't be," Johnson said, floored once more. "What in hell am I going to do, sir? I planned to put in my twenty and take retirement. I kinda like this gig lately."

"That's why I'm telling you this now, boy," Bryant growled. "You've got a couple years to think about that."

"Shit, sir, all I know is fixing cars and what I do here."

"I'm sure you could join a police force somewhere," Bryant offered.

"I wouldn't make a good cop," Johnson said, and Bryant thought about it.

"No, probably not," the colonel agreed. "What about your girl?"

"Don't even ask, sir," Johnson waved it away. "I've been going round with the State Department for the last two weeks since we got back from Grenada, trying to get her in the country but it's being blocked in channels, I'm told. I don't have any leave coming until next year either, so I can't get back there anytime soon to take care of the marriage requirements."

"I can grant you emergency leave," Bryant said. "But you'd better have a real good story about how you came back with a wife and how that was an emergency."

"I've already thought that over, Colonel," Johnson smiled. "I'd rather not break the law if I have other options," he said.

"Smart move, Rick," Bryant nodded. "How's your mom?"

"She's good, sir, thanks for asking," Johnson smiled. "But my dad's working his ass off, trying to keep the business going."

"That's right, he's a defense contractor," Bryant remembered.

"Yes, sir, but the aircraft industry is moving off Long Island. He's lost a lot of work over the past few years," Rick told him. "He's humping to keep the place alive and he looks like shit."

"Give them my best, son."

"I will, sir, thank you." Johnson left and spotted Nate Beu on his way to the NCO Club.

Beu jumped out of his car and ran over to him, shoving a cigar in his face. "I'm gonna be a daddy," he grinned. "We just found out today."

"Congratulations, pal," Johnson tried to sound cheerful as he accepted the cigar. "Give Alexa a kiss for me."

"Try to sound a *bit* more enthusiastic," Beu nudged him.

"I just found out I'm going to SAC. I'm gonna be a coat carrier for a maintenance chief on a B-52 base. Can you *stand* it? I'm sorry if I'm a little down, but Stonewall took the opportunity while I was there to inform me that what I thought would be an illustrious Air Force career was going to crash and burn when it came time for reenlistment," Johnson said disgustedly.

"I'm sorry," Beu meant it.

"So much for my visions of grandeur," Johnson shrugged. "I'm gonna head over to the NCO Club for a couple."

"Why don't you come over to the house?" Beu offered.

"This is supposed to be a happy day for you, Nate. You don't need me moping around. I also don't need to see *you* with everything I want, a beautiful wife and a baby on the way, not on the day that the dream was put even farther out of reach. I'll come over to visit in a couple days, I promise."

"Are you sure?"

Johnson bit off the end of the cigar and lit it, grinning broadly. "Yes, I'm sure. Go home to your wife and be happy."

"Hey," Beu nudged him again before heading for the car. "Can you *believe* that I am going to be a father?"

"Officers shouldn't be allowed to breed," Johnson jibed. "Let's hope the kid takes after your better half."

"You got that right, boy," Beu said before driving away.

Johnson waved and turned in the other direction, resuming his trek to the NCO Club. It was a short walk and he gave a nod to a couple Marines he knew who were coming out when he arrived. Inside, he found Hermann Wood at the bar. "Hey, man," Rick sidled up to him. "A shot of Jack Daniel's and a Bud," he said to the bartender.

"What's up?" Wood asked.

"They're gonna deny me reenlistment and send me to SAC," Johnson said as he knocked back the shot. "Stonewall gave me the word a half hour ago. Did you hear about Nate?"

"Yeah, lucky bastard," Wood raised a shot of Bacardi 151 and downed it, chasing it with a beer. "Did you ever think he'd turn around like this?"

"Alexa rides herd on him," Johnson agreed. "She's the best thing that ever happened to him."

"What about *your* girl?"

"Don't ask. I don't know when I'm gonna get back there," Johnson said sadly. "I'll have to write to her and tell her the news." He finished his beer and stood.

"Where are you going?"

"The barracks," Johnson replied. "The last thing I need is to sit here and get blasted. I'll see you." Johnson left, the alcohol numbing him as he stepped into the warm Florida evening. He stopped at the post office and received three letters, one from his mom, one from Yung Shu, and a third from his bank containing the payment book for the loan he took out while on leave. The baby blue 1970 Chevelle SS 454 sat parked in the lot next to the barracks reminded him every day and the first payment of $247.50 was due in fifteen days.

"Yeah, that's what I need now, a fucking hot rod," he cursed at himself as he crossed the street and saw his car, shining in the late day sun. He needed all the money he could acquire to get him to Korea and back with a wife. It was why he took the loan instead of paying cash, so he could keep his liquid assets liquid.

Entering his room, he saw that his roommate, Staff Sergeant Alex Deere, was gone and that was good. He didn't feel sociable tonight and Deere could talk a blue streak. Opening the letter from his mother, he got a chuckle. She always kept him up to speed with what was happening in the old neighborhood.

Yung Shu's letter, on the other hand, gave him pause; a feeling and he didn't want to open it. He did so slowly, unfolding the page but not focusing on it. She was always so upbeat and optimistic, and he had none of those emotions right now.

Rick,

It was good to get your last letter and I am glad you came through your dangerous mission without getting hurt. Your words however, were sad. I know you are agonizing over our situation, my love, but I am beginning to think mother was correct.

She has not been feeling well of late and I finally talked her into going to the doctor. Her heartbeat has irregularities, the doctor said, and she can no longer keep up her routine. Therefore, I must take over her duties here at the club. Other things have changed as well, and I can no longer foresee leaving Korea anytime in the future. Maybe after mother passes, but I cannot leave her alone here and she would not come with us as long as she has the club. As you know, the love of her life built this place and she could not turn her back on it.

I know you have two years left with the Air Force, but I will always be here for you if you decide you could live here with me. In light of the present situation, I do not believe you should hold yourself to the commitment you made to me. I know it goes against your character, but you made that commitment with a completely different set of assumptions and I will not hold you to it.

I will always love you, Rick, and will treasure the time we spent together, but we are of different worlds, as mother said, and your destiny is certainly not your own. Maybe God never intended us to be together, who knows, but we will always have the love we shared. Remember me well, my love.

Yours always,

Yung Shu

"She's dumping me?" Johnson said as a tear fell from his cheek to the page. "Or at least letting me off the hook." He got up and went to his locker, digging out a small flask of Jack Daniel's that he kept for what he called 'in-room emergencies', and this certainly qualified. Johnson took a long swig. "So, she sees it too," he said as the liquor heated his gut. "The old crone was right," he gave a sardonic laugh when he thought of Yung Shu's mother. While he was fully prepared to marry Yung Shu and bring her back to the States, the old lady too if she wanted, living out the rest of his life in Korea was something altogether different.

While he would probably manage the club for Mama-san, he didn't think he was up to the task. "I'm no businessman and I'm no . . . *manager.*" He said the word with disdain. Being a manager meant, to Johnson, somebody sitting in the rear away, from where the action was. Richard Edward Johnson, if anything, was a man of action, someone who had to be at the pointy end where the rubber met the road. Managing meant getting soft, fat, and routine and that was definitely not he. "And I don't want to live in that asshole of a country until the old lady kicks off."

He took another swig from the flask before lying down on his bed fully clothed. He didn't care. He didn't care about anything right now because everything he cared about was taken from him in the last twelve hours. He thought of Beu and the wonderful news he carried this afternoon. "The guy who never wanted it got it in spades," he said as the tears ran down his cheeks. "And the guy who wants it so badly will never get it."

The Kremlin, Moscow, Soviet Union

"The Grenada initiative was a waste of resources," Kosarev said to Andropov. "Cuba itself is a waste of resources and financing that airport for them was ridiculous."

"We need Cuba, especially now with the rumblings in the Balkans," Chairman Andropov shot back at him.

"And did you not think the Americans would take action?" Kosarev was incredulous since he'd received the report this morning. "They will not allow another Cuba in the Caribbean. You saw what they did to that little madman in Korea."

"He is demanding more assistance," Andropov told him, moving the subject away from the fiasco in Grenada. "Zhukov's weekly reports detail the pressure the North Koreans are placing on him."

"I have heard from Zhukov, it is Park's usual ranting," Kosarev waved it away.

"We hear that his government is willing to part with some of its hard currency for more advanced . . . expertise," the Chairman said.

"He should not be given the wherewithal to field offensive nuclear weapons," Kosarev said. "He will destabilize the continent."

"It is not just he, Comrade Kosarev," Andropov growled. "Major Park has to follow the edicts of the North Korean government."

"Park has dirt on all of them, Mr. Chairman," Kosarev snapped. "And he is an insane, power hungry little deviant. He can do what he wants, or half of their Politburo would be looking for work in the rice paddies."

"We are not the only ones with nuclear technology to sell," Andropov told him. "You know about the South Africans?"

"Let *them* make their deals with the Devil," Kosarev spat. "It is not worth the money."

"Yes, it *is*. We will have advisers there, Yevgeniy Stepanovich. We can keep an eye on them."

"This is a foolish pursuit," Kosarev told him.

"Then you will make sure we do not make fools of ourselves."

"Yes, I will," Kosarev said as he stormed out of the Chairman's office.

The time was coming closer and over the last three months, he'd spoken to more old friends, military men who'd served with him against the Nazis and pledged their support to him when the time came. More importantly, they pledged their support to Gorbachev.

Chapter Fifteen
Carswell Air Force Base, Fort Worth, Texas
21 February 1984

"You got a call, Sarge," the crew chief called from the flightline truck. "They want you in the FMS orderly room."

"Right," Johnson yelled back and turned back to the two engine shop troops. "How long before she's flyable?" They were standing in front of B-52D; machine 59-063, currently missing two of its eight engines, destroyed when they ingested several gulls each.

"Tomorrow afternoon, Sarge," one of them said. "That's about as fast as we can do it and still do it right."

"Fine," Johnson replied. "Let me know if anything unforeseen comes up." He left them to their work and hopped aboard the truck that took him from the flightline to one of the hangars used to house the gigantic bombers. 7th Field Maintenance Squadron's orderly room was on the second floor. "I have a phone call?" He said to the airman sitting at he desk.

"Here you go, Sergeant Johnson," she said with a smile, indicating the flashing line.

"Johnson," he said.

"Richie?"

"Mom? What's wrong?" He could hear it in her voice.

"Your father ... he ... he had a heart attack at work this morning," she got out before breaking down.

"Where is he, mom? What hospital?" But he knew they were the wrong questions to ask; if his father were in the hospital and alive, his mother was strong enough to keep it together. And he felt another of the dull spears slam into his chest.

"He didn't make it to the hospital, Richie," she cried.

"Shit," Rick sighed. "Are you with somebody?"

"Yes, your aunts are here," she said, regaining her composure.

"I'll be home in a couple days at most," he said. "I have to talk to my CO. Is there anything you need me to do from here?"

"No, but hurry home."

"I will, mom. I love you."

"I love you too, Richie."

"Shit," he said again as he hung up the phone. "Can you get me in to see the old man? It's an emergency," he said to the WAF.

"Sure thing, Sergeant, go right in," she saw that whatever news he'd received had seriously deflated the normally gregarious Johnson.

The 7th FMS commander approved his leave request almost immediately and passed along condolences on behalf of all. A trip to the travel office got Johnson a seat on an American Airlines red eye leaving tonight from DFW to JFK in New York and he called his mother again to let her know.

Sitting in his barracks room, he wondered what else could go wrong. Over the past few months, he'd written to Yung Shu on a regular basis, but her replies were becoming less and less frequent and he'd begun to think their relationship was finally over. He was starting to come to terms with that, starting to let the reality sink it and now this.

"Dad's gone," he said aloud. And he was surprised that he felt worse for his mother than he did for his father. "But I didn't know him that well." Yes, they'd gone on family vacations once a year and yes, he'd done many of the dad things, taught Rick to play sports and went to many of his junior hockey games when time permitted, but Richard Johnson Senior was a small businessman. From the time Rick was young, his most vivid memories of his father were the things the elder had missed, the late hours, and the constant chasing after a dollar. It was his mother who'd been the parent to him, an only child.

"I'm sorry, mom," he said, again to his empty barracks room. "I could have been a better teenager. I promise I'll be a better son from now on."

***

Johnson landed at JFK just after midnight and picked up his rental, a piece of shit Chevy Cavalier that couldn't get out of its own way. Thankfully, traffic was light, and he didn't have to drive in rush hour traffic. It took him about forty-five minutes on the Long Island Expressway out to Suffolk County and saw the lights were on in his mother's house when he pulled in.

"Hi, ma," he said as she met him at the door.

"Oh, Richie ..." she sobbed, and he held her.

"How're you doing?" He asked as he got her up the stairs.

"Not good," she said in her clipped German accent. She pointed to the table in the dining room, littered with documents. "You know the business was not going well," Maria Johnson said rhetorically.

"Yeah," he nodded.

She stopped and took him in. "You look good in your uniform," she smiled. "I remember when your father came back from Korea. You remind me of him then," Maria said sadly. "The house has three mortgages on it," she went on. "There isn't much left of the business and I can't keep it running. Your father was working fourteen hours a day and I can't do it. I have Felix looking into buyers already; maybe I can sell it before the banks take it. I won't be able to keep the house if they foreclose on the business. He should have sold that damn business when Republic Aircraft left Long Island." She began to cry again.

"I'll stop over at Felix' office tomorrow," Rick said. Felix Carlsson was the family lawyer. "And I'll figure out what we need to do. Why don't you get some rest?"

"I can't sleep," she waved him away.

Rick went into his bag and came out with a pill bottle. "Here," he handed her two of them.

"What are these?"

"They gave them to me when I was in the hospital a couple months back," he told her. "They're for pain, but they'll put you out. I'll take care of everything in the morning."

Maria looked at her son appraisingly. "You've grown up, Richie," she said. "And it becomes you." She smiled and kissed his cheek.

"Look, ma," he stopped her. "I'm sorry for being such a shit when I was a teenager. I'm sorry for putting you and pop through all the juvenile delinquent bullshit."

"I knew you would mature someday," Maria patted his cheek. "Don't stay up too late."

"I won't," he kissed her on the forehead, and she went to her bedroom.

He found himself picking papers up at random, gazing at them as if he knew what they actually meant. All he knew was they represented several hundred thousand dollars of equity in the house in which he stood. *I can't let her lose the house*, he thought. He thought of the love his mother put into the yard that resembled a park, with manicured bushes and a rose garden that made strangers stop on the street to take pictures. It was her home, her sanctuary, and it was so since he was a little boy. "I *won't* let you lose the house," he said softly, foregoing the papers for the liquor cabinet, smiling when he opened the door. His mother had a small bottle of Jack Daniel's for him. "You're the best, mom," he said as he found a shot glass. While he did it all the time, drinking out of the bottle was forbidden in his mother's house and he wouldn't dare under her roof. And he laughed as he poured himself a shot.

Moscow, Soviet Union

They were all there, Kosarev, Popov, Gorbachev, Konstantin Chernenko, Colonel-General Iosef Kharlamov, and General Mikhail Lovenko, a half-dozen conspirators gathered in what many in the Soviet Union would consider treasonous circumstances. They waited in a room not far from the Kremlin, an apartment owned by Chernenko.

"You will assume your rightful place tomorrow, Konstantin," Kosarev said. "They should never have given the position to Yuri Vladimirovich," he chuckled. "The call should be coming any minute."

"And I can count on your support?" Chernenko asked.

"We are here, aren't we," Kharlamov growled. He too served with Kosarev and Popov in the Patriotic War, Lovenko also, though he was a flyer and now in command of the Air Defense Forces/South Asia.

"And this will not be traced to me?" Chernenko worried.

"Stop whining like a girl," Lovenko barked.

"It will not be traced to anyone," Kosarev smiled, and the phone rang.

Chernenko answered it. "Yes? How long ago? Yes, I will be there directly," and he hung up looking at the other five, each in turn. "General Secretary Yuri Vladimirovich Andropov was found dead in his study, presumably from natural causes. No obvious evidence of foul play has been detected. They want me at the Kremlin."

"There will be a vote in the Politburo tomorrow," Gorbachev said. "I will second your nomination for General Secretary, Konstantin Ustinovich," he told Chernenko.

"And you will head the Komitet?" Chernenko asked of Kosarev.

"That is my price for delivering the support of my patriotic comrades who have joined us tonight, thus delivering the support of the Politburo." Kosarev smiled broadly. "I have just given you the Soviet Union, Mr. General Secretary, and you will give me the means to hold it together in these urgent times."

"And when you tire of me as you tired of Andropov, Yevgeniy Stepanovich?"

"The power is in the Secretariat, you know that, or you wouldn't be here," Kosarev barked. "Should we drink to our fallen comrade and to the new leadership of the Party?" He asked as Lovenko brought a bottle of vodka and six glasses. *You should worry I might tire of you,*

244

Konstantin Ustinovich, Kosarev thought as he drank his vodka. *You could be fertilizing a collektiv next to Andropov.*

Chapter Sixteen
Carswell Air Force Base, Forth Worth, Texas
22 May 1984

"Yeah," Johnson said as he ran for the phone.

"Boy, you'd better get down here as soon as you can."

"Nate?" Johnson hadn't expected a call from him.

"How much leave you got saved?" Beu went on.

"A couple weeks."

"Good, get here."

"Why?"

"Because I just became a daddy twenty minutes ago and Alexa and I want you to be Katie's godfather."

"Katie?" It took a second for Johnson to digest. He'd just come off a month of twelve-hour shifts, most of which lasted sixteen, and was exhausted. "You had a daughter? Shit, I hope she doesn't look like *your* big ugly ass. Why in Hell would you want *me* to be her godfather? I ain't seen the inside of a church in fifteen years except for weddings and funerals."

"Because if it weren't for your help, Alexa and I would never have gotten together," Beu told him. "And when you get here, you can congratulate me on two accounts. I made lieutenant colonel."

"I always said bullshit floats to the top," Johnson laughed. "I'll be there by the weekend. I'll call you after I pull a leave slip out the old man's ass."

"How is it there?"

"It's SAC, twenty year old tankers and thirty year old bombers waiting to fight World War Three with nukes," Johnson told him. "These guys are more interested in the stray threads on your uniform than whether you can get the job done. Some maggot gave me a hard time about it in the Base Exchange."

"That's because they know they will never be called upon to fight unless the Soviets decide to nuke us," Beu said. "They need something to do."

"Don't remind me. I'll talk to you soon, say hi to Alexa for me."

"Will do, pal," Beu said and hung up.

"At least he's happy," Rick muttered as he collected his toiletries and headed for the shower. If Johnson were the type to admit it, he was probably suffering from clinical depression, but he wouldn't. He and Yung Shu had effectively lost touch, although he thought of her often. He'd helped his mom save her house, arranging the sale of the business and consolidating the mortgages on the house *and* guaranteeing the bank a little over four hundred dollars a month for five years after all was said and done. He felt good that his mother didn't have to move, but he'd used up much of his savings helping her out.

"Hey, I got my Chevelle," he said sarcastically as he turned the water on and adjusted the temperature. At close to twenty-four years old, his total worth was a fifteen year old hot rod and whatever clothes filled the locker in his barracks room. He could pack his entire life into the trunk of his car. He also had no desire to seek out female companionship, the ache he felt for Yung Shu still burned in him. "I have nothing to show for twenty-four years of life but a car, a stereo, twenty t-shirts, ten pairs of jeans, and a bunch of green clothes; just fucking wonderful."

After the shower, he dressed in his best fatigue uniform and headed out to his car. Through he could have walked, he drove the half-mile over to the 7th Field Maintenance orderly room. It was a short walk from the parking lot to the hangar and then upstairs.

"Hi, Christine," Johnson smiled as he entered. "Is the old man in?"

"Sorry, Sarge," Senior Airman Christine Armstrong replied. "You just missed him. Anything I can help you with?"

"Shit, I wish. Can you forge his signature on a leave slip?" Johnson grinned. "I have to be in Fort Walton Beach by the weekend. I'd like to leave Friday morning if at all possible."

"Got a hot date?" The pretty Afro-American asked him.

"Don't I wish," he replied. "I'm gonna be a godfather. My best friend had a little girl an hour ago. Well, his wife did all the hard work," he grinned.

"Congratulations," she said with a warm smile. "I'll have one typed up and on his desk first thing in the morning," Armstrong volunteered. "When are you coming back, Rick?"

"Never," he kidded. "Ah, Monday or Tuesday."

"Stop by when you go to the chow hall at lunch tomorrow," she told him. "It'll be signed by then."

"You're the best, Christine," Johnson said, considering her. They'd always been cordial in the two months since Armstrong arrived, joking occasionally and meeting at parties thrown by mutual acquaintants. "Speaking of chow," he said, not used to this at all. "Would you be willing to join me for dinner tonight? Nothing fancy, just a little steak place off base. This *is* Texas, you know."

She looked him over once. "Sure," she smiled. "I just never thought ..."

"What?"

"Word is you're in love with a Korean girl, that you haven't dated since you've been here and you didn't bring a wife with you," Armstrong smiled sheepishly. "I was curious about you and I asked around," she admitted. "I also was wondering if you just weren't interested in black girls like some of the rednecks around here."

"I'm no redneck," he said. "And *all* women interest me," he smiled back. "I just didn't want to jeopardize what I had ... let's just say I've come to the realization that it's not going to work out."

"Then I'll see you later, Sergeant Johnson," she said as the squadron executive officer came into the room.

"Thank you, Airman," Johnson said and then turned to the officer. "Captain," he nodded before leaving and got one in return. *I got a date*, he thought when he got outside and for the first in a long time his smile was genuine.

Wantagh, New York

Connie Wasserman's hands shook when she opened the envelope. She was late to work for her summer job at Jones Beach, but she didn't care. She'd been anxious since she'd taken her finals and the results and her final grades were here. Her hands shook when she opened the envelope, trying to do it neatly at first but eventually tearing it apart in fervent anticipation.

Scanning the page, a bright smile came to the surface her lowest grade a B. "Yes," she breathed, looking around the empty house. There was no one home to share the good news with and she was late to work. Connie stuffed the envelope in her bag and headed to her car, the smile still present. Her grades were good enough to continue in her new major, which would please her mother greatly. She'd gotten grief about the change from economics to the law but now she'd proven this was the path she would take. Her grades had been far better than any she'd received in her economics classes the year before. While she had problems staying awake in class then, the law intrigued her, kept her interest and curiosity peaked.

"I'm going to be an attorney," she said as she merged onto the Wantagh Parkway from Sunrise Highway. Granted, her degree was still two years away, but after the next year, she would be halfway there. "I'm going to be a *fucking* attorney," she said again as the perfect, bright, beautiful smile beamed even brighter.

Fort Worth, Texas

"Oh shit, oh *yes*," Armstrong moaned as her climax approached. She held him by a handful of his dark brown hair as his tongue probed her most secret places.

Dinner had been just what he'd promised, a little steak place just off base, and she'd asked him back to her apartment afterward. Thankfully, her roommate was on temporary duty somewhere and they would be alone. Both feeling amorous after the drinks and conversation over dinner, they failed to make it to her bedroom, remaining on the couch instead.

He rose from between her legs and she returned the favor as he stood, taking him in her mouth and pleasuring him before urging him to enter her. He made love to her furiously, passionately and she began to moan again as he used his fingers in conjunction with his manhood to bring her release once more. Johnson's followed, erupting in violent orgasm as he liberated all of his pent-up emotions.

"Damn," he breathed as she pulled him to her, kissing him deeply.

"I see you needed this as much as I did," she said.

"I guess I did," he agreed, though now he felt like shit, felt as if he'd cheated on Yung Shu. *She probably has someone else by now anyway*, he thought as he gazed at Armstrong's lithe body. Christine rose and took him by the hand, leading him into the bedroom. She wanted more of him and tonight he was more than willing to oblige. *I'll deal with the guilt in the morning*.

Pensacola, Florida

Things had gone well for Alan Holmgren since the day he committed murder. A promotion had come, and he now wore the single silver bar of a first lieutenant. He'd also begun to implement his career plan. He was at this very moment at the caterer's, sampling hors d'ouvres for his upcoming nuptials.

He'd met a girl, plain but on the pretty side, and courted her like a gentleman. In fact, he still hadn't slept with her and that was fine by him. She was the second daughter of the senior senator and, over the last eight months, Holmgren had earned the father's respect and admiration. He treated her like a southern belle, put her on a pedestal and bowed to every whim, and Jessica Latour had many.

I chose well, he thought as he listened to Jessica and the caterer make the arrangements, giving the appropriate nods and agreeing with her whenever necessary. His bride-to-be was cultured, educated, and pretty, but most of all, her father was a ranking member of the Senate Armed Services Committee. Ernie Latour was a very powerful ally to an ambitious young lieutenant in the United States Air Force.

Holmgren had courted Ernie through his daughter, researching the man and his foibles. Alan had even gone as far as taking up the same hobbies, golf primarily, and developing a taste for country music, two things he'd found distasteful before. He would marry the daughter and she would be the perfect officer's wife, and Ernie Latour would be a very helpful father-in-law.

"What do you think, Alan?" Jessica asked him about the cracker with the cured salmon slice and dollop of caviar.

"Can your dad eat it?" He asked, a concerned look on his face. "You know how his stomach is and we wouldn't want . . ."

"Say no more," she smiled at him, her blue eyes twinkling. "You're always so thoughtful."

"So, it's no to the salmon and caviar," the caterer said, rolling his eyes. The two young people's affectations were making his stomach turn.

"No," Jessica said sadly. "Let's go to the next one."

And Alan smiled passively and continued his charade. He would only have to keep it up for a few years until he got what he needed, until he made new connections in Washington and could further his career on his own.

Chapter Seventeen
Fort Walton Beach, Florida
26 May 1984

"You're looking good, Rick," Hermann Wood said as he came over.

"You too, Woodsy," Johnson handed him a beer. "Nate makes nice kids."

"Sure does," Wood agreed. "Nate told me about Yung Shu, sorry."

"That's life, man," Rick shrugged. "Her mom got sick, my dad died, and it just put everything out of reach. I met somebody the other day," he said conspiratorially.

"Is it serious?"

"Man, *nothing's* serious anymore," Johnson told him. He looked over at Beu, flipping burgers on the grill. "It's like my life and his flipped. Look at him; all happy he has a wife and kid. If you would have told him a year ago that he'd be playing dad a year later, he'd have laughed in your face."

"I figured you'd be the one married by now," Wood said.

"So did I, man."

"You figure out what you're gonna do when you get out?"

"Nah," Johnson waved it away. "I gave up thinking long term. As long as I wake up in the morning, my arms, my legs, and my prick still work, I'm a happy man. I'll deal with it when they give me the heave ho."

"Why don't you talk to somebody, Rick?"

"What are you saying, my outlook on life sucks?"

"Yes," Wood said. "You used to be a dreamer, boy, a romantic dreamer. Now you're just cynical."

"Let's just say that all my long-term goals became irrelevant over the past year," Johnson growled. "No use planning for shit that never happens." He looked back to Beu. "Look at him, tell me *he* planned for this. Last year this time, he'd spend half the nights of the week passed out in my spare room. Now he's the King of Suburbia."

"You *are* a cynical bastard," Wood said. "The man I knew would have been thrilled at the passion and romance of it."

"I gave up on passion and romance. I'm just happy to get laid again," Johnson shrugged.

"Burgers are ready," Beu called over.

"It's about damn time," Johnson said as he and Wood came over. "I took leave so I could see the baby and all I get to look at is your big ass in shorts."

"Babies need sleep," he said. "She'll be up from her nap soon. Have a burger, Rick."

"Thanks," Johnson said. He'd seen the baby at the christening this morning of course, but beautiful little Katie, Katherine Alexandra to be exact, had spent most of her time either sleeping or breast feeding. He looked around the yard, a little over an acre, and thought this suburb a fine place for her to grow up. *At least for the near future*, he thought. Beu would get orders somewhere or another eventually. *And then you'll have some decisions to make.*

It was always harder when a military member had family, whether to take them along or leave them stateside when going overseas. *And you have to be careful where you go, don't you, Alexa?* Beu had never given him the truth about what happened that night a little less than a year ago, but if she were a Soviet defector, certain parts of the world would not be safe for her.

"Here's the munchkin," Alexa said as she came out of the house carrying the baby.

"I didn't think anyone could be prettier than her mother," Rick said as he took the little girl in his arms gingerly. While he would willingly walk into the face of overwhelming enemy fire, babies scared him. They were so fragile, so delicate, he was afraid he might hold them too tight or not hold them correctly. He must have been doing something right because little Katie reached up for him and then yawned. "But you are a beautiful little lady," he smiled at her. He looked up at the proud parents. "Good job, guys," he grinned, looking back down at the child in his arms. "Your Uncle Rick loves you, Little Katie, and he'll be here whenever you need him."

***

There was a knock on the door and Beu rose to answer it, leaving his wife in the living room with the baby. His breath was taken away when he opened the door.

"Congratulations, Nathan," Yevgeniy Kosarev said as he took his son-in-law's hand.

"Come in, Colonel," Beu stammered, checking the street to see if any of the neighbors saw Kosarev.

"It is general now," he corrected Beu and stopped when his daughter appeared with a bundle in her arms.

"Papa," Alexa breathed.

"Is this my grandchild?" The bear of a man smiled as he took the little one from her mother.

"Katherine Alexandra, papa," Alexa said. "We named her for mama."

And the proud Russian looked at them both with tears in his eyes. "Thank you," he said, taking Beu's hand once more.

"From what Alexa tells me of her mother the name was appropriate. Katie is a feisty one," Beu told him and on cue, the little girl stuck a finger up her grandfather's nose.

"She has her grandmother's eyes," Kosarev confirmed with a laugh and a tear. "You have made me very proud," he said.

Chapter Eighteen
Key West, Florida
30 June 1984

It was a splendid wedding at Senator Ernie LaTour's vacation home on the island, the guest list including some of the most powerful people in business and political circles. Latour called it his 'cottage' but in reality, it was a thirty-room mansion on the eastern shore of Key West. Reverend Beecher from the First Baptist Church of Fort Walton Beach performed the service, Ernie Latour a member of the congregation. The reception was also being held here and the new bride and groom were about to make their appearance.

There was a strong military contingent here as well, mostly uniforms of Air Force blue, but others sprinkled in as well, some friends of Holmgren, others, the higher-ranking ones, friends of the senator. Holmgren's friends were saying goodbye tonight also, for he was leaving shortly for a new assignment in Washington, one of the many wedding presents his new father-in-law lavished upon the young couple. They would also take over the house Latour kept in Georgetown and make it their own.

"Talk about a career boost," one of the guests, an Army officer said to another.

"Yeah, it doesn't hurt to marry well," the other said with a laugh as the applause started. 1st Lieutenant Alan Holmgren appeared with his new bride on the veranda overlooking the beach. Jessica waved to the guests and Holmgren just beamed.

"Where's he going?" The Army officer asked.

"National Reconnaissance Office," the naval officer replied. "They say no one knows East Asia like he does. He's been on the ground there on and off for a couple years now, speaks Korean, Chinese, and Japanese."

"Nice résumé," the other agreed. "You know CIA will get him soon enough."

"That's the way it works, doesn't it," the Navy lieutenant junior grade said with a shrug as the newly married pair made their way among the well-wishers. "And you can bet daddy will get him a good job over there too."

***

For his part, Holmgren was enjoying himself, though he couldn't get his mind off the young Spanish boy who worked for the caterer. He'd gone too long without and the boy in the kitchen was just delicious in his opinion. *There will be time for that*, he thought. This was not the time to indulge his cravings. Jessica would give herself to him tonight and her body would have to do until they were settled in Washington. He would give her children also for that was how he would advance. Ernie Latour would never turn his back on the father of his grandchildren. Holmgren smiled as he watched his wife dance with her father. *Yes, there will be time for everything, and everything will be possible.*

Jessica would be pregnant by Christmas, of that he was sure and if not, they would see a doctor to find out why. There would be at least one child for Ernie Latour to dote on, the child of his youngest, to assure that his son-in-law would always be in a position to provide the best.

"Come, Alan, dance with me again," Jessica left her father and went to her husband.

"Yes, my darling," he replied with a smile as he took her hand and allowed himself to be led to the dance floor. *Anything you want, I will give it to you, my dear Jessica, and your father will give me what I desire.*

Wantagh, New York

"*Why* won't you marry me, Connie?" Jay Moskowitz asked plaintively. They'd been seeing each other for a year now, Moskowitz also in law studies at C.W. Post. "I know you love me."

"I *care* about you, Jay," she said, tears forming at the corner of her eyes. She'd hurt him and she'd done it publicly, not that anyone in the restaurant noticed. At least, she thought no one had noticed the young man handing her the box with the ring and her putting it back on the table without opening it. "But I still have two years of college left. It's not time for me to settle down."

"But I can support us," Moskowitz protested. "I have a guaranteed job at dad's firm, and you'll be able to stay home and be a mom to our kids."

"I don't know if I even want to be a mom, Jay," she replied. "And I'm pretty sure I don't want to be a housewife. I'm not in law school just *because*," Connie went on. "I want to *be* a lawyer."

"So, we'll wait until you get your degree to start a family."

"I want to be a *practicing* lawyer," she said firmly. "I want to take the bar, I want to work, and I want to be in the courtroom where the action is, not sitting at home with a useless degree on the wall. I want to be known as a good attorney, not as the *wife* of a good attorney. Can you understand that?"

"No, Connie, I can't," his tone suddenly surly. "Do you know how many women want to marry me? They know I can keep them in style and luxury."

"I don't want to be *kept*," she hissed back. "So why don't you ask one of *them* to marry you?" She stood, dropping her napkin on the table. Connie turned to leave but he grabbed her by the arm.

"I don't want any of them, Connie, I want *you*," he held her wrist firmly.

"I won't marry you, Jay," she said, pulling her arm free. "If you can't deal with that, then I'm sorry." She didn't look at him.

"So am I," he said and looked away.

Connie regarded him for a moment before leaving the restaurant and getting into her car. She hopped on the parkway and headed south, to the place where she could always find peace and solace. Keeping her composure until she pulled into Field 6 at Jones Beach, the tears began to fall as she walked out onto the sand, coming in torrents by the time she sat down on the shore.

Jay was a nice guy; adequate in bed and, most importantly in a Jewish family, her mother liked him. Rita Wasserman had hinted to her daughter, none too subtly, that Jay would make an excellent choice for a husband. The youngest son of a wealthy, respected family, Jay had an unlimited future and he was Jewish. Both of Connie's older brothers had married outside the faith, much to Rita's consternation. Connie was her last hope for one of her offspring to marry correctly and would not be pleased to hear that Connie declined his proposal.

"The man I marry has to set me on fire," she said with determination. "It has to be right the *first* time."

Connie Wasserman had definite feelings about divorce and none of them good. She felt very strongly about love and commitment, and divorce was not the same as a do over. When she made the vow to commit to someone, it would be forever. She would be absolutely sure before taking that step. Her future husband would be a man she loved passionately and there would be no doubt of her commitment to him. "And Jay isn't the one," she said to a seagull who'd stopped to check out the human on his stretch of beach. He squawked at her and flew away. "Now I have to go home and break the news to mom," she chuckled. Her mother would take it worse than she did.

Chapter Nineteen
Lubyanka Prison, Moscow, Soviet Union
10 March 1985

"Is it done?" Kosarev asked when Zhukov returned from the Kremlin.

"It will be," Zhukov told him. "Things are in place and we shall have news in a few hours."

"Good."

"This will not look good, Yevgeniy. It is just a year since Andropov..."

"I give a damn how it looks," he growled. "Konstantin Ustinovich has outlived his usefulness." Kosarev looked up at his friend. "Go back to Pyong Yang, Marko, it might not be safe for you in Moscow in a few hours, it might not be safe for any of us."

"There have been rumors Colonel Park has been speaking with the South Africans," Zhukov said as he turned to leave. "We believe he is negotiating for a delivery system."

"I know," the KGB Chairman said. "I want to know exactly with whom he is speaking, Marko. He has to be prevented from purchasing the missile bodies."

"What about their breeder reactor program?" Zhukov asked. "They should be online in a year or two."

"We are using other assets in that regard," Kosarev said. When Kosarev became head of the KGB after he and his cohorts had Chernenko installed as Party Chairman and General Secretary, he'd promoted Zhukov into his old position as the Pyong Yang *rezident*. The existence of the sleeper agent was unknown to Zhukov; Kosarev still chose to run Soon Yat Oh personally. Soon was the only asset the Soviet Union had within the North Korean nuclear program and the less anyone knew about him the better.

"Colonel Park will have his nuclear missiles, my friend, regardless of what you do to stop him. He wants the entire Korean Peninsula under Communist rule," Zhukov informed him.

"He's wanted that since he assumed control of their internal security division," Kosarev told his friend. "I want you to explore the options of Colonel Park having an accident of the fatal sort. It might be the only way we can stop him."

"He has excellent security," Zhukov relied. "If he were to be neutralized, an accident would be difficult to arrange. An obvious assassination would have far better chances of success."

"We cannot be seen as taking an active hand in their internal politics," Kosarev warned. "Our Chinese comrades would take exception to that and I have worked too hard to keep them out of Siberia. We could lose much more than we intended. I would rather Park remained healthy and in power than risk war with the Chinese. Not in the current state of the Soviet economy at least. We cannot afford a major war at this point in time, not with the drain on our budget trying to hold Afghanistan."

"We should leave it to those barbarians," Zhukov spat.

"And the Americans will move right in," Kosarev said with a raised finger. "Their CIA is already arming the Mujahidin, Marko. Go back to Pyong Yang and leave the rest to me."

Washington, D.C.

Holmgren felt good as he left the Pentagon, the brisk wind off the water stinging his lungs. Things were looking up this cold March morning, Jessica expecting their first child in a few months and his promotion to captain scheduled to come around the same time. It was why what happened next took him totally by surprise. As he walked to his car, another nondescript sedan came up alongside.

"Lieutenant Holmgren?" The driver asked as he put down the window. Holmgren noticed the man, obviously of Spanish descent, wore the uniform of a Marine Corps major.

"Yes?" And then he saw the dart gun come up in the driver's right hand and he saw two others emerge from a van parked nearby. The dart struck him in the chest, and he felt his knees go to rubber almost instantly. His last conscious thought was being hauled into the van.

***

He regained consciousness extremely disoriented and cold, and then he noticed he was naked and unable to move. His wrists, ankles, and waist were secured to a chair. *What is going on?*

The door opened and he recognized the man who'd now changed from his Marine Corps threads. "So, you're awake, Lieutenant," he smiled.

"Who are you?" Holmgren asked.

"My name is Hector," the swarthy man replied.

"Are you going to kill me?"

"Oh no, you will be quite safe, provided you cooperate," Hector said.

"What do you want?"

"I want to watch a movie with you, Alan," Hector smiled as he dimmed the lights. He produced a remote from his pocket and turned on the TV in the corner of the room. "Let's go back a few years." The videotape ran and Holmgren's eyes widened. Hector saw his reaction and laughed. "Yes, you recognize the star of this movie, don't you?"

"Oh ... my ... God," Holmgren whispered as he watched himself cavorting with Quanh in the *Tongdaegu-jang Yogwan* and the *Olympia Hotel*. And then he realized what else happened that day at the *Olympia*. And then he watched the mutilation and murder of the young man in the bathroom. "How ..." there were no more words to be found and he just sat and stared, watching his whole life flushed down the toilet.

"You see, Lieutenant," Hector continued as he brought the lights back up. "Quanh worked for us and his loss was significant for my employers. Fortunately, he alerted us to your potential before you so brutally killed him. You can compensate my employers for their loss of a good operative with your cooperation. On the other hand, you can refuse to cooperate, and copies of this tape will go to your wife, her father, the South Korean government, and the Air Force Office of Special Investigations."

"Who are your employers?" Holmgren asked.

"That is not your concern just yet," Hector said as he raised an index finger. "You will deal exclusively with me for the time being."

"What do you want me to do?"

"You will be advised." Hector pointed the remote at the TV, shutting it off before pointing it at the chair to which Holmgren was restrained. A press of a button sent a low voltage charge through the seat, harmless but excruciatingly painful when applied to a man's genitals. Holmgren screamed. "If you are willing to sacrifice your career, your freedom, and your marriage for some reason and decide to turn on us, you will die slowly and horribly," Hector warned as Holmgren tried to regain his composure. "Your savage act has condemned you to this life, Lieutenant, and your only way out is death. It is your only escape, be it at your hand or mine."

"I can't do it," Holmgren wavered, and Hector waved the remote again, this time holding the button down a little longer. Holmgren screamed bloody murder and then vomited from the pain.

"You should have no problems with your conscience," Hector proclaimed. "If you can live with what you did to Quanh, you can live with this. You *will* find a way, Alan, or you will die." Hector released him from the chair, allowing him to fall to his knees on the floor, as his two comrades entered the room. "Clean him up and get him dressed," Hector ordered and then regarded Holmgren. "Go home to your wife.

I will contact you with instructions." They dragged him out by his arms.

***

Holmgren stared out over the steering wheel trying to keep his hands from shaking violently. It was his worst nightmare come true. After positioning himself perfectly, his impulsive act nearly two years before threatened to ruin him. But Holmgren was a survivor; he'd proved that by keeping it together after Roger's death and then pulling off the murder without even coming under suspicion.

"And I will get through this," he said aloud. Starting the car, he pulled out of the lot and began to wonder whom Hector's employers were. Assuming he was telling the truth, Quanh worked for them and that meant it was probably the North Koreans or the Chinese who were running him. "I have to find out." But he was an intelligence officer and he had resources at his disposal. If he wanted his career to move forward, he would have to play Hector's game, but he would not play without compensation.

"I will not be blackmailed," he said. "But I will be rewarded for my efforts." He smiled.

Holmgren crossed into Georgetown feeling better about the situation and by the time he pulled into his driveway, the afternoon's events were put away. He stepped back into the persona he'd so carefully cultivated, the devoted husband and model military officer.

"Hi, darling," he said brightly when he walked through the door. "I'm home."

Chapter Twenty
Wantagh, New York
20 February 1986

"Yes, thank you," Connie Wasserman said. "I'll be there first thing tomorrow." She hung up the phone and wanted to scream with delight. She'd applied for numerous internships, but this was the one she wanted. Epstein and Associates was a prestigious Manhattan defense firm with a Seventh Avenue address and a reputation for defending the wealthy and famous. Nary a week went by where the residents of New York City would not see the face of Chaim Epstein giving a press conference on behalf of a client or corporation he represented.

The ever-present smile remained as she gathered her books. The last half of her third year of law school was starting, and she was beginning to see the light at the end of the tunnel. An internship, if successful, could turn into a permanent position at the firm and that would certainly be welcome. While Connie's only goal at this point was to be an attorney, she would much rather practice her chosen craft at Epstein and Associates than Jacoby & Myers.

Fort Walton Beach, Florida

Beu answered the knock on the door, knowing who was there before he opened it. The throaty rumble of the big Chevy motor foreshadowed its owner's identity. "Hey, pal, what are you doing here?"

"I'm a free man with DD Form 214 in hand," Johnson grinned. "I separated yesterday and I'm on my way home. I wanted to see you and the family once more. Who knows when we'll get the chance again?" Rick looked around at the boxes stacked in every corner of the room. "Going somewhere?"

"I got orders to Spain," Beu told him as he offered a beer, which Johnson accepted. "We're gone day after tomorrow on leave. We're gonna visit my dad in Texas for a couple weeks before heading out. What about you?"

Rick shrugged. "Who knows?" He took a gulp of the beer. "Mom's got a list of shit for me to do around the house that should keep me busy for a month or two. I'll look for a job in between doing chores," he laughed.

"I figured you'd try to go back for Yung Shu," Beu said.

"With what? I've been helping mom out with the mortgage for a couple years now, you know. I don't have enough cash to pay attention let alone start a family. Besides, I haven't heard from her in over a year. She's probably with someone else by now anyway." Rick looked around. "Where's the wife and munchkin?"

"They went to the hospital for a checkup," Beu told him as they walked out into the yard. "This is it, isn't it?"

"What?" Rick asked.

"Today," Beu took a sip of his Budweiser. "We're gonna shake hands, promise to keep in touch, and eventually lose track of one another."

"Who knows, man," Rick shrugged again.

"I've seen it before." Beu thought of the friends he'd lost touch with over a fifteen-year career. "Try, pal," he said as he looked Rick in the eye. "I want Katie to know you."

"You make nice kids, you know," Rick said. "Are you gonna have another?"

"That's in God's hands." That earned a look from Johnson.

"Are you turning into a bible thumper on me, man?"

"You look at shit differently when you have a kid, Rick," Beu explained. "You don't take as much for granted."

"You're getting old, boy," Johnson laughed.

"Wait until you have kids someday," Beu gave him a knowing look. "You'll say the old man was right."

"Don't hold your breath."

"What about that girl you were seeing?"

"Christine?" Johnson shook his head. "That was never serious. We just had fun and enjoyed each other's company."

"Anyone else?"

"Nope, didn't think it was worth the effort being that I was leaving. I didn't want to get something started that I couldn't end when I separated from the Air Force," Johnson replied. "Maybe I'll look up some of the girls I used to see when I was in high school when I get home."

"Never look back, Rick," Beu said with a smile.

"You've got a point, my friend, you've got a point."

***

Johnson wiped a tear away with a sleeve as he steered the Chevelle onto I-10 just west of De Funiak Springs. From here out, he would stop only for gas and refreshment and, hopefully, in a little more than twenty hours he would be back on Long Island. He thought about what Beu said, turning it over in his mind. *I want Katie to know you.*

"How?" Johnson said as he kept the car in the middle lane and the speed a steady sixty-five. In this part of the south, even though he had Texas plates on the car, his New York accent would get him more than a cursory look-over from a cop. He had a bag of weed tucked under his seat and a seal of cocaine in his pocket, insurance he would stay awake on the long drive. He didn't need a hassle from some southern lawman that enjoyed giving Yankees a hard time. "When in hell will I ever going to see them again?"

They were going to Spain for a three-year tour, Beu taking an assignment as the executive officer of a chopper squadron at Torrejon Air Base. Johnson was sure he would never get there. "I'll see them if they pass through Kennedy on leave or on the way home," he said to himself as the radio blared the Rolling Stones' *Honky Tonk Woman*. Beu had his address and he would write when they were settled. *I hope*, he thought. As he drove on into the night, he felt like the loneliest person in the world.

Washington, D.C.

The Washington Monument stood over him like a glowing phallus in the cold night and Holmgren shook off the thought. He'd only sought sexual gratification twice over the past year since Hector made contact with him and he had a yearning. Yes, he'd made love to his wife dutifully, but it gave him no pleasure, fantasizing he was making love to a beautiful boy in order to keep himself turgid as he pleasured her. Tonight would be no different when he got home, but first he had to meet Hector. There was information vital to his employers whom Holmgren had verified were the Chinese under the guise of the North Koreans.

Holmgren had learned much over the past year, especially how the two Communist countries operated their intelligence services. Both also had alliances with the Cubans, relatively recently arrived at, ever since the Soviet Union could no longer afford to be as supportive as they had been in the past. Hector Reynaldo was an American citizen from the Little Havana section of Miami, yet worked for the Castro regime, mainly against the efforts of the anti-Communist Cuban exiles in the States. Holmgren surmised the Cubans loaned him to the Chinese or North Koreans for operations over here.

"They're so stupid," he muttered. "The Communists won't last twenty years. The Russians are bankrupt already and the others aren't far behind." He saw the car slow down and he clutched the envelope in the pocket of his overcoat. The light turned red and the car came to a stop, the driver lowering the right-hand window. As Holmgren entered the crosswalk, he discreetly dropped the envelope on the passenger seat and kept walking. The driver raised the window, the light turned green, and as quickly as that, the information was on the way.

Holmgren was on his way also, in his car and down K Street before one of his father-in-law's friends or any he worked with at the Pentagon spotted him on the street. Tonight was his daughter Megan Ashley's first birthday and he could not be late for the party at the senator's new home just up the street from theirs. "What kind of dad would I be?" He laughed, knowing there would be another ten thousand in his account at the Bank of Singapore, remuneration for the package just dropped into the anonymous automobile.

"And they'll never catch me at it," he said brazenly while negotiating the traffic. And he was not far off base. Most of the information he'd passed on over the past year came to him from the lips of his father-in-law. Ernie Latour, like any politician, had a big mouth and he liked to show off to his young son-in-law. He let Holmgren in on many little secrets he'd learned as a member of the Armed Services Committee and those tidbits served to line Holmgren's pockets.

Pulling into the long drive through the gated access, he didn't have to buzz in for he had a key card; he saw several cars of the Cadillac and Lincoln persuasion. Latour couldn't fail to invite several of his most trusted cronies on the Hill and at the Pentagon and Holmgren could imagine which of them would help celebrate his daughter's birthday. Ernie answered the door himself.

"I hear the traffic was a bear, son," he said.

"Yes, sir," Holmgren handed his coat to Latour. "I got hung up at work also. Sorry."

"Nonsense," Latour hung Holmgren's on the banister and brought him into the study. "I hope you don't mind but I invited some friends." There were several men in uniform and the rest in suits. "You know General Joe Wingate, the Army Chief of Staff, Senator Dick Robertson from my home state, CIA Director Louis Guerin,

Senator Harold Duquesne from the great state of Louisiana, Senator Phillip Boylan of Georgia, and General Tom Gibbets, Air Force Chief of Staff."

"Gentlemen," Holmgren shook hands with them all.

"So, you're the intelligence prodigy the senator has been crowing about," Guerin said.

"I don't know if I'd go that far, sir," Holmgren said sheepishly. He'd practiced for this day. He'd be humble and obsequious, deferential to this man for by the end of the evening, his transfer to the Central Intelligence Agency would be discussed. Holmgren would be offered a job; he was certain of that for Ernie Latour waited until just this occasion to arrange it.

Latour had given Holmgren a year and a half to prove himself, as a good husband to his daughter, as a good father to his granddaughter, and as a capable intelligence officer. This party was arranged because Holmgren had passed the tests. The Air Force Chief of Staff was here, Holmgren's transfer from the Air Force to the Agency required only a nod from Gibbets and Guerin was here to see Holmgren for himself. Again, the job at the Agency only required a nod from him to make it a reality.

Ernie Latour had his own reasons for wanting Holmgren at CIA, far removed from helping his son-in-law take a step up. He wanted eyes and ears there belonging to someone he trusted. Though Latour considered Guerin a friend, he trusted him only so far. Alan would give it to Latour straight, for his job would not require justification to Congress. Guerin told Latour what he wanted to hear; Holmgren would tell him what he needed to know.

Keep believing that Ernie, Holmgren thought as he accepted a scotch from his father-in-law. The move to the Agency involved a promotion to captain and he would be one step closer to unloading Ernie Latour and his spoiled brat daughter along with Megan Ashley, who was sure to grow into another spoiled brat like her mother.

The Kremlin, Moscow, Soviet Union

"It is a surprise to see you here, Yevgeniy Stepanovich," General Secretary Mikhail Gorbachev said. "Have I outlived my usefulness as Andropov and Chernenko did?"

"Don't be a fool, Mishka," Kosarev waved him away. "I came to discuss the problem in North Korea. I have been getting updates from Zhukov, you know."

"I should hope so," Gorbachev grumbled. "Are you still obsessed with that man?"

"General Park is a danger to the region and to the Union. He has finalized an agreement with the South Africans for a medium range ballistic missile body. He will receive thirty-two of them over the next few years," Kosarev advised.

"What do you propose?"

"An intervention program of sorts. We have the resources to intercept the missiles as they are delivered," Kosarev explained. "And we will be able to do it covertly," he added.

"And what of the Chinese, Yevgeniy," Gorbachev said. "What will they say when our part is revealed through the inevitable leaks? You were the one who told me they were selling the Kalashnikov rifles we licensed them to make to the Americans, so *they* can give them to the Mujahidin to fight against us in Afghanistan."

"Afghanistan is a lost cause, Mishka, we have to get out of there."

"In time, Yevgeniy. There are some here who are not as eager as you are to dissolve the Union and I fear that dissolution will bring about civil war. A sudden pullout from Afghanistan or a conflict with the Chinese in an effort to stymie Colonel Park's plans might be the trigger for such a war."

"This cannot wait," Kosarev insisted.

"It will have to, my friend," Gorbachev countered. "Or there will be no Union and no Russia. You will have your chance, but we cannot risk what we have worked for over the last decade. Think about this objectively, Yevgeniy. For the good of Mother Russia and her children, put this aside until we are in a more stable position. We cannot do too many things at once and the economic reforms have caused enough hardship."

"You are right, of course," Kosarev surrendered. There were other less official ways to deter the North Koreans from their nuclear goals. "I *will* desist, Mishka," he smiled. "But I will *not* forget about Colonel Park."

Chapter Twenty-One
Islip, Long Island, New York
19 June 1987

"Hey, ma," Johnson said when he got home from work. "What's up?"

"A woman called for you," she said. "Do you know someone named Cheryl?"

"Yeah," he chuckled, remembering the sex he had with her the night before. "I went to school with her."

"Are you chasing the same little sluts you did in high school?" His mother hissed. "What's happening to you, Richie?"

"What do you mean?"

"When you came home from the military, you were a different man," Maria told her son. "Now you're hanging out with the same bunch you walked away from close to ten years ago."

"They're my friends, mom. I don't believe we're even having this conversation. I'm twenty-*six* years old," Johnson tried to get to his room, but she blocked his way.

"Richie," she put a hand on his arm. "I'm your mother, I love you more than anything else in the world."

"I know that and the feeling's mutual."

"It's been good to have you here for the last year and a half and I appreciate all the work you've done around here, but it's time for you to get your own place," she declared. "Living here is turning you into the man you were when you were a teenager. You're falling into old habits and that's not good. Your old friends are too close and so are your old girls. I know what pot smells like, your room is starting to smell like it again, and God knows what else you're doing. Are you at least using protection when you're with those nasty little girls?"

"Ma!"

"I mean it, Richie. I'm a nurse, take it from me, AIDS *will* kill you."

"I'm not queer."

"You don't have to be to get it, you idiot," she spat. "This is New York, Richie, not middle America. You grew up here, you know how things go."

"So you're throwing me out?"

"In a way," she kissed his cheek. "In the Air Force, you had a sense of honor and pride, you lived by a code. I've been watching all that slip away since you've been home. I know you, Richie, better than anyone else knows you, better than you know yourself."

"So, what do you want me to do?"

"Stop drinking so much, stop smoking pot, and make some new friends. Get an apartment and find a nice girl," Maria said. "I will always be here for you and this will always be your home but living here is not good for you."

"So, this is thirty days' notice," he growled.

"Don't be an idiot," she hissed back. "But you know I'm right."

"Yeah," he replied, and she let him into his room where he shut the door, turned on the stereo, and promptly rolled a joint. He took a long hit and slumped back on his bed, holding in the smoke as he tossed the joint into the ashtray. "She *is* right," he said aloud, the smoke released with the words. Looking back over the years, he realized she usually was.

"And here I am," he looked around his room, the same room he occupied before he enlisted. "And I'm that same kid who lived here then. I joined the Air Force, became my own man, loved a good woman, and now I'm a teenager again. I just *look* older."

He was not happy with the direction his life was taking, but he didn't see anything he could do about it. Rick was making enough working at an independent automobile repair shop and enjoyed his job and the people he worked with, but his future was strictly blue-collar. Eventually he would find a woman to settle down with and he would continue his blue-collar existence until he retired or died, whichever came first.

"I *do* have to find my own place," he agreed. It was difficult to bring women here. While Rick loved his mother, living in her home afforded little privacy and was generally accompanied by an interrogation of the woman he was with at the time. "But then, I have yet to meet a woman here I'd even consider marrying."

There had been none with whom he'd even felt the pangs of love, none that he'd felt anything near what he felt for Yung Shu, and a tear fell from his cheek when he thought of her. He relit the joint and took another hit. "I should have married her when I had the chance."

Epstein and Associates, New York, New York

Connie could barely keep the smile from her face. She'd received her grades from school, and she'd passed her last year with brilliance. The next step was to take the New York State bar exam and she was confident the result would be the same. That confidence came from working at Epstein and Associates, learning from their team of accomplished partners and crack associates. Chaim Epstein himself took to writing her performance reports and today he'd called her into his office just before quitting time.

"I have been informed of your final grades by Dean Shapiro," Epstein said in his thick Israeli accent. "I would like to think your internship here has something to do with it."

"I couldn't have done it without the help everyone here has given me, Mr. Epstein," Connie beamed.

"It is a pleasure having you here," he nodded. "And you have shown a talent for investigation. I would like to offer you a position, Connie," Epstein continued. "I spoke with the partners and they are in agreement. Your potential is a resource we would like at our disposal and you play a critical part in our long-term plans. Would you be interested?" Epstein gave her a knowing smile. There was no way she could turn it down, *anyone* in her position would accept an opportunity such as this. "We would be willing to pay you this to begin, until you pass the bar of course." He pushed a folded piece of paper across the desk.

Fifty thousand dollars, she thought, nearly falling off the chair. "I would be honored ... I *am* honored you regard me so highly." Her eyes kept going back and forth between the paper and the grandfatherly Epstein.

"We do, Connie," he stood and offered a hand. "Welcome aboard."

"Thank you, sir," she shook it firmly, wanting to scream with delight.

The Kremlin, Moscow, Soviet Union

"It is working," Kosarev said as he entered Gorbachev's office, tossing a magazine on the desk. "The Americans love you."

"*Time* magazine has voted me Man of the Year?" Gorbachev was pleased and astonished at the same time.

"They trust you," Kosarev went on. "They see you as the one that will send the Communist Party to its eternal sleep."

"The economy is in ruins, Yevgeniy," Gorbachev replied. "The time is not yet right. The economic situation has to be repaired before the Party is dissolved."

"When, Mishka?" Kosarev asked him. "You've had two years."

"Ah," Gorbachev waved it away. "Spies and soldiers," he spat. "You don't want the politicians telling you how to run your operations, yet you want us to listen when you tell us how to run ours? The Old Guard is still well entrenched in the Politburo, my friend, and we still have to meet with the Americans and the Israelis later this year. If we want cooperation, we cannot present a fractious Union to the West."

"How long," the Chairman of the KGB demanded.

"Four years," Gorbachev declared. "It will take four years for the reforms to take effect, provided we can implement them with minimal opposition."

"Four years, Comrade," Kosarev said with raised index finger. "We have fallen too far behind the Americans and soon they will have an insurmountable lead."

"We cannot do it without money and that is what they have more than any other," Kosarev informed him. "The economy first, Yevgeniy," Gorbachev said. "And *then* we will be able to save Mother Russia."

"Four years," Kosarev said again. "And *no* longer."

Wantagh Train Station, Wantagh, New York

The grin on her face remained as she left work, during the commute on the railroad, and now as she sat in her car at the Wantagh train station, two hours later. "Well so much for my worries about repaying my student loans." Connie laughed aloud at that. "And maybe I can afford to move out of my parents' house."

But that was not a necessity right now. What *was* necessary was to mark this most fortuitous confluence of events with a party, a big one. Another wonderful coincidence was that her parents were in the Catskills for two weeks and she had the house all to herself.

Chapter Twenty-Two
Civil Court of the City of New York, Part IX, New York, New York
8 April 1988

"I can't even make love to my wife," Woodrow Madison said from the stand. "I have no feeling in my privates thanks to their negligence." He pointed to the defense table, occupied by two executives of the IGA supermarket chain and their attorney.

"I have no further questions, Your Honor," his lawyer said before taking his seat.

"My sympathies to your wife," Connie Wasserman said, throwing a knowing look to the jury and the court. "But could it be, Mr. Madison, that the lack of ability to make love to your wife could mean a lack of *desire* on your part?"

"I love my wife," Madison spat back.

"Well if you loved her, sir, you shouldn't consort with prostitutes," Connie said casually and let it hang.

"I object, Your Honor," the plaintiff attorney was on his feet. "Ms. Wasserman has no basis …"

Connie went back to the defense table and picked up two envelopes. One she tossed in front of her opponent, the other she handed to the judge. "This is defense exhibit eight, Your Honor," she said. "These photos document Mr. Madison leaving his home in the Beach section of Brooklyn at approximately eight p.m. last night and driving to Long Island City in Queens. At eight forty-five, approximately, Mr. Madison is shown soliciting the services of a known prostitute."

"I object again, Your Honor," the plaintiff attorney shouted again after consulting his notes. "The woman in the picture is a cousin of Mr. Madison. He was giving her a ride home."

"I have a copy of an arrest report stating the woman in question was arrested just two nights ago on prostitution and pandering charges. She might be your cousin, sir, but she's a hooker too," Connie did not take her eyes from the plaintiff attorney. "Is her home the Kew Motel in Kew Gardens, Queens?" Connie shot back. "And I have *many* cousins, Mr. Moskowitz," she went on. "We *never* get *this* friendly."

She'd taken a picture from the evidence packet not included in Jay Moskowitz', showing a hooker with Madison's erection in her mouth, and propped it on the easel in front of her opponent, the young man who'd proposed to her almost four years ago.

"Now, Mr. Madison," Connie turned back to him. "It certainly seems to me," she looked at the picture appraisingly. "That you have *full* feeling in your privates, judging by the look on your face." Connie looked up at the judge. "Your Honor, the defense moves to have this case dismissed and Mr. Madison arrested for conspiracy to defraud. Also, Your Honor, the defense requests the court invoke sanctions against the plaintiff firm of Moskowitz, Finkel, and Kaplan for aiding Mr. Madison in his conspiracy."

"I'll consider the sanctions, Ms. Wasserman," the judge said. "But this case is dismissed." He rapped his gavel and looked to one of the uniformed personnel. "Will one of the court officers take Mr. Madison into custody pending the filing of charges with the District Attorney's office?" One of the burly New York City COs took him by the arm.

"No, you can't do this," Madison howled. "You fucking *bitch*. I'll *kill* you." He went to lunge at Connie, but the court officer disabled him with a crack from his baton.

"I'll stop at the DA's office and proffer charges," she said to the judge.

"You're a sharp one," Jay said to Connie after Madison was hauled away. "We could have made a good team."

"Representing slime like that?" She laughed. "I seriously doubt it."

"Are you married yet?"

"I didn't realize it was a race, Jay," Connie said as she packed her briefcase.

"I've got two kids and a house in Locust Valley," he said. "You could have been part of that."

"I'm still living with my parents," she replied proudly. "And I'm glad you *can't* list me as one of your possessions," she added with a hiss.

"Whatever," he shrugged. "I'd caution you not to go through with the sanctions," Moskowitz said as he turned. "It might not be good for business."

"I'll pass it on to Mr. Epstein," she said, pushing past him.

Connie made it out of the courthouse twenty minutes later after corralling Manhattan Assistant DA, Anthony Cippoletti and advising him that IGA would be pressing charges against Woodrow Madison. "Yes," she breathed as she hailed a cab. It was her first case in the lead chair, and she'd destroyed the plaintiff's credibility convincingly. "I'm not just an attorney," she said as the cab pulled over. "I'm a *good* one."

Queens Village, New York

"Honey," Doreen McCormick whined as she came into the bedroom. "Get dressed."

"Why," Johnson replied lazily. They'd just finished some outstanding sex when the phone rang.

"A friend of mine is having a party tonight," she said as she began her shower.

"Not insurance people again," Rick growled. "Jesus, all they talk about is lawsuits and negligence." Doreen was in the insurance business, a subrogation person for a niche corporation of which there were many in New York.

"Just come on," she urged. "I've told her about you and now I can show you off."

"Aw Jesus, Doreen, can't we just stay home and fuck?"

"Is that all you want me for?" She hissed.

"You say it like it's a bad thing," Johnson said as he stood and came over to her, kissing her lips. "What kind of clothes do I have here?"

"I washed some of your jeans the other day," she said as she stepped into the shower. "Look in the drawer."

This was Doreen's apartment; Rick had almost forgotten what his looked like. And although her sexual skills were excellent, and the blonde was very easy on the eyes, the relationship was mostly one of convenience for him. She lived a mere two blocks from his job and the bar they both hung out in was almost exactly between them. It was where they met a little over six months ago. Not the brightest bulb, she annoyed him with her inane prattling most of the time, but there was the convenience of the situation. "Where is this party?"

"At Buttle's," she called over the running water. Former New York Jet, Greg Buttle owned the place just off Hempstead Turnpike.

"I have to go all the way to East Meadow to party?" Rick called back, yanking a pair of Levi's 501 jeans, a sleeveless t-shirt, and a leather vest from the drawer. He dumped the clothes on the bed, joining her in the shower.

"Get away," she giggled as he grabbed for her. "We'll never get there."

"That's the idea."

"We *have* to go," she insisted and stepped out. Doreen dressed in leather pants topped only with a camisole under a leather jacket and he looked at her appraisingly when he got out.

"Are you sure we can't stay home," he said hungrily.

"No," she said as she watched him stiffen. Doreen dropped to her knees in front of him. "If I do this, will you go willingly?"

"Yup," he grinned, and she took him in her mouth.

Buttle's, East Meadow, Long Island, New York

"They look like fucking lawyers," Rick growled when they walked in. He stood on the balcony overlooking the lower level of the club where the party was in full swing. He checked the two helmets with the coat girl.

"They *are* lawyers, honey. My friend's firm is our defense counsel," Doreen explained.

"If you would have told me before, I wouldn't have come," he said.

"I know," she smiled and led the way down the steps.

Johnson felt out of place among these yuppies, the mutant bottom feeders who made their money on people's despair. They were all so well-groomed, neatly trimmed hair and moustaches, the shoes with the little tassels on them, he wanted to puke. He and Doreen stood out in this crowd for most of the women here were in business suits as well. They drew stares, but almost all withered under his gaze. Rick did look menacing, having avoided the barber and the razor since he'd separated from the Air Force. His brown hair hung midway down his back and the full beard was of a length to bring the members of *ZZ Top* to mind.

"*There* she is," Doreen squealed with delight, a sound that Rick swore could deafen a dog in a second.

"Where?" Rick paid little attention to her, looking over the room instead, first for threats as his Special Forces training taught him, and then for the beautiful women. One with dark hair and dark eyes caught his eye immediately. The impeccably tailored business suit betrayed her well-endowed form.

"There," she pointed, and Rick realized they both were watching the same woman.

"The one with the tits?" He confirmed.

"I thought you'd like her," Doreen smiled knowingly. The person in question noticed them and changed her course.

"Hi, Doreen," Connie Wasserman said when she approached. "Is this him?" She looked Rick over.

"Rick Johnson, this is Connie Wasserman," Doreen made the introductions.

"You need a haircut," Connie said in a husky voice that Johnson found he couldn't get enough of.

"Nice to meet you too," he smiled. "What's the occasion?"

"I won my first case today," she told him, her eyes remained locked on his.

"Congratulations," he replied. "I guess you're one of *them*." Connie laughed at that.

"Yes, I'm a lawyer." She couldn't tell if he was kidding or not, but he intrigued her. Connie expected the biker type, Doreen favored them for some reason, but he wasn't like the others she'd met. She could see the intelligence in his eyes, and she believed there was a handsome man hidden under all that hair. Her friend could have done worse. As she considered him, she saw something else in those eyes also. She saw the same look in her father's eyes when he told her his stories of flying B-17s over Europe during World War Two, knowing he was sanitizing them for her benefit. *I'll bet you can tell those same kinds of stories, hairy man.* She was certain this man had done and seen things civilized people never should.

"Ah, we all have our faults," he said. "Nice party."

"Thanks," she smiled as they walked to the bar. "You're direct."

"See," Rick smiled. "As a lawyer you can't appreciate that. With me, everybody knows where they stand. With lawyers, you can never tell. Give me a shot of Jack Daniel's and a Molson," he said to the bartender.

"I get the feeling you don't like me," Connie said.

"Then feel again, my dear," Rick smiled. "If all lawyers looked like you, I might even start a fan club."

"I'm going to the ladies' room," Doreen said, essentially ignored since Rick and Connie shook hands. She reached into his pocket and snatched his vial of cocaine before leaving.

"You're a funny guy," she smiled back as their drinks came, watching him toss back the shot, savoring the flavor. "Aren't you going to chase it?" Connie asked him as she sipped her vodka on the rocks. She made a face, imagining how the bourbon must taste.

"I'm a purist, Connie," he said, lighting a cigarette before going on. "I like the taste of Jack Daniel's and I don't like messing it up with anything. The beer is to quench my thirst, *not* to chase my bourbon."

She fished one out of her purse and he lit it for her. "Thanks. What is that; the World According to Rick?"

"I know what I like," he told her with a smile, finally taking a sip of his beer. "Do you feel better now?"

"Yes, much," she shuddered involuntarily. "I guess you don't drink anything else?"

"Nope. Are you married?"

"That's out of left field," she said.

"Hey, you're a beautiful woman and I'd like to get to know you better. Asking for your number in front of Doreen would have been a little tacky, don't you think?"

"Asking me for my number while you're dating my friend is tacky whether she's here or not," she told him.

"What if I break up with her?"

"What if I tell Doreen?"

"So? You don't see a ring on my finger, do you?"

"Don't you care?" She asked him.

"Look, Doreen is okay, but we both know that she's an airhead coke fiend. Call me a bastard, but to have an opportunity with a woman like you is worth cutting her loose."

"And what is to say that you wouldn't dump me for another when you got tired of me?"

"So, you'll go out with me?"

"No, I was speaking hypothetically," another smile.

"Then hypothetically, counselor," Rick said. "Any man who would get tired of a beautiful, multi-faceted woman such as yourself would be a fool."

"You're a serious bullshit artist," she laughed.

"I guess we'll never know then," Rick shrugged. "Your loss."

"*My* loss?"

"Of course, my dear. I'm a hell of a guy."

"That's what Doreen says," Connie told him.

"I know."

"Confident, are you?"

"Yes, ma'am. If I have faith and confidence in anything, it's me."

"Well, I hope you and Doreen are very happy."

"You'll be sorry," he said with a smile. "One day, I'll cut my hair and put on a suit, maybe you'll change your mind."

"Do you even own a suit?"

"Don't judge a book by its cover, counselor," Rick warned and went to stand. Another man muscled in between he and Connie. "You might be missing an entertaining novel."

"Hey, man," the young lawyer said. "This is a *private* party."

"Who the fuck are *you*?" Johnson growled.

"It's all right, Mike," Connie said to one of the junior partners of Epstein and Associates. "He's a guest."

"What are you doing hanging around with riffraff like this, Connie?" Mike Porter asked her. "The partners all want to talk to you."

"You're drunk, Mike," she said. "Leave it alone."

"Riffraff?" Johnson asked, amazed that the skinny yuppie even considered talking to him like that.

"You heard me, Neanderthal man."

"Mike, no ..." Connie didn't get to finish.

Johnson spun him around and cracked him across the jaw. He went to swing back but failed to retain conscious thought and his legs buckled under him. "Yuppie scum," Rick spat.

"Very good, asshole," Connie said. "You just punched out one of my bosses."

"Sorry, but he asked for it," he shrugged as people began milling around.

"What happened?" Someone asked.

"Mike had a little too much to drink," Connie told them and then turned to Rick. "Help me with him."

"Why?"

"Because I *said* so," she hissed.

Rick picked him up and put him on his shoulder. "Where to?"

"Take him to my car," Connie ordered.

"Lead on," he gestured with his free hand.

"Nice bike," Connie said when she saw the chopped, raked, and flamed Triumph Bonneville parked at the curb.

"Thanks," Rick said as they passed it.

"That's *not* yours," Connie stopped and turned back to it.

"Yes, it is; built it myself," he said proudly. "If you like cars, I have a '70 Chevelle SS too."

"I love riding," she told him.

"See what you're missing out on," he smiled.

"That's obvious," she said. "You're a bully." Connie continued the walk to her car.

"I didn't start it," Rick said as he dumped his charge in the passenger seat. "Tell butt-boy here to keep his mouth shut unless he's prepared to back up his bullshit."

"You're *not* impressing me, Rick."

"I didn't think I had a chance anymore," he shrugged.

"You don't strike me as the type of man who takes no for an answer."

"If a woman tells me no, then it's no. Have you changed your mind?"

She reached in her purse and pulled out a card. "Call me when you're free of your obligations," Connie smiled. "Maybe you can take me for a ride?"

"Does Doreen count as an obligation?"

"She's the biggest one," Connie told him. "I won't go *anywhere* with you behind her back."

"Well what do you know, a lawyer with principles," Rick laughed.

"And I won't go anywhere with you if you do drugs."

"Understood," Johnson said with a nod.

"Make sure you dump the coke when you dump Doreen."

"But you just don't want me to dump her on your account."

"If she makes you as miserable as you say, you *shouldn't* be with her in the first place. It's not fair to you and it's *certainly* not fair to her. In case you didn't notice, she's looking for a husband and if you're not willing to fill those shoes, you should get out of her way,"
Connie informed him.

"Are you looking for one too?"

"Are you proposing?"

"No," he laughed.

"When I get married, it will be to the right one," Connie said.

"Does Mr. Right ride a motorcycle and fix cars for a living?"

"I never pictured him that way," she smiled. "And you're moving awfully fast. I only consented to letting you give me a ride."

"She just wants me for my bike," he kidded. "*Letting* me? You're *dying* to take a ride."

"And you just want to feel my tits against your back while we're riding," she whispered.

"That would be nice, but I want you for *so* much more," he grinned.

"Remember what I told you," she wagged a finger at him as she got in the driver's side of the car. "Clean up your life."

"Is that a promise?"

"No promises," she said. "Call it friendly advice."

"Fine," he replied as she drove away. "Now that's one hell of a woman," Johnson said aloud as he walked back to the bar.

***

He lay in bed, Doreen's breathing regular and shallow beside him. They had sex when they got back to her place and she fell asleep directly. Conversely, Rick was wide-awake, thoughts of the beautiful attorney meandering in his mind. He felt foolish now, acting like some hard up fifteen year old in front of the woman, willing to agree to anything in order to take her out.

What in Hell would she want with me, he asked himself. *I probably amused the shit out of her.* And it was an epiphany of sorts. He had nothing to offer her, earning three hundred bucks a week; Rick was in the same boat he was when he left the Air Force a little over two years ago. Aside from having a few more clothes and a motorcycle, his situation was unchanged.

She must make seventy-five grand a year and she's just starting out. In ten years, she'll be clearing a hundred and fifty and I'll be making thirty. While Connie Wasserman seemed to be everything he wanted in a woman, she was out of reach. *Don't I know about that?* Accessible now, she would outgrow him soon enough. He could only slow her down. *It's not the kill . . .* but he couldn't play that game with her. If he won her, he would never want to let her go, of that he was sure. And he was unsure his heart could take the letdown when she came to her senses and left him.

I'm not in her league, he thought and shrugged, rolling over and getting comfortable. Now that he'd made up his mind about the attractive lawyer he could sleep, even though it was the first time he'd admitted defeat before he even tried. *I guess it's time to start fighting the battles I can win.*

Chapter Twenty-Three
Mineola, Long Island, New York
21 May 1988

"Hello?" Rick answered the ringing phone, wondering who might be calling him at eight a.m. Most of his friends were still comatose at this time on the weekend.

"For a guy who was determined to get my number, I figured I'd hear from you sooner," Connie said without preamble. "Doreen said you broke up with her a little over a month ago."

"I changed my mind," he said. "How'd *you* get my number?"

"I'm a lawyer, I know how to get phone numbers," she said, sounding a bit disappointed. "What do you mean, you changed your mind?"

"I realized I was reaching a bit high," he told her. "Sorry about that night, for your boss, and for my pestering you."

"So that's *it?* You didn't strike me as having confidence problems," she countered.

"Look, I realized your boss was right just before I punched him out," Rick said. "You don't need to be hanging around with guys like me. You can do a lot better."

"Suppose I think you might be worth the effort?"

"Save your energy for the courtroom, honey," he replied. "I'm the boy your mother warned you about, you don't need the hassle."

"Fine," she hissed. "Will you still take me for a ride?"

"No."

"You can be a prick when you want to be, can't you?"

"Okay, okay, I'll pick you up at your place in a couple hours," he surrendered. "Where do you live?"

"Do you think I'm going to tell you where I live?"

"I won't rob your house."

"My parents' house," she corrected. "And I know you won't rob them, but my father would kill both of us if he saw me getting on a motorcycle. I'll meet you at your place in an hour."

"I suppose you know where I live."

"I know Mineola."

"Did you run me for warrants and priors too?"

"You've got a couple unpaid parking tickets in the Bronx and a speeding ticket in Suffolk that you should clear up," she laughed.

"I'll see you in an hour and a *half*. I want to make sure the bike doesn't quit while we're out and I have to walk to a phone, or are you going to have us followed?"

"No," she said. "I've received good references." She gave another laugh. "See you then."

"This is *not* good," he said as he hung up. He picked up her card that lay right next to the phone, looking at the number he'd wanted to call many times since he broke up with Doreen. After six weeks, he was just about to throw the card in the trash. "And she had to call now."

He'd known if he called her, he would want her; hell, he wanted her now, but he would never want to let her go. Having known the love of beautiful, intelligent women, he could never bear to go through the loss of it again. "It'll just be a ride," he said. "Nothing more."

But would he ever have the opportunity to meet a woman like her again, someone who had the chemistry, the total package of looks, poise, and brains to consume his fantasies and dreams? He'd only known her for an hour, and she'd got him thinking about the future again after all these years, about a real relationship and commitment.

And it was a different feeling than he had when he first met Yung Shu, she'd stimulated different parts of him, or the same parts in different ways; he didn't know, but he knew he could fall for Connie if he'd let himself and if she were willing. "Then why did she call?" And he laughed. "She wants me for my bike."

***

Connie pulled her Hyundai into his driveway and saw him coming out the side door, dressed almost the same as the night she'd met him. She noticed he'd shaved the beard away, leaving only the moustache, and she smiled. "Did you shave for me?" She said when he opened the door.

"I was hoping to get a rise out of you," he said with a smile. "It's good to see you again."

"You have a handsome face; you shouldn't hide it."

"It's the makeup," he kidded. "What are you doing driving this puddle jumper? I figured lawyers drove BMWs or Mercedes Benz'."

"Jews don't drive German cars, at least my family doesn't," Connie said. "Besides, I only drive it to the station."

"Well then you'd better stay away from my mother, she has a microwave that seats six," he said casually, noting the look of horror on her face. "I'm kidding," he chuckled. "But she *is* German, right off the boat from the Fatherland. So, *your* mother's gonna *love* me, right?"

"I don't think she'd get past the hair to find out if you were German or not." She looked at him and shook her head. "You're a piece of work, you know that?"

"You got that right, ma'am," Rick said with a nod. "Care for a cup of coffee?"

"I'd rather get on the road," Connie said, wondering about his strange sense of humor.

"As you wish, Madame," he smiled, handing her a helmet. "Do you know how this works?" He went to help her with the chinstrap.

"I've been on bikes before," she said, turning away from him.

"Fine," he threw up his arms in surrender. He got a look from her when he donned his helmet, a replica of the German Army steel helmets of World War Two. A pair of aviator goggles went along with it. Rick gave her a grin. She shook her head but couldn't keep back the smile.

"What did I get myself into?"

"Just a ride, Connie," he said, smiling as he threw his leg over the bike and kicked it to life. "Get on." She did. "Oh, by the way," he added. "This is a hard tail, there's no suspension in the rear."

"*Wonderful*," she groaned as she put her arms around his waist and held on tightly.

"Perfect," he smiled as he felt her ample, firm breasts against his back.

"Where are we going?"

"Do you like seafood?" He asked, dropping the bike in gear.

"I thought this was just supposed to be a ride."

"I lied," he smiled and looked back at her, her face inches from his. She was smiling too.

"Yes, I like seafood," Connie said over the noise of the engine.

"Good."

"Where are we going?"

"Montauk," he replied. "We should just be getting there around lunchtime." He let out the clutch and blipped the throttle, the Triumph moving into traffic with ease.

***

"Do you mind if I order lobster?" Connie asked him sheepishly. "It's a weakness of mine."

"My mother says you shouldn't take someone out if you aren't prepared for them to order anything they want on the menu," he smiled as their drinks came. They'd gone for a walk out on the beach at Montauk Point and then stopped at a roadside seafood shack in the town of Amagansett.

The walk had taken them several hours, though they hadn't planned it that way. They talked about everything, from his love of science and engineering to auto racing, the first woman he'd ever met who'd enjoyed it. She told him about the nuances of the law and her strategies in the courtroom and he actually was intrigued. Her recount of how she ambushed Woodrow Madison to win her first case won

Rick's admiration. He found he could listen to her for hours and that's what he did. The sun was on the downside of the sky by the time either of them thought to check a watch.

The idea of a late afternoon early dinner seemed natural to both of them and they continued their conversation stopping only to order drinks quickly. They felt as if they'd been friends for years.

"A good philosophy," she agreed as she raised her vodka and grapefruit juice. "It avoids embarrassment."

"Agreed," he clinked his shot glass against hers. "You don't mind if I drink and drive, do you?"

"Do I have a choice?"

"No." He tossed the shot back and she shivered involuntarily again, causing him to laugh. "Are you going to do that every time I have a shot?"

"You mean there will be a next time?"

"If you want," he said.

"You didn't want to come out *today*. You didn't want anything to do with me."

"I told you," he said as he took a sip of his beer. "Don't judge a book by its cover."

"I thought people knew where they stood with you? I don't."

"You're different."

"How?"

"Never mind."

"No," she grasped his arm. "How?"

"Have you ever been in love?"

Connie paused to consider that her dark eyes resting on his. "I don't know."

"Well, I have," he said wistfully. "And I know how it feels to say goodbye to someone you love."

"So what does that have to do with me?"

"You're special, Connie. At least, you are to me." He caught the look she gave him. "Yeah, I might be a little nuts, but I told you, I know what I like and you've got a lot of things I like."

"So, what's the problem?" She said this with a Yiddish accent, and he smiled.

"I don't want to have to say goodbye to you someday. I don't want this to get started so it doesn't have to end. Do you understand that?"

"You said something about reaching a bit high," Connie said as she sipped her drink.

"Well, yeah," he said. "Look at you. You're a lawyer in a ritzy-titzy firm and I'm just an auto mechanic with a bad attitude. I'm just a bit dangerous to you and you're curious because you're an over achiever and you only dated nice boys through high school and college. Nice Jewish boys who your mother would want you to marry," he added.

"They weren't *all* Jewish," she told him.

"My point is that you're just at the beginning of a career and I've shot my load, so to speak," Rick said. "I'm gonna be a mechanic until the day they put me in the ground but you'll end up like your boss, probably owning your own firm with a nice house on the North Shore, the two and a half kids, and the stone fence with a couple Volvos in the driveway. In a few years, I'll just be baggage."

"Do you think so little of me to believe that I would discard the love of my life like an old suitcase?" And she realized that their eyes were locked once again. They'd been doing that all day and she felt the same things he did. She'd enjoyed his company and his straightforward attitude. He was up on current events and showed a love of the political system and his country. Connie could picture herself with him in the big house with the stone fence and she was feeling things she didn't think she would. "If I *were* to marry someone, they would *have* to be the love of my life," she explained and looked away. She didn't want him to get the wrong, or right, idea. *Not yet anyway*, she thought. "Why are we talking about marriage anyway?" She looked at her watch. "We've known each other six hours."

"So, why *did* you call me this morning?" He said with a smile as a plate of cherrystone clams on the half shell was placed in front of him.

"For the reasons you stated," she replied as she accepted the order of calamari from the waiter. Rick ordered a couple two and a half pound lobsters for them. "I'm curious, especially since you're smarter than the type Doreen usually goes for."

"I didn't go out with Doreen for intellectual conversation," he smiled knowingly.

"I'm sure," Connie chuckled. "And I saw something in your eyes that I see in my father's."

"I'm afraid to ask," he grinned as he signaled for another beer.

"Were you in the military?"

"Yes."

"What did you do?"

"Maybe when we get to know each other better," he smiled sadly. "When can I see you again?"

"What are you doing tomorrow?"

"Do you like baseball?" He said.

"I'm a *big* Met fan," she smiled.

"Well I'm glad," he smiled back. "I happen to have a few tickets to the game; the Dodgers are in town."

"How did you know?"

"Honestly, or do you want the line of self-aggrandizing bullshit I have prepared?"

"Honestly," she urged with a giggle and a playful swat.

"My dad had season tickets before he died and I held on to the subscription," Rick told her. "Pick you up around noon?"

"I'll meet you at your place," she said. "I'll have to prepare my mom for you."

"Are you already planning to introduce me? We've only known each other *six* hours," he kidded her.

"Mike Porter was right, I don't hang around with guys that look like you," Connie said. "My mother wouldn't believe you're just a friend."

"Do you consider me more than that?"

"Not yet," she teased. "But you'll know when I do." She looked up to see the waiter coming with two bright red crustaceans. "*This* is what I've been waiting for."

"Okay, so you only want me for my bike and a lobster dinner," he joked as she tore a claw loose.

***

"I can't believe we rode back in *that*," Connie laughed as they nearly broke through the door of his apartment. Perfect timing, the sky opened up as they got back on the road and driving summer rain pelted them for the seventy-five mile trip back to Mineola. Rick pushed the bike to eighty mph once he got on the Long Island Expressway, but Connie hadn't complained.

"Are you okay?" Her laughter was contagious. "I was hoping you didn't drown back there."

"The rain hurts," she said as he took her coat and handed her a towel. "How fast were you going?"

"Did I scare you?" He grinned.

"No," she smiled. "You're pretty good with that thing."

"I can fix anything from lawnmowers to jets and drive anything with wheels," he said proudly. "And a few other things that you'll find out about later on."

"I can just imagine," she said sarcastically.

"No you can't," he said in all seriousness.

"I should go."

"I'd rather you didn't," Rick came to her.

"I'm soaked to the bone and I didn't expect to be gone this long," Connie said. "I'm sure my folks are worried." She looked up at him and he kissed her, and she kissed him back passionately.

"Are you sure you don't want to stay?" He urged.

"Not tonight, handsome," she said, kissing him lightly once more. "Thanks," she breathed. "I had a great time."

"Be careful driving," he warned.

"See you at noon," she waved and ran into the rain.

This is going to get complicated quickly, he thought as he closed the door, tasting her kiss once more. *And I don't care.*

***

"Oh boy," she said to herself once she got on the Meadowbrook State Parkway. Connie hadn't lied to him; she'd had a wonderful time, the day breezing by too quickly. "I almost stayed," she said it aloud as if to confirm it to herself. "Good thing he didn't push the issue."

Connie brought her fingertips to her lips and smiled at the feeling of his moustache against them. "He's a gentleman," and it was another surprise. The wild ride down the highway on the motorcycle pumped him, she could feel it as she held onto him for dear life, feel how his muscles tensed, feel his heart beating madly in his chest, and she saw the smile on his face when she dared take a peek. And she saw it in his eyes when they got to his apartment, a fire burning there, and she also saw the hunger, something she'd never seen in a man before. And she knew he had a hunger for her, not a lust, not something so esoteric, but a hunger driven by instinct, almost as predator toward prey, and it aroused her.

There was no fear of him, and she thought him gentler than she'd anticipated, thoughtful and compassionate, but she also realized he was much more dangerous than she could have guessed. While there was passion in those eyes, that other characteristic was there as well, the look that said he'd seen and done things none should have to. "I'd hate to see him angry," Connie said to the car, thinking that Mike Porter got off easy several weeks before.

"He could have killed the skinny twerp with half the effort," Connie shook her head and understood the self-control this man had. *When a woman tells me no, then it's no*, she thought about what he'd said in the parking lot six weeks ago and he lived up to it tonight. As soon as Connie said she wouldn't sleep with him, he pushed the hunger and the adrenaline away and gave no argument. "He has principles," she smiled. *And he's a good kisser*, she thought as she drove into the rainy night.

Chapter Twenty-Four
The Kremlin, Moscow, Soviet Union
22 May 1988

"And what will you tell them, Mikhail?" Kosarev asked.

"I believe we must make the world aware of our situation and this speech will do it. If we want the West to trust our intentions when we need them to most, we have to become more straightforward," Gorbachev explained. "We will need their money, Yevgeniy Stepanovich, we need it *now*." Gorbachev, his popularity in the West growing, had been invited to speak at the United Nations in a little over three weeks.

"Reagan will take advantage if we admit to troop reductions," the KGB chief said.

"He knew we would do it when we began pulling out of Afghanistan last week," Gorbachev shot back. "He knows he's won, my friend, and he will allow us to admit defeat gracefully. You knew this five years ago."

"We don't need the Americans stirring the pot with the problems we already have in the Balkans and Armenia," Kosarev warned. "We will dissolve the Union, but it can't be torn apart, there are too many lives hanging in the balance. Look what happened when the British left India, Pakistan, and the Holy Land. We cannot allow that to happen in Europe, not if we want the support of the West."

"Then we will have to move up the timetable," Gorbachev said. "Reagan will be out of office in January and we will find a way to work with the new man."

"Bush," Kosarev declared. "Bush will win. He has Reagan's momentum, and everyone is making money in the stock market." There was a knock on the door and Lieutenant Boris Popov entered demurely.

"I beg your pardons, Comrade Secretary, Comrade General," Popov said.

"What is it, Boris?" Kosarev growled.

"There is a message from Comrade Colonel Zhukov, it is urgent."

"Tell him I am with the Secretary, Boris. I will contact him later," Kosarev barked.

"I did, sir, and he said to tell you there was news from Low Chen," Popov said and backed from the room.

Kosarev looked to Gorbachev. "I have to go."

Mineola, New York

"Do you want to grab dinner?" Rick asked her as they pulled into his driveway.

"I can't, I have to go," Connie said as he shut off the engine. "I hadn't planned to blow the whole weekend. I have a case starting tomorrow and a pile of work to go over."

"Well I'm glad you did," he said as he put the kickstand out and rested the bike. "I guess you won't have time for dinner during the week with this case and all."

"Yes I do," she smiled. "In fact, I was going to ask if you'd allow me to cook dinner for you one night."

"Here? I don't even know if the stove works. I'm a fast food junky."

"No at *my* house," she replied, handing him her helmet.

"You'll give your mother a heart attack," he joked.

"She won't be there, just my dad," Connie went to him, pulling him close. "I think he'll like you and he can give a good report to mom when she gets back from Florida." She kissed him then holding him there. "I haven't had a weekend like this in recent memory. Thanks, Rick."

"The feeling's mutual, darling," he kissed her again. "I just wish you'd stay."

"There will be time for that," she assured him. Turning for her car, she stopped. "I know what you meant yesterday," Connie said. "You're special to me too."

He waved as she drove away, watching as the car turned the corner onto Mineola Boulevard before heading in. "I want that woman," he muttered as he grabbed a beer from the fridge. She excited him, even though she dressed conservatively, tastefully, unlike most of the other women he'd known since Yung Shu, yet she had an unbelievable sexiness that made him want her even more so. And he didn't want her just for her body, but for her company, after just two days with her, he felt that something was somehow wrong when she wasn't there.

Rick felt so comfortable with her, as if he could be completely himself and she'd accept him for it. "So, she has bad taste in men," he laughed and took a healthy swallow. "Either that or she finally acquired some good taste." Another swig. "And I wonder if she tastes good," and he laughed at that. If her kisses were any indication, he would enjoy exploring the rest of her. Rick realized how stupid he sounded and knew he'd been smitten.

"Shit, she's gonna introduce me to her dad," Johnson appreciated just what he'd agreed to. "That's how it starts." And he realized Connie did feel the same way about him. He'd never believed in love at first sight and she didn't give him the impression either, but they did have chemistry. At least, that's all he'd admit to now. "And I'm gonna have to bring her home for inspection too."

Rick wasn't too worried about his mother. After all the women of the looser variety she'd seen him with in the past two years, Connie was a very big step up. "With my luck, mom will love her and then they'd gang up on me." And it was then he realized he wouldn't mind it in the least.

"But we've only known each other a couple days. Why am I thinking about all this *now*?" He took another swig of beer and stood, heading back out to put the bike in the garage. "Because I'm going to meet her dad this week," he told himself. "This is moving *far* too quickly."

Moscow, Soviet Union

    Kosarev leaned back in his chair and stared out the window, looking at nothing, thinking of his daughter and his granddaughter and glad they were far away from here. The Union was crumbling faster than he and his cohorts had planned, and they'd never planned for Gorbachev to be so popular in the West. He'd spoken with Zhukov and learned the Ukrainians, who planned to have a stockpile of nuclear warheads available in the near future, had approached the North Koreans. "Bastards," he muttered. "But they see it coming too."

    The Ukrainians could see the end was near after the losses in Afghanistan and the unrest in the Balkans, not to mention the half-hearted cleanup attempts at Chernobyl. They could see there was no money for them, and they were willing to sell their nuclear stockpile to the North Koreans for hard currency as soon as the Soviet Union collapsed. "We have to bring those weapons to Russia," he said.

    But that was not easily accomplished. Allegiances to Moscow weakened with distance and local commanders were territorial. They would not give up what they saw as a source of revenue in the coming hard times willingly. "We cannot risk civil war," he repeated to himself. "And I have to sit back and let this happen."

    He did and he would, but he still had Low Chen and that was his trump card. The meek Korean engineer was the Soviet Union's last chance to assure the nuclear balance was not upset. Soon Yat Oh, by virtue of his position, was able to give real time intelligence on Kim Sun Park's progress and that gave Kosarev some solace. He would know when the North Koreans' arsenal was about to become operational and he could deal with them then, one way or the other. Kosarev knew Gorbachev was right, and the economy was their priority. The last thing they needed at this point were the cold, hungry masses to start a revolution this winter and destroy his well-crafted plans. "We will survive this," he said with determination before leaving the office for his empty house.

Chapter Twenty-Five
Mineola, Long Island, New York
9 September 1988

"Hi," she said dreamily when her eyes opened to the smell of fresh coffee.

"Good morning," Johnson replied, handing her the mug. His eyes went to the parts of her body the sheet didn't cover. After three months, she decided last night would be when they made love, although she hadn't informed him until after dinner. And he was glad they'd waited so long, now anyway. Their relationship was not about sex, not at all, and they'd become just a little more than close friends since they met. Until last night, and he conceded once again it was worth the wait. Their lovemaking had been outstanding.

"You're the best," she said after taking a sip. "The only way you could be better is if you brought me a cigarette." She smiled warmly, for she too thought it was worth waiting for. Doreen had hinted at his expertise in bed and he'd proven it several times last night. He came back from the living room with her bag.

"I'm not sticking my hand in there," he said. "What in Hell do you keep in this thing? It weighs a ton."

"I knew I'd be spending the night," she grinned. "It takes a lot to make me pretty in the morning."

"No, it doesn't," he said honestly, taking her in as she fished through the bag that resembled luggage. She had a natural beauty and a smile that was infectious, even first thing in the morning *without* makeup. She looked up and shared that smile with him.

"You're biased but thank you."

"If I'm biased it's because I love you," he said casually, and she stopped. "What?"

"Did you hear what you said?"

"As if it isn't obvious by now," he shrugged. "I haven't been interested in anyone else since I met you and we spend almost every bit of spare time together. God, Connie, you're the best thing that's ever happened to me." He bent over and kissed her, though he felt a pang of guilt when he said that. The image of Yung Shu appeared in his mind.

"I love you too, Rick."

"That's good to know," he said with a smile as he went back to the kitchen.

"Rick?"

"Yes?"

Connie put on the robe she brought with her and followed him. "You said you were in love before."

"Twice."

"Did it feel like this?"

"Different, but they were different women," he explained. "And I was a different man."

"Do you feel comfortable with me?"

"Very," he replied. "That's one of the things I love about you. I feel as if we've known each other for years."

"Tell me about them," she urged.

"Maybe someday."

"Tell me about what you did in the military."

"Maybe someday," he grinned.

"Why not now?"

"Because I don't want to scare you off."

"Did you kill people?"

"A few," he said solemnly.

"Why did you get out?"

"They didn't like my attitude," he chuckled. "They showed me the door after six years."

"That hardly seems fair."

"The military isn't fair, Connie," Rick said. "The Air Force had something called a Quality Force Program and if you didn't follow the program exactly, you were denied reenlistment. It didn't matter how good you were at your job or anything more than the opinions of a few at the top. I guess I told too many people where to get off."

"*You?*" Connie said sarcastically. "Never," she laughed.

"They couldn't appreciate true greatness the way you can," he joined her at the table.

"You've never had an ego problem, have you?" She leaned over and kissed him.

"Nope," Rick shook his head. "I've always been able to do what I put my mind to." He gazed at her. "This is your last chance, you know."

"For what," she leaned over and kissed him.

"To come to your senses. God, Connie, you have your whole future ahead of you, what in hell are you doing with a guy like me. You could do so much better."

"*That* sounds like an ego problem to me," she chuckled.

"I'm serious," he shot back. "I don't have an ego problem because I'm with you, am I not? Or were the last three months a fantasy?"

"The last three months have been fun."

"I agree, but I'm a high school dropout with a GED diploma. You're a college grad, you work for one of the most prestigious defense firms in New York; do you think they're going to make you a partner if you're married to *me*? I punched out Mike Porter, remember?"

"Mike doesn't remember anything," she waved it away and looked at him squarely "You're more intelligent than *most* of the partners in the firm and you're one of the best engine builders in this area," she countered. "You're handsome, strong, kind and compassionate, and I feel like being in your arms is the safest place in the world for me. Are you proposing?" She elbowed him playfully.

"No," he said honestly. "But I've pictured us married. I don't know if I'm ready to take that step though."

"I don't either," she agreed with a nod. "It's a *big* step."

"Your father offered me money," a big grin crossed his face. He and Murray Wasserman had hit it off from the minute they met, both ex-Air Force, Murray a flight engineer on B-17s during World War Two, they each had a new audience for their war stories. Connie was sure that in the last three months, Rick learned things about her father that she never would and vice versa.

"To *marry* me?" Connie looked shocked.

"Yup," he took a sip of his coffee. "You're close to thirty years old and still living with your folks. The poor guy is tired of having *two* women nagging at him."

"He is *not*," she swatted him.

"So you *do* admit you nag the man, counselor," he grinned.

"I don't nag," she declared.

"I wish I had a recording device," Rick said. "I'll remind you of that statement in five years."

"Do you see us together in five years?"

"Unless you kill me in my sleep first," he joked.

"Or I *nag* you to death." She poked him in the ribs.

"That too."

"I think we should just take it as we have been for now," she became serious. "No pressure, no expectations."

"I'm not complaining," he said, going to kiss her but stopping suddenly. "We're going to continue having sex, right?"

"Most definitely," Connie grinned before kissing him. "Truthfully, I wanted to sleep with you the first time we went out."

"And you made me wait *three* months?"

"We *both* waited," she corrected. "But a good friend told me to wait until you and I became friends first."

"You're my best friend, Connie," he took her hand in his.

"You too," she gave his hand a squeeze. "Rick?"

"Yes?"

"Don't ever think I'm just spending time with you until someone better comes along, or someone my mother approves of. I'm in this all the way, for however long it lasts. Okay?"

"Okay." Rick kissed her. "She hates me, doesn't she?"

"You're an acquired taste, Johnson," she said as she ran her fingers through his hair. "She'll get used to you."

Chapter Twenty-Six
Falls Church, Virginia
24 December 1988

"Come on, Meagan Ashley," Jessica Holmgren pleaded as her almost-three year old squirmed in the seat as she tried to secure the seatbelt. "We have to get home before daddy does." The child finally relaxed, and she snapped the belt, closing the side door of the brand new Chrysler Town and Country her father bought them for Christmas. She went around front to the driver's door and that was when she saw him.

The man with the ski mask grabbed her before she could close the door and forced her across to the passenger side. "Shut up," he yelled and waved a gun at her as she screamed bloody murder. "Shut that kid up too," he ordered when the child began to wail. He started the car and drove out of the Safeway parking lot and directly to the highway, taking it north, away from the Capitol.

"I have a few hundred dollars in cash," Jessica offered. "Please take it and let my daughter go."

"Shut up," he growled before backhanding her.

Jessica brought a hand to her lip and saw she was bleeding, though she didn't feel pain above her terror. When the man pulled over, she saw they were in a densely wooded area. "What are . . ."

"Get out," he ordered, and she did, looking back to the child. He came around the van and pushed her to the back roughly, forcing her to open the rear gate. Pushing her down in the cargo area, he ripped her coat open and then her shirt, all the while keeping the gun trained on her head. "Take off your jeans," and she did as she was told.

"Just don't hurt Meagan," she sobbed as he opened his own trousers, exposing his rigidity. The assailant pushed himself inside her roughly, forcing her to cry out at every stroke. She went numb then, barely noticing when he flipped her over and forced himself into a more private place, only the tiny yelps of pain escaped her lips with each trust.

Jessica could hear her daughter crying over her attacker's grunting as he neared release, filling her a second later. He dismounted and she attempted to turn her head, to plead for her daughter's safety once more, but it would never happen. She didn't hear the two pops from his pistol, nor did she feel the two lead slugs smash through the back of her skull into her brain. Another shot followed and the child remained quiet as well.

The man walked to the edge of the dirt road as another car approached and came to a stop. "Is it done," Hector Reynaldo asked.

"She had two hundred and fifty bucks and a bunch of credit cards," he waved the wallet he'd taken from Jessica's purse. "You wanted it to look like a robbery, right?"

"Fine, just get in," Reynaldo said and turned the car around. He saw the semi-nude body in the back of the minivan and could see his man had been thorough. Leaving the scene quickly, Reynaldo took the man back to Anacostia and pulled over next to an alley dark enough for his purposes. "End of the ride, my friend," Hector said.

"Thanks for the lift," the hired attacker said. "Where's my jack?"

"Right here," Hector raised his silenced pistol and shot the man between the eyes before opening the door and pushing him out on the curb.

Islip, New York

"Merry Christmas, Connie," Maria Johnson said, handing her an elegantly wrapped box. "Have you ever celebrated Christmas before?"

"I've had Christmas dinner with some of my Christian friends previously, Mrs. Johnson," Connie said, opening the package to reveal a beautiful sweater that Maria knitted herself. "It's gorgeous."

"I wish you'd call me Maria," Rick's mother said as she put her arm around the younger woman.

"I know you've told me before, but I'll get with the program one day. Thanks, Maria." Connie replaced the sweater and picked up a light blue bag. "I got something for you, too."

"From Tiffany's?" Maria appraised the bag with a raised eyebrow before looking at her son. "Why haven't you married her yet?"

"I'm slowly letting her see the real me, so I don't scare her off," Rick joked.

"If your hair didn't scare her, your personality won't," his mother observed, looking to Connie. "I can't believe you go out in public with him looking like that." Rick gave them a face as they had fun at his expense, but he was glad Connie and his mother got along well. They didn't always agree, especially when it came to him, but they could discuss things calmly and intellectually and come to some sort of agreement. Rick knew now how Connie's father felt with a couple women telling him what to do all the time.

"It isn't much," Connie said as Maria opened the box that contained a crystal paperweight in the shape of an apple, a view of the New York City skyline etched into it. "But I know how you love crystal."

"She does?" Rick said.

"Men," Connie groaned as she indicated the cherry wood cabinet containing his mother's rare crystal collection.

"I just thought it was pretty glass shit," Rick shrugged, and the women rolled their eyes.

"What are you doing with *him* anyway?" Rick's mother asked Connie. "I've known him all his life and he can be such an idiot. Couldn't you find someone better."

"*Ma*," Johnson looked shocked. "Jesus Christ." He shook his head.

"You're such a nice girl, Connie," Maria went on with a smile and Connie broke into laughter.

"It's a good thing I love you, Rick. Your mother won't even give you a good reference."

"He's good to have around the house though," Maria said. "He can fix anything."

"I need a beer," Rick threw up his hands and walked into the kitchen.

"You're the best thing that's ever happened to him," Maria whispered when Rick was out of earshot. "He needs a woman with a firm hand."

"You raised him well, Maria," Connie replied. "He's a good, kind man."

"I tried, but his father spent all his time with the business. Richie was wild when he was a teenager and I couldn't control him."

"You did fine," Connie put her arm around the woman she'd come to consider a close friend. "And the military built on what you did. I intend to polish him the rest of the way."

"So you *are* getting married?"

"He hasn't asked me yet," Connie said. "But we're in no rush. I don't think he planned to fall in love again." And then Connie got curious. "Did you ever know any of the other women in his life?"

"There was Sabine, of course. She's a nice girl and I was hoping they would end up getting together, but the distance …"

"She's German?"

"Yes, my oldest friend's niece," Maria replied. "But they lost contact when Richie went into the Air Force." She shook her head sadly. "I don't know of any others he cared about; I saw him with a few of the little chippies he liked but that's all."

"Chippies?" Connie chuckled.

"You know, sluts," Maria said. "I'm glad he got some sense when he met you."

"I thank you, Maria," Connie kissed her cheek. "I'm glad he did too."

Georgetown, D.C.

"They found the van, Senator," Ernie LaTour's chief of staff said as he entered; the man looked shaken. Holmgren and Latour turned to face him. "I'm ... I'm sorry, Captain Holmgren, Senator Latour, but Jessica and Megan Ashley were ... they were murdered."

Atlanta, Georgia

"This is CNN Breaking News, I'm Victoria Simpson in Atlanta. CNN has just received word that Jessica Latour-Holmgren, daughter of Senator Ernie Latour, and her three-year-old daughter Meagan Ashley were murdered earlier today in an apparent carjacking attempt. Witnesses say that Ms. Holmgren was kidnapped as she left the Safeway in Falls Church. Her Chrysler minivan was found about eighty miles outside Washington at a secluded spot in the Virginia hill country and police sources say both her body and the body of her child were inside. Both had been shot in the head and Ms. Holmgren was sexually assaulted before she was killed. There has been no comment as of yet from Senator LaTour's office. We will break into *Newsnight* in about thirty minutes when the Virginia State Police hold a press conference. More news as it happens; I'm Victoria Simpson at CNN Headquarters.

Islip, New York

"That name sounds familiar," Rick said as he shut the TV off.
"What name?" Connie asked him.
"Holmgren," Rick said. "Where do I know that from?"
"That poor woman and child, murdered on Christmas Eve," Maria observed.
"There is *no* good day for murder, ma," Rick growled.

"You know what I mean," she snapped back. "She had a family and they were all in the Christmas spirit, preparing for the holiday, and now this horrible act will always be connected with Christmas for them. Heartless bastards," she spat. "They should find the ones who killed them, put them up against the wall, and shoot them at dawn."

"Her German is coming out," Rick whispered to Connie, who grinned. "The Krauts always like to have their shootings at dawn."

"Don't be an idiot, Richie," Maria swatted her son playfully.

Chapter Twenty-Six
RAF Mildenhall, Suffolk, United Kingdom
28 December 1988

"Congratulations, Nathan," Yevgeniy Kosarev said as he stood at the door of Beu's quarters. "A command brings a promotion and such a beautiful house? Full colonels in my day lived in the same accommodations as lieutenants," the big man clapped his son-in-law on the back and gave a hearty laugh. "You're getting gray, Nathan, but that is what wives and children do to you." Beu checked outside to see if anyone had spotted the Russian, but the head of the KGB wasn't that sloppy.

"Grandpa!" Little Katie Beu came running out of the kitchen and Kosarev gathered her up in his arms. "You are old enough to remember your grandfather now?" She just nodded and put her arms around his neck, hugging him as tightly as her four-year-old limbs could muster.

"Katherine Alexandra," Alexa Beu's voice came in pursuit of the youngster. She appeared a second later. "Papa?"

"Hello, my love," he held his granddaughter in one arm and took his daughter to him with the other.

"It's good to see you again, sir," Colonel Nathan Beu, new commander of 21st Special Operations Squadron said.

"Yes, papa," Alexa said. "But it's only been three months since your last visit."

"Can't I see my two girls on a more frequent basis?" He winked at Beu. "And Saint Nicholas left something for my dear Katherine in Moscow, so I thought I should bring it."

"What is it, grandpa?"

"I left it outside, why don't you go and look," he patted her bottom as she ran for the door.

"Put a jacket and some shoes ..."

314

"I remember when you'd run into meter-deep snow in your bare feet, my dear," Kosarev wagged his finger at Alexa. "And you are none the worse for it." Katie came back struggling with a stuffed bear that was as big as she was.

"Thank you, grandpa," she reached for him and he picked her up so she could kiss him.

"You are welcome, my dear," he laughed. "And this is for her when the time comes, when it is time for the university," Kosarev said quietly to her father and mother. He pulled an envelope from his jacket.

"Papa," Alexa gasped.

"I can't accept this," Beu said. "If I open a bank account with this much ... the IRS ... *generals* don't make this much in a year."

"I understand," Kosarev took the bank draft back. "It will be waiting in Switzerland when she needs it."

"That's not necessary ..."

"Yes, it *is*, Nathan," Kosarev insisted. "What kind of grandfather would I be if I did not provide for Katherine's future when I could do so comfortably? If she does not get a good education, it will be because she does not want it, not because she cannot afford it."

"Is something wrong, papa?" Alexa could sense something weighing heavily on him.

"I told you of the changes coming within the Union when you agreed to help me bring Alexa to the West," Kosarev said to Beu.

"Yes," he nodded.

"The time of change is upon us, my children. Things will move quickly in the next few years and I do not know when I will see you again. I cannot stay long, but I had to see all of you once more," the Russian explained.

"Don't make it sound so final, papa."

"It just might be, my love," he caressed her cheek. "These are critical times; you will see that soon enough." He hugged the little girl and her mother to him. "But enough of this maudlin talk. I *know* you have some vodka in this house."

Georgetown, D.C.

They buried Jessica and Meagan Ashley next to each other that afternoon and Holmgren was finally alone in the house, the first time since the day of the murders. He'd poured himself a scotch and sat in the soft leather wingback, once owned by President Hayes, and looked upon the Capitol Dome, tinseled with a fresh dusting of snow. The ring of the doorbell surprised him, but then again it didn't. He'd given the governess the night off and he walked to the entry foyer to answer the door himself. "Hello, Hector," Holmgren said.

"What you asked has been done to your specifications," Reynaldo said.

"Indeed, it has," Holmgren poured him a brandy and pointed to a briefcase on the floor next to the umbrella rack. "And that is what I promised *you*, the specifications for the latest in the 'Keyhole' series of satellites."

Reynaldo considered him for a minute. "You play the game well, Captain Holmgren, or should I say Major Holmgren?"

"How did *you* know my promotion came through? I only heard it from my father-in-law this afternoon at the funeral," Holmgren was amazed at the depths of Reynaldo's network.

"As I said, you play the game well, you should know better than to ask that question," Hector smiled and knocked back a good portion of his brandy.

"Where is the one who did it?" Holmgren asked.

"Taking a long rest," Reynaldo chuckled and finished the drink. "You will call when you have anything of interest?"

"I always do," Holmgren smiled. Reynaldo grabbed the suitcase and left. "I always do," he said again as he contemplated his scotch. With this promotion came a new assignment at the East Asia desk at CIA. He'd proven himself over the past few years at Langley, thanks to his cooperative relationship with the North Koreans and Chinese through Hector Reynaldo. They'd fed him enough information to make Holmgren's analyses look like flashes of genius and he'd repaid them with more salient and classified information as he advanced. It was a symbiosis that profited both sides and Holmgren's murder of Quanh, the bartender/prostitute so many years ago, paled in comparison to the treasonous acts he'd committed against his country.

"But I live in Georgetown and I have more money than I know what to do with," he laughed. Ernie Latour loved his dedicated son-in-law and made certain Alan, Jessica, and Meagan Ashley wanted for nothing. There was also the fact that he would be receiving a payment on Jessica's life insurance with an amount in the millions. "Yes, I *do* play the game well."

Paulie's Tavern, New Hyde Park, New York

They'd stopped in for a drink after he picked her up at the Long Island Rail Road station, several of Rick's friends drifting in as the evening wore on. Mostly he and Connie stayed to themselves, saying hello and exchanging a few words with some of his friends, but mainly doing what they liked to do most, just sit and talk. A few times a week, they'd stop in at Paulie's to unwind before heading back to his apartment. Connie had practically moved in there since she'd stayed overnight the first time.

"We should get going," she said to him. "It's a school night," she joked.

"Well, I wanted to do this in public," Rick stammered.

"Do what?"

He reached in the pocket of his coat and pulled out a box, thrusting it at her. "I did this once before and it never came to pass. I was determined to do it in front of witnesses this time." He got down on one knee.

"You're drunk," she laughed, becoming serious when she opened the box.

"Sorry, it's the biggest I can afford," he said as he put the ring on her finger.

"You're *serious*?"

"Damn it, Connie, of *course* I am. I love you more than anything," Rick said. "Will you marry me, *soon*?"

"*How* soon?"

"We can go to the County Seat tomorrow," he offered.

"No, damn it," she said before kissing him passionately to a chorus of cheers and applause. "I'm going to be thirty years old and I've never been married. I want to be Cinderella and I want you to be my Prince Charming. I'm going to have a *real* wedding, Rick Johnson, I'll be damned if I elope. I'll marry you, but we're going to do it *right*."

"How soon," he asked this time.

"Three months," she said. "You can't spring this on people on such short notice and there are things to arrange."

"Three *months*?"

"You waited that long to sleep with me, you can wait that long to marry me," she insisted.

"What's your mother going to say?"

"She'll have a small stroke," Connie smiled. "But she's not marrying you, *I* am."

"Are you sure, Connie?"

"Are *you* sure, Rick?"

"Yes," he said as he took her to him.

"So am I," she agreed, kissing him deeply and the applause started again.

Chapter Twenty-Seven
Mineola, Long Island, New York
12 February 1989

"Is there anyone else you might want to add?" Connie asked him as she went over the guest list.

"Nope," Rick said as he cracked a beer.

"No friends from the Air Force?"

"Nope," he grabbed the remote and started scanning the channels for the NASCAR race.

"I thought people made close friendships in the military. My father still sees his friends from the war," she pushed.

"We lost touch," he waved it away. "They're all a bunch of crazy bastards anyway. Here we go," Rick found the correct channel. "I doubt your family would appreciate them. Hell, my family wouldn't appreciate them."

"Shit, Rick, half of your friends are bikers," Connie countered.

"They're sane compared to the guys I served with," he stopped and stared off into space. "But Nate Beu would get a kick out of it."

"Who's he?"

"A chopper pilot I knew, nice guy. He found a decent girl and settled down. I'm his daughter's godfather, that's if I haven't been replaced by now," Rick told her.

"You should try and find him," Connie insisted.

"We'll stick with who we have," he said with finality.

"Why don't you ever want to talk about your military career?" She asked him. "It was six years of your life, Rick."

"And I left it behind," he barked. "It was a different life and I was a different man. That life is over."

"But you want to go back, don't you?"

"What?"

"I see it sometimes, usually when we're at my folks' house and my dad starts into one of his stories. You get all glassy-eyed and this little smile crosses your face," she caressed his cheek. "Either I'm missing out on some good stories or you're thinking about a woman."

"Both," he said and gazed at her. "And I do miss it sometimes, but my life is here and now, with you. There's no point going over the past."

"Was she beautiful?"

"Yes." He was successful keeping the tear from escaping when he thought of Yung Shu. "But it was something that couldn't be."

"Am I like her?"

"Not really, except your kindness. You have that in common," he shook his head. "I don't want to talk about it anymore. It has nothing to do with our lives or our future."

Connie shrugged and went to the kitchen to make some lunch for them. He watched her go before turning back to the TV. *What will happen to fuck this up*, he thought as reflections of Yung Shu spun round his brain. *I can't go back*, he thought. *And Connie is my future.* He saw it as very bright, while still harboring concerns that he would not be able to keep her. *She has her shit too together and I don't.*

Connie was unlike any woman he ever knew, determined, self-assured, and independent in addition to her looks. She didn't need him, didn't need any man to make her what she was, and that is what appealed to him. It made him smile to think she *wanted* him.

Connie Wasserman was a woman who didn't have to settle, didn't have to marry for money, or out of desperation. If she didn't marry him, she would get other proposals; she was desirable both physically and intellectually and he was ecstatic she desired him. *I have to get my act together.* And Rick realized his soon-to-be mother-in-law was partially right. *I look as if somebody lifted up a rock and let the Wildman of Borneo loose.* "Hey, baby?" He called to the kitchen.

"Get your own beer," Connie called back. "I'm cooking."

"I'll say," he said when he walked in, sliding his arms around her waist. He bit her neck playfully.

"Get away," she pointed the knife at him. "But remember that for later. I'll be done in a little while," she smiled seductively.

"Yes, you will," Rick agreed with a lecherous laugh. "But that's not the reason I'm bothering you. Do you know anyplace I can get this mess cut?" He grabbed a handful of his hair. She dropped the knife.

"Are you *serious*?"

"I'm sure you'll want to show off the wedding pictures. Do you want me looking like *this* in them?"

"How much to you plan to cut off?"

"I figure I'll have it neatened up a bit," he was noncommittal.

"I'll make you an appointment and I'll go with you," Connie declared.

"Adult supervision?"

"Exactly," she kissed him. "Try this." Connie popped a piece of beef in his mouth.

"Excellent as always," he said, picking in the pan for another piece.

"Enough," she slapped his hand. "We'll eat in a little while."

"What about …" he grabbed her again.

"After dinner, you little hornster." She wiggled away from him.

"Don't I have to wait a half hour before exerting myself?"

"That only pertains to swimming, not sex. Now leave me alone." She kissed him again and Rick believed he was the luckiest man in the world to have loved three exceptional women in his short life.

I'm glad I found Connie last, he thought as he took another beer from the fridge. *She's the best.*

The Kremlin, Moscow, Soviet Union

"They have already overrun the government forces," Kosarev told Gorbachev and Air Defense Commander General Mikhail Lovenko. "Those barbarians are going to take that country back to the Dark Ages."

"The British gave up on those savages a century ago," Lovenko spat. "The Islamists would rather beat their woman and fuck their goats than have running water. I cannot believe how much we wasted there."

"Afghanistan is a closed chapter in the book of Soviet history," Gorbachev said as he leaned back in the ornate chair. "It is the Americans' problem now and we have more pressing concerns."

"Ah, the elections," Lovenko laughed. "Are you both getting worried?"

"Several candidates in the local races could be troublesome," Gorbachev said. "Yeltsin in particular. He has designs on Moscow and he is positioning himself."

"I will deal with Yeltsin, one way or another," Kosarev muttered.

"This cannot work if the KGB resorts to its old tricks," Gorbachev spat. "He cannot have an accident just before the election, Comrade Chairman," he lectured. "Unless you certainly want civil war."

"He is one of the people *and* a Party member in good standing since that foolishness a few years back, Mikhail Sergeyevich, he might not be satisfied to be the self-proclaimed Mayor of Moscow," Kosarev warned. "You should ask the Americans about the nuances of public opinion. Better a little prudence now …"

"*No,*" Gorbachev shouted. "I will take my chances against Yeltsin. We can have what they have someday, if not in our lifetimes, then our children's, but we cannot do it if we play by the old rules. There can be no question of impropriety or our years of planning will be wasted. Your attention should be on the dissidents in Georgia, not letting Shevardnadze make them promises of a sovereign nation."

"The dissidents are in hand; Eduard Avrosiyevich is one of them and he will keep them under control for now. And I will remind you of this conversation when they vote you out of office, Comrade Gorbachev," Kosarev said before leaving. "And I will not deal with Yeltsin as you think," he said under his breath as he walked to his waiting limousine.

Anacostia D.C.

"Why do you have to meet here?" Holmgren asked Hector Reynaldo.

"No one who'd recognize you would be caught dead down here," Reynaldo told him. "What do you have?"

"Maybe nothing, maybe everything," Holmgren shrugged. "Depending on whether your superiors are still working on their nuclear program."

"I wouldn't know what you're talking about," Hector smiled.

"They're talking about a new satellite over at NRO," Alan said. "A satellite that can detect nuclear material anywhere in the world. They're talking about building a fleet of them so they can watch almost everywhere simultaneously."

"I see," Hector fell into thought. "Did you hear about a deployment date?"

"I thought you didn't know what I was talking about," Holmgren smiled maliciously.

"Answer the question, Alan."

"I don't know, but I will find out eventually," Holmgren said nonchalantly.

"As soon as possible then," Reynaldo told him.

"I do expect some show of gratitude," Alan demanded. "When I get this, I want something more."

"As was done to your wife and child?"

"Nothing so drastic," Holmgren waved it away. "Money, my friend. The FBI is not as inept as they used to be. I will not go to jail and I will not live my life on the run. I want enough to leave the country and live happily ever after in the Far East. As you know, I have a style that has to be maintained so I need money and lots of it."

"Need I remind you we have you on tape ..."

"Need I remind *you* I am in so deep that the stupid tape doesn't matter anymore? They'll hang me for treason long before they put me away for murder one," Holmgren shot back. "And the fact that I'm gay will mean even less. If your friends want this intelligence, they'd better be willing to pay handsomely for it. We're talking millions, Hector, I'm not taking this risk for a piddly hundred grand."

"I will have to run it past my superiors," Hector said.

"Make sure it *flies*, Hector, or your superiors will have the same problems they did when they tried to build a breeder reactor," Holmgren advised. "If this new satellite comes online, they won't be able to sneak a *gram* of plutonium into the country, let alone enough to achieve critical mass. They *need* me and they're going to start paying for it."

"No man is indispensable, Major Holmgren."

"But no man is in the position I am either, Hector, and it's about time I got paid for it."

Chapter Twenty-Eight
Brooklyn, New York
15 April 1989

"Jacob," the old man grinned. "Come in, please," he coughed a bit and spat in the basin.

"Hello, grandpa," Thirty-two year old Jacob Levy said, coming to the bed and kissing the old man's cheek.

"You have that look," Rabbi Avram Levy said. Avram was old, in his nineties, and his body was failing, but his mind was still sharp. "The way your cousins look when they come to borrow money." And Avram had lots of it.

"No, grandpa," Jacob said. "My practice allows me to live comfortably. I am in need of something else."

"That's why you're my favorite, Jacob. You always had your priorities straight," Avram hacked again. "Although I would have loved to see you find a bride before I passed on. I would have loved to perform the service." The old man got wistful. "What do you need, my boy?"

"I am in need of your influence, grandpa. I want to run for the Senate next year," Jacob explained, and the old man laughed.

"From New York?" Jacob nodded. "On the Democratic ticket?" Another nod from his grandson. "Impossible, they already have a candidate who's electable. You have no name recognition, Jacob. You are an outstanding young man with solid ethics and principles, but you can't raise money, not in the amounts the party needs from a U.S. Senator. Even *with* my influence, you'll never get listed on the ballot."

Jacob's face fell when confronted with the hard, political reality. He was a lawyer, a fair one who'd struck out on his own five years before. He wasn't rich, but he was comfortable, and he felt it was time to give back. The incumbent was retiring, citing family concerns, and Levy thought it an appropriate way to fulfill his ambition for public service. He'd psyched himself up, talked it over with his parents, and they'd sent him to the Rabbi, his father's father. The grandfather who'd immigrated to America with his family from Austria just after Hitler came to power in Germany. Avram Levy was respected in the New York Jewish community, aside from being the icon of the largest congregation in the country, and his word swayed a large block of votes. Over the past forty years potential candidates learned quickly that if they wanted the Jewish vote, they would have to get Avram's support.

"That doesn't mean you can't run as an Independent," Avram raised a gnarled index finger and coughed again.

"But what kind of chance would I have?"

"All the chance in the world," Avram smiled. "With my support, of course," he added.

"But, grandpa, your health …"

A raised hand stopped him. "I might not live to see you with a family, Jacob," Avram hacked once more. "But I *will* live to see you in Congress."

Lake Success, Long Island, New York

And he stepped on the glass, and it shattered, and it was done. "You may now kiss the bride," Rabbi Robert Agin said. And Rick did.

The kiss seemed to last forever as the applause began along with the music, sufficiently loud enough to drown out his rowdy friends in the rear. *It is done and she's mine*, he thought as he heard the rabbi clear his throat. They came up for air and began their walk down the aisle as everyone stood. "It's too late to change your mind now," he said through the smile.

"I was about to say the same thing to you," Connie told him as she accepted congratulations from a guest.

He stopped halfway down the aisle and turned to her. "I love you, Connie Wasserman, and that's forever."

"I love you too, Rick," and she kissed him again.

Chapter Twenty-Nine
Moscow, Soviet Union
9 November 1989

"It has come apart," Gorbachev said as he hung his head. "It is inevitable."

"It was inevitable in 1917, Mikhail Sergeyevich," Kosarev said.

"They opened the Berlin Wall a few hours ago, that is the latest. Those stinking Germans are taking to it with picks and hammers," Gorbachev looked up to the much larger man. "The strike continues in the Ukraine, Siberia, and the Kazakh, civil war rages between Armenia and Azerbaijan, and the Baltic States are steps away from declaring independence. Is this what you envisioned, Yevgeniy Stepanovich?"

"And there will soon be a McDonald's on Gorkiy Street," Kosarev added. "It could have been much worse. We will get through this."

"And what about Georgia?" Gorbachev stood. "We have troops in the streets of Tiblisi. The Caucasus has gone the way of Eastern Europe."

"There is talk now, but they cannot stand on their own," Kosarev soothed. "But you have to keep your focus. Times are hard, but you have to continue the accelerated economic reforms. If we want to survive the next few years, we have to keep the economy going."

"There are others who would stop it, it would not take much, a large influx of currency to the banks for instance. There are those who would advocate that, Geraschenko for instance," Gorbachev warned. "Yeltsin has also become worrisome since he and Sakharov were elected to the Congress of Deputies by such a margin."

"Need I remind you about my warning at the beginning of the year?"

"He will *not* be killed."

"No, he will not be," Kosarev smiled. "To do so now would be counterproductive. We will work with him." What Gorbachev did not know was Kosarev's secret meetings with Yeltsin since he'd regained his power in the Congress. It was a matter of survival he did, for Gorbachev would not last long, a year or two at most. He was walking a fine line between Gorbachev and Yeltsin, but he had to in order to survive. While Gorbachev was in decline, he was still powerful, and Yeltsin would not come to Kosarev's aid if the General Secretary felt it necessary to crush him. "You should begin to make overtures to him Mikhail Sergeyevich. It might spare your life if he gains more popular support."

"I will consider it," Gorbachev turned back to the window. "I have much to consider."

Georgetown, D.C.

"I have to go for shots today," Venice said to him as she got out of bed. The term 'she' applied loosely in this case. Venice, one name only, began life as Carlos Lopez and as long as she didn't strip below the waist, none could have differentiated her from a natural born woman.

"You should stay at your place tonight," Holmgren said. "The senator is coming over tonight. He believes I am still in mourning and it would not do to have him see you."

"I understand, baby," Venice said as she sat before the mirror, brushing her long brown hair. She smiled as she made eye contact with him. She was nineteen and overwhelmed, and she would do anything he asked.

Holmgren found Lopez prostituting himself in a nasty little club in D.C. and made him an offer. Lopez was destitute and desperate, a transvestite with a family who didn't understand, he found himself on the streets a year ago. His father and stepmother showing him the door after catching him dressed as a cheerleader and servicing one of the football players on the high school team. Carlos' mother, still residing in Puerto Rico, was supportive of her son but finances and a thousand miles kept them separated.

Carlos had a sweet young face and a hairless body, a twink, and was desired by the family men who stopped by his corner on their way home. For twenty dollars, he'd satisfy them orally, a few minutes of anonymous, forbidden sex with a young man who dressed as a little girl. Nine months ago, Alan Holmgren offered him so much more.

There were the gifts, of cash and jewelry, and the hormone therapy followed by breast implants, it was overwhelming to the young man and he went with it. He'd wanted this long before he'd met Holmgren, always felt out of place in his own body, and his Prince Charming had given it to him. Venice loved him for it and knew that eventually Alan would allow her to get the final operation, to remove the appendage that still defined her as a man.

Venice would stay at her apartment tonight, a beautiful place in the Watergate that Alan also subsidized and read or watch TV; Cinderella waiting for her prince. She no longer sold herself, had no need to, and Alan treated her with love and admiration. Soon, after Alan deemed it appropriate, he would take her out among the powerful in Washington that were his friends. And that's what overwhelmed her. In a year, she will have gone from prostitute to one of the Washington society ladies.

Holmgren, on the other hand, had no such feelings, and no plans to give her the final operation. To him, Venice was an investment, money well spent to assure he could fulfill his desires without drawing suspicion to himself. He'd chosen Lopez carefully, a young runaway without any who cared whether he lived or died. He was a beautiful boy and an even prettier girl with the desire to be a princess. Holmgren made that dream a reality and created the beautiful girl he could be seen with, but with the parts of a boy that counted.

"That's my girl," he said, rising as well. He ran his fingers through her hair as he passed, heading for the shower.

"Mind if I join you," Venice asked him, obviously aroused as she followed.

"Of course, darling, there's no better way to start the day." Holmgren smiled as he too felt a stirring between his legs.

Chapter Thirty
Yong Hung, North Korea
22 March 1990

It was crisp and cold this morning as Major Kim Sun Park stood above the excavation. The weather finally allowed this; the horrible winds from the north came for the last time a month before and work could continue on the open hole in the ground. There were others, smaller in area but equal to the hundred-foot depth. Park's assets in the U.S. National Reconnaissance Office had imparted timely intelligence the previous year and this was his solution.

It would be called the Sung Rocket Complex when it was finished, and it would house the launch facilities for twenty-four intermediate range nuclear weapons. The missiles would be housed below ground; over a hundred feet down and away from the prying eyes of the U.S. reconnaissance satellites. Within five years, the facility would be operational and be able to deliver its lethal stores as far as Japan. Within ten years, North Korea would be once again in a position to move across the border with impunity, uniting the peninsula under one flag. The Sung Rocket complex would be North Korea's trump card, giving them the ability to hold the Americans at bay.

Park envisioned a lightning strike across the DMZ with air power; armor and infantry to follow along with a coordinated naval barrage. The missiles in the Sung Complex would be used against American bases in Japan to discourage reinforcement of their units on South Korean soil, keeping some in reserve as a threat of more destruction should surrender not be forthcoming. "The Americans would not risk nuclear confrontation over Korea," he assured himself as he watched the first of the heavy equipment move in. "I will unify the Koreas and lead them into the twenty-first century," Park declared as he walked back to his car. He had an appointment in Pyong Yang later in the afternoon.

CIA Headquarters, Langley, Virginia

"Hey, Alan," U.S. Army Lt. Colonel Jerry Duff said, dropping a satellite photo on his desk. "Look who's in Pyong Yang?"

"Oleg Zinoviev," Holmgren smiled. "Head of what is effectively the Ukrainian KGB. When was this taken, Jerry?"

"Couple hours ago. Why do you think he's there?" Duff asked. "The Soviets can't afford to subsidize the North Koreans anymore."

"Maybe he's not there on behalf of the Soviets?" Holmgren offered. "Maybe he's there on behalf of the Ukrainians? Is Zhukov still Moscow's Pyong Yang rezident?"

"As far as we know. We can't tell if Zinoviev met with him or not," Duff said.

"Who's this?" Holmgren pointed to a man to Zinoviev's right, much smaller than the Ukrainian. He wore the uniform of the North Korean People's Army, the rank of major and the badge denoting the Internal Security Division.

"We *think* it's Kim Sun Park," Duff explained. "We don't have much on their internal organization, only things we get from Chinese and Russian defectors."

"Let me make some calls," Holmgren said. "I still have some connections over there. How much do you want to bet Zinoviev is there on a sales call?"

"Nukes?"

"Maybe," Holmgren shrugged. "The North has been trying to join the nuclear club for ten years. I'll let you know more when I check a few things."

"You're the best, Alan. Thank God you did some time over there," Duff said as he took the picture. "You know how those people think."

"Can I keep that, Jerry?" Holmgren took the photo back. "I want to run it by a defector that lives in the D.C. area. He might be able to confirm this little guy is Park."

"Sure," Duff smiled. "I'm glad they put you in the East Asia section," he added. "You're the best analyst we've got and your next FITREP will reflect that."

"I appreciate it," Holmgren said humbly.

"You know," Duff confided. "When you came here eighteen months ago, we figured it was thanks to your father-in-law, but you've proven yourself. Keep up the good work and you'll make light colonel in no time."

"Thank you, Colonel," Holmgren said. "That means a lot." Duff waved and walked back to his cubicle.

Alan smiled and leaned back in his chair. He'd come far for a man with three murders on his hands and he would kill again if it were required. Even Venice was more than he expected since he'd introduced her to his friends. He'd not flaunted her in front of Jessica's family just yet, but she'd charmed all of his contemporaries and none were the wiser. Better yet, the officers' wives loved her too and that was what counted in Washington. They all said it was about time the handsome young widower got on with his life and the sultry young Latina was just the thing to do it. And he remembered Hector Reynaldo's words when he came for the payoff in return for the lives of Jessica and Meagan Ashley. *You play the game well.* "Yes, I do."

Brentwood, Long Island, New York

"Hi, I'm Jacob Levy and I'd like to be your senator," he said, shaking the hand of a Dominican woman as she approached the IGA. "I'm running on the Independent line and I'd like your support." Jacob handed her a flyer and a voter registration card.

"Thank you," she smiled and continued her shopping. In the parking lot, a white microwave truck with the number 12 emblazoned on the side pulled to a stop and a pretty blonde emerged, followed by a cameraman.

"I'm Janet Hanson from News 12/Long Island," she said, offering a hand. "Are you Jacob Levy, the guy who's been driving a beat-up old Chevy all over New York campaigning for the Senate?"

"Yes, pleased to meet you," Levy shook her hand heartily. "I've been from Schenectady to Sag Harbor and now I'm going to the points in between."

"Do you think you'll win?" Hanson asked him. "I mean, this is a grass roots campaign and you haven't bought any TV time. Do you think this personal approach will work?"

Levy smiled as he took her in, reminding her a bit of an older Tom Cruise. "The ads will begin running next week, Ms. Hanson," he said. "By then, everyone will know about the crazy Jewish boy from Crown Heights who wants to be a politician. Congratulations, you're the first TV crew to break the story. I guess I'm going big time."

"What's with the old Chevy?"

"It's called keeping campaign costs to a minimum. I have been telling the people of New York that I will treat their money as I do my own," Levy explained. "When I get to the Senate, I will run my office the way I run my campaign with minimal staff and maximum productivity. I care about the people of New York, and I care about the way their money is spent by the people in Washington. There is a lot of waste and I'm going to find it and end it."

"You seem pretty confident, Mr. Levy," Hanson said as a crowd gathered.

"Why not, Ms. Hanson?" he turned to the crowd. "How many of you have met one of your elected representatives?" None signaled yea. "When I am in the Senate, the people of Brentwood will know that I took the time to see them, to talk to them and listen to their concerns. The people of Brentwood, and Briarcliff and Buffalo, will know their senator came to their town to meet them before he went to

Washington. They will know that I am representing *their* interests, not the political power bosses and the *special* interest. The *only* special interest I am beholden to is the people of the great state of New York."

And the crowd grew as Levy spoke, just as they had done in the other towns and cities he'd already visited. He would be in Manhattan on the weekend for his first fundraiser. The price of the tickets was kept low and the general public was invited to attend. It was what Rabbi Avram Levy, self-appointed campaign manager had scripted. Jacob would slide in under the radar using the gimmick; the old Chevy Malibu that belched smoke every time he took off. People knew him for that and his fiery speeches that riled them. It was stump politics in its purest form and Jacob found that he did it well.

Growing up in Crown Heights, he was exposed to many cultures and ethnic groups, and he could talk to them all. He was one of them, a fellow New Yorker from the streets of Brooklyn who'd made good and was now giving back to the community. He would go to Washington to watch out for them, the guy in the Chevy with the fire in his eyes.

"Other candidates make the rounds, Mr. Levy."

"Yes, but I was here first. I didn't wait until the weather warmed up. I was out here all winter, driving around the state, talking to people wherever I could get a crowd together, learning what was important to them. I went upstate and downstate, from the Catskills to the Finger Lakes, from Niagara Falls to New York City, I went to the people and personally asked them for their vote and their confidence."

It would be that way for the next few days, Levy giving more and more interviews to news crews who'd noticed his story on the wire. It would be only a few weeks more until his name would be included on all the polls by the major network affiliates and another week before he was doing the morning shows. By the time the frontrunners took him seriously, he was in the thick of the race.

Arlington National Cemetery, Arlington, Virginia

They met at the cemetery, Holmgren stopping at the grave next to the one at which Reynaldo seemed to be paying his respects. "Your little friend ought to be more careful," he said, not looking at Hector.

"What are you talking about? What is so important?" Reynaldo hissed.

"Kim Sun Park," Holmgren said. "We have imagery of him meeting with Oleg Zinoviev earlier today in Pyong Yang. My section chief thinks they were talking about nukes. I'd tell the Major to be careful."

"You are assuming much, Alan," Hector said, but Holmgren could see he looked worried. "I don't know who either of those men are."

"Suit yourself," Holmgren crossed himself and turned to leave.

"What about the satellite, the new one?"

"I haven't heard anything yet," Holmgren said. "You'll know as soon as I do."

"My superiors are amicable to your terms. Meet me at the Vietnam Memorial tomorrow at the usual time," Hector said. "You will receive a . . . down payment; a little monetary motivation, so to speak."

"See you then," he said over his shoulder, smiling when he turned back. They had to play his game for he could expose them easily. The North Koreans needed to know the capabilities of the new bird, its deployment date, and its viewing window for the Korean Peninsula. The fact they'd spotted Park with Zinoviev confirmed it; the Koreans had the hard currency, Japanese yen, German marks, and American dollars that the Ukraine needed to survive the fall of the Soviet Empire. The Ukrainians possessed the nuclear warheads that the North Koreans needed to threaten the democratic nations on the Pacific Rim; there was little chance the subject of their conversation was anything but about nuclear weapons.

"You will pay handsomely for what I know," he said as he drove out of the cemetery.

Chapter Thirty-One
Mineola, Long Island, New York
12 June 1990

"Who'd have thought it," Rick said as he watched the news. "For fifty years the Soviet Union was the only threat to our existence and now it's falling apart before our eyes. The Russians just declared themselves independent."

"You have that faraway look again," Connie said as she sat on the couch across from him.

"When I was in the service, we trained for the war that never came," Rick said wistfully. "It was even worse when I got to a B-52 base. They had ten bombers loaded with nukes on alert all the time. The crews slept near the planes and could get them airborne within minutes."

"Thank God it never came," Connie agreed.

"Oh, there were other little wars we fought by proxy or covertly," Rick said. "The casualties were usually chalked up as training accidents. I know of three families who think their fathers and sons died for nothing." He got up and went to the box he kept under his side of the bed, rummaging through it for a minute and coming back with an eight by ten photo and a small box. "Here," he handed her the picture.

"Nice looking bunch," she said as she studied the ten men wearing tiger-stripe camouflage, sporting black berets. "A-Flight," Connie read the caption handwritten on the bottom. "Holy shit, is that *you?*"

"You have a good eye," he kissed her. "I was twenty at the time." Rick pointed to three men in the picture. "These three never made it back from a mission."

"Do you recognize him?" Johnson pointed to one of the Afro-American members of the team.

"He looks like that rich guy in Chicago, Emory I think."

"You're good," Rick smiled. "Jerry and I were tight back then. It's nice to know one of us made something out of himself."

"What exactly did you do when you were in the Air Force, Rick?"

"Mostly pickups and deliveries," he grinned. "But we got to break some shit too. Did I tell you I helped liberate the island of Grenada?" Rick went to the liquor cabinet and poured himself a shot of Jack Daniel's and her vodka with Seven-Up.

"Why are you telling me this now?" Connie asked him, accepting her drink.

"It's about time you knew almost all of my deep, dark secrets," he replied.

"Almost?"

"There are a few subjects that are still a bit raw. It's been four years since I left the Air Force and it's time you knew."

"What about the woman you were in love with?"

"That's one," he said. "I'll tell you about her someday, I promise."

Connie opened the box to find the Silver Star, his marksmanship medals, and his unit citations. "They gave you a medal?"

"The Silver Star," he answered. "I got it for getting the guys out of a tight spot, the same place we lost three of our own. These two were killed by a rocket propelled grenade," he pointed to Chief Corlies and Lieutenant Jenkins. "And this guy was cut down by machine gun fire. I carried him out, but he was dead when I got him to the chopper." Rick shook his head. "What a waste."

Connie just gazed at him, a million questions running through her head, but she couldn't verbalize them. Only one would pass her lips. "Would you go back to that life?"

"They wouldn't want me."

"Just say they would, just say they wanted you to go to Kuwait and they came begging you," she postulated. "Would you?"

"I'd consider it," he said honestly. "Why do you ask?"

"Because I know that look, Rick, and I know you'd do more than consider it. You loved it, didn't you?"

"It doesn't matter, Connie. I wouldn't do anything that would jeopardize our relationship, *nothing*. I give you my word on that and not just on this subject. I love you more than I've loved anything or anyone and I would never do anything to hurt us."

"I know," she nodded, her eyes becoming moist. "And I know I'm not being rational, but I feel as if you had a whole other life before you met me, that you were a different person."

"I was, darling," he threw his arm around her. "But I'm not going back to that. I am where I want to be and I am *who* I want to be, your husband, *this* is the life I want and no other."

Chapter Thirty-Two
The Waldorf Astoria, New York, New York
6 November 1990

"I give you new the junior senator from the State of New York, Jacob Levy," his chief of staff Sandra Weitz said to the crowd of about five hundred. Weitz was a petite, pretty blonde, a former Democratic party operative until she defected to Levy's camp when he offered her the chance. Levy bounded up to the lectern with his usual enthusiasm, giving Sandra a hug.

"Thanks, Sandy," he said. "And thank you all," he said to the group of volunteers. "I couldn't have done it without you." And there was more applause. "Today, the people of New York spoke overwhelmingly in favor of responsible government and I thank them profoundly as well. To my two opponents, I would like to give my thanks for a good race. We'll be going to Washington in a little while to take the fight against fraud, waste, and abuse to the floor of the Senate."

Until this morning, all of the opinion polls called for a tight race between Levy, the Independent, and the candidates representing the Democrats and the GOP. By noon, it was evident Levy was going to win in a landslide. When the polling places closed at nine p.m., Levy had taken seventy three percent of the vote. The major networks declared Levy the winner by seven and the Cinderella story was written. The unknown lawyer from Brooklyn wins it all in a runaway.

Mineola, New York

"Well, I'll be damned," Rick said as he took a sip of water. "The Jewish kid won."

"He's the one with the old car, isn't he?" Connie asked.

"Yeah, he's been killing mosquitoes all over the state with it for a year," he laughed. "I wonder if he'll take it to Washington with him."

"They say he's a decent guy," Connie offered.

"He's a politician," Rick muttered. "Just a new crook in Congress."

"You're so cynical," she giggled.

"The people who'd be good at the job don't want it," he said. "And the people who do are on a power trip."

"I suppose *you'd* make a good politician?" She considered her husband skeptically.

"Hell no," Rick grinned. "I see me as more of the King type."

"Do you?"

"Sure," he smiled. "I know the way the world should run."

"Oy," Connie shook her head and went back to the *TV Guide* crossword. "I could *just* imagine."

"Okay, so I might have all the stupid people shot," he joked.

"And they thought Hitler was bad," Connie said, not looking up at him.

"Well, it's the German in me. We all want to take over the world."

"Oy," she said again. In the eighteen months they'd been married they'd gotten comfortable and both thought that was a good thing. They were friends first, best friends, and both thought the other's company superior to all others. They were happy and though they had adjustment issues, neither would change the situation. The sex was still passionate, both were happy in their work, and neither felt ready to have children. Rick and Connie were still having too much fun.

Chapter Thirty-Three
Port of Odessa, Ukraine, Soviet Union
26 May 1991

Oleg Zinoviev watched as the ship cast her lines and set out across the Black Sea. Rubbing the two-day growth of stubble on his chin, he pulled his fisherman's cap low as he turned and left the pier. It was a glorious Sunday morning when the *Rula Dhergham* slipped her moorings and he felt a twinge of guilt as he opened the back door of the dusty old Mercedes. Within the Rula were twenty-four nuclear warheads capable of decimating several cities and that gave Zinoviev cause for reflection. *In the wrong hands* . . . But he never finished, for he could not be certain that the North Koreans would wield their new power responsibly. *And the money will keep my people from starving*, he rationalized, though a large chunk of it would end up in the pockets of those aware of its existence, Oleg Zinoviev being one of them.

Moscow, Soviet Union

"Ah," Kosarev spat. His operative in Odessa had just relayed the news that the *Rula Dhergham* had slipped her moorings. "I have failed." He shook his head and walked to the sideboard, pouring himself a glass of vodka. The door burst open and Boris Popov entered in a dither, three men followed him. "What is *this?*" Kosarev boomed as he went to the top drawer of his desk, removing the 10 mm Makarov pistol in a flash. Two of the arrivals were faster and a standoff ensued.

"Please put the gun down, Yevgeniy Stepanovich," Vladimir Kryuchkov, the unarmed member of the trio said. "This is not the place for bloodshed."

Kosarev studied the men for a minute and did not doubt their resolve. He'd kill one of them, but he would die here too. And he saw the face of his beloved Katherine Alexandra, his only grandchild, and his purpose for taking the risks he had over the last few years. This would be a moment of reckoning, one of many that would come over the next year. Kryuchkov was a member of the Old Line, the Communists who wanted a return to the old ways. They had taken Gorbachev's ear and Kosarev was counting on the fact the Union would be gone before this day. Kryuchkov and his associates held the power at this critical time and Kosarev knew the end was near for he and Popov. "You are making a mistake, Vladimir," Kosarev barked, looking to Popov. He lay the pistol on the desk. "At least let the boy go."

"My place is by the General's side," Popov said. "Do your best."

"Please to not help him, Boris," Kosarev said.

"Your time here is over, Comrade Kosarev," Kryuchkov said. "This can be done in a civilized manner or they can drag your bodies from the building. The choice is yours."

"We will not be a problem," Kosarev assured him. He and Popov fell in between the armed men as they left the office, heading directly to the elevator. The young man, Popov, was sheet white when Kosarev gazed at him. "There are worse things than dying, Boris," Kosarev chuckled.

"I couldn't think of any at this time, Comrade General," Boris trembled.

They stepped out on the ground floor and walked directly outside where a Zil limousine idled at the curb. "If you would get in, gentlemen," Kryuchkov ordered as he opened the back door. At that moment, two shots rang out in Red Square and Kryuchkov's bodyguards fell dead. Kryuchkov himself dove into the back of the limousine as it took off, leaving Kosarev, Popov, and the two bodies on the sidewalk. Another car squealed to a stop a few seconds later and two Red Army officers of the lieutenant rank stepped out. Kosarev saw they were wearing the badges of the Spetsnaz, the Soviet Special Forces.

"Comrade Yeltsin regrets the close timing of the operation," one of them said to Kosarev. "If you and Lieutenant Popov would come with us, we will see to your safety."

They got in the back of the car, Popov still pale, still staring at the bodies as they drove away. He looked back to Kosarev. "You knew, Comrade General?"

"Kryuchkov and his people have Gorbachev's ear," the big man replied. "I would not be surprised if Vladimir is in my office before nightfall."

"There is no place safe for us in Moscow," Boris said and then he got even whiter. "My father ..."

"He will be fine, my boy," Kosarev assured him. "He, Lovenko, and Kharlamov have insulated themselves." He looked to the driver. "Take us to Sherematyevo quickly."

"Yes, Comrade General."

"Where will we go?" Boris asked him.

"Away from Moscow for a while," Kosarev said, his eyes saying more. The car most likely was bugged and the fewer who knew of Kosarev's plans the better. It was up to Yeltsin now, for he would be the bait to ferret out those who would return to the old ways. Kosarev had set the wheels in motion, brought the Union to the brink, and now it was Yeltsin who would push it over the edge. There would probably be a coup attempt within the year and Kosarev was in no position to help him, not if he wanted control of the KGB or whatever materialized from its ashes. When the fall came, it had to be Kryuchkov or one of his cronies at the helm and that was assured today.

The Pentagon, Washington, D.C.

"Shit," Colonel Nathan Beu read the dispatch.

"What is it?" Navy Commander (Captain selectee) Paul Wallace asked him. Beu handed him the page. "It's getting dicey over there, isn't it?"

"You know it is when the head of the KGB disappears," Beu agreed. "I've gotta go."

"What's up?" Wallace asked. They'd met a month ago, both new arrivals to the Pentagon, and hit it off immediately. The two officers had much in common, careers on the fast track thanks to distinguished service during Desert Storm, married with young children, both were rising stars in their respective branches of service.

"Alexa has an appointment with the doctor, and she wanted me to go with her. I'll talk to you later," Beu waved and hurried out to the lot, heading directly to the house they'd rented in Arlington. Wallace could never know the truth, could never know his wife's true identity or the life Nathan Beu built for himself would come crumbling down in an instant. As he drove home, he could imagine the consequences of helping Yevgeniy Kosarev bring his daughter out of the Soviet Union. His wife was at the door by the time he made it up the walk.

"Why are you home so early?" She asked, knowing her husband well. "What's wrong?"

"Let's sit down," he urged her to the living room. She sat and regarded him, her eyes becoming moist. "We got some intelligence from Moscow," Beu began. "Your father and his aide, a Lieutenant Popov, have disappeared. There's been a shakeup at the top of KGB and a guy named Kryuchkov is in charge now. I'm sorry, sugar," he took her to him. "They were last seen outside Lubyanka in an altercation where two of Kryuchkov's men were killed. Witnesses say that your father and Popov got away."

Alexa just held him, sobbing as she tried to form words. "They will kill him," she cried.

"The most I can do is keep an ear to the ground, honey," Beu held her tightly. "But he's a resourceful guy. Look how he got you out of Russia."

"I just wish we could help him."

"So do I, sugar."

"Why is mommy crying?" Six-year-old Katie said from the door.

"It'll be okay, Katie honey," Beu said, reaching for her. "She's not feeling well, that's all."

Chapter Thirty-Four
Moscow, Russia
21 August 1991

Minister of Internal Affairs Boris Pugo placed the key in the door of his apartment and entered quickly. There were papers to retrieve before he left Moscow, probably for good. And then he heard a voice he never thought he'd hear again. Two men stood in the corner of the darkened room.

"Good morning, Minister Pugo," Kosarev said.

"It is good to see you are still with us, Yevgeniy Stepanovich," Pugo said nervously. He recognized Ivan Popov's son as well, the same Ivan Popov whose tanks were guarding the streets. "Where have you been hiding?"

"I always loved Switzerland," Kosarev replied and stepped out of the shadows, the Makarov pistol firmly in his left hand. "Your feeble coup attempt is over. Kryuchkov has been arrested along with a few others, Yazov and Tizyakov. I am doing my part to clean out the trash and I'm going to Lukyanov next"

"Do you think you and Ivan's skinny boy can arrest me?" Pugo laughed.

"No," Kosarev said and fired, the ten-millimeter slug blowing the side of Pugo's face off." Young Popov went white again and Kosarev dragged him from the apartment.

The Pentagon, Washington, D.C.

"It's over," Paul Wallace barged into Beu's office. "The coup is over, and Yeltsin is *still* there. They arrested a bunch of them, a couple ministers and the KGB chief."

"No shit?" Beu followed him out to the situation room.

"Look," Wallace pointed to the monitors. Boris Yeltsin was giving a speech in front of the White House, the Russian Parliament building.

"It looks like the Old-Line Communists are out," the Assistant Secretary of Defense turned to them. "If this holds and Yeltsin can consolidate his power with the military, this could be the end of the Soviet Union as we know it, gentlemen."

"He's already done that, sir," Beu said pointing to the scene unfolding before them. "Look who's with him; that's Iosef Kharlamov, commander of the 42nd Guards Regiment, and there's Lovenko, one of the regional Air Defense Commanders, and Ivan Popov, commander of the Ministry of the Interior troops. We've been hoping for this day for years, Mr. Secretary."

"Remember what they say about getting what you wish for," the Assistant Secretary cautioned. "We might find it was easier to deal with the Supreme Soviet than with a dozen smaller republics, most in a state of anarchy."

"Yeah, let's hope we don't long for the good old days," Wallace added as they watched history unfold.

"At least Russia stayed intact and the transition to democracy was relatively orderly," Beu observed as two more men joined the group standing behind Yeltsin. "And the KGB is on board as well."

"Who's the big, old guy?" Wallace asked.

"That's the Russian Bear himself," the Secretary said, wondering how Beu knew one of the most secretive men in the world on sight. "That's Yevgeniy Kosarev and the young guy next to him is Ivan Popov's son, Boris. He's Kosarev's aide de camp, almost like a chief of staff. You've done your homework, Colonel Beu."

"I learned all about him when I was attached to NATO in their Intelligence Division a couple years back," Beu lied. "We have to assume he is back at the controls of the Komitet." He was elated and had to stifle his impulse to call his wife immediately, but the good news would wait until he got home.

Mineola, Long Island

"Can you believe these Russians?" Rick pointed at the TV. The footage of several of the coup conspirators being led out of their offices ran over Peter Jennings' narration. "I wonder what they're doing with the nukes."

"What do you mean?" Connie finished loading the dishwasher.

"The Commies had nukes in almost all of the Republics," he explained. "The satellite states are leaving the Union like rats from a sinking ship and the Russians are going to be the ones left holding the bag. All of the decisions in the last seventy-five years have come out of Moscow, the power was there and they're going to answer if any of them get loose."

"Where would they go?"

"To anyone with money, honey," he grinned. "I could think of a few countries who'd love to have one or two. That nut in Iraq for one, and that other nut in North Korea, just to name a few. Just think what a terrorist organization would do with one if they could set it off in Tel Aviv."

"That's scary," she blanched.

"The world's a scary place," he threw his arm around her. "That's why I don't like the idea of you working in the city. New York is a prime target for a madman with a bomb."

"I love New York, Rick," she insisted. "We always have this talk when someone is mugged in the Subway. There are eight million people in the city, the odds of my being in the wrong place at the right time are incredible."

"Uh huh," he muttered. They did have this talk before and she always won, just as she had today.

Yong Hung, North Korea

It was the last of the excavations to be covered over and the largest, the maintenance/launch facility. Kim Sun Park smiled as he watched the heavy equipment grading the area to its original topography. There would be a few low buildings constructed above the sprawling complex; elevator and maintenance structures additional to the tunnel system that had been constructed to allow large trucks to be driven directly inside the complex. In a few weeks, the final part would be in place, the missile warheads waiting at a secure location just across the border from China at Sinuiju. Twenty-four agents of death that would put North Korea on par with the West and allow the unification of Korea under the government in Pyong Yang. *It will be a glorious day*, Park thought as the hot wind blew the humidity in from the west.

The Washington Monument, Washington, D.C.

Holmgren put the camera bag down and framed Venice in the lens as she posed in front of the tall, slender building. He was taking a chance today having her along when he met Hector, but there would be no real contact and she was part of the cover. Holmgren had spotted Reynaldo about fifty yards away and exchanged a nod.

"The sun is perfect here," Reynaldo said as he came up next to Holmgren. "Do you mind if I get a picture of her?"

"Not at all," Holmgren smiled, and Hector set an identical camera bag next to Holmgren's.

"Pretty girl," Reynaldo said, snapping off a few shots of the Latina in miniskirt and halter-top. He picked up Holmgren's bag and nodded. "Thanks."

"No problem," Holmgren smiled.

"Thank you," Hector said to Venice before walking away, disappearing into the crowd.

"Who was he?" Venice asked when she got to where Alan stood.

"Some guy enthralled by your beauty," Holmgren kissed her before reaching down to pick up the bag. The only difference between Reynaldo's bag and Holmgren's was that Holmgren's carried the specifications to the new KH-26 intelligence satellite, due to be launched in the fall of next year.

Part Three:

Effects

March 1995

Chapter Thirty-Five
Kadena Air Base, Okinawa, Japan
Wednesday, 1 March 1995

The C-20A business jet taxied up to the parking spot and the band began to play. As the door opened, Brigadier General Nathan Beu stepped onto the tarmac. "I didn't want this," Beu whispered to Lt. Colonel Mark White as he stepped up and saluted.

"Yes, you did," White grinned. "Or you wouldn't have stayed in this long. Welcome to Kadena, General."

"Thanks, I think," Beu said as he stepped up to the podium. Kadena Air Base was the largest U.S. facility in the Pacific and Beu had been given command of the base in conjunction with his promotion to brigadier general. "Alexa would have loved this."

"I thought she'd be coming with you," White said as they waited for the band to finish.

"Katie came down with strep-throat for the umpteenth time," Beu explained. "They're *finally* going to take her tonsils out and Alexa wanted it done at Walter Reed instead of out here. They'll be out next week."

"Do you have a speech?"

"I thought I'd wing it," Beu smiled and stepped up to the microphone as the last bars faded into the breeze.

Sung Rocket Complex, Yong Hung, North Korea

Soon Yat Oh knew this would be the end of his work for the Russians. What Kosarev asked him to do this time could only lead to his discovery. There would be an investigation and eventually the evidence would point to him, but this was his doing. He was the one who'd heard General Park talking with a few of his maintenance men and reported the details of the conversation to the KGB. They didn't call it that anymore, officially, but as long as Kosarev was running things, it would be.

Kosarev had given Soon his promise; this would be the end. He would be extracted from North Korea along with his family, wife and five daughters, and resettled in the West as payment for his exceptional service. Prior operations only involved information gathering but this was sabotage and General Park would not rest until the conspirators were found and punished. Soon could only imagine what would happen to his wife and daughters should he be discovered. But this had to be done; it was the only way Park's plan could be exposed.

Why did they have to launch that satellite, Soon asked himself as he rewired the limit switch on one of the lead lined missile silo doors. In a few hours, just after the American KH-26 satellite made its pass, a test would be done on the silo doors. This door would open as advertised but would refuse to close. By the time the troubleshooting checklist was run, the satellite will have made another pass and will have discovered the missile waiting in its silo twenty-two thousand five hundred miles below.

Lubyanka, Moscow, Russian Federation

"Begging the Marshal's pardon," Captain Boris Popov said as he entered the office.

"What is it now, Boris?" Kosarev growled as he looked up from his PC.

"I have been considering the operation Low Chen is undertaking," Popov said.

"I did not put the question up for consideration," Kosarev said. "When I want your opinion, I will give it to you."

"But, sir, will not the Americans act once they detect the North Koreans' weapons?" Popov ignored Kosarev's warning, one of the few people who could without receiving his nine ounces.

"That depends on their President, Boris," Kosarev waved it away. "Was there something you wanted, or will I have to put up with your diatribe until you spit it all out?"

"What if the Americans do act? What will become of Low Chen? You made him a promise, Marshal," Popov reminded him.

"Damn it, when did you become my *mother*?" Kosarev rose from behind the mahogany desk and Boris backed up a step. "The Americans will *not* send a squadron of bombers to destroy Yong Hung," he declared. "But they will exert pressure on the North Koreans at the U.N., and *that* is the outcome we are seeking. Once the world knows of their existence, that miserable dwarf will not be able to use them. The element of surprise will be taken from him."

"I see," Popov fell into thought. "What if ..."

"*Nothing*," Kosarev slapped the desk. "The Americans will not be foolish enough to attack. The President does not want to explain to the American people why he began another war in the Far East. They still remember Vietnam, just as Afghanistan leaves a sour taste in the collective mouths of the *Rodina*. This conversation is *over*, Boris."

"Yes, Marshal," Popov bowed and left the room.

Kosarev turned to the window. "You are not that stupid, Mr. President," he said to no one. It was a chance Kosarev was taking, but the odds the American President would precipitate a war on the Korean Peninsula were infinitesimal. Launching a few cruise missiles at that maniac in Iraq every so often was one thing, but an attack on North Korean soil would probably draw the Chinese into the situation. Things could escalate quickly from there and while Kosarev did not like the man very much, the President was no fool.

I should handle this myself, Kosarev thought, feeling a twinge of guilt for laying it at the Americans' feet, but the Russians could not be seen to be involved. With the economy in its fragile state, they could not afford sanctions for meddling in the affairs of a sovereign state. It could also push the Chinese to enter Siberia and that was something to be avoided at all costs. There was also no money to properly equip the military and the units who would be first to meet the Chinese were woefully undermanned and under equipped. *The Americans are the only ones who can do this*, he assured himself.

CIA Headquarters, Langley, Virginia

"Whoa," the technician said when the hardcopy spat out of the laser printer. He took the photos and headed upstairs to the Intelligence Directorate. "Mr. Rice?" He knocked once on the partially open door of the Deputy Director (Operations).

"Sit," David Lawrence Rice said to his assistant, Timothy Gordon. "What is it?"

"The latest download from the –26 overflight of the Korean peninsula twenty minutes ago," he said. "Look in the southeastern quadrant, sir."

Gordon looked over Rice's shoulder, their eyes going wide at the same time. "Is that a silo?" Rice asked the Navy chief petty officer.

"Yes, sir," he nodded. "When I saw it, I printed it and brought it directly here. My assistant is running a copy to the DDI as well."

"Thanks, Chief," Rice said. The tech nodded and left Rice and Gordon alone. "I want a meeting with the Director and all the Deputy directors in ten minutes, Timmy. We will also have to brief the President."

"How did we miss it until now?" Gordon asked, more rhetorically than of his boss.

"That's what the President will want to know. I want that hotshot who runs the East Asia desk at Asian Pacific Analysis up here too. I want to know why *he* didn't know about this."

"Colonel Holmgren?"

"Yes," Rice nodded. "We've had that satellite up there four years; I want to know why we got surprised by this and I want to know how those warheads got there without us knowing about it."

"Yes, sir," Gordon nodded and left for his office. Rice just sat there, considering the implications of this new piece of information.

Yong Hung, North Korea

"The doors are closed, General Park," the maintenance supervisor said. "We bypassed the hydraulics and cranked them closed."

"Twenty minutes too late," Park hissed. "How did this happen?"

"I do not know, General. I am beginning my investigation as soon as I leave your office. Our priority was getting the launch doors closed. I will inform you as soon as I know something," he promised.

"See that you do," Park declared, the man departed, and his secretary entered. "Inform Pyong Yang I will require an audience with the Intelligence Minister." She nodded and left hurriedly. "We must prepare for the Americans to come," Park said to the empty room.

Langley, Virginia

"We didn't receive a whisper from our people on the ground," Holmgren said, looking at the faces around the table. "We saw the excavations from our overflights, but we never got any indication it was a launch facility. All our people said it was a mining project."

"It looks like they've been mining plutonium," CIA director Louis Guerin barked as he tossed the false-color image from the –26 on the conference table. "Jesus, Alan, this is a pretty *big* miss."

"With all due respect, Mr. Director," Holmgren said. "We did the best we could with the assets we had. We don't have many human intelligence assets on the ground over there and the satellites can only tell us so much. I brought some of our old data." Holmgren spread overhead photos of the Yong Hung facility before the Director. "They dug it up just like a strip-mine," Holmgren showed them the gaping hole in the ground and the smaller ones on the perimeter. "Our people thought it was a control center for the mine and the smaller ones were shaft openings. That area is littered with mines, coal, copper, iron, and lead to name a few. That's probably how the –26 was fooled," he offered. "I'd bet there's enough lead in those hills to mask the radiation."

"It sounds farfetched to me," Guerin said. "Has anyone talked to the South Koreans?"

"They haven't heard anything either," Holmgren said. "They believe the area is part of a mine complex as well."

"Can we get boots on the ground?" Deputy Director (Intelligence) Ron Mitchell asked. "Do you think the President will let us put some people in there?"

"I don't know," Guerin said, turning back to Holmgren. "Why did we get an indication of nuclear material *today*? Why not yesterday, or last week?"

"We think they must have had one of the doors open, sir," Holmgren said. "The indication was not present on the next pass of the satellite. I agree with Mr. Mitchell. We should get some people on the ground."

"Mr. Rice?" Guerin looked over at the DDO.

"It's not easy to get people in there," Rice said. "We could ask the South Koreans to loan us some folks to get a look see," he shrugged. "It's dicey, especially since we improved trade relations with the Taiwanese. The Chinese might take umbrage with us for playing around in their backyard some more."

Holmgren had a kernel of a thought blossom in the back of his mind, something he hadn't thought about for a long time. His thoughts of revenge had mellowed, still cursing Johnson and his comrades for forcing him to take the risks he'd had to, but he was able to put them away for a while. He'd let them age, and soften, until a second ago when the rage returned when he was reminded of the expense, for Venice and for the lifestyle, that he'd had to endure because Roger's absence had brought him to Quanh. "I might have an idea," he volunteered. "But I'll have to do some research first. I'll need six to eight hours and I should know if it's workable."

"You want to use Americans?" Rice was surprised.

"If I can find the right ones, Mr. Rice," Holmgren said with a nod. "I don't know if any of them are still in the military."

"I want everything run through Bobby before it goes to the House," Guerin warned. "I want no loose ends that will embarrass the Administration." Bobby was Deputy Director Robert Holt. "Take the night, Alan," Guerin said. "I want this gamed out, best-case, break even, and worst-case scenarios. Beside Colonel Holmgren, this is restricted to Directorate heads and above." Guerin got nods from all of them before turning back to Holmgren. "And make sure the Senator and his friends don't get wind of it. I don't want to hear any screaming from the Hill on this one. If we go forward, it will have to be done quietly, with none of that Somalia bullshit of a few years back."

"Yes, sir," Holmgren said, a broad smile creasing his face.

Chapter Thirty-Six
CIA Headquarters, Langley, Virginia
Thursday, 2 March 1995

"Oh boy," Holmgren rubbed his eyes as he leaned back in his chair. Checking his watch, he was surprised it was after midnight. He punched a number into his phone.

"Hello," Venice's voice was sultry.

"Hi, darling," Holmgren smiled. "I don't know if I'll make it home tonight."

"Sorry to hear that, lover," she said. "I'll keep your place warm just in case."

"I'll see you when I get home," he promised and hung up. He leaned forward and considered the information before him. Out of the seven who'd survived the operation at Nam Po in July of 1983, only one remained on active military duty. There were one or two who might prove to be troublesome, but he was certain all were accessible. One name in particular caught his attention. Taking out his cell phone, he dialed a number from memory and then deleted it from the phone's directory.

"It is late," the voice on the other end said.

"Do you run?" Holmgren asked.

"Yes," the voice replied.

"Rock Creek Park, five a.m.," Holmgren said and hung up.

***

Holmgren was on a high by the time he got to the park, getting home around three, pleasantly surprised Venice was awake and horny, but then, she was *always* horny. She felt dominant this early morning and took him forcefully, using skills to control him and bring him to an incredible orgasm that energized him. A shower and more coffee were just the thing before heading back out. Hector was on the trail by the time Holmgren got out of the car.

"What is it?" Reynaldo asked when Holmgren caught up to him.

"Your masters are slipping up," he said. "Eighteen hours ago, our –26 showed a bright blue spot in the Yong Hung area of North Korea. Somebody left a door open," he wagged his finger and laughed. "It was smart, hiding the weapons in among the lead mines but somebody got careless."

"What will happen?"

"It's going to the President in a few hours. He'll have an op-plan in his hands by tonight. Within the next six months, your boss can expect a visit."

"How?"

"Who knows?" Holmgren said as they jogged over the bridge. "I'm not with the Joint Chiefs' Office; maybe a stealth bomber attack, maybe a special ops mission," he offered. "But you can bet they'll try to shut him down."

"What about the CIA?"

"We don't have the assets over there, and I doubt they'd leave this to the South Koreans," Holmgren informed him. While he was alerting Reynaldo of the discovery, he was also planting the seed that an American attack on the Sung Rocket Complex was inevitable. *It will be if I have anything to say about it.* "It will be a military operation."

"I will have to consult higher authorities. Will you have access to the mission details?"

"Probably," Holmgren nodded. "Assume I will until you hear differently. Inform your higher authorities that I expect a show of gratitude of the same caliber as last time, when I gave you the specs to the satellite."

"I am certain your cooperation will be appreciated," Reynaldo agreed.

"I should hope so," Holmgren smiled as he veered off the path and headed back to his car. He was now in the game, not just as a conduit of information, but also as a player. The headiness of it got to him and he slowed. He would be manipulating two nations toward a confrontation, possibly nuclear, and that gave him a rush. And he realized it was the power he craved.

The U.S. and North Korea would be brought to the brink, a standoff that would most certainly end in the Americans' favor, but he cared not how it would end. His only concern was his revenge, and that desire would be satisfied. For though the North Koreans would eventually lose their weapons, Richard Johnson and his comrades would not survive the confrontation. They would be the tips of the spear that would be seriously blunted when the dust settled.

***

"Christ, Alan," Louis Guerin said as he watched the presentation. "I can't fly this past the President."

"I realize it's a bit unorthodox, sir, but it offers us success in the best case and deniability in the worst," Holmgren explained. "And the entire operation can be run by the Agency. Only three or four active duty troops would be directly involved and less than a hundred in an ancillary capacity."

"The President would never approve it," Guerin shook his head.

"Would he approve a reconnaissance mission?" Holmgren offered. "We'd put the team in place and then play it by ear from there. The President can make the final decision once they are on the ground and we know what's *really* there."

"What *about* this team?" Guerin asked him. "Why are there no specifics?"

"I'd classify them as temporary employees, sir," Holmgren said, keeping the grin from his face.

"We had our problems with mercenaries in the past, Colonel," Guerin eyed him narrowly. "Congress won't let us use them."

"Neither Congress nor the President need to know the manpower details, Mr. Director," Holmgren said.

"Look, Alan," Guerin said as he rose. "I agreed to listen to this because of my relationship with Senator Latour, but I can't see the feasibility of it. I don't believe the President would approve it, and I will not leave myself or the Agency open to criminal charges."

"As you wish, sir," Holmgren said sadly.

"I admire your initiative," Guerin admitted.

"Thank you, sir." Alan went to leave but then turned around. "Might I have authorization to game this out a little more in depth? Maybe I might come up with something a little more palatable to the President?"

"It can't hurt," Guerin shrugged. "Take a couple days to work the problem. I'm on my way to the White House. We'll see what the President wants to do."

Pyong Yang, North Korea

"Our security has been compromised," Kim Sun Park said to Zhang Tae Woo, Interior Minister of the Democratic People's Republic of North Korea. "We have confirmation from one of our sources in the American Central Intelligence Agency that their satellite observed one of our missiles when the silo door malfunctioned."

"Can we expect some sort of reaction?" Zhang asked.

"The source believes so," Park nodded. "I suggest we plan for an attack of some sort. I believe we should begin to reinforce the security contingent at the Sung Complex."

"Will we have advance warning of an attack?"

"Possibly, Minister Zhang," Park replied. "Our source has been advised of our . . . interest."

"I need not remind you of the expenditures we have undertaken to make the Sung Complex a reality," Zhang warned. "Security is your responsibility, General Park, and you *will* be held responsible should the American attack be successful."

"I understand, Minister Zhang," Park bowed and retreated. Zhang was old and powerful and a warning from him was best heeded. Park would one day hold Zhang's position, but he could not arouse the old man's displeasure lest Park spend the rest of his days managing a labor camp in the hilly interior.

Langley, Virginia

"I would like to know why we weren't informed about this directly," Chen Hua Li demanded.

"We are still trying to confirm our intelligence, Mr. Chen," David Rice said. "There was no need to create an incident over a computer glitch."

"*Was* it a computer glitch?" Chen, the liaison from the South Korean Central Intelligence Agency, asked him.

"We don't know yet," Rice shrugged. "Previous and subsequent passes of our satellite show nothing there but a mining complex."

"Are you planning some sort of operation?" Chen still fumed.

"We're talking about some things. We'll let you know once the President is made aware of the situation. The Director is at the White House now."

"What about *my* people?"

"You know what I know, Mr. Chen," Rice said. "You can inform your government that you will be advised in real time."

"We will be their first targets, Mr. Rice," Chen insisted. "We will not allow the North to have nuclear weapons that can threaten our cities. One of your analysts said that there were rumors the South Africans sold the missile bodies to the North Koreans several years ago, yet this is the first I've heard of it."

"You'd have to talk to Ron Mitchell in Intelligence," Rice put up his hands in surrender. "But I don't think we could confirm that either."

"I'd appreciate being advised if you decide to run an operation," Chen said as he turned to leave. "We will pursue our own avenues to confirm your suspicions."

"As always, you will have our full cooperation," Rice said as Chen left, Timothy Gordon entering after an appropriate second. "Who's been talking to the Koreans?" Rice demanded.

"I don't know, sir," Gordon shrugged.

"Keep an eye on Chen, Tim," Rice ordered. "I want to know what they're up to. If they're willing to do a recon of the North Korean missile complex, we'll let them. Also, get me an appointment with the Director."

"Yes, sir," Gordon nodded. "Did you see Holmgren's presentation?"

"No," Rice looked up.

"I hear he took it to the Director," Gordon said conspiratorially. "Even took it over Bobby Holt's head, but you can do that when you were once married to Senator LaTour's daughter."

"*He* was the one?"

"Yes, sir, I thought you knew," Gordon looked surprised.

"It's a shame what happened to that poor girl," Rice shook his head. "And the baby too. What about his op-plan?"

"I hear it involved mercenaries and a couple of active duty troops," Gordon grinned. "They'd be inserted a couple miles from the complex, and they'd find a hole to watch the place from for a couple days; maybe even get inside to get a couple pictures."

"Let's see what the South Koreans come up with," Rice smiled. "Holmgren's commando raid is a cluster fuck waiting to happen."

***

"Hi, Alan," Chen Hua Li said when he arrived at the East Asia section.

Holmgren looked up from his PC and smiled. "Hi, Li. What brings you here?"

"I just left a meeting with the DDO," Chen sat heavily. "The lines of communication are not what we would like them to be."

"Sorry about that but you know how this business is," Holmgren shrugged. "What are you going to do?"

"I am certain my superiors will want to know more about what's going on in Yong Hung," Chen said. "Your government does not have the same urgency as we do. It is a certainty those warheads are targeted on our major cities. Your President's motivations would be different if they could reach Los Angeles or San Francisco."

"That's a fact," Holmgren chuckled. "Maybe you should talk to the Japanese," he offered. "They might be targets as well. Maybe they're willing to share the risk of an operation with you."

"Good idea," Chen said, standing suddenly. "Can you keep me apprised of developments here?"

"I'll do what I can," Holmgren promised. "That works both ways, you know," he added.

"I understand," Chen nodded. "Thanks for your help."

"Not at all, my friend," Alan smiled as Chen departed. The push had begun, and from an unexpected sector. The South Koreans would exert pressure on the Americans and so would the Japanese, making it more difficult for the President to ignore the situation. *And you will not be able to ignore my plan.*

Chapter Thirty-Seven
Kadena Air Base, Japan
Friday, 3 March 1995

"Hello, General," Colonel Elizabeth Callahan gave him a smile and then a hug when he arrived. Callahan was the CO of the 909th Air Refueling Squadron based at Kadena and a friend from Beu's posting at Mildenhall.

"Hi, Liz, it's good to see you again," Beu said. "I heard you got a command and it's about damn time."

"As long as I get to fly," she said. "Congratulations on your promotion. Do you get any seat time anymore?"

"Once in a while," Beu admitted. "I keep qualified on the –53s but I can't keep up with the kids anymore. I'm not as aggressive as I used to be."

"That's because you're a dad," Callahan said.

"It's because I'm forty-five, darling," Beu drawled. "When I was *twenty*-five, I was too stupid to be afraid of dying."

"Oh, to be young and stupid again," Callahan smiled wistfully. "How are Katie and Alexa?"

"Getting over a tonsillectomy," he said. "Katie, not Alexa. *She's* fine and they'll be along in a couple days. She wanted the surgery to be done at Walter Reed."

"I can understand that. Do you want to come along?"

"What?" Beu looked at her strangely.

"It's time to play gas station for a flight of F-15s," Callahan said. "Do you want to tag along? Vinny's flying lead today." Colonel Vincent Ubriaco was commander of the 12th Fighter Squadron and Callahan's husband.

"I was looking for an excuse to get out of the office," Beu grinned.

"You can even sit up front with the grownups, General."

Pyong Yang, North Korea

"The Americans are using the South as proxies," Kim Sun Park said to his aide. "Our source in Washington believes something will happen shortly."

"What will we do?" The aide asked.

"The 201st Mechanized Infantry Regiment is on its way to Yong Hung was we speak," Park said. "We will be waiting for them."

Aboard Air Force 85-779

"Hound Dog Leader, you're clear to the boom," the nervous airman first class said over the radio to the F-15C Eagle approaching the rear of her KC-10 Extender. The boom engaged the fuel port of the fighter plane. "We have a fuel flow," she said under the watchful eye of her supervisor as she used the controls to keep the boom steady. The youngster was doubly nervous because a general officer was peering over her shoulder as well.

"I've been on the other side many times," Beu said. "But it never fails to amaze me how it works from this end."

"Mother Goose," the pilot of the F-15 said. "This is Hound Dog Leader. I hear General Beu is aboard."

"Yes, sir," the boom operator said. She handed the headset to Beu.

"Hey, Vinny," Beu smiled as he saw Ubriaco wave at him from behind the canopy of his bird.

"Nate Beu, you old rotor head," Ubriaco called back. "Are you making time with my old lady up there?"

"She's flying this beast, pal, she's got no time for me," he kidded. "How's things?"

"Up here, everything is beautiful," Ubriaco replied. "Stop by and we'll crack a beer tonight, bring the wife and kid along."

"They're not here yet, Vinny," Beu told him. "But I'll take you up on it."

"I'll be back by seventeen hundred. Be at the house by nineteen thirty and you can partake in my famous lasagna," Ubriaco promised.

"You got a deal," Beu grinned. He missed his wife's cooking but Ubriaco's ethnic specialties came close.

"Fuel transfer complete," the boom operator said.

"I'm done here," Ubriaco said to Beu. "See you later, General."

"Take care, Vinny," Beu said as the –15 broke the connection and peeled off to the right. "Thanks, Airman, Chief," he said as he left the boom operator's position. "I'm coming to your place for dinner," Beu told Callahan when he arrived on the flight deck.

"That's nice," she said. "You bring the beer."

CIA Headquarters, Langley, Virginia

"It seems the South Koreans and the Japanese caught wind of our little discovery," DCI Louis Guerin said at the meeting of his senior staff. "They are annoyed with us for not informing them and the President is feeling the heat. We're going to let them do the dirty work, but we will give them technical backup."

"What does that mean, sir?" DDI Ron Mitchell asked.

"That means you'll fill in the gaps in their overhead surveillance, you and the boys in Fort Meade," Guerin informed him.

"That means we're out of it." Deputy Director (Operations) Rice asked hopefully.

"For the time being, Dave," Guerin nodded. "For now, we're going to let State handle this through the U.N. quietly."

"That's a relief," Rice said. "I thought we were going forward with Holmgren's operation."

"Not yet," Guerin said. "But the President has been advised we are gaming it. I'd like you to give Holmgren the help he needs to refine it a bit."

"He wants to use mercenaries," Rice complained.

"No," Guerin raised a finger. "Temporary employees," he corrected. "Holmgren is looking into the feasibility of recalling several former military personnel."

"We're going to *draft* them?"

"Something like that," Guerin waved it away. "There is a clause that applies to personnel with a special skill or knowledge."

"Who are these people?" Rice asked, not liking this idea at all.

"I'm not sure of all the details but that will firm up. Holmgren says there's an old Special Forces unit that had experience in North Korea," Guerin explained.

"We had units in *North* Korea?" The question came from more than one.

"About a dozen years ago the Air Force did some things over there. Holmgren was involved with them at the time," the DCI told them. "But we're not at that point yet. We'll wait and see what the Japanese and the South Koreans do."

"Oh joy," Rice muttered.

"Is there are problem, Mr. Rice?"

"None at all, sir."

"Then this meeting is over," Guerin said, and the participants filtered out.

"How well do you know Holmgren?" Rice asked Ron Mitchell.

"He's competent and intelligent, knows that part of the world well," Mitchell advised.

"But?" Rice looked at him as they walked to the elevator.

"He's an apple-polisher, Dave. Senator Latour treats him like the son he never had, and Guerin is close with the senator. Guerin is also an ambitious cocksucker who wants an ambassadorial posting during the President's next term," Mitchell explained. "If Guerin thinks

Holmgren's plan will get him there, he'll shove it down the President's throat."

"Yes, but if it goes to Hell, Lou will be the one swinging for it," the DDO offered.

"Guerin and Holmgren both know how to cover their butts, Dave," Mitchell wagged a finger at him. "Make sure yours is too if this game ever gets off the ground."

"Thanks for the warning," Rice groaned as the elevator opened.

Mineola, Long Island, New York

"Make sure you're there on time," Connie said as she kissed him.

"I'll be there, baby," Rick promised as she shut the door. He watched as she climbed the stairs to the platform of the Long Island Rail Road station. There would be a party tonight at Epstein and Associates, not at the firm but at the *Russian Tea Room*. Normally, old Chaim Epstein did not invite him to corporate functions but tonight was different. "The old geezer knew I'd twist his neck until it snapped if he banned my ass tonight," Rick said aloud as he threw the Chevelle in gear and turned out of the parking lot. Tonight, his wife would become the newest junior partner of the firm and there was no way he wouldn't be there to help her celebrate her success.

Kadena Air Base

"What are you thinking about?" Liz Callahan asked Beu as he stared at a picture over the fireplace.

"That picture of Vinny in New York," Beu pointed. "I knew a couple guys from there, one in particular, a stand-up guy like Vinny. I haven't thought about him in a while, he's Katie's godfather, you know."

"Shouldn't she have a godfather who's in her life?" Callahan said.

"Probably," Beu nodded. "But I know that if anything happened to Alexa and me, he would step up. I know he would keep her safe and make sure she was provided for, or he'd die trying. Without him, I probably would never have married Alexa either," he added. "He was my best man."

"And you lost touch?" Callahan seemed surprised that men so close would fall out of contact.

"He separated from the Air Force," Beu shrugged, knowing it was no excuse. "And our lives changed. It was as if we switched lives when we met. He was in a stable, loving relationship and I was determined to die a bachelor." He laughed. "The last time I saw him he was sleeping with any woman who'd let him and determined never to get close to anyone again. We just had less and less in common and we stopped writing …" Beu thought about it. "Jeez, it's got to be about seven or eight years."

"So Katie doesn't really know him?"

"I doubt she'd remember," the general officer nodded.

"Hey, why is everyone looking like their puppy was just run over?" Vinny Ubriaco asked when he returned from the bathroom.

"Call him, Nate," Callahan said, ignoring her husband. "If he's the type of man you say he is, Katie should know him."

"I'll think about it."

Chapter Thirty-Eight

CIA Headquarters, Langley, Virginia
Monday, 6 March 1995

"They're going tonight," Rice told Holmgren. "I want you downstairs with us when it happens, Colonel."

"Yes, sir," Holmgren smiled.

"How are you coming with your production?" Rice asked him.

"I'll need a week to put it into motion," Alan said confidently. "Depending on what the South Koreans do tonight," he added. "Is their op strictly reconnaissance or will they try to take the warheads out?"

"They say they're just going in for a look," Rice told him. "Chen will be with us so be careful what you say in there."

"How are they going in?"

"They've got a couple frigates and a destroyer in the Sea of Japan," Rice said. "The team will be put ashore by helicopter five miles from the complex."

Holmgren looked at his watch. "How much time to I have?"

"Four hours."

"I have some things to finish," Holmgren lied. "Thanks for the opportunity."

"You'd better hope the Koreans don't screw this up or your butt will be in the hot seat," Rice warned. "The Director seems to like your little paramilitary game, especially since you're not using Agency personnel." Rice leaned forward and looked the younger man over. "If I were you, I'd make sure your team doesn't make it back, whether they are successful or not."

"What are you saying, Mr. Rice," Holmgren looked shocked. He wasn't, for he'd entertained the same thoughts. It was his motivation, the impetus for taking the risk that could cost him everything he'd worked for, to see Rick Johnson and his cohorts perish on the same soil where they let Roger die.

"I'm not saying anything, Colonel Holmgren," Rice leaned back. "But I don't know if I'd want a dozen people running around who know the details of the mission after it's over."

"I'm not doing anything illegal," Holmgren shot back.

"Bringing these people back into military service is legal only by the finest split of a hair," Rice laughed. "That might work with your father-in-law and the Director, but those of us who have to work for a living over here know what kind of shit will hit the fan if the general public ever finds out about this, let alone the Chinese or North Koreans. We've been taking a tough stand with them over Taiwan and I don't think they'd appreciate it if we went diddling around with North Korea. It's too close to home."

"We'll make them sign secrecy directives," Holmgren offered.

"Okay," Rice shrugged. "But if this comes back to bite the President in the ass, *your* ass will be in some listening post in the Aleutians for the remainder of your career."

"So, what do you suggest?"

"I told you, I'm not suggesting anything." Rice shook his head. "I'll deny we had this conversation, but I just gave you something to consider. Just look at history, the times our operations came back to bite us in the ass, Cuba, Angola, Vietnam, someone always talked, and someone's career was flushed every time. I'll tell you right now, I won't be the one called on the carpet over this. Neither will Lou Guerin." Rice looked at his watch. "Do what you have to and be back here at thirteen hundred. I have a meeting." The DDO stood signifying the meeting was over.

"Thank you, Mr. Rice," Holmgren said as he headed to the elevator. The timing would be close, but he had to get a message to Reynaldo. The South Koreans could not be allowed to succeed, or his vengeance would not be sated.

Sea Cliff, Long Island, New York

It wasn't the engine shop he was used to, but Rick was happy here. He'd been here two years and couldn't think of any place he'd rather work. Located right next to the post office, G&H Auto Repair was in the heart of the one square mile town on Long Island's affluent North Shore.

It was a little shop, just he, another mechanic, and the owner, who also turned wrenches whenever they were swamped. They usually were, for Harry ran an ethical place and word had spread. Most of the clientele were rich north shore types who were tired of being taken for a ride by the specialty shops. There were no cappuccino machines here, no TV, no waiting room playing light jazz or classical music, no smartly dressed service advisers falling over them; the place was about auto repair, strictly, and turning out the best product possible. Harry would settle for no less. But there *was* personality here.

Harry was a unique individual, a man of values and ethics, incredibly honest in action and word. Rick respected him as he did Colonel Bryant and others of that breed. Harry was also ex-Air Force, serving in Vietnam before coming home to open his shop. He was speaking with a customer when Rick arrived at work this sunny, crisp March morning.

"But my car was in here three months ago," the woman said. "Why are my brakes squeaking now?"

"We did an oil change," Harry said as he rummaged through the file cabinet, looking for her file. He saved everything, and Rick and the other mechanic, Mike, could never make sense of the system he used. Harry, on the other hand, could find it faster than if he had it on a computer. He found the paper when Rick walked in. Harry and the customer ignored him. "And I made a note on here that your brake pads should be changed but you didn't want to then."

"I don't remember that," she said.

"That's why I wrote it down," Harry said. "I knew I wouldn't either."

"How do I know your men didn't do something when they were working on it?"

"Just what are you accusing me of?"

"Uh oh," Rick muttered.

"Well," the woman went on. "When I brought my car to another place, they broke my heater when they worked on something else. When I brought it back, they charged me to fix it."

"Look, lady," Harry said, trying to keep his cool. The easiest way to get on Harry's bad side was to question his integrity. "There are enough broken cars out there. I don't need to make more work for myself."

"All mechanics are crooks," she said haughtily.

"Oh boy," Rick said as Mike arrived. "It's gonna hit the fan now."

"Oh yeah," Harry growled at the woman as he opened the cash register. Checking her bill, he removed the forty dollars she'd paid for the oil change and twelve thousand mile service and threw it at her. "Take your money and shove it up your ass. Don't ever come back here again. Find someone else to rip you off." He turned and stormed away from her, out into the shop. "What are you two assholes laughing at?"

"Your charming personality, boss," Mike replied.

"Fuck her," Harry shot back. "Nobody accuses me of being a crook. I don't want her money, or her business." He made a show of ripping up her file and tossing it in the trash. "Neither of you better make her an appointment if she comes back. Her ass is banned."

"No way," Rick said as Harry marched back into his office. He looked to Mike, a man he also respected, just as the men of 23rd he'd served with, and grinned. "The old boy is pissed."

"His hip is acting up again," Mike said, sipping his coffee. "He'll be in a bad mood all day, especially since Mrs. Moskowitz fired his ass up first thing on Monday."

"He should get it replaced," Rick said.

"He doesn't like doctors," Mike explained. "He had the other hip done, but he dragged his dead leg around for five years until the pain got too much for him to bear." Mike was that way, another who spoke plainly, and another with whom there was no doubt where you stood. "He'll wait just as long with this one."

Langley, Virginia

"We have the feed, sir," the technician said without looking up.

"There's the chopper," Holmgren said as the Japanese Self-Defense Forces MH-60 flew into the scene displayed on the large monitor on one wall of the room.

The helicopter flared and set down, discharging a KCIA paramilitary squad comprised of six men. Seconds later, the chopper lifted off and turned east toward the Sea of Japan. As it was about to fly out of range of the satellite's high-resolution infrared camera, there was a flare of bright white on the ground.

"What the ..." Several people began to ask the question, but it was answered when a surface to air missile raced toward the fleeing helicopter. It impacted two seconds later, the fireball causing the people assembled to shield their eyes. Looking back to the center of the screen, they saw the forest erupt in gunfire as the South Korean team came under fire. It was over in minutes.

There was stunned silence for a minute before all eyes turned to Chen Hua Li. A single tear ran down his cheek as he witnessed his countrymen die. "They knew we were coming," he said without emotion. "I have to contact my superiors."

"I'm sorry, Li," Holmgren said to him as he passed.

"They knew we were coming," he whispered again as he left the room.

"They've got a leak in either Seoul or Tokyo," DDI Mitchell said as he shook his head. "The North Koreans knew they were coming and knew what they were coming *with*."

"This could get ugly, depending on how far the North Koreans want to push it," Jimenez, the State Department liaison said.

"I have to get to the White House," Guerin said as he turned to Holmgren. "I want your operation ready to go on seventy-two hours' notice."

"Yes, sir," Holmgren nodded as the DCI left just after the State guy did. Holmgren was alone with Rice, Mitchell, and DDCI Holt.

"You got what you wanted," Rice chuckled. "But if I were you, I'd figure out a better way to insert your team."

"I want Evans to look it over," Bobby Holt said. William Evans was the Agency General Counsel. "If he doesn't like it, it doesn't fly."

"I'll need a code word, sir," Holmgren said.

Holt thought a minute. "No, Colonel Holmgren, I think this operation will remain between the four of us for now. There will be no official record of this unless it is absolutely necessary."

"I don't like this," Mitchell said. "This can't stink from square one."

"It was rotten from the beginning," Rice said. "I get the funny feeling we were meant to see the missile and they're counting on us to act."

"Why, Dave?" Holt asked. "Have you read Colonel Holmgren's brief? There were several engagements with North Korean troops during the early eighties, the largest of which was at a foundry well within North Korea. They probably figured we sabotaged their plant and I am sure they would expect us to take action again if we found out about their missiles. Why would they want us to see it? How would they know we have a satellite capable of detecting their weapons if they *did* want us to see it?"

"Maybe we have a leak," Rice shrugged. "Maybe *we* are the ones who've been compromised?" He looked at them all. "We'll brief

380

Evans in an hour," he said to Holmgren. "Be in my office with your product in thirty minutes."

"Yes, sir." Holmgren left the room.

"If this blows up ..." Mitchell threw up his hands. "This is happening too quickly and without proper oversight."

"It all depends on the President," Bobby Holt said. "We'll see when the Director gets back. Until then, it stays on this level."

Rice and Mitchell nodded and waked together to the elevator. "I don't want any part of this, Ron," Rice said when they were safely inside the elevator car.

"It's in your shop now," Mitchell said. "CYA is the watchword."

"Amen," Rice said with a smile as he stepped out, headed for his office, motioning for Tim Gordon to follow him. "Close the door," he said when they were both in the office. "Who do you know at S&T that won't require a formal request for some hardware?"

"I have a connection over there," Gordon said with a nod.

"I need a small recording device, maybe even a remote transmitter to my computer," Rice said. "And I want one that works inside this building."

"Woof," Gordon scratched his head. "They might want to have some documentation of need, sir."

"See what you can do, Tim," Rice patted his shoulder. "It might mean keeping our jobs after this Korean thing goes down."

Lubyanka, Moscow, Russia

"Marshal," Boris Popov said as he entered. Kosarev looked up. "Colonel Zhukov is here."

"*Here?*" Kosarev stood and Popov confirmed with a nod. "Send him in." His face grew a broad smile when Marko Zhukov entered. "What are you doing here, my old friend." They embraced warmly.

"I wanted to talk to you about this face to face, Marshal," he said when Kosarev released him. "As you know, I have been in contact with Low Chen." Kosarev nodded before Zhukov went on. "I was in Tokyo when he contacted me and came directly here. I was hoping I would find you working late, but that has become your habit since Alexa and Katherine …"

"There is *nothing* at home," Kosarev spat. "What did he say?"

"The Japanese and South Koreans sent a reconnaissance team to the Sung Complex last night," Zhukov said. "They were engaged immediately and killed; their air assets destroyed."

"The little bastard's tentacles reach farther than I thought," Kosarev shook his head. "He must have someone in Seoul or Tokyo, maybe both."

"Low Chen wants to leave," Zhukov offered. "He fears General Park will find he was the one who sabotaged the door."

"Tell him we will get him out, but he will have to remain a few weeks, maybe a month," Kosarev said. "If the Koreans failed, the Americans would surely try, and I want him in a position to help them."

"He might not have that long, Yevgeniy."

"He knew the risks when he chose to betray his country," the Chairman of the Federal Security Service insisted.

"He sees himself the patriot," Zhukov said.

"He will only be a patriot if he is successful, Marko, or he will die a traitor."

Langley, Virginia

"Given enough time," William Evans said. "This thing will be picked apart by some smart lawyer. Are these 'temporary employees' Americans?"

"Yes," Holmgren replied.

"Not good," Evans shook his head. "I don't believe the Agency can be held criminally responsible, but we could be exposed to civil liability, Colonel Holmgren. That's not accounting for the damage to the foreign policy of the United States if your men are discovered."

"That's why we are using these particular personnel, Mr. Evans," Holmgren said.

"We shouldn't be doing this at all," Evans shot back.

"While I agree with you, Bill," Dave Rice said. "This isn't our call. It seems the Director and the President want this to go forward."

"Maybe I should speak with the White House counsel," Evans said and picked up the phone. "This is Evans at Langley, is Jeff in?" He said to the phone. Rice and Holmgren waited through a collection of yeses, nos, and uh-huhs for five minutes before he turned his attention back to them after exhaling loudly. "Why in Hell does he have to have a midlife crisis?"

"Excuse me?" Rice asked though he knew what Evans was saying.

"The President feels this would be a good way to strengthen our image in the region," Evans said. "The only reservation they have over there is the deniability angle."

"Oh, this will be deniable," Holmgren assured him. "If it goes bad, which it won't, only the military should have any exposure."

Evans computer beeped and he hit a key, revealing a letter of authorization on White House letterhead. He gave a command to the printer and handed the paper to Holmgren.

"You've got the ball," Rice said as Holmgren read it. "Don't drop it because I'm not the one that will have to pick it up."

"I don't understand," Holmgren said.

"Look at the paper," Rice said. "Your name and the Director's are the only ones on it, and I don't want to be connected to it. This is *your* operation, Colonel, make sure the Agency is not embarrassed."

"Yes, sir," Alan said and left the office.

"They're letting their ambition lead them," Evans said.

"Of course," Rice laughed. "The President wants to show the North Koreans and Chinese that he has a set of testicles, Guerin wants to be Ambassador to France, and Holmgren wants to be CIA Director." Rice thought about that. "He might be the only one of the three who benefits from this."

"What does Bobby Holt say?"

"He's washing his hands of it, just like I am," Rice explained. "And I'm going to see the Director when he gets back from the White House to advise him of that. When Holmgren goes down, I'm *not* going with him."

Chapter Thirty-Nine
The Capitol, Washington, D.C.
Tuesday, 7 March 1995

"Bases should be closed overseas first," Senator Butch Overton (R-Mississippi) said. "We're putting Americans out of work while we're supporting foreign economies. We're wasting money …"

"Wasting money?" Jacob Levy cut him off as he rose from his seat near the back of the chamber. "Wasting money? You have the nerve to stand up in this committee chamber and talk about wasting money?"

"There is no need to be adversarial, Mr. Levy," Overton shot back.

"Oh *no*?" Levy began turning red, a sure sign he was displeased. "To me, a waste of money is the two cruise ships being built in your state that no one wants. The company who began building them went out of business and you managed to obligate the government to finish them. So far, you have spent a quarter of a billion dollars and will waste another fifty million before they are complete. None of the cruise lines have shown an interest of them so the taxpayers will own two brand new cruise ships that will remain tied up to the pier in Pascagoula."

"The Navy has agreed to accept delivery of them if they cannot be sold," Overton growled.

"I have *yet* to talk to an admiral who wants them, Senator Overton," Levy spat. "And if the Navy *does* take them, it will cost an additional ten million apiece to convert them for troop carrying duty. How can you keep a straight face when you tell the public you are crusading against fraud, waste, and abuse?"

"I can sleep at night."

"Yes, because you don't have to tell the people of *your* state that they are paying all that money to subsidize five thousand workers on the Mississippi coast. You show the greatest amount of fiscal irresponsibility in this Congress, Mr. Overton. There isn't one appropriations bill coming through here without it being loaded with pork for the state of Mississippi. What I want to know is; where do you get off, sir?"

"That tone will not be tolerated on this floor, Mr. Levy," Overton shouted back at him. "You will have your chance to speak before this body."

"Why would the American people not want to hear the truth, sir? My chance to speak will come when the chamber is empty, when one of the senior members decides to yield me several minutes out of pity. All of you here had better remember this, ladies and gentlemen. I will *not* be silenced. I intend to inform the American people exactly what goes on here and if I have to interrupt you to do it, then that is what I will do. We are here because the people trust us to do what's best with their money, for the good of the nation, not just our little corner of it, but what do we do? We add riders to appropriations for projects that do the country as a whole very little good.

"Oh yes," Levy went on as the acting President of the Senate rapped his gavel and ordered him to sit down. "It's nice to go home and say, 'look what I've done for you', especially in an election year. I'm sure you'll get *all* five thousand votes at that shipyard, Senator Overton, but at the cost of a half billion dollars that could be more wisely spent for the good of the whole, not the very few. There are some among you who feel as I do, but the rest of you disgust and embarrass me."

"That will be *enough*, Mr. Levy," Dick Robertson (R-Florida) said.

"Sit *down*, Jacob," Phillip Boylan (R-Georgia) barked.

"Come on, Jacob," Barbara Kristoll (D-Massachusetts) urged him with a tug on his sleeve. "They're going to censure you one day."

"*Let* them," he hissed at her.

"Goddamn it, Levy, sit down or I'll knock you down. This is the United States Senate, for God's sake," Ian Jensen (D-California) growled.

Levy ignored them, but he did sit down, leaning over to talk to Kristoll. "You feel the same way I do, Barbara," he said. "Why don't *you* say something?"

"Because there is a process," she told him. "A process we've refined over two hundred years."

"Do you call this *refined?*" Levy slumped in his chair. "All they've refined is the methods they use to screw the average citizen. They should all thank God every day that the average joker on the street doesn't have a clue what we do here, or they'd drag us all out and string us up on the Mall."

"They've gotten too used to their power," she said, looking around the chamber. "And there is nothing you can say or do to make them give it up. Look at Hal Duquesne over there." Duquesne (R-Louisiana) was the Senate Majority Leader. "Have you ever been to his place in Georgetown? Have you ever seen his place in New Orleans?"

"I'm the *last* person he'd invite to his house," Levy laughed sardonically. "Hell, I'm not even a Democrat, let alone from his own party."

"He has those things because he's been here for thirty years, and for all of those years, he's brought appropriations to Louisiana. What have you brought to New York, Jacob? What can you point to in election season, something tangible and say to your constituents 'I did this for you'?"

"That's not the point, Barbara," Levy shook his head as Overton continued his monologue. "The point is we are a *representative* body. We represent our home state and all the people within it. They trust us to spend their money here the way they do at home. Deficit spending is something that only happens in Washington because the average Joe would go bankrupt in no time. Do you realize the kind of crap we could cut out of a budget if they wouldn't attach all this additional spending?"

"But they would lose jobs in their home states, or not create any new ones, and eventually lose theirs," Kristoll said.

"If we invested the money they waste to build ships in new technology, they would create more jobs than they save," Levy countered.

"Politics is local, Jacob," she replied. "Five thousand jobs in his home state are worth more to Overton than a hundred thousand in New York or Boston, or wherever because they don't vote for him. It might be better for the country, but not for Butch if he wants to come back here, and he wants to be like Hal Duquesne when he grows up." Kristoll smiled. "Besides, if you keep getting so worked up, you'll have a stroke before they have a chance to censure you."

"I wouldn't give them the satisfaction," Levy grinned back.

CIA Headquarters, Langley, Virginia

"We can begin on Friday, sir," Holmgren said to Louis Guerin. "I have six teams enroute."

"We're walking a thin line here, Alan," the DCI replied. "I'm counting on you to do your usual exceptional work, but the stakes are high. The repercussions of failure could affect many powerful and influential people."

"I understand," Holmgren nodded. "I have every contingency planned for, from best case to worst case."

Guerin raised his hand to stop Holmgren. "The less I know, the better," he said. "Just make sure any contingencies are handled *quietly*. This will do neither of our careers any good if word gets out."

"Yes, sir," Holmgren took his paperwork and returned to his section. He'd worked the deception well, Guerin and the President grasping at the opportunity he gave them, yet not wanting to know too many of the details in case the operation went bad. Holmgren would make sure it did; he would as soon as he verified the deposit in the Bank of Singapore.

The money would be there, as it always was, but this would be the biggest payment yet, enough for him to leave when the operation was over. Holmgren would have to; it was too dangerous for him to stay once failure was imminent, but he would be near his destination when it became obvious. There were many islands within the Indonesian Archipelago, and he'd made arrangements to own a section of one of them when he began a relationship with Hector Reynaldo and his employers. The end would come soon but he had to make his life less complicated before then, make it easy to leave. Holmgren picked up the phone.

His first call was to a real estate agent, the second to American Airlines. With the first call, he put his house in Georgetown up for sale; with the second, he bought one round trip ticket to Puerto Rico. Holmgren made a third call, to a different real estate agent, and advised he was in the market for a small apartment. Another call was made to his home number.

"Hi, darling," he said when Venice answered the phone.

"Hi, baby," Venice said in her usual sultry voice.

"I've got a surprise for you," he told her. "How would you like to visit your mother for a week? I know you've been talking about going back home to see her."

"I love you, baby," Venice said.

"You leave on Sunday," Holmgren replied. "I thought I'd tell you now so you could shop for some new clothes."

"You're the best, Alan," she said. "Will you come with me?"

"I'll be home in a little while," he promised and hung up. "And so it begins," he said quietly as the wheels were set in inexorable motion.

Sea Cliff, Long Island, New York

"Hey."

Johnson looked up at the sound of the male voice. He was alone in the shop, Harry and Mike at lunch. "What can I do for you, buddy?"

"Are you open on Saturdays?"

"You bet, at least in the morning," Rick said with a nod as he grabbed a rag. "You'll have to have it here at 7:30, pick it up before noon. What do you need?"

"Just an oil change," the man said.

"Sure," Rick went to the appointment book. "Name?"

"Cooper."

"Make and model?"

"'94 Ford Crown Victoria."

"V-8?"

"Yes," Mr. Cooper replied.

"Good man," Rick smiled as he looked past the new customer at his car. "Police package, huh?"

"Yeah, bought it at auction," Cooper told him.

"One of the best cars Ford ever made," Johnson agreed as he finished writing the pertinent information into the book. Rick looked up and appraised the man. "You've never been here before, have you?"

"No, I just moved here, but my neighbors say that this place is the best around."

"They got that right," Johnson pointed at the sign that hung over the appointment desk. It said 'Zero Defects, Zero Tolerance for Mistakes'. "We do it right the first time; Harry wouldn't have it any other way."

"That's good to know," Cooper turned toward the door.

"7:30 Saturday, Mr. Cooper. Don't be late, I like to get out by twelve," Rick warned.

"You'll be working?"

"Yeah, we rotate Saturdays," Rick nodded. "It's my day this week. Thanks for your business, Mr. Cooper."

"Who was that asshole?" Harry asked as he returned from the deli around the corner to see Cooper drive away.

"A new customer," Rick replied. "He heard about your charming personality from his neighbors," he kidded his boss.

"I'm here to fix cars, not to make friends," Harry growled as he put his lunch on the desk. "Looks like an unmarked cop car," he observed as Cooper passed on the street."

"It is," Rick nodded. "Bought it at auction, he said."

"He looks like a cop," Harry said. "So does his buddy." He went back to unwrapping his sandwich.

And it was then Rick felt something he hadn't in many years. It was a tingling at the back of his neck and a slight ringing in his ears. It wasn't something he could control, and he'd had this feeling several times before. The tingling always got worse before it got better, and the ringing would become clanging alarm bells before silence returned. It was the feeling he had when going into combat, his instinct telling him there was imminent danger surrounding Mr. Cooper. And then he thought he was being foolish. Even if Cooper were a cop, there would be no reason for Rick to worry. He didn't break the law. "I'm being an idiot."

"It's about time you realized that," Harry said with a full mouth. "Is that brake job done?"

"No."

"Then get back to work, fuck face."

"I love you too, boss," Johnson laughed as he walked back into the shop.

Hurlburt Field, Fort Walton Beach, Florida

"Do you have any questions, Chief?" Colonel W.A. Choudry asked him.

"No, sir," Chief Master Sergeant John Reasoner replied. "But the orders seem awful cryptic. I suppose it will all be explained at the appropriate time."

"Indeed," Choudry shook his head. "I can't say I like this, but it comes from the top and they didn't ask my opinion."

"Who exactly is running this operation anyway?" Reasoner asked him.

"You'll report to a Lieutenant Frank Roman, he'll be your CO. The command authority is a Colonel Alan Holmgren, from Air Force Intelligence," Choudry told him.

"That sounds like a euphemism for the CIA, Colonel."

"It probably is," Choudry nodded. "Have you picked your weapons specialists yet?"

"Petersen and Coles will come along," Reasoner replied. "They share a SAW and they know their way around C-4 and Semtex. I'm taking Joe Rockwood too, I want at least one NCO with me I can trust, sir."

"So, I'll be losing four of my best people," Choudry grumbled. "They assured me it wouldn't be for long."

"How long is this supposed to be, sir? I'd like to tell Angie something about when to expect me home."

"They tell me a month or so."

"Sounds good," Reasoner said. "This is the strangest TDY I've ever been on. Never have I been assigned to my own base temporarily, let alone act if I've been sent somewhere on the other side of the world. They won't even let me call home."

"I don't understand it either, Chief, but you've been in the game long enough."

"That I have, sir." Reasoner nodded and left, wondering who would comprise the rest of the temporary unit. *This is too weird*, he thought as he walked to his car.

Chapter Forty

Kadena Air Base, Okinawa, Japan
Wednesday, 8 March 1995

"I just got a weird call," Colonel White said as he entered the office of the commander, 18th Operations Group.

"What about?" Beu asked as he looked up from his paperwork.

"They're sending a special ops unit here in a couple weeks," White told his boss. "They want use of a hangar for an indeterminate amount of time and a security cordon set up around it."

"They aren't getting shit without the proper authorization," Beu muttered. "Am I supposed to pull a spare hangar out of my ass? We'll have to take one away from one of the flying units and I don't want to hear the screaming."

"They're faxing over authorization as we speak, General," White said.

"Who are *they*?"

"Special Operations Command, sir."

Beu gave him a sideways look and picked up his phone. "Ellen," he said to his secretary. "Get me Lieutenant General Harley Clay at MacDill. I don't care if it's three in the morning yesterday over there, get him out of bed if you have to." He hung up and looked back to White.

A female chief knocked and entered, handing a fax to White before departing. "Here you go," he dropped it on Beu's desk.

Beu let out a whistle when he read the signature at the bottom. "This comes from the President."

The intercom buzzed. "General Clay for you, sir," the secretary said.

"Harley," Beu said. "What's this they just sent me from Washington? Two weeks is no time for us to prepare to add another unit here."

"Sorry, Nate," Clay replied. "I got the same orders you did. I'm giving up one of my planes and an aircrew for this, as well as a section of one of my bases, and I don't know why either. When I called the Pentagon, they told me to give my full cooperation and mind my own business. That came from the Air Force Chief of Staff."

"So what, I have to put your people up for *however* long until whatever it is they're doing is finished?"

"And give them your full cooperation, don't forget that," Clay kidded. "I hear there's some Intel officer running this. You might want to corral him when he gets there and squeeze him a bit. Let me know what you get out of him because they aren't telling me shit here."

"Thanks, Harl," Beu said. "I'll let you know when I hear something." He hung up and looked to White. "Go see Liz Callahan and tell her the next phase bird will have to be done outside on one of the spots."

"She won't be happy," White warned.

"Tell her to see me if she has any questions."

"Better you than me," White said and set off for the 909th Orderly Room.

Washington, D.C.

"Hi, Bob," Levy said when freshman congressman Robert Clarke (D-Massachusetts) sat down. They met at one of the local restaurants that catered to the Beltway crowd. "What's so important?"

"Jacob," Clarke said as he looked around. "I have a friend who works for Air Force Intelligence, we went to college together. He knows I'm on the Committee and he wanted me to know a few things that worry him." Clarke was the junior Democratic member of the House Intelligence Oversight Committee.

"Why are you telling me?" Levy asked after the waitress took their order. "Bring it up to the Committee."

"Because it involves Senator LaTour's son-in-law," Clarke whispered. "He's a colonel in AFIS and politically connected."

"And you figure I don't care whom I piss off?"

"Something like that," Clarke said sheepishly.

"So, what's going on?"

Clarke waited until their salads were served. "My friend says there's been a lot of interest in North Korea in the past week and there are rumors that the South Koreans ran a reconnaissance operation there that failed miserably. From what I hear, *we're* going to try it next."

"What's so important that we are willing to risk war over there?" Levy asked and Clarke shrugged. "Are you sure this isn't some rumor your friend bought into."

"I've known him since my freshman year at Yale," Clarke said. "He was my best man when I married Jen, I trust his judgment and his sense of perspective. He wouldn't have gone out of his way to tell me if he weren't damn sure."

"Who's running the operation?"

"A guy named Holmgren," Clarke said. "As I said, he's LaTour's son-in-law and came up through Air Force Intelligence. Word is he's with the Operations Directorate over at CIA now. It seems he's been ruffling feathers from Florida to Japan to get this thing off the ground."

"Is he using Air Force personnel?"

"I don't know, Jacob," Clarke said. "I know you know some people over at the Pentagon and Langley, you might be able to see what this is all about."

"Surely the President must know about this," Levy offered. "Wouldn't they need his authorization to pursue an operation over there? I mean, Americans on North Korean soil could cause them to attack South Korea. It could cause the Chinese to get involved."

"That's what worries me," Clarke admitted. "And that's what worries my friend. This was laid on too quickly to be kosher; if you'll pardon the expression." Clarke leaned closer.

"Look, Jacob, I was the Boston D.A. for eight years and I know when something smells fishy. The CIA Director and Senator Latour are good friends and Holmgren is LaTour's widowed son-in-law, do you think it's a coincidence he's running the thing? Latour is one of the most vociferous anti-Communists in Congress and Louis Guerin is one of the most ambitious men in Washington. Do you think the President had a chance against that kind of political capital? Besides, he's worried that he doesn't look tough enough. He'd probably agree to anything that would help him look manly in that area."

"But that's not a good enough reason to go to war, or at the least light the fuse," Levy said.

"I told you all I know, Jacob," Clarke said. "If I hear anything more, I'll let you know."

"I'll ask around," Levy tried to sound disinterested. Once Clarke got wound up about something, there was no stopping him. It was why the man was such a good district attorney.

Levy liked Clarke, a man of principle and ethics, he was still getting the feel of the place and was a bit overwhelmed, just as Levy was when he first got here. *He'll go far*, Levy thought as he watched Clarke cut his filet. *He'll get the hang of this place and teach them all a thing or two*. It took Levy nearly a decade to see how prophetic his thoughts were.

Chapter Forty-One
Sung Rocket Complex, Yong Hung, North Korea
Thursday, 9 March 1995

General Kim Sun Park checked the computer in front of him, satisfied the entire complex's systems were operating within specified limits. It was the first time a full power, full systems test was run, and he was a bit nervous. It was the culmination of over a decade of work and the incident with the missile door worried him, but no other glitches had been found. He was pleased with his source in the American CIA for alerting him to the recent threat from the South Koreans and the forthcoming one from the Americans.

The ease with which his men dispatched the South Korean team and the Japanese helicopter gave him confidence that the Americans would be dealt with just as quickly. There would also be more, for he would move against the South using the American incursion as the catalyst. It was something he'd only dreamt about, never thought he'd be in this position, but he had the troops and he had the will, and once events were set in motion they would be very difficult for Pyong Yang to stop.

Hurlburt Field, Fort Walton Beach, Florida

The dawn was turning into early morning, the sun casting long shadows on the four men as they arrived at the expanse of marshland that seemed to stretch forever to the north. It was known as Area 1A, a fifty square mile area encompassing a mockup of a quaint European village. It was a remnant of the Cold War, a place where Special Forces could train for the operations in Western Europe that would never occur now that the Soviet Union was just a bad memory.

"That's one big ugly sucker," Airman First Class Coles said.

"He'd make a nice pair of boots," Sergeant Joe Rockwood added.

"Make that a pair of boots, a belt, and a wallet for all of us," A1C Petersen said.

"That's a beautiful animal," John Reasoner said with admiration as he traded stares with the fifteen-foot long male alligator that watched the four men from the marshy swamp twenty feet away. The gator floated on the surface at the edge of the marsh, presumably debating if the men were a viable food source. On shore, they didn't qualify but once in the water, in the alligator's living room, they just might. "Besides, he looks too well fed to bother with us."

"Have you heard anything more, Chief," Coles asked Reasoner.

"Nope," he shook his head. "All I know is the rest of them will be here Saturday morning."

"What unit are they from?" Petersen asked.

"They didn't tell me."

"Who is the CO?" Rockwood asked.

"Again, I don't know," Reasoner said firmly. "He'll be here on Friday." Reasoner looked up at Rockwood. "I know; I don't like this either."

The alligator snorted and looked them over once more before submerging.

Lubyanka, Moscow, Russia

"There is a communiqué from Colonel Zhukov, Marshal," Boris Popov said handing the envelope to Kosarev. "It came in the diplomatic pouch."

The big man gave his aide an annoyed look before opening the letter. As he read his hands began to shake, guilt and anger filling him. "And they will die as well," he whispered.

"Excuse me?" Popov said.

"I have done a terrible thing," Kosarev said, looking up at the young man, studying Popov's wiry frame and ferret face. "Zhukov learned that General Park has someone in the American CIA, Boris," he said softly. "The Americans will die just as the Koreans did. I assumed he had someone in Seoul; Park might be insane, but he *is* good. He will know how and where the Americans will come, and he will slaughter them. And I caused this. You were right, we should have undertaken this endeavor ourselves. I might be causing the thing I was trying to prevent."

"Can we help them?" Boris asked.

"The Americans?"

"Yes, sir."

"And how do you propose I do *that?*"

"General Beu is in Japan ..." Boris' voice trailed off when Kosarev stood. The only thing in his mind was whether Kosarev would kill him with the Makarov in his top drawer or his bare hands.

The Bear stood transfixed, as if Popov had slapped him in the face and he was unsure whether the young man was insane or just that stupid. And then he wondered how he'd found out. "Do not *ever* mention his name in here again," Kosarev growled through clenched teeth, the steel blue eyes burning hot and ice cold, and Boris wilted. "How did you know?"

"I saw you writing a letter ..." Boris paused. "I thought Alexa was dead, Marshal?"

"She *is* as far as you are concerned."

"And she is married to the general?"

"And I have a lovely granddaughter named Katherine Alexandra."

"For your late wife."

"Yes, Boris. General Beu is not to be contacted by anyone from this office; this information will not leave this office, even if it means the death of Mother Russia. I will *not* have my family used or put in danger."

"How ..."

"He did me a favor many years ago, when he and I were both stationed in the Far East," Kosarev explained.

"He helped Alexa defect."

"Yes," Kosarev smiled when he thought about that night.

"But the Soviet Union is gone, Marshal," Boris suggested. "You could continue your relationship with them now."

"No, I cannot," Kosarev shook his head sadly. "What do you think would happen to Nathan Beu's career when it is learned he is married to the daughter of the KGB Chairman? People would make assumptions about him that are most certainly untrue. He is a loyal officer who made the mistake of doing the right thing when he was young and foolish, and I will not make him pay for that now. He is a good husband to Alexa and an exceptional father to Katherine."

"But if we could get word to him …"

"No, Boris." Kosarev took his seat. "The American team will die. General Beu is not an option."

"But it is not just the American team, Marshal."

"I believe you have work to do," Kosarev barked, still debating whether to have Popov killed rather than let him carry the information he had in his head.

"But, Marshal, why did you have Low Chen sabotage the missile door in the first place, what was your motivation?" Kosarev just glared at him but said nothing. "Suppose General Park uses the American operation as an excuse to move against the South. He has the nuclear advantage now and you and I both know the Americans will not bring their nuclear arsenal into play on behalf of the South Koreans. We also know they will be hesitant about attacking the North because of the probable Chinese response. A Chinese entry to the conflict would escalate things dramatically. I haven't run it past the analysts yet, but if General Park goes south, the Americans will let him have it."

"And since when are *you* an analyst?" Kosarev muttered.

"Since I became your aide," Boris ventured a small smile. "You are always using me as a sounding board, sir. I do believe some of it is rubbing off on me."

"Maybe so," Kosarev replied. "Maybe you're just a nosy little bastard." He stared at Popov and raised an index finger. "So help me, Boris. I have known your father for fifty years, but I will not hesitate to kill you with my bare hands if anything said here leaves this office."

"I will give my life before I divulge your secrets, Marshal," Popov said.

"Yes, you will."

Chapter Forty-Two

CIA Headquarters, Langley, Virginia
Friday, 10 March 1995

"I'll be leaving later this afternoon," Holmgren said to David Rice. "The retrieval operation will begin tonight."

"Don't make a mess of this, Colonel," Rice warned. "Need I remind you it is illegal for the Agency to operate on U.S. soil."

"There will be no connection to Langley," Holmgren said in an annoyed tone. He was tired of all the warnings, from Rice to Mitchell, to Bill Evans and Bobby Holt, they'd been relentless, but he cared not about any damage this would do to the Agency. Once he left Washington he would never return, never have to answer for his actions, never have to face the relatives of the men he'd sent to die, and never have to take responsibility for the events he'd set into motion that could very well put millions of lives in jeopardy.

Rice waited until Holmgren left before picking up the phone. "Jay," he said to his secretary, Jay Lewis. "See if the Director has a few minutes for me."

"Yes, Mr. Rice," Lewis replied as he called up to the seventh-floor office of the DCI. "He can see you now, sir."

"I'm on my way up," Rice replied as he headed for the elevator, the miniature recording device installed under the lapel of his jacket. Tim Gordon had come through and none aside from the two men and an S&T specialist were aware it was in Rice's possession.

It was a short trip upstairs via the elevator and the Director's secretary showed Rice directly to the inner office. "Good morning, Dave," Louis Guerin said as he looked up from his PC.   "What can I do for you?"

"Good morning, sir," Rice said. "I came to talk to you about this operation of Colonel Holmgren's."

"You have reservations?"

"Many of them, sir," Rice nodded. "The biggest is that this was laid on too quickly."

"The President agreed that speed was of the essence," Guerin replied. "The consensus is that the North Koreans would not be expecting another operation so soon after the first one, *especially* after the first one was such a failure."

"But there is a leak somewhere, sir," Rice insisted. "You can't believe the North Koreans were that lucky to be in the right place at the right time to thwart the South Koreans' operation. They knew to expect them and I'm afraid they will be expecting our people as well. We should wait until we learn where the North Koreans got their information."

"That could take an indefinite, indeterminate amount of time, Dave," Guerin soothed although the DDO sensed Guerin's displeasure at this line of questioning. "We are certain the details of the raid were not leaked by the Agency and the South Koreans and Japanese have been kept out of the loop."

"I believe we are making a mistake, sir," Rice offered. "And I can't believe the President would authorize this with so many questions still left unanswered."

"The President was not made aware of all the facts, Mr. Rice," Guerin admitted. "But he will be once this operation reveals the true nature of the North Korean nuclear program. It will yield the answers we are looking for."

"And suppose it ends in failure just like the first operation?"

"We have learned from that one, learned what the South Koreans and the Japanese did wrong." Guerin insisted.

"And suppose one or more of our team is captured or killed? Suppose the North Koreans learn the identities of our people and use it against us?"

"You're dealing in speculation, Mr. Rice," Guerin hissed. "But I can assure you that deniability is built in."

"Did Holmgren tell you that?"

"Yes," Guerin barked. "And I have *every* confidence in his abilities."

"I'm glad *you* do, Mr. Director," Rice shot back. "Because I don't trust him as far as I can spit into the wind."

"Are you afraid for your job?" Guerin asked maliciously. "Holmgren is one of your people, are you trying to submarine him?"

"It will be a cold day in Hell when that upstart works me out of a job, sir. My only concern is this half-assed operation going wrong and how it will affect the Agency," Rice said angrily. "And I'm not the only one," he went on. "Bobby Holt doesn't even want to put this one on the books. We're financing it through the back channels, nothing going through the official accounting process, and Bobby is the most hawkish guy here."

"It will be done retroactively, when the mission ends successfully," Guerin said.

"So you have as much confidence in Holmgren as I do."

"I didn't say that, Dave," Guerin was adamant. "The appropriate Members of Congress and the President have been advised and that is all that is required at this point."

"As if Senator Latour would voice objections about the man who is the son he never had," Rice said disgustedly.

"I do believe you are out of line, Mr. Rice," Guerin said, his voice rising a few decibels. "The senator is a good friend of mine who lost a daughter and grandchild to senseless violence and I will not stand for your disparaging remarks."

"Well you and the senator will hang alongside Holmgren when this goes awry," Rice stood. "If the President is caught in the middle of this, you'll be going to jail."

"Do not threaten me ..."

"No threat, sir," Rice said. "But you said so yourself, the President was not made aware of all the details."

"And if you repeat that outside this room, I will see you in jail, Deputy Director Rice, never forget that. The operation will commence in a few hours and I expect you to give Colonel Holmgren your full cooperation and support or you *will* be out of a job."

"As you wish, sir," Rice growled and left, breaking into a smile as he stepped into the elevator. His smile got wider when he returned to his office and found the new file his computer had created in a new directory. The sound file contained everything he and the Director had discussed for the five minutes he was on the seventh floor. "No, Director Guerin, it will be *you* who goes to jail."

Georgetown, D.C.

"When will you be back, baby?" Venice asked him as she nuzzled him.

"In a month or so," Holmgren replied. "I wish I didn't have to go, but you know the military." His hands went to her abdomen and then lower and she spread her legs apart for him.

Through the silky spandex he could feel her arousal, the stiffness that she would keep tucked up between her legs when they were out in public. Even with the hormone shots that softened her voice and kept the body hair from appearing, Venice could still become fully erect and she slipped her pants down before stepping out of them. She forced him to his knees and pulled his face to her, pushing herself past his lips, and he gobbled her in hungrily. "I'm going to miss you, Alan," she said as a moan escaped her.

More than you know, Holmgren thought as Venice pushed farther down his throat with each thrust.

Prescott, Arizona

"Yeah," Nick Mason said as he applied power to the recently restored 1978 Harley Davidson Electra-Glide. The reworked V-twin engine roared with delight as the big bike bounded down the dirt road as Mason steered into the desert. The sun was beginning to set, the orange ball flattening as it fell behind the mountains.

Mason didn't notice the thump-thump of the rotor blades over the sound of the 1200cc motor thanks to the large pipes and their throaty roar. Only when the chopper was nearly on top of him did he feel the rotor wash and look up. "What the fuck?"

The helicopter was Vietnam vintage, a Huey still painted the original olive drab, the side door pulled back. A man was taking aim at him with a rifle when he looked up and then Mason felt the dart hit him in the shoulder and he saw his world go black.

Memphis, Tennessee

"Good gig," Jake Guthrie patted his band mates on the shoulder as they passed him on their way out to their cars. He was always the last to leave, driving the van that carried their instruments and amplifiers. The band, *The Tune Masters*, was a popular cover group in the Memphis area, playing all the country hits from the last thirty years and the staples required of a group that made its money playing weddings.

The parking lot was empty as he did a final check of the van, making sure the back doors were fully closed and smiling when he thought about the incident on I-40 where they lost half their equipment. A strong yank confirmed they were shut, and he came around the driver side. There were two men in business suits waiting at the door.

"Senior Airman Guthrie?" One of he asked.

"Senior Airman?" Guthrie laughed at the moniker. "I haven't been called that in over a decade. It isn't something I brag about."

"We'd like you to come with us," the man said, and Guthrie was instantly on guard.

"Are you cops?"

"No," the other said and plunged a syringe into his bicep. The narcotic worked quickly, and Guthrie fell limp into their arms. He was dumped into the trunk of a waiting car and whisked away.

Dallas, Texas

"Thanks for coming, ladies and gentlemen," the PA announcer said to the crowd who'd just witnessed one of the most exciting bull riding competitions in the history of the Professional Bull Riders circuit. "We'll be back in Dallas in a couple months when the PBR returns with Chuck Campbell and all of your favorite stars."

"How are you, Chuck," Dawn Canfield asked her boyfriend when she found him in his motor home.

"I'm a little sore, darlin'," he said with his ever-present grin. "Ol' Thunder's got it out for me." Thunder was reputed to be the toughest bull on the circuit and Campbell had ridden him for a full eight seconds before being chased from the ring by the ornery critter. "Thank God for the clowns," he chuckled. "I think that bull wants to kill me."

"Well, I just want to love you, baby," Dawn said as she came to him, spinning wildly when she heard the door fly open. The first dart buried itself in her chest and she fell to the floor. Campbell was on his feet but stopped when he saw two 9mm Berettas pointed at him.

"Sergeant Charles Campbell?" One of them asked.

"What did you do to her?" Campbell screamed as he looked upon his girl.

"She will be fine," the man assured him. "But you won't be if you don't answer my question. *Are* you Sergeant Charles Campbell?"

"I used to be," Campbell admitted. The man raised another pistol and fired a dart into Campbell's chest.

Fells Point, Maryland

It was a slow night; an off night for most hockey teams and the last game had ended an hour before. The big screen TVs in *Capitol Sports* were now showing the obscure contests that only ESPN2 was capable of bringing into people's living rooms. Jack George was wiping down the bar as the last of the patrons waved goodbye, a ritual he did every night at closing time.

Finished with the bar, he checked to see the progress the dishwasher was making with the last of the dirty dishes. "I gotta get a new one," he muttered aloud as the old unit moaned and groaned as it did its work. It took George by surprise when the door opened and two men in suits walked in.

"Sergeant Jack George?" One of the men asked.

"I haven't been called that in years."

"You will be again," the suit replied and sprayed George with an aerosol mist.

George raised his hands but was too late. He'd only inhaled a small amount, but it was enough to put him under. They dragged him out the back door.

Anacostia, D.C.

The place was a wreck, but that was the way of a crack house. There were ten to fifteen of them, sitting around an open fire that burned in what was once a basement. It was a miserable place but a sanctuary of sorts for the addicts and users, a place away from the prying eyes of the police and nosy citizens bent on cleaning up their neighborhood. It was here, in the wee hours of the morning, that Ron Gibbs found himself this night. He took a long hit on the glass pipe, heating it with a small torch to gasify the white rocks in the bowl. It took everyone in the filthy basement when the door at the top of the stairs burst in, blown from its hinges by a small explosive charge.

Gibbs dropped the pipe and the torch, taking cover behind the bug-infested couch as a small group of men gained entry. He heard the distinctive zip of silenced bullets flying through the air and the slap as they connected with flesh and bone, and he knew this was more than just a police raid. He'd been through those before and these men were not looking to make arrests. *I'm gonna die here*, he thought when the shooting stopped.

Peeking up from behind the couch, he saw all of his cohorts either dead or dying on the floor around the fire. One of the men spotted him and raised his pistol. "Senior Airman Ronald Gibbs?" He asked the frightened man behind the couch.

Y-yeah," Gibbs replied shakily.

"If you don't want to end up like them, you will come with us," the man said.

Chapter Forty-Three
Sea Cliff, Long island, New York
Saturday, 11 March 1995

Cooper was waiting when Rick pulled up in front of the garage at 7:30. There was another car parked there as well, an almost identical Crown Victoria to Cooper's. In it was the man who'd accompanied Cooper when he made his appointment. *Either they're the Blues Brothers or a gay couple*, Johnson thought as he shut off the big 454. And he felt the tingling at the back of his neck again and the ringing in his ears was back as well. He stepped out of the car as Cooper approached him. "Good morning, Mr. Cooper," he said brightly.

"Good morning," Cooper returned the smile. "Tell me, you wouldn't be Sergeant Richard Johnson of the United States Air Force; would you?"

Rick stopped. "How in Hell do you know *that*?"

"A good guess," Cooper said, spraying the aerosol fully in Johnson's face.

"I'll shave your ass and make you walk backwards, you son of a ..." Rick lunged for him before falling face down on the pavement.

Chicago, Illinois

Jerome Emory always worked Saturday mornings. It wasn't as if he liked it, he had a lovely wife and two beautiful children, a boy and a girl, and everything a man could want, but he did it to set an example for his people. JE Enterprises was a shining star, the most successful black-owned businesses in Chicago, save Oprah Winfrey's Harpo Productions.

Emory built his business from next to nothing, first as a general contractor and then making a name by restoring many of Chicago's lakeside row houses. Ten years later, Emory and JE had left the contracting business behind and now concentrated exclusively on the sale and lease of upscale properties in the Metro Chicago area.

"Hey, Mr. E." Darnell the weekend guard said as he passed by Emory's open door.

"Good morning, Darnell," Emory said, proud he remembered the names of each of his two hundred employees. It was part of the example he tried to set, the work ethic, the closeness between he and his employees, and the respect he'd given them was returned willingly. "How are the wife and kids?"

"Just fine, sir," Darnell said with a nod. "Thanks for asking."

"Your youngest has a birthday coming up, doesn't he?" Emory said. He liked to remember personal things about his employees too, their marital status, the number of kids they had and the names of each. His employees were devoted to him, loyal to him, and most had been with him from the beginning. Darnell was not one of those, but he was starting his fourth year at JE and had never worked a Saturday where the boss didn't.

"Yes, sir, Tuesday," Darnell agreed and then turned his head toward the roof. A helicopter was flying low and the building began to shake. "Sounds like he landed on the roof," he said. "I'll check it out. Please stay put until you hear from me, sir." Darnell turned to walk toward the elevator.

Emory jumped when Darnell's body flew backward past the doorway, blood streaming from the gaping hole that was once his face. "What the …" he said, rising from the chair and reaching for the pistol he kept in his briefcase.

"Don't move, Mr. Emory," a man in a business suit said. "You have a chance to live so long as you don't go for your briefcase."

"What do you want? I don't keep any money here," Emory replied as he stepped out from behind his desk.

"Just your services, sir," the man in the suit said.

"You want to buy some property?"

"No, sir," the man shook his head. "You have other talents, namely the ones that pertain to plastic explosive." And another man walked into the office, firing a dart into the middle of Emory's chest.

Georgetown, D.C.

"Yes, thank you," Holmgren said as he hung up the phone. He smiled, having just received confirmation of the success of the retrieval operation. All seven former members of Alpha Flight, 23rd Special Tactics Squadron, 1st Special Operations Wing were now in custody and one of the most difficult phases of the operation was complete.

"How does this look?" Venice asked him, as she appeared from the bedroom in a drastically short miniskirt. She'd not bothered with underwear and her penis peeked beneath the edge of the skirt.

"Delicious," Holmgren said as he took her to him, pulling her onto his lap.

"I'm going to miss you," Venice said as she kissed him. She felt him stir and she wiggled her butt to arouse him further.

"Me too," he agreed. "But we'll be together again soon," he promised, his erection straining the material of his pants.

Venice stood and took him by the hand, leading him into the bedroom. "Make love to me until I have to leave," she insisted.

"My thoughts exactly,' Holmgren smiled as he let her remove his pants.

Mineola, Long Island

"You're doing this on purpose, Rick," Connie muttered. He should have been home from work a half hour before, but they had to visit her parents, something he tried to avoid whenever possible. She'd wanted to call, but she knew he'd get annoyed, probably having to extricate himself from under a car to answer the phone at the shop. Instead, she flicked on the TV.

Atlanta, Georgia

"This is CNN Breaking News, I'm Lou Saunders. Details are still sketchy, but we have word out of Chicago of a break in at JE Enterprises. Chicago millionaire and philanthropist Jerome Emory has been reported missing; yet no ransom demand has been given. Metro Police sources say that one security guard was killed, probably trying to defend Mr. Emory from his abductors. We will have more on this story as it comes in.

Mineola, Long Island

Connie shut off the TV, feeling as if she'd been punched in the gut. She knew not why the abduction of a man her husband knew over a decade ago bothered her so much, but a sense of great dread enveloped her. "No, it couldn't be," she said aloud as she went for the phone. Her hand shook as she dialed the number. "Answer the phone, damn you," she said as it rang and rang. "Shit," she hung up and dialed another number. That one was answered on the first ring.
"Hello?"
"Hi, Harry, it's Connie. Have you been to the shop today?"
"Nah," Harry replied. "Rick had a light morning."
"He still isn't home, and he doesn't answer the phone," she told him. "Is there any way you can swing by and have a look?"
"Sure, I'll call you back," Harry hung up.

The five minutes it took for Harry to get in his car and drive the three blocks seemed interminably long and Connie paced around the living room, flipping through all of the cable news channels to find out anything more about Jerome Emory's abduction, but it was too soon for any sort of detail. The phone rang and she sprinted to it.

"Hello?"

"His car is here, Connie, but the shop is locked up tight," Harry said. "I called the alarm company and they said it was never deactivated this morning. It's like he got here but never opened up."

"Is he in the bar?" Connie asked knowing that her husband and Mike liked to go the tavern across the street at lunchtime and throw darts.

"Nope, I checked there, and no one saw him today," Harry told her.

"Call the police, Harry," Connie demanded. "I'm coming up there."

***

There were three Nassau County Police cars surrounding her husband's Chevy when she pulled into the lot and Harry came over to her. "One of the neighbors heard him pull in this morning," he told her as she got out of her car. "But they didn't hear anything after that."

"Are you his wife?" A uniformed officer joined them.

"Yes, officer," she said trying to hold back her tears.

"Were you having any sort of marital problems?" The cop asked.

"No," Connie said defiantly.

"Money problems?"

"No," Connie hissed. "No problems. We have a wonderful relationship."

"Guys don't show up to work and then disappear, Mrs. Johnson," the cop said suspiciously.

"It's Wasserman," she corrected. "We have different last names. And my husband *wouldn't* do that."

"You're not the first wife whose husband left town with a woman he was having an affair with," the officer countered.

"Rick *wasn't* having an affair," Connie spat. "He didn't have time; we spent every spare minute together. We love each other."

"He left here every night and went straight home, officer," Harry agreed. "Rick wasn't the type."

"One of his friends was abducted this morning too," Connie offered. "Jerome Emory, the wealthy businessman, disappeared without a trace too."

"Rick knows him?" Harry was surprised.

"They were in the same unit in the Air Force," she told them.

"Were they in touch regularly?" The cop asked.

"I don't think Rick has spoken to any of them since he left the military," Connie replied.

"When was this?"

"1986," Connie said.

"I'll pass it on to the detectives," the cop said.

"That's it?" Connie asked.

"We're dusting his car for prints, maybe that might tell us something, Ms. Wasserman, but I wouldn't get my hopes up."

"So, what am I supposed to do, sit at home and wait?"

"There is nothing else you *can* do, ma'am," he said. "Let us do our jobs."

"My ass," she said, turning to Harry. "Can I leave his car here for a while?"

"Do you have an extra set of keys?"

"Yes, I brought them," she handed them over and headed back to her car.

"Where are you going?"

"I'll be at my parents' house," she said and threw the car in gear.

Fort Hamilton Armed Forces Processing Center, Brooklyn, New York

"Jesus Christ," Johnson groaned when he opened his eyes. His head was pounding, and he was disoriented. "Where in hell am I?" He looked around and realized he was in a jail cell. Hearing voices coming from outside the cell, he tried to stand and walk to the door but the pain in his head forced him to sit back down.

"He's up, Major," a voice said from outside the cell. A short man in U.S. Army uniform appeared at the door.

"Good evening, Sergeant Johnson," he said. "I am Major Espinal."

"What, the Army doesn't have height requirements anymore?" Johnson growled.

"You're a comedian," Espinal laughed sardonically. "Do you have any other comments before I administer your Oath of Enlistment, Sergeant?"

"Oath of *Enlistment*?" Johnson laughed heartily. "The military and I parted company ten years ago and not on the best of terms. There must be some sort of mistake because they didn't want me back."

"Well, it seems they want you now," Espinal said. "Raise your right hand ..."

"Hell no," Johnson shook his head. "I'm not doing anything until I talk to a lawyer."

"That is not an option, Sergeant."

"Then I'll just sit here," Rick said.

"That isn't an option either," Espinal told him. "Look, I don't claim to know what is going on, but I have orders to give you the Oath and get you over to McGuire Air Force Base."

"Don't you think it a bit strange that you're inducting a thirty-five year old into the service?" Johnson asked him.

"I've seen stranger things during my career," Espinal shot back.

"I was abducted and brought here, Major," Johnson shouted. "We fought the War of 1812 to stop the British from doing that very thing to our troops. Don't you at least question the legitimacy of your orders?"

"I have not been ordered to do anything illegal, Sergeant Johnson. Besides, this comes from the top, the *very* top," the Army officer said.

"The President?"

"So I am told," Espinal nodded. "Your country needs you."

"Fine," Rick barked. "Then why didn't the Air Force just come to me and *ask* for my help?"

"I can't say," Espinal shrugged.

"I have to call my wife," Rick said. "She's got to be worried sick."

"I'm afraid that's impossible," Espinal shook his head.

"Then you can go fuck yourself," Johnson crossed his arms on his chest.

Espinal raised his index finger and lowered his voice. "Look, Sarge, you were brought here by guys who wear suits for a living."

"FBI?" Johnson asked and Espinal shook his head. "CIA?"

Espinal nodded. "They don't care whether you take the Oath or not. They will take you out of here whether you cooperate or not. After you leave here, they can do anything they want to you and none would be the wiser. You best shot is to cooperate fully."

"Or what, they'll make me disappear?"

Espinal shrugged. "Who knows, but you can safely assume that you and I are the only ones who know you're here. I looked at your service record. You've worked with them in the past and you know how they operate. The choice is yours, but I'd go along with this until I found a way out."

"Did they tell you to say that?"

"No, just speaking from experience," Espinal said. "And you know I'm right."

Wantagh, Long Island

The tears flowed freely down her cheeks when she arrived at her parents' house twenty minutes after leaving Harry and the cops. Her father answered the door and immediately took her into his arms.

"What's wrong?" He asked. "Where's Rick?"

"He's been kidnapped," she sobbed.

"What?" Murray said skeptically.

"He went to work this morning and disappeared," she said. "God, I have to tell his mother." Connie was not looking forward to that. "I can't tell her over the phone, I have to go see her."

She went to turn back out the door, but Murray grabbed her. "Just sit down a second and talk to me," he said.

"Okay, dad," she sniffed and took a seat in the living room.

"How do you know he's been kidnapped?"

"What else could it be?"

"Why would anyone want to kidnap him?"

"I don't know," she insisted. "But one of his friends from his Air Force days was kidnapped this morning too."

"How do you know?"

"It's on the news," she said. "Jerome Emory was kidnapped from his office this morning." And she stopped. "What did Rick do when he was in the service, dad?"

"I don't think he wanted you to know about that," Murray shook his head.

"I don't give a damn what he wanted," she spat. "It could explain why he and Emory were taken."

"That's a reach, Connie," Murray said.

"You asked the question, dad. Why *would* someone kidnap him?" Connie stood. "We're comfortable, but we don't have the kind of money to pay any worthwhile ransom," she said.

"Maybe it has something to do with a case you're working on," Murray offered.

"I'm a defense attorney, dad, I defend our clients against people trying to sue them. If I were with the district attorney's office, I'd consider that argument but there are better ways to influence me than to kidnap my husband. And that doesn't explain Emory's disappearance."

"Suppose it was just coincidence?"

"If the police don't come up with something by Monday, I'm going to check that angle out myself," she said adamantly. "Now I have to get out to Islip and give Rick's mother the bad news."

"Have you considered the possibility he might have left for some reason?" Murray asked as she headed for the door.

"I *refuse* to consider that possibility, dad," she said, letting the door slam shut behind her.

Chapter Forty-Four
Dulles International Airport, Washington, D.C.
Sunday, 12 March 1995

"Have fun, lover," Holmgren said to Venice at the security area. "I'll see you in a few weeks."

"I miss you already," she said as she kissed him once more.

Holmgren watched her go through the checkpoint and waited until she was out of sight before walking back out to his car. He showed minimal surprise that Hector Reynaldo was waiting in the passenger seat.

"If I didn't know better, I would say it was a waste to dispose of such a beautiful woman," Reynaldo said with a chuckle. "But she has a bigger prick than I do, doesn't she?" He laughed again.

"Is there something you wanted?"

"Just a status report on your operation," Reynaldo said.

"The team is enroute to the training area," Holmgren said. "If they're not too out of shape, they should be ready to go in a few weeks."

"You will advise when they are ready?"

"Yes," Holmgren nodded, looking over at Reynaldo. "What will happen to them?"

"I don't know, it is not my business," Hector said. "I am merely a conduit. Are you having second thoughts?"

"No, but they cannot come back alive," Holmgren was adamant. "I insist on that."

"Why?"

"Have you ever been in love, Hector?"

"Yes."

"I was, once," he said wistfully. "Thanks to those bastards, I lost the love of my life. I've waited twelve years for this."

Mineola, Long Island

"No, I haven't heard anything yet, Maria," Connie said. "I'll call as soon as I do." Connie hung up, not able to sit on the phone and dwell on what might have happened. Her mother-in-law was losing it and Connie didn't need to be dragged into a funk. She was determined to find her husband and crying over him would hinder her investigation.

Connie found the box that Rick kept under his side of the bed, never having opened it before, always respecting his wishes. He'd shown her some of its contents several years before, just after they were married. She set the thing on the coffee table, contemplating it for a while before deciding to look inside.

Opening the cover, Connie found the things she'd already seen, the photo of his old unit and the velvet box that contained his decorations, and then she dug further. There was his DD Form 214, his discharge papers, which she looked over carefully, making notes of his postings and assignments. After that were his training records and reading them gave her pause. "How many ways does he know how to kill people?" And she realized why he was so close-mouthed about his military career, why her father was reluctant to divulge the secrets Rick had shared with him. And then she saw something that took her breath away.

It was a picture of a girl, one of the most exquisite women she'd ever seen. Turning it over, she read the inscription on the back. 'I will always love you', it said, and it was signed Yung Shu.

For a fleeting second, Connie thought Rick had decided to go back to her, to renew the love of a beautiful China doll but pushed it away. "He's not that kind of man," she said aloud. Their relationship was too good, too solid for him to just up and leave in an attempt to rekindle an old love. He was also a man of principle and if he did have such desires, he would have been man enough to tell her so, not run like a thief in the night. "I'll find you, Rick, and we'll be together again soon."

San Juan, Puerto Rico

Venice sashayed her way through the Aeropuerto Internacional de San Juan, never being happier. She'd found a man who treated her like gold, a man with money and influence. One day, he would give her the opportunity to transition and she loved him for what he'd done for her and what their future together would bring.

"Taxi, mamacita?" The driver said when she made it out to the curb. He held the door open for her and gave her a hand in.

"*Si, gracias,*" she said and gave him a seductive smile.

"Where to, pretty lady?" He asked.

"265 Arroyo Street," she replied, and he put the car in gear, leaving the airport by the west exit. "Pardon me, but I think you're going the wrong way," she noticed the unfamiliar route almost immediately.

The driver stopped at a red light and turned around, pointing a silenced Sig at her. "No, lady, you're the one who's going the wrong way." Before Venice could speak and before the light turned green, he fired two silenced shots into her chest. She flopped over in the seat, her body sliding onto the floor as the car drove away. The police would find what was left of Venice washed up on one of the local beaches in a month, the damage done by the marine life in the warm water precluding any identification.

Area 1A, Hurlburt Field, Florida

"Isn't this a motley fucking bunch," Johnson laughed when they threw him in the cell.

"Well, that's all of us except J.R.," Chuck Campbell said from his cot. "How're you doing, Rick?"

"As well as you are," he growled. "Pissed off enough to kill some-fucking-body." Rick looked over to Emory. "I thought you rich guys knew about security."

"They killed my guard," Emory said.

"Killed a bunch of my friends too," Gibbs said from the back of the room. "They tell you why we're here?"

"Nope," Johnson shook his head.

"I say we jump the guard the next time they come, kill their ass, and get the fuck out of here," Nick Mason said. "Cocksuckers shot me off my ride."

"Do you know where we are?" Johnson asked him.

"No," Mason shook his head, his dirty, shoulder length red hair swishing back and forth.

"Do you remember Area 1A?" He got nods from them all. "There's nothing but swamp on the north side and we're twenty miles from any-fucking-where on the other three. Either we'll end up as gator shit or they'll round us up before we get off the base. If we go along with this, we at least have the chance to survive and get home."

"What makes you think we're gonna get home?" Jack George asked him.

"They need us for something," Jake Guthrie took up for Johnson. "Something that an active duty unit can't do. They can't force us to do something without dangling a carrot before us."

"They'll kill us if we don't cooperate," Gibbs said.

"They wouldn't have gone through all this trouble just to kill us," Campbell said.

"I ain't doing shit," Mason declared. "They can shoot my ass if they want."

"That's smart, Nick," Campbell muttered. "Fucking moron."

"I happen to have a life that I'd like to get back to," Guthrie said.

"Hear, hear," Emory agreed.

"What do you think they want us to do?" George spoke up again.

"Fucking kill somebody," Guthrie hissed. "Isn't that what we all did so well?"

"Hey, Rick?" Campbell yelled over with a grin on his face. "Do you think our pictures are on the back of milk cartons yet?"

***

"Ten-hut," Joe Rockwood said when Holmgren and an Air Force 1st Lieutenant arrived in the Orderly Room.

"At ease, men. Take your seats," Holmgren said. "I am Colonel Holmgren, and this is Lieutenant Roman." He looked to Reasoner. "I assume you're Chief Reasoner?"

"Yes, sir," he nodded.

"Have you read the mission brief?"

"Yes, sir," Reasoner nodded again. "Are you the CO?"

"In a manner of speaking," Holmgren smiled. "Lieutenant Roman will be the commander of your unit and he will report to me."

"The brief was a bit vague, Colonel," Reasoner continued. "I gather this is a CIA op?"

"Indeed," Holmgren nodded. "Lieutenant Roman will fill in the details later, once training begins."

"And the rest of our unit, sir?" Joe Rockwood asked Holmgren.

"They are already here, Sergeant," Holmgren smiled again. "They are in building 5672. You will meet up with them after we are finished here."

"Who are they, sir?" Petersen asked.

"They are from Alpha Flight, 23rd Special Tactics Squadron, 1st Special Operations Wing," the smile never left Holmgren's face.

"That can't be, sir," Reasoner said. "23rd was disbanded ten years ago. Even 1st Special Ops doesn't exist anymore."

"True," Holmgren nodded. "This unit was just reactivated for this mission because of their special skills."

"Reactivated?" Reasoner became instantly skeptical. "Are you saying that you brought the members of my old unit back into the military?"

"Yes, Chief," he nodded. "It is why I requested you specifically for this mission. They have been separated from the military for ten years and they were less than cooperative when recalled. I'm counting on you to motivate those men and get them back into shape."

"With all due respect, sir," Reasoner said. "These guys had bad attitudes when they were on active duty. I seriously doubt they have improved over a decade of civilian life."

"Chief Reasoner," Holmgren said patronizingly. "You didn't become the youngest chief in Air Force history because you couldn't motivate your troops. You spent four years of your life with these men, I trust in your skills and your knowledge of their foibles to keep them on the path."

"Thank you, sir, but …"

"The subject is closed," Holmgren said with finality and then turning to Roman. "You have just over two weeks, Lieutenant. I expect daily status reports on the progress of A-Flight's training."

"Yes, sir," Roman said with a nod. Holmgren looked at them all before departing. "Failure is not an option, gentlemen."

"I don't like this, Chief," Rockwood said when Holmgren departed.

"You're not paid to like it, Sarge," Roman growled and turned back to Reasoner. "Come on, Chief, let's go see what we have to work with."

***

"Well, look who it is," Gibbs said as he rolled off the cot. "Figures *you'd* still be in."

"Always knew you were an ate up maggot," Mason said as he approached the bars. "Is this your idea of a joke?"

"This isn't my idea of anything," Reasoner shot back.

"Hey, J.R.," Campbell said. "Are you here to spring us?"

"Your country needs you," Reasoner said.

"Did they tell you to say that, John?" Johnson said as he rose from the cot in the rear of the cell.

"Hello, Rick," Reasoner said, a small smile crossing his face. "You of all of this bunch should understand how things go."

"I know that you aren't in control of your destiny," Johnson replied, his eyes never leaving Reasoner's. "Just as we aren't. How are Angie and the boys?"

"Good, good," he said pensively. "You know I had nothing to do with this, don't you?"

"When did you find out they brought us here?"

"About an hour ago," Reasoner replied.

"We should take him hostage," Mason offered. "Threaten to cut him up into little pieces unless they let us go."

"Shut up," Johnson barked and turned back to Reasoner. "Why are we here, John?"

Reasoner looked away, somewhere off into the middle distance before turning back to him. "They want us to go back into North Korea," he said softly.

"Fuck that," Gibbs said.

"I am authorized to offer you all a settlement," Reasoner said. "In the seven-figure range if this mission is completed successfully."

"Each?" Emory asked.

"Each," Reasoner confirmed. "But all of you have to agree. If one of you opts out, all of you are out."

"What exactly does that mean, John?" Johnson asked. "Does that mean if I tell you and the Air Force to go fuck yourselves, we can all go home?"

"I don't think so," Reasoner shook his head. "This isn't an Air Force op, Rick. You know that as well as I do."

"So, either we're in and take their money when we're done, or we disappear?"

"You know how they can be," Reasoner said with a chuckle. "If it means anything, I don't like this any more than you do."

"And what do you get out of it, you ass-kissing motherfucker?" Mason growled.

"*Nothing*," Reasoner spat. "I'm just doing my *job*."

"What makes you think we won't kill you when you let us out of here?" Gibbs said.

"Aside from the fact that we used to trust each other with our lives?"

"Yeah, aside from that, John," Guthrie hissed.

"Killing me will have the same consequences as if you refused to cooperate," Reasoner told him.

"But it would make us feel better," Mason added.

"Nobody's killing *anyone*," Johnson growled. He turned back to Reasoner. "Get out of here for a while, John. Let me talk to these guys."

"Our CO wants to brief us," Reasoner insisted.

"He isn't our CO yet, damn it," Johnson hissed at him. "You said it yourself, this is your job, it isn't ours anymore. We've been taken from our homes and families against our will. You tell him that if he wants our cooperation, he'll have to do it our way. Either that or they can assemble the firing squad right now."

"I'll talk to him," Reasoner surrendered. He turned to leave and then looked back. "Talk some sense into them, Rick. It's just a couple weeks and you'll be able to go home a million dollars richer."

"Or in a body bag," Johnson added. "Give me a couple hours, John."

"I'm not bullshitting you, Rick, I told you everything I know."

"I believe you," Johnson gave him a single nod. "And I still trust you with my life."

Mineola, Long Island

Connie hadn't slept the night before and tonight was no different. After years of marriage, she'd become accustomed to Rick's body next to hers. The pillow soaked from her tears, she never felt so alone in her life. Many things coursed through her mind, all sorts of terrible circumstances that could have befallen the man she loved. The police had frustrated her, not wanting to accept the connection between Rick's disappearance and that of Jerome Emory and told her to go home and leave the job to professionals.

Rising, she went to the box that still sat in the living room and found the picture of A-Flight. Turning it over, she copied the names and hometowns of the men who'd seen combat with her husband. Connie had friends, one in particular, with the resources to determine the whereabouts of the rest of them. In the morning, she would approach him with her dilemma. "I just hope he'll put friendship before duty," she said as she formulated her plan of action.

Chapter Forty-Five
Area 1A, Hurlburt Field, Fort Walton Beach, Florida
Monday, 13 March 1995

"Time's up," a voice boomed from the door of the holding area and the owner of the voice was met with laughter when he appeared.

"How old are you; twelve?" Campbell asked of Lieutenant Roman.

"Damn, he's a little kid," Guthrie added with a chuckle. "Did you stop breast feeding last week?" It was met by more laughter from the lot of them.

"This is our CO, Lieutenant Roman," Reasoner said.

"CO?" Jack George said. "I'll bet he's still in diapers."

Roman looked to Reasoner who just shrugged. Though he was twenty-six, Roman did look young, it was something he'd been kidded about since he'd received his commission in the Air Force. "I need an answer, gentlemen," he said, ignoring the catcalls.

Johnson came toward the door and considered Roman for a minute. "What *exactly* are we expected to do?"

"What are we expected to do, *sir*," Roman corrected him.

"You'll get us to call you sir when you earn our respect," Rick said. "And not a second before. The best way to do that is to be honest with us from jump street."

Roman looked to Reasoner who gave him a nod. "Intelligence believes the North Koreans have built a ballistic missile facility outside the city of Yong Hung. We will be inserted in order to verify that fact."

"So this is strictly a recon mission?" Johnson asked.

"For the time being," Roman replied. "If it is determined that they do have a missile base there, they might want us to take it out."

"Just the nine of us?"

"I'm sure Chief Reasoner advised you will be well compensated," Roman shot back. "But there are three members of the team you haven't met."

"Jesus, J.R.," Campbell said to Reasoner. "Didn't you tell this clown what happened the last time we took out one of their factories?" He jerked a thumb in Roman's direction. "Your son's godfather died on that mission along with Roger Hoffman and Lieutenant Jenkins. What makes you think this will turn out any different?"

"That was a long time ago," Roman said. "Technology is better, communications are better, and we will have support."

"And you, like the rest of us, have no control over this," Johnson said to the young lieutenant. "Do you?" Roman looked away. "Yes, Lieutenant, just because you are on that side of these bars doesn't mean you are any better off than we are. Think about it, both of you," he looked back and forth between Reasoner and Roman. "Your futures depend on a successful completion of this mission, just as ours do. If we tell you to fuck off right now, you both will meet the same fate as we."

"I don't think so," Reasoner said. "We're active duty ..."

"So what?" Johnson shrugged. "I'd bet that Angie doesn't know you're here, and I'd venture that your families are just as ignorant of your circumstances as ours are. You know too much about our situation to escape the consequences should we not cooperate. I've known you a long time, John. Would you let them kill us all? If they did, would you let them get away with it?"

"No," Reasoner said softly.

"Then you will die along with us. I suggest the two of you do some thinking yourselves. Think about the legality of what you've been drawn into," Johnson said.

"It is not up to us to determine whether a mission is legal or not. We get our orders and we obey them," Roman said.

"Hopefully, you'll live long enough to learn the difference between orders and a death warrant, sonny," Johnson barked. "Why do you think they recalled a bunch of out of shape, bad attitude assholes like us? Don't you think there are five hundred guys on active duty who could do this job with a lot less hassle to the government?" Rick looked at them both. "No, you didn't until now, did you?" Reasoner and Roman remained stoic. "Figures," he chuckled. "They don't expect any of us to come back."

"So, you won't cooperate?" Roman asked finally.

"No," Johnson shook his head. "I'm in, just to prove them wrong. I'm gonna survive this, collect the million bucks, and then shove it up the President's ass, one dollar at a time." He turned back to the rest of the men. "What about you clowns? Do you want to come to Washington with me when this is over?"

"Fucking A right," Guthrie stood. "I'm in."

"Me too," Campbell said.

"What the fuck," Emory shrugged.

"If it goes bad, I'm gonna kill the skinny officer before they get me," Mason said, looking at Roman with disdain. "But I'll go."

"You'll have to beat me to it," Gibbs said to Mason. "Cause I'm gonna fuck his ass before I kill him. Count me in."

"Jack?" Johnson looked at George who'd said nothing.

"I got a bad feeling about this, Rick," George said. "But if I'm gonna die, I'd rather it was in a blaze of glory with you guys than being fed to a crusty old alligator." He rose and walked to the bars, getting as close to Roman as he could. "No bullshit, Lieutenant. We're with you, but you have to be honest with us at all times. If I think you're not, I'll kill you out of hand, no questions, no warning." He looked back to the rest of them. "You've got your unit, Lieutenant Roman. Don't fuck it up, for yourself and us."

"Ten-hut," Johnson said, and instinct took over. All of them came to attention. Rick turned to Roman and rendered a snappy salute. "A-Flight awaits your orders, *sir*."

Mineola, Long Island

Connie stepped onto the Long Island Rail Road train at the front and began to walk toward the back. When she got to the third car, she spotted her quarry about halfway back, a large red-haired man in a business suit. He was sleeping and she sat down heavily next to him. He stirred and looked over at her.

"Hey, good looking," Special Agent Francis Xavier O'Connor said with a sleepy smile. "What's the matter?" He asked when he noticed her discomfort.

"I need your help, Frank," she said, trying to keep her tears in check.

"Personally, or professionally?"

"Professionally," she replied. "Rick was abducted Saturday morning."

"Have you called the cops?"

"They don't want to believe he was kidnapped. They're of the opinion that Rick left on his own accord."

"Why do *you* believe he was?" She opened her briefcase and withdrew the picture of A-Flight, circa 1982, and handed it to him. "Good looking bunch," he said sarcastically.

"This is Rick's unit when he was in the Air Force," she pointed to her husband.

"*That's* Rick?"

"Yes," she nodded. "And *this* is Jerome Emory."

"That name sounds familiar," O'Connor said.

"Your Chicago office is probably working the case," she told him. "*He* was abducted Saturday morning too."

"The rich guy?"

"The same," she nodded.

"Shit," FBI Agent O'Connor whistled. "What about the rest of them?"

"That's what I need *you* to do," Connie said. "Here." She handed him a list of names and hometowns. "They might not live in the same places but I'm sure you can run the names on some sort of database. Please," she added with a smile.

"What exactly did Rick do when he was in the service?"

"I don't know, he never told me," she shrugged. "My father knows, but he was evasive as hell."

"Are you still with Epstein?" O'Connor asked as he tucked the list in his pocket.

"Yes."

"I'll call you after lunch," he promised.

"You're the best, Frank," she said as he kissed his cheek.

Hurlburt Field, Florida

"If I'd have known we'd have to get haircuts, I would have told you to fuck yourself," Mason said to Roman when they were finished at the base barber shop. "Sir," he added with a devious smile.

"Get in the truck," Roman said, exasperated. Shepherding the retreads around to their various appointments, haircuts, clothing issue, and processing, was like babysitting a bunch of nine year olds. None had anything resembling military bearing and their attitudes were worse than Reasoner led him to believe. He watched Mason climb in the back of the venerable deuce and a half, the others already up there made faces at him. Roman got in the cab with Reasoner and Johnson, who was driving. "How did you guys ever get into the Air Force in the first place?"

Johnson laughed. "I didn't have a choice, Lieutenant," he said. "I got busted for stealing a car when I was seventeen. It was either enlist or spend six months in juvenile hall. I don't know about the rest of them."

"What a collection of nuts," Roman muttered.

Johnson and Reasoner traded a mile. "They might be all sorts of fucked up, sir," Reasoner said. "But there isn't another group of guys who I'd rather go into combat with."

"I'll take your word for it, Chief," Roman grunted. "What happened to *you*?"

"John's always been a poster boy, sir," Johnson said as he threw the truck in gear and dumped the clutch to shake up the guys in the back. They responded by pounding on the roof of the cab. "I don't know if you're old enough to remember how things were in 1980, but the economy was for shit. It was difficult to find jobs and many guys who normally wouldn't have enlisted took that option then. This clown was the only one of us who came in with the idea of making it a career." He looked at Reasoner. "I'm glad you got what you wanted, John. I'm happy for you."

"Thanks," Reasoner nodded. "What happened to you after you got out?"

"I'm an auto mechanic," Rick said. "About five years ago, I found a woman whom I have no right being with and she actually agreed to marry me. I wouldn't trade what I have for anything."

"Kids?"

"Nope," Johnson shook his head. "Connie's set on having a career first. We put the kid thing off until she gets a full partnership in the firm."

"She's a lawyer?"

"Yeah, and a damn good one," Johnson beamed with pride. "She just became a junior partner."

"Whatever happened with Yung Shu?" Reasoner asked him and Rick felt as if a knife was jammed in his gut.

"She and I fell out of touch about a year after we left Korea," Johnson told him. "I think about her once in a while but that's about it."

"Does your wife …"

"No," Rick cut him off. "I never told her." And they fell into silence as Johnson steered the truck back out to Area 1A.

New York, New York

"Connie," Anita Maldonado said. "You have a call from an FBI agent."

"Thanks," she said to her secretary and punched the button next to the flashing LED. "Hi, Frank."

"I checked what you wanted," he said cryptically. "But I can't talk on the phone. Take me to dinner tonight?"

"Sure," she said, wondering what he'd found. "Where?"

"T.G.I. Fridays in Westbury," he told her.

"Okay, see you around six," Connie said. "I'll be in the smoking section."

"I thought you quit?"

"I started again," she said before hanging up.

Hurlburt Field, Florida

"Where are they now?" Holmgren asked Roman.

"Out on the firing range, Colonel."

"Do you think it was wise giving them weapons so soon?"

"These guys are the farthest thing from military, sir," Roman said. "But I believe I can take them at their word. They trust Chief Reasoner implicitly."

"Do you think they are capable of completing the mission successfully?"

"If you'd asked me that yesterday I'd have told you no, sir. But I think that if anyone can do it, they can. They can still shoot as if they have been doing it every day," Roman said, surprised he was looking forward to working closely with these men who'd called him every name in the book.

"Very well, Lieutenant," Holmgren said. "I'm pleased you are so optimistic. Thank you for your report."

"Yes, sir," Roman came to attention and departed.

Holmgren stood and looked out the window, his stomach fluttering in anticipation. He was so close now, only a handful of days until he could avenge himself on the men who'd allowed Roger to die, and he wished time would move faster, wished he could fast forward to the day when all of them would die. "Patience," he said aloud to the empty office.

Westbury, Long Island

"Hey, beautiful," O'Connor said as he slid into the booth across from her. The waitress came over directly and he ordered a Guinness. Connie already had her vodka on the rocks and a cigarette burned between her fingers.

"What did you find out, Frank?" She said, doing away with any greeting or niceties.

He exhaled loudly as he opened his pad. "I got a line on five of the six others who are still alive," he began. "This guy Gibbs looks as if he dropped off the face of the Earth, though he was arrested on drug possession charges twice in the D.C. area a few years back. One of them, a guy named Reasoner, is still in. The rest of them were reported missing either Friday night or Saturday morning."

"What does this mean?"

"That's why I wanted to do this away from the office. I took the liberty of requesting their military records from the Air Force Personnel Records Center in Denver. About ten minutes later a funny thing happened," he chuckled. "I got a call back saying that there is no record of any of these men, even the one on active duty, ever being in the military. I checked with the Army, Navy, Marine Corps, and the Coast Guard, just to be sure. Nothing. When I called my connection in D.C. who gave me the line on the active duty guy, he said he must have made a mistake."

"What does that mean?" She asked and O'Connor smiled, raising a finger.

"It gets better," he said. "I know a guy who was in the Corps, Force Recon. He said he worked with your husband's guys about ten, fifteen years ago."

"All Rick said was that they made pickups and deliveries," Connie informed him.

"Yeah, picking up CIA agents and delivering them into Communist countries during the height of the Cold War. My guy says they also did some sabotage work, blowing up things and killing enemy agents, that kind of thing," O'Connor said, and Connie blanched. "If I had to guess, I'd say the CIA brought them back to do a job for them. Either that or Rick has been working for them all this time without your knowing. There is one other possibility, but it seems unlikely."

"What is that?"

"I'd rather not say until I know more," O'Connor said.

"*Tell* me, damn it," Connie hissed, taking a gulp of her drink before ordering another.

"The Agency could have decided that these men knew too much about some operation or other and silenced them."

"You mean *killed?*"

"Yes," O'Connor nodded sadly, seeing a tear roll down her cheek.

"No," she said firmly. "I'd know it."

"How?"

"I don't know," she shook her head. "But I *would* know if my soulmate was dead." Their meals came but Connie didn't touch hers. "I'm going to find him," she said with determination.

"How in Hell are you going to do that, Connie?"

"With the FBI's help," she said with conviction. "*You're* going to open the case."

"Whoa there, lady," he raised his hands in surrender. "All we have here is a lot of conjecture."

"*What* conjecture?" Connie slapped the table with her palm. "Five, maybe six men have disappeared over the course of eighteen hours, all serving in the same military unit over decade ago. What are the odds of *that*, Frank?"

"Do you want the truth?"

"Please," she demanded.

"I brought the same argument to my boss," O'Connor admitted. "He didn't want to touch it."

"Why?"

"Because it has the Agency's fingerprints all over it. Damn it, Connie, we have a rocky relationship with them as it is, and we need their cooperation with our overseas investigations. SAC New York doesn't want to make waves in Washington. I'm only telling you this because you and Rick are friends of mine. My boss explicitly told me not to."

"So I'm supposed to sit back and wait until Rick comes home, maybe in a coffin? I don't think so."

"What do you plan to do?"

"I'm going to Washington and you're going to get me into the Hoover Building to see the FBI Director," she insisted. "If I don't get the FBI's cooperation, I'm going to call every newspaper and TV station and raise Holy Hell. I swear, Frank, when I get done, the President won't be able to hold a press conference without someone asking him about it."

"What if Rick went willingly?"

"No," she shook her head again. "He wouldn't do that to me. He wouldn't just up and leave without letting me know he was going to and when I could expect him back. He just wouldn't, Frank, he's not the type."

"I could lose my job," he suggested.

"For what, upholding the law? It's your boss who'll lose his job when I'm finished."

***

Pete McTavish smiled as he listened to the conversation in the booth behind him. The crime reporter for the *New York Times* smelled a story and the way the woman threatened to go to the press made him think some big fish were involved. He waited for them to finish their dinner and then followed them out. He saw they'd come in separate cars and decided to follow the woman. The man, obviously an FBI agent, would spot his tail and take action. McTavish hoped that if he got an address on the woman, he would be able to find out more about her, find a way to follow her and learn more about the mystery she was trying to investigate. *This is gonna be a killer story*, he thought as he pulled up in front of the house on Cleveland Avenue in Mineola.

Chapter Forty-Six
Mineola, Long Island, New York
Tuesday, 14 March 1995

McTavish was startled when he heard the door slam. He'd fallen asleep parked on the street in front of Wasserman's house. Thankfully, most people in this town parked their cars at the curb and his didn't stand out. Watching as she got in her Hyundai, he followed her to the train station, four blocks away.

McTavish parked near her and walked up to the platform, nonchalantly picking up a *USA Today* and mimicking the rest of the commuters who made this trek daily. The train came presently, and he took a seat behind her, pleasantly surprised she took a seat next to the FBI agent she'd spoken with last night. He put the paper down and feigned sleep.

***

"I used to like you," O'Connor said to her.

"And now you don't?"

"No, you activated my conscience," he smiled. "I didn't get much sleep last night, thinking about Rick's predicament."

"Good," she said adamantly.

"I'm taking some personal time to help you, but you have to make me a promise," he said.

"What?"

"When this is over, you have to promise to defend me against any internal charges they might try to pin on me," O'Connor said.

"I'll even do it *pro bono*," she gave him a smile and a kiss on the cheek. "Thank you, Frank."

"What's your plan?"

"I'm taking a couple weeks off and going down to Washington," she told him. "I'm going to do whatever I have to in order to find these men and bring them home."

"I hope you know what you're doing, Connie," O'Connor said with a shake of his head. "I might not be able to protect you."

"Just do your best, Frank."

Hurlburt Field, Florida

Mark Coles enjoyed playing the bugle, having taken up the instrument when he was a Cub Scout. Lieutenant Roman thought it a good idea if he played *Reveille* this fine morning to wake the troops. As the first notes left the horn, the members of A-Flight began to rise, not in a particularly good mood. He dove for cover as they threw projectiles at him, combat boots, articles of clothing, and other miscellaneous items. The words 'Shut the fuck up', were shouted at him by almost every member of the team.

"All right, girls," Lieutenant Roman's voice boomed through the squad bay. "Let's go, wake up. I want you all outside and formed up in three minutes. For every minute you're late, I add another mile to the run this morning."

"I told you we should have killed him, Rick," Mason said as he fell out of bed. He stayed on the floor until Johnson prodded him with a foot.

"Get up, man, a run will do you good," he laughed.

"We're already up to five miles, ladies," Roman bellowed, unable to keep a smile from his face as they stumbled into their uniforms. "Let's go, let's *go*."

"I'm with Nick," Emory said. "Let's kill the boy."

New York, New York

"Hey, Al, "Pete McTavish said when he knocked on the open door of his editor, Al Pritchett. "Can I see you a minute?"

"What's up, Pete?" Pritchett looked up from his copy.

"I'm gonna need some time and an expense account. I've got a lead on something hot," McTavish replied.

"What?"

"I'm not exactly sure, but I think the CIA has abducted a group of men who were part of an elite military unit about ten years ago," he said proudly.

"What evidence do you have?" Pritchett asked skeptically.

"Just a few overheard conversations between the wife of one of the men and an FBI agent."

"It's thin, Pete," Pritchett shook his head.

"It's *good*, Al," McTavish countered. "One of the guys who's missing is Jerome Emory."

Pritchett raised an eyebrow and leaned back in his chair, giving McTavish his full attention now. "*Ebony* magazine's Man of the Year on two separate occasions? The same Jerome Emory who owns a good part of Chicago? The same Jerome Emory who is being considered the head the NAACP?" He was met by an affirmative nod after each question. "Are you saying that Emory is part of this group?"

"You bet," McTavish nodded hard enough for Pritchett to think his head would come loose from his neck. "The wife saw Emory's story on the news and made the connection between him and her husband. Her husband was taken the same time Emory was and the rest of their unit as well. From what I gather, they were Air Force Special Operations."

"What do you need?"

"The wife is going to Washington with the FBI agent," McTavish said. "I want to follow her and see what she shakes up."

"Have you approached her?"

"From what I overheard, going to the press is her last resort. I don't want to scare her off until I know more."

"Does she have a chance of success?" Pritchett pushed.

"I checked her out," McTavish smiled. "She's a lawyer, one of Chaim Epstein's shining stars, she just was made a junior partner. If she's right, and she has the resources of Epstein and Associates at her disposal, she could make life very difficult for the CIA if she wanted, the President too."

Pritchett considered him for a minute. "How much time, Pete?"

"A couple weeks," McTavish shrugged.

"Fine," his boss said. "But if she does decide to go public, it had better be under your byline first."

"Damn right it will be," McTavish nodded enthusiastically again.

"I want you to check in with the Washington bureau when you get there, and I want daily status reports. I don't want you to waste your time on a dead end."

"Will do, Al, and thanks."

"Just bring me a good story," Pritchett said as McTavish headed off to make arrangements.

Hurlburt Field, Florida

"Yeah, Rick," Mason said as he fell to the ground next to Johnson. "A run will do me good. How good do *you* feel, *ass*hole?"

"Fuck ... you," Rick gasped as he lay there, panting like a dog in the summer heat. The only ones who were still on their feet after the five-mile run were the active duty personnel. "I need a cigarette."

"On your feet, ladies," Roman said. "You aren't finished by a *long* shot."

"I changed my mind," Jack George said. "Feed me to the alligators."

"On your *feet*," Roman said again. "We have an appointment on the flightline."

"What for?" Guthrie asked as he helped Campbell to his feet.

"It's time to see if you old guys remember what you learned at jump school," Roman replied as Reasoner drove up with the deuce and a half.

"You're going to make us jump out of a perfectly good airplane just to test a parachute?" Emory said as he climbed onto the truck.

"Come on, old man," Petersen said to Mason, offering a hand.

"I might be older than you, boy," Mason growled, slapping the hand away and getting himself up. "But I can still kick your ass."

"Maybe, if you could catch me, gramps," Petersen laughed.

"Both of you, on the truck *now*," Lt. Roman ordered and stared at Petersen. "These guys will be going home when this is over, Airman," he said. "You'll still be on active duty, so don't let their attitude rub off or you'll be joining them."

"Yes, sir," Petersen said sheepishly.

"Tight ass," Mason said under his breath so Roman couldn't hear, getting a giggle from Petersen and Coles. The two young airmen enjoyed hanging out with the older guys, listening to their stories, and admiring their Devil may care attitude. Rockwood and Reasoner weren't pleased that the two young men looked up to the retreads.

"I don't want these guys to ruin Petersen and Coles," Roman said to the sergeants when they were in the cab. "I know you can't do much for the old guys' attitudes, but I want you to get on the young guys. Keep them straight, gentlemen," he ordered.

"Yes, sir," Reasoner said with a nod as Rockwood drove to the flightline.

Aboard the Delta Shuttle, LaGuardia Airport, Flushing Meadows, New York

"My boss isn't happy I'm taking time off," O'Connor said as he and Connie were seated on the MD-80.

"He should be happy I'm buying your ticket," Connie joked.

"If they file charges against me, your boss will be paying a lot more," he replied.

"Are you kidding?" Connie laughed. "This is something Chaim Epstein lives for. Do you realize the kind of publicity he'd get out of defending an FBI agent against the Bureau, especially if the agent were doing the right thing? When I told him what we were doing, he offered to defend you himself if need be. The firm is behind us with all its resources if we need them."

"Well, that makes me feel better," he said genuinely.

"Where do we go first?" Connie was up for the first time since Saturday, she had a something to do, a direction with which to pursue her husband's disappearance.

"I have some friends in Washington who'll do me an unofficial favor or two," O'Connor informed her. "We'll take what we learn from them and plan our next move."

***

McTavish wished he could hear what they were saying but that was life. He considered himself lucky that one of the computer geeks at the *Times* was able to hack into Delta's SABRE reservations system to find out what flight Wasserman was on. He also learned the name of the FBI agent, Frank O'Connor, a hotshot from the Boston office who'd helped the local D.A. clean the Mob off the Boston waterfront. District Attorney Robert Clarke took his popularity and ran for Congress and O'Connor was transferred to the high-profile New York office.

McTavish could see they were speaking animatedly ten rows ahead of him, wondering what the pair planned to do. He was confident they would head to the Hoover Building first, the headquarters of the FBI and familiar ground to O'Connor. McTavish knew people there too; an agent who'd begun his career with the NYPD and another he'd met when working the World Trade Center bombing two years before.

He leaned back and smiled, knowing that he might just be onto the biggest story of his career and he had just about every angle covered. His reporter's instinct was sharp, it's what got him the job at the *Times*, and the instinct told him that Wasserman and O'Connor were his tickets to a Pulitzer.

Aboard an MC-130 Combat Talon, 1500 feet over Area 1A

"Hey, I can see my house from here," Johnson grinned as he stood in the open cargo door of the −130, the hot wind buffeting him.

"Shut up, smartass," Jack George said, just before retching into the puke bag.

"Man, what's wrong with you?" Johnson looked at him strangely. "You used to love flying."

"It's not the flying part that bothers me, it's the falling part," George groaned. "I got stuck in an elevator a few years back that fell three floors before it stopped. I haven't been right since."

"You've *never* been right," Rick replied with a laugh as he pushed George off the cargo deck into the sky. "Tally ho!" He said as he jumped after his friend.

"Silly bastard," Campbell said as he jumped after them, the rest of the team following.

Roman was the last of them to jump and he counted eleven good chutes in the air. In the distance, he could see Jack George making derogatory hand signals to Johnson as he floated next to him. Roman wished he could hear what George was saying. He had to admit that though his men had no military bearing and seriously bad attitudes, they were fun to be around. They constantly played practical jokes and always had a comment, and the morale of the unit was high.

Though they bitched and griped, they looked at every test with a can-do attitude. The run this morning surprised him and showed him just what these men were made of. He'd expected them to fall out within a mile, never even considering they would finish the five-mile run, but they did. They pushed each other, drew strength from each other, and though Roman thought they might die at the end, they did finish. He smiled again when he looked down and saw Johnson and George hit the ground.

George was out of his harness first and ran to where Johnson was trying to get out of his rigging. He tackled Johnson and the two of them rolled around in the dirt, George trying to get a good punch in, but the rest of the team managed to pull them apart. "You fucking asshole," Roman heard George scream as he hit the ground and rolled out. Four team members kept George from going after Johnson. "You could have *killed* me."

"Ah, quit your whining," Johnson laughed. "Your chute opened, didn't it?"

"You *dick*," George spat.

"Come on, Jack," Johnson's grin got wider. "That *was* fun, wasn't it?"

"I'll show you some fun," George growled, struggling to get loose.

"At ease, boys," Roman said, getting in Johnson's face. "If you ever do that again, I'll put you in confinement. Do you understand me, Sergeant Johnson?"

"Yes, sir," Rick said, coming to attention. "It won't happen again."

"And if you don't calm down," Roman said to George. "I'll have you locked up along with him."

"Yes, sir," George relaxed, and they turned him loose. He ran over to Johnson and punched him in the gut, doubling him over. "Now *that* was fun," he laughed.

"Truce?" Johnson said as he caught his breath.

"You bet, Rick." George smiled. "We're even now."

"Fucking idiots," Roman muttered, unable to keep the smile from his face. "Flight, form up," he ordered. "We're heading back to the barracks." They all looked around for a truck or some sort of conveyance that would take them the two plus miles back to their lodgings. "No boys, we're not riding, we're running," Roman chuckled. "You can thank Johnson and George for it. Double time, *march*!" And they all set off at a run.

Falls Church, Virginia

Connie flipped off the TV and mixed herself a drink. She was exhausted and they hadn't done much this day. O'Connor had been off talking to a few friends at the Bureau and she'd been left alone once they got to D.C. She'd taken the time to see some of the sights around the Capitol and returned to the Holiday Inn, waiting for him to return.

He did not bring good news, not bad either, but she'd expected results. All O'Connor said was that his friends would look into the case and that didn't satisfy her. It did frustrate her though and the television did nothing to alleviate it.

"This is taking too long," she said aloud as she took a gulp of her drink. Another cigarette followed. She wanted to do something, but knew not what, knew not what actions to take to make the man she loved come home faster and in one piece.

Hurlburt Field, Florida

"You wanted to see me, sir?" Reasoner said when he appeared at the door to Roman's office.

"Come in, Chief," Roman indicated a chair. "I wanted to talk to you about the incident this afternoon."

"What incident, sir?"

"The deal in the –130," Roman looked at Reasoner as if he lost his mind.

"Sir?"

"Johnson and George, when he pushed ..." And Roman realized what was happening. "I get it, Chief," he nodded. "And if I ask Sergeant Rockwood, or Coles, or Petersen, I'd get the same blank stare too, right?"

"I doubt they noticed anything either, sir," Reasoner shrugged.

"Very well, Chief," Roman sighed. "You're dismissed. Get some sleep."

Reasoner stood and came to attention. "Yes, sir," he said and left.

Roman leaned back in his chair and had to smile. They'd become a cohesive unit in less time than he'd thought possible. None of them, not even the active duty troops would admit that anything untoward happened aboard the C-130 this afternoon. Regardless of the squabbling between them, none would betray any of the others. The young lieutenant had to admit it was a good thing, yet it nagged him that the two young airmen would develop bad habits hanging around with the others. He decided to let Chief Reasoner handle any disciplinary problems Coles and Petersen might develop. "Shit, he wouldn't tell me about it anyway," Roman chuckled as he turned off the lights and closed the door.

Chapter Forty-Seven
Hart Senate Office Building, Washington, D.C.
Wednesday, 15 March 1995

"Jacob?" Sandra Weitz said as she entered his office, dropping a large manila envelope on his desk. "This was sent over from Congressman Clarke's office. The messenger said it was urgent."

"Ugh," Levy groaned when he opened the package.

"What is it?" His chief of staff asked him.

"Bobby's got a wild hair over a rumor that's going around," Levy said as he looked over the paperwork. A handwritten note fell out of the stack of documents. 'It's already in the works', it said. Levy then went to a clipping from the front page of the *Chicago Sun Times*, detailing the abduction of Jerome Emory. There was another note scribbled on the side of the page. It said, 'He's one of them'. Levy looked up to notice that Sandra had come around the desk and was reading over his shoulder.

"It looks like it's more than a rumor," she said. "Considering his record as the Boston D.A., I don't think Congressman Clarke deals in speculation, Jacob. What does he want you to do?"

"He wants me to investigate this on the Senate side," Levy muttered. "He thinks it has something to do with Senator Latour and he doesn't want to make waves."

"That's understandable," Sandy nodded. "The Republicans have control of the House and the Speaker is a close friend of LaTour's. They could make life difficult for him."

"I have to run for reelection next year too, you know," Levy turned to her, catching a whiff of her perfume. He thought her attractive, drawn to her from the first time they met, but he'd never acted upon the feeling. They had an excellent working relationship and he didn't want to ruin that by adding romance to the equation. And though he knew she considered him a good friend; he had never noticed any signals she'd wanted him for anything more than that.

"I'm confident you'll win," she smiled warmly. "You've endeared yourself to your constituents by doing what's right, regardless of political correctness."

"So, I *should* grab this by the horns?"

"You know you want to, Senator," the smile remained. "Especially if you can slap the Republicans in the process," Weitz added and Levy grinned.

"I'll slap anyone if they need it," he smiled back.

The J. Edgar Hoover Building, Washington, D.C.

Thomas Archambeault was the FBI's General Counsel and he regarded Francis Xavier O'Connor, and the woman he'd brought with him, with a critical eye. "I'm surprised you even got involved in this, Agent O'Connor, let alone do an end run around your boss. This is purely circumstantial, and you could leave yourself open to departmental charges."

"Are you planning to file charges against Agent O'Connor?" Connie asked him as she handed him a business card. "Because if you are, the Bureau can consider itself on notice that Epstein and Associates are Agent O'Connor's attorneys of record. We are prepared to defend him with every resource the firm can muster. I will then proceed to call a press conference as soon as we leave this office."

"I am just stating possibilities, Ms. Wasserman," Archambeault backpedaled.

"Since we're talking possibilities," Connie said as she tossed Johnson's DD Form 214 on his desk. "These are my husband's discharge papers from the U.S. Air Force. How is it possible that the personnel records center has no record of him? The man was awarded one of the highest decorations he could receive in the line of duty and he was part of an elite unit; six years of service is documented on this form. Why does the Air Force say he never served?"

"Maybe you should ask the Air Force," Archambeault shrugged.

"They are my next stop," Connie hissed. "My point is," she threw the group picture of A-Flight in front of him. "The Air Force says that *none* of these men ever served. *All* of them had their records deleted from the personnel archives." Connie shot daggers at him from her dark eyes. She stood and leaned over Archambeault's desk, pointing to one of the men in the picture. "*This* is Jerome Emory." She paused to let it sink in. "Yes, sir, there is no physical evidence of a crime, but there is too much of a coincidence here. If you doubt me, show my evidence to *any* of the field agents and they'll tell you the same thing. Show it to any district attorney worth his salt and he'd start drawing up indictments."

"Leave this with me and I will bring it to the Director's attention," Archambeault surrendered.

"I will leave you *copies* of this information," she said. "Over the past few days, I've developed a large distrust of government institutions." She tossed a package on his desk. "If I don't hear from the Director or the Attorney General's Office in forty-eight hours, I'll be back with a cadre of reporters."

"Don't threaten me, Ms. Wasserman," the FBI Counsel warned.

"No threat, just a promise," Connie shot back and then turned to O'Connor. "Come on, Frank, our next stop is the Pentagon."

Hurlburt Field, Florida

"A .50 caliber Remington," Jack George said as he opened the case Roman gave him. "Nice weapon."

"Your records indicate you were the most proficient marksman of the group," Roman said. "Can you still shoot?"

"I could hit a quarter at a mile distance with this thing," George said proudly.

"Well, let's see you do it."

"Yes, sir," George replied as he pulled the rifle out of the case.

Roman reached in his pocket and pulled out a quarter, flipping it to Reasoner. "Take it out to the end of the range, Chief."

"Yes, sir," he hopped into the Humvee parked nearby and drove out to the sand bank a half mile away.

"He can't hit that," Coles said as George assumed a prone position on the mat, resting the barrel on a small sandbag. Reasoner looked tiny in the distance, standing next to the Humvee.

"Ten bucks he does it on the first shot," Guthrie said to the young airman.

"You're on, Sarge," Coles said. Johnson held out a hand and both deposited a ten-dollar bill in it.

"Kids today," George muttered as he sighted in the rifle. He waited until Reasoner was positioned on the other side of the Humvee before bringing his finger to the trigger. Taking a few deep breaths, he began to regulate his respiration as he brought his eye to the telescopic sight. Johnson gave Guthrie a wink as George pulled the trigger. Less than a half second later there was a puff of sand downrange. Reasoner walked over and rummaged in the dirt for a second before finding the coin. He flashed the lights of the Humvee twice.

"I'll take that," Guthrie snatched the two tens from Johnson's hand.

"Man, he's good," Coles said.

"I'm the best, sonny boy," George said with a smile.

The Pentagon, Washington, D.C.

"I'm sorry, Ms. Wasserman," the Army sergeant said. "If you don't have an appointment with the Secretary ..."

"You tell the Secretary," Connie cut him off. "I'm ready to drive over to the *Washington Post* and bring a reporter back with me. If he wants the press camped out at the front door it's fine by me."

"What does this pertain to?"

"As you say in the military, that's classified, but he can be certain the FBI is aware of the situation." She pointed to O'Connor. "This is Special Agent O'Connor, by the way. Tell the Secretary I only need five minutes of his time."

"Yes, ma'am." The sergeant made call, spoke quickly, and then hung up. "I'm sorry, but he is in conference right now. Is there any way he can reach you when he's finished?"

"I'm at the Holiday Inn in Falls Church. He can leave me a message when he will be free."

"Yes, ma'am."

Connie turned and led O'Connor out to the car. "Shit," she said when they were inside. "I thought I could bully my way in there."

"It was a good try," he nodded, looking at his watch. "What do you say we get something to eat?"

"Yeah," she agreed. "Do you know anyplace good?"

"A friend told me about a place in Georgetown, maybe we can get in before the lunch crowd. Supposedly, all the big shots on the Hill eat there."

The Hart Senate Office Building

"Come on, Jacob," Sandra Weitz said. "You've been in that stuff from Clarke all morning, let's get some lunch."

"Can we order in?" He asked. "Or we can go to the cafeteria."

"No," she shook her head. "You need to get out of the building for a while, get some fresh air. Let's go to that new place in Georgetown."

"Is it expensive?" Levy asked.

"Jacob," Sandra said, putting her hands on her hips. "You are frugal with the taxpayers' money and that's a good thing, but I'm beginning to think you're just downright cheap."

"Cheap?"

"Cheap," she replied with a smile. "How are you ever going to find a wife if you don't splurge now and then?"

"Did I ever say I was looking for a wife?"

"You're forty years old, it's about time you had one."

"Is that so?"

"Okay, forget the wife thing. Let's just go to lunch and be happy that it's probably not as expensive as the dinner menu," she insisted.

"Well, since you put it that way …"

"I do," she handed him his coat.

Georgetown, D.C.

"I know who he is," Connie whispered to O'Connor, indicating a table near the far window. "He's the senator from California, what's his name, Jensen I think."

"I wouldn't know one of those clowns from another," O'Connor muttered.

"May I help you?" The Matre'd asked Connie.

"A table for two, please," she said with a smile.

"I'm sorry, Madame, but there are no tables available," he said haughtily.

"There are six empty tables over there," Connie pointed to the back corner.

"Those are reserved for Members of Congress," the Matre'd told her.

"But the sign says you don't take reservations," Connie insisted, pointing at the small sign near the door.

"I am sorry, but there is nothing available," he repeated.

"You've got to be kidding me," O'Connor said, opening his wallet and flashing his ID.

"This is no joke," the man said. "We have no tables."

"Hmm, I wonder if I should put in a call to the Health Department," O'Connor asked him.

"You may call whomever you want, sir, it will still not get you seated."

"That's a crock," Connie spat.

"Yes, it is," said a voice from behind them. "What is the meaning of this?"

"Ah, Senator Levy," the Matre'd looked past Wasserman and O'Connor. "A table for two?"

"A table for *four*," Levy barked. "And I have a good mind to inform the other members of your discriminatory policy." He winked at Connie who'd turned to face him. "These two fine people are my guests."

"Yes, sir, immediately."

"Thank you, Senator," Connie said. "You didn't have to …"

"Nonsense," Levy told her, extending a hand. "I'm Jacob Levy and this is my chief of staff, Sandy Weitz. From your accent, I'd say you're one of my constituents."

"Yes, sir," Connie said. "My name is Connie Wasserman and my friend is Special Agent O'Connor from the New York office." They shook hands and followed the Matre'd to a table, a good one.

Levy turned to Weitz. "I'll never eat here again," he said under his breath. "Pompous bastards." He gave a nod to Jensen across the room and took his seat.

"Yes, Jacob," Sandy said and looked to Connie. "Are you on vacation?"

"I wish," Connie said. "I'm trying to fight the bureaucracy."

"Ah, a woman after my own heart," Levy clutched his chest, drawing a giggle from Connie. "Is there any way I can help?"

She looked to O'Connor who shrugged. "Maybe, sir," she began.

"Jacob, call me Jacob," Levy insisted.

"I believe my husband has been abducted by the CIA and I'm trying to find him."

"*Why* do you believe that," Levy pressed.

456

"Because he was part of an elite Air Force unit a little over a decade ago and now all of them have disappeared," she said. Levy looked over at Sandy and raised an eyebrow. Connie didn't know how to read that, figuring he thought she was some kind of nut or conspiracy theorist. "Did you ever hear of a man named Jerome Emory, Senator ... Jacob?"

"The businessman?" Levy became intent as Connie fished the photograph from her briefcase.

"Yes," she pointed out Emory and then her husband.

"Damn," Levy whistled. "Bobby was right."

"Excuse me?"

"Well, Connie," Levy shook his head. "I've heard rumors about something like this happening." He turned to O'Connor. "Is the FBI involved in this?"

"Not officially," he admitted. "Rick and Connie are good friends of mine. I've taken some time off to help her. The Bureau doesn't want to open that political can of worms if possible."

"Oh, they *don't?*" Levy said. "We'll see about that after lunch."

***

"Isn't *this* a combination," Pete McTavish said to himself as he saw the foursome leave the restaurant, Levy and his chief of staff returning to their car, Wasserman and O'Connor following them to the Hart Building. He wondered if Wasserman had sought Levy out or if this meeting was purely coincidence. McTavish knew of Levy's idealism, the trait that got him elected in New York and what accounted for his overwhelming popularity in his home state. That coupled with Wasserman's tenacity, he'd done his research on her too and found she was a dogged investigator, would move their inquiry along more quickly. "That is if he's helping her." McTavish could have been reading this all wrong too, but he doubted Wasserman would pass up the opportunity to enlist the senator's aid. "This just gets better," he muttered as he clicked off a few pictures of them entering the Hart Building.

***

"You certainly have done your research, Connie," Levy said. He'd been comparing her facts with the material he received from Bob Clarke.

"I had to," she said. "I was prepared to do this alone." They were sequestered in Levy's office; he'd cleared his schedule for the rest of the day for this was the type of thing he lived for. "I didn't expect to run into *you*," she smiled.

"Lucky you," he returned the smile. He looked to Sandy. "I'd like an appointment with the CIA Director first thing in the morning."

"I'll work on it," she promised and returned to her office to begin her arm-twisting.

"I was at the Pentagon this morning," Connie offered. "But the Secretary of the Air Force wouldn't see me. I threatened to go to the press, but the most I got was a promise of an appointment sometime."

"They'll probably hand you off to a public affairs officer," Levy suggested. "If there are no records of these men's military service, the DoD won't care if you go to the press or not."

"We were also at the Hoover Building this morning," O'Connor said. "Connie managed to threaten the FBI General Counsel too."

"I knew I liked you," Levy grinned at her. "I think it's time we gave Director Atkins a call."

FBI Headquarters, Washington, D.C.

FBI Director Julius Atkins hung up the phone and then asked his secretary to have Thomas Archambeault report to his office. Atkins had the distinctive honor of being the first Afro-American FBI

Director. That carried both good and bad connotations. Good, because it was about time someone of ethnicity broke through the glass ceiling erected by the white male clique that dominated the Bureau at the highest levels. Bad, because he was under constant scrutiny by that same group, ready to pounce should he make the smallest of mistakes. Atkins was a veteran of the streets, a product of the D.C. Police Department who reached this level by hard work, honesty, and a dedication to the law.

"You wanted to see me, sir," Archambeault said from the open door.

"Sit down, Tom," Atkins said as he sat up in his leather chair. "I just got a call from Senator Levy's office. He's coming over here tomorrow with a woman named Wasserman." Archambeault blanched. "The Senator said she was here this morning with one of our people from the New York office and you turned them away."

"I was led to believe she was a nut case, sir. She struck me as one of those conspiracy theorists," Archambeault replied.

"I know Frank O'Connor, Tom," Atkins shot back. "He has fifteen years of exemplary service with the Bureau, what made you think he would be swayed by this woman if she were some kind of nut?"

"SAC New York didn't want to touch the thing, Mr. Atkins," Archambeault replied. "I assumed that if O'Connor's boss didn't want to know about it, her accusations were baseless. You must admit, sir, her allegations seem a bit farfetched."

"Not too farfetched to gain the support of one of our best field men and the junior senator from New York," the Director said. "Where is the material she left with you?"

"In my office, sir."

"I want it sent to Estevez immediately," Atkins ordered. "When the Senator arrives, I want this office to be prepared for him. The last thing we need is a congressional inquiry and the ramifications of the press finding out about this. I also want you to put the Attorney

General's Office on notice that we might be in need of a court order or two if this woman's information is as solid as Levy believes."

"Is that all, sir?"

"For now, Tom," Atkins said with a nod. He watched Archambeault leave and shook his head. "This is going to bite us in the ass," he said to the empty office before picking up the phone and dialing the extension for Special Agent Jorge Estevez.

Hurlburt Field, Florida

"You guys are coming along well," Reasoner said to Johnson. They were sitting outside the barracks, the rest of the team already turned in for the night.

"Did you have any doubt," he grinned.

"Many," Reasoner nodded. "You were out of control back then. I figured you'd be worse now."

"Hell, John," Rick said. "I've mellowed with age; it looks like the rest have too." Johnson considered him for a minute. "You know, I get this feeling that there's something more to this than just taking a look-see at the North Koreans' rocket facility."

"What do you mean?"

"Come on, John, look past the Air Force blue glasses you wear," he snapped. "They don't need us to do this. They could send Marine Force Recon or Army Special Forces, Navy SEALs even, why would they need a bunch of old retreads? Didn't it strike you as strange they chose us? Didn't it seem strange they'd waste the time and money on us?"

"Someone must feel that we're the best for the job," Reasoner offered. "We were the last American unit on North Korean soil, we know how to operate there."

"Shit, it's no different than operating in Europe, the same type of terrain, basically the same climate. Damn it, think objectively for once in your life."

"Unlike you, I'm not a troublemaker," Reasoner spat. "I don't go looking for ways to thumb my nose at the system."

"If they needed me so badly, they could have asked. I would have come running, I'm sure the other guys would have too," Johnson countered.

"Did you ever think of the security situation?" Reasoner asked him. "Do you realize the risk they would run if they'd done it your way? Too many people would know about our mission, too many of the wrong people."

"Easy for you to say," Rick said. "Your wife knows you're TDY somewhere. Mine probably thinks I walked out on her or I was the victim of foul play. You'd feel differently if you were picked up off the street and dragged here against your will. You'd be one pissed off Mohican too."

Reasoner thought about it for a moment. "I guess you're right," he said. "But that doesn't discount the fact that the country needs us, all of us."

"I hope *you're* right," Johnson nodded. "But I still think there's something more going on here, something none of us will find out until it's too late."

Chapter Forty-Eight
Kadena Air Base, Okinawa, Japan
Thursday, 16 March 1995

"Okay," Liz Callahan said when she arrived in Beu's office. "We've vacated our phase hangar and it's been empty for two days. What's going on?" She gave Beu no indication she was even remotely happy.

All he could do was shrug. "I don't know," he said.

"It happens to be the rainy season here, you know."

"No shit," Beu replied looking up at her. "Do you think this is *my* idea?"

"Damn it, Nate, you're the base commander, this is *your* patch of dirt."

"And I take my orders from the Joint Chiefs and the President," he growled. "Don't you think I screamed all the way to the top?"

"I guess," she looked away.

"Look, Liz," he softened his tone. "I don't want your maintenance people working under tarps any more than you do, but I've been told, in no uncertain terms, to shut up and cooperate."

"So what are you going to do?"

"Shut up and cooperate, by golly," he told her. "And I'll continue to do that until I can find out the whole story."

Lubyanka, Moscow, Russia

"Begging the Marshal's pardon," Boris Popov said, handing an envelope to Kosarev. "Another message from Colonel Zhukov."

Kosarev snatched the message from Popov and tore it open. "Ah," he spat disgustedly. "That insane little bastard."

"Bad news, sir?"

"The Americans are in the process of assembling a team," Kosarev told his aide. "And the North Koreans are beginning to reinforce the Sung Complex. General Park has the extraordinarily good fortune to have an agent privy to the details of the mission."

"Why doesn't he just make the Americans' intentions public, sir?" Popov asked. "They would have to abort the operation."

"Because then the Democratic People's Republic of Korea would have to admit they have nuclear weapons," Kosarev shot back. "Such an admission would force the Americans to suspend the food aid they've been sending to North Korea and that would destabilize the country. No, Boris, the North does not need a civil uprising on their hands and that is what they will get if the people begin to starve."

"We have to help the Americans, Marshal," Popov insisted.

"I will *not*," Kosarev slapped his desk. "And I will not hear any more of this."

"Suppose General Park uses the American incursion as an excuse to launch," Boris shot back.

"Then millions of South Koreans will die," the head of the FSK replied.

"Maybe some Japanese too," Popov added. "Maybe some *American installations* in Japan might be potential targets, wouldn't you think, sir?"

"Do not try to manipulate me, Boris," Kosarev warned. "And do not use my family to make your point. I know the risks to them."

"And are those risks greater than the one you would take by contacting General Beu?"

"Not nearly as great as the risk you are taking now," he barked. "So help me, Boris …"

"I will leave you with your conscience, Marshal," Popov bowed and backed out of the room.

"Damn him," Kosarev said as he looked out the window. "Damn them *all*. Damn this world and the all the people in it."

The J. Edgar Hoover Building, Washington, D.C.

"Welcome, Senator," Julius Atkins said when Levy and the small entourage entered.

"Thank you, Director Atkins," Levy said before he made the introductions. "Have you had a chance to look over the information?"

"I have one of my best people on it," Atkins replied, looking at his watch. As if on cue, there was a knock on the door and a tall Latino entered.

"George?" Frank O'Connor said as he stood.

"Hi, Frank," Special Agent Jorge Estevez said, taking the other FBI man's hand and shaking it. "It's been a long time since Boston."

"Agent Estevez will be running the Bureau's end of this," Atkins explained. "And I'd appreciate it if he did it out of your office, Senator."

"Why is that?" Levy asked him.

"George?" The Director looked to Estevez.

"Well, Senator," Estevez began. "Just the nature of this operation, and the players involved demands the utmost secrecy on our parts." He looked to Connie. "While your evidence is compelling, Ms. Wasserman, it's circumstantial, and I doubt we'd find anything conclusive if word gets out the Bureau is opening an official investigation. Someone wants to keep this secret for a reason. If we go making waves, your husband and his friends might disappear permanently. We should keep in mind that those men's lives depend on our being discreet."

"Which means," Atkins picked up for him. "That Agent O'Connor will be on a flight back to New York before the end of the day. Too many people here know who you are," he said to his agent. "And they will begin to wonder why. I'd rather people not ask too many questions."

"But ..." O'Connor began to protest.

"Don't worry, Frank," Estevez said. "I'll look out for Ms. Wasserman."

"So, where do we start?" Sandra Weitz asked.

"I have an appointment at the Pentagon this afternoon," Connie offered.

"Then that's where we'll start," Levy said. "I'm coming with you."

"And I'll check out this guy Holmgren," Estevez said. "We'll meet at your office around four, Senator?"

"Sounds good," Levy said.

"It sounds very good," Connie agreed, finally getting the feeling they were making progress.

Hurlburt Field, Florida

They were tired as hell but none of them looked like the human wreckage they did at the beginning of the week. Their bodies were responding to the exercise and the grueling routine and beginning to lose some of their flab. There was less bitching during the run, now up to seven miles, and all kept in step and in formation. There were no stragglers this time.

"You girls are doing better," Lieutenant Roman said when he brought them to a stop. "Not great, but better."

"Tight ass," Mason muttered. It had become his pet name for the young lieutenant.

"*Your* ass will be in a sling if you keep it up, Sergeant Mason," Roman barked.

"Yes, sir, *Lieutenant* Tight Ass," Mason grinned in reply.

Roman shook his head in exasperation. "Everybody on the truck," he ordered. Joe Rockwood was behind the wheel and he drove to the edge of the mock European town. They dismounted and Roman looked over the area. "We're going to break up into two groups," he said. "You're in command of the retreads, Sergeant Johnson, and I'll take the active duty guys. Tonight, your group will infiltrate the town and mine will be the defending force. Any questions?"

"Can we use live ammo?" Johnson asked him with a smile.

"Very funny," Roman growled. "The idea is to get in here *without* firing a shot, Sarge."

"I got ya," Rick saluted.

"We'll separate after lunch and we won't have any contact until you show up with your team," Roman told him.

"*If* we show up," Rick replied, his grin remaining. "The Mets are playing the Yankees in spring training and the game's on tonight."

"If you don't, you'll be sleeping with the alligators," Roman threatened, but he too was smiling. He couldn't help it.

"Gotcha," Johnson said. "We'll just have to get you guys quickly, so I won't miss too much." He turned to the men. "I want this wrapped up before the third inning starts."

"You're a cocky, arrogant bastard," Roman said.

"Yes, sir," Johnson kept smiling.

The Pentagon, Washington, D.C.

"I ... I didn't receive notice that you would be accompanying Ms. Wasserman, Senator." The Air Force captain was taken completely by surprise when Levy arrived with Wasserman. The public affairs officer was advised to listen to what Connie had to say, make a show of caring about it, and then send her on her way. That plan had crashed and burned. There was no way he could pull that on a member of Congress, especially one that sat on the committee that held the military's purse strings.

"I know," Levy smiled. "I would appreciate you informing the Secretary that I would like to speak with him immediately, Captain."

"Yes, sir." The captain made a call and spoke in hushed tones for a few minutes before hanging up. "The Secretary will be here presently," he said to them. "May I get you some coffee or something to eat?"

"No thank you, Captain," Levy said. "You've done everything I needed you to."

Not thirty seconds later, the door to the conference room opened and Manny Green, Secretary of the Air Force, entered. The captain departed hastily. "Welcome to the Pentagon, Senator Levy," Green said brightly. "Had you informed my people you were coming I would have arranged a tour."

"Cut the crap, Mr. Secretary," Levy said as he took his seat. "I already had the tour. I'm here on a *serious* matter."

The smile vanished from Green's face instantly. "What is it that is troubling you, Senator?"

"This is Ms. Connie Wasserman," Levy began. "Not only are she and her husband constituents of mine, but they are also my friends." Levy did not elaborate on the depth of their friendship or that he wouldn't recognize Rick Johnson if he fell over him in the street. "I would like some information on the 23rd Special Tactics Squadron."

"Is that a flying unit, Senator?" Green asked.

Connie pulled the photo out of her briefcase and slid it across to Green. "This is Alpha Flight, 23rd Special Tactics Squadron. The squadron was disbanded in 1985," she informed him.

"It seems you know more about it than I do," Green said.

"It *seems*, Mr. Secretary," Levy said as he leaned forward. "That this unit has been reactivated recently."

"I have heard nothing …"

"These men have all had their service records deleted from Air Force archives," Levy pointed to the photograph. "It seems a strange coincidence that all of them have gone missing within eighteen hours of each other; wouldn't you say, Mr. Secretary?"

Green picked up the photo and read the caption on the front and the names on the back. "Are you implying they were brought back to active duty, Senator Levy?"

"I'm not implying anything yet," Levy shot back. "But I would like to know why there is no record of them being on active duty in the first place."

"I honestly don't know, sir," Green shrugged.

"Well, find out," Levy demanded.

"This will take some time."

"Find out *now*," Levy insisted. "Or this conversation can take place in a Senate hearing room."

Pensacola, Florida

"What is the matter now, Alan?" Hector Reynaldo asked when he met Holmgren.

"There is a senator asking questions in the wrong places, Hector," Holmgren said.

"And you want him . . . discouraged, I presume?"

"I won't swing alone if this goes badly," Holmgren said. "And this operation will not go forward without me in control. Remind General Park of *that*."

"Who?"

"Stop playing this game, Hector, I know he is the one who pulls your strings," Holmgren hissed.

"You may believe what you want," Reynaldo said. "I will pass your concerns on to my superiors."

"This has to be done soon or Levy will trace this to me," Holmgren urged. "And if they come to me, I will send them to *you*. Tell General Park that if he doesn't want his missiles blown out from under him, he will do something about Senator Levy."

"As you wish, Alan," Reynaldo nodded and walked to his car.

The State Department, Washington, D.C.

"We have concerns, Ambassador Jiang," Secretary of State John Stanfield III said to the North Korean ambassador to the United States. "As you know, your government signed a treaty last year promising not to develop nuclear weapons and in return the U.S. obligated itself to providing fifty million metric tons of fuel oil per year to your country along with substantial food aid."

"Yes, indeed, Mr. Stanfield," Jiang nodded.

"Sir," Stanfield went on. "We have credible intelligence that your government is pursuing a weapons program in direct contravention to the treaty."

"Then I would have to say that your intelligence is *not* credible, Mr. Secretary," Jiang told him. "The DPRK honors its agreements, sir."

"So, I may tell that to the President with utmost confidence?"

"Yes, sir," Jiang reiterated. "The DPRK is *not* pursuing a nuclear weapons program. Any nuclear material on North Korean soil is only used for the purpose of generating electricity."

"Very well, Ambassador," Stanfield said. "I thank you for clarifying your position."

The Pentagon

"This is quite strange," Green said when he returned from his office several minutes later. "AFMPC in Denver can't find their records anywhere."

"So, what have you done with my husband and his friends?" Connie demanded.

"I have done *nothing*, Ms. Wasserman," Green snapped. "There has to be some sort of reasonable explanation for this."

"I've been waiting to hear one, Mr. Green," Levy said.

"Do you think the Air Force has a use for a group of men in their mid to late thirties most of whom have been separated for ten years, Senator?" Green asked him. "We have younger men on active duty who can do any job we ask of them. Besides, the draft ended after the Vietnam War. As you know, it would take an act of Congress to reinstate it."

"So how do you explain these coincidences, Mr. Secretary?" Connie insisted.

"I *don't*, Ms. Wasserman," Green said. "And I don't have to. I can say with maximum surety that the United States Air Force did *not* recall your husband and his cohorts to active duty."

"Do you have any operations ongoing that would require troops with the same skills as these men?" Levy asked him.

"You can safely assume, Senator, any operation requiring their skills would probably be classified," Green said. "I suggest you go through proper channels to gain access to that information."

"That would take too long," Levy said. "There are seven lives that are hanging in the balance."

"I am truly sorry, Senator," Green said. "But I have done all I can."

"That's not enough," Connie said.

"Why don't you talk to that bunch at Langley," Green suggested. "If you're right, I'd wager the Agency was behind this."

"You'd better hope so, Mr. Secretary," Levy warned. "Or you will be explaining your actions on the Hill and I can guarantee you I *will* have someone's head."

Hurlburt Field, Florida

Johnson removed his night vision goggles and pointed to the upper story of a building made to look like a farmhouse. "He's yours, Jack," he said to George. "Take Gibbs with you." George went to move, and Johnson grabbed his arm. "Make sure you wait for me."

"Right," he whispered and tugged on Gibbs' shirt. They disappeared into the scrub.

Johnson returned the NVGs to his eyes and spotted another of the OPFOR on a rooftop several yards down the dirt road. "Can you still climb, Nick?"

"Yeah," Mason nodded.

"Then that one's yours," Johnson said. "Go." Mason also disappeared. He saw movement behind an old shack. "There's the rover, Jerry," he said to Emory.

"I got him," he declared, vanishing in the darkness.

Johnson scanned the ersatz town once more looking for the remaining two. "Shit, I don't see them. They've gotta be inside one of the buildings. I'll be you it's the ell-tee and Reasoner."

"I agree," Campbell whispered.

"Okay, I want you two to follow that ditch and wait for them to come out into the open. Just keep your heads down and wait for me to do my thing."

"You got it, Rick," Campbell replied, and they set off for their destination.

Johnson checked his watch, giving his men three minutes to get in position before stepping out onto the road and walking toward the town. As he approached the structures, he began whistling the Air Force theme.

***

"Is he crazy?" Coles said to himself softly as he went to the window to see Johnson meandering down the road. He did not expect to be grabbed from behind, a hand going over his mouth. He was dragged down the stairs and his wrists and ankles were duct taped together. Another piece of tape was plastered over his mouth.

***

"What the fuck?" Petersen said from the balcony of the two-story house. As he raised his M-16 loaded with blanks, two arms enveloped him, relieving him of the rifle. His legs were kicked out from under him and he too received the duct tape treatment.

***

"Fucking morons," Rockwood grumbled as he watched Johnson walk leisurely down the street, wondering why neither Petersen nor Coles spotted him. He raised his rifle and took aim just before feeling the cold steel of a gun barrel behind his left ear.

"Drop the gun, Sarge," Emory said. "And put your hands behind your back."

***

"Who is it?" Roman whispered to Reasoner.

"Johnson," he replied, taking the NVGs from his eyes.

"Why haven't we heard a shot from one of our guys? They should have spotted him by now."

"I don't know, Lieutenant, but I don't see any of his team," Reasoner explained. As he came closer, they could hear him singing softly.

"Off we go, into the wild blue yonder ..." they heard a second before they felt rifle barrels at their back.

"Bang, bang, you're dead," Guthrie said from behind them.

"Hello, gents," Rick said as he walked through the front door. "I do believe you're my prisoners."

"Where are the rest of my men?" Reasoner asked him.

"In a second," Johnson raised an index finger. Mason was the first inside, Petersen slung over his shoulder. He deposited the young man on the floor. Gibbs and George were next dragging Coles between them, and he was set down next to Petersen. Emory was last, marching Joe Rockwood in at gunpoint. "Can I go and watch the game now, Lieutenant?" Rick said with a grin.

"You son of a bitch," Roman said.

"Don't say things like that about my mother," Johnson chuckled. "And never underestimate us again."

Hart Senate Office Building, Washington, D.C.

"Holmgren was an analyst with Air Force Intelligence until he went to work at CIA," Jorge Estevez told them. "It seems the guy knows his way around the Far East and his fitness reports reflect that. It doesn't hurt that he was married to Senator LaTour's daughter until she was murdered. From what I got out of Congressman Clarke's friend, most of the people in Holmgren's section figure that's how he got the job at Langley in the first place. The senator and CIA Director are close friends."

"What did Clarke's friend say about Holmgren's involvement with the disappearance of these men?" Levy asked him.

"He believes what Ms. Wasserman does, and he believes that Holmgren is the one running the operation. According to him, Holmgren's been temporarily reassigned, by the way. He's been incommunicado since Sunday night," Estevez replied.

"Where is he?" Connie asked this time.

"No one knows, ma'am," Estevez shrugged. "At least, no one who I've talked to."

"Well then," Levy said. "In the morning, I'll have to speak with someone who does."

Chapter Forty-Nine
CIA Headquarters, Langley, Virginia
Friday, 17 March 1995

"Sir," the DCI's secretary burst into his seventh-floor office. "Senator Levy is here, and he wants to see you."

"The Jew?" Louis Guerin asked.

"Yes, sir," the young man nodded. "The one from New York."

"Tell him I'm not ..."

"Not *what*, Director Guerin?" Levy said as he walked through the open door with Connie in tow. "Not willing to answer a few questions from a representative of the American people?"

"It depends, Senator," Guerin spat. "I've seen your witch hunts and I won't let you vilify the CIA as you've done in the past."

"I haven't told you why I'm here yet," Levy said with a devious smile.

"The only time you have contact with this agency, Senator, is when you sense some perceived wrongdoing. Your track record speaks for itself," Guerin said.

"That is a good thing, Mr. Guerin," Levy said. "I won't have to spend so much on campaign ads."

Guerin shook his head disgustedly. "And who the hell are *you*?" He asked Connie.

"My name is Connie Wasserman, sir, and I want to know what the *hell* you've done with my husband."

"I don't know what you're talking about," Guerin replied. "Get out of here."

"You can answer my questions here or on the Hill," Levy warned.

"Summon me to the committee room, Senator, if you are able," Guerin declared. "Until then, I will not answer *any* questions."

"You're making a mistake," Levy said.

"No, I'm not, Mr. Levy. You are a security risk and you threaten to compromise a whole host of ongoing operations, and I don't even know how to classify *her*," he pointed to Connie.

"She is a woman whose husband this agency has taken against his will, and I am her advocate, Director Guerin."

"We don't abduct Americans, Senator Levy," Guerin replied.

"Then *prove* it," he spat. "I want to speak with an Air Force colonel named Holmgren."

"Who?"

"He's Senator LaTour's son-in-law, don't feign stupidity," Levy hissed. "You know him well enough."

"This interview is *over*," Guerin announced.

"I'll see you in the hearing room, Director Guerin," Levy promised.

"Best of luck to you, Senator," Guerin gave them a two fingered salute as they left. He immediately grabbed his phone and dialed a number from memory. It was answered on the first ring. "Hi, Ernie," he said. "It's Lou Guerin. We have a problem."

***

"He's hiding something," Connie said when they were in his car.

"You noticed," Levy agreed with a smile as he threw his old Chevy in gear.

"Well, it's obvious he doesn't like you," she said. "But I think his attitude was more than just a genuine dislike."

"If he doesn't know what Holmgren is up to, I'll buy a new car," Levy grinned.

"You should buy a new one anyway," Connie advised as he turned onto the George Washington Parkway. "I'm sure your constituents won't hold it against you. Besides, this thing smokes so much it qualifies as a superfund cleanup site. You don't want us to think you're a hypocrite on the environment; do you?"

"Very funny, Ms. Wasserman," he looked over at her, just taking her in. "Do you mind if I ask a personal question?"

"No, ask away."

"How is your marriage?"

"Why? Do you think Rick left me?"

"No, he'd be an idiot if he did," Levy said. "I guess I'm hoping you're undertaking this crusade out of a sense of duty instead of your love for the man. You are an exceptional woman, Connie. I guess I'm asking if …"

Connie realized what he was trying to say. "Believe me, Jacob, I'm flattered, but I love Rick more than anyone I've ever known, and I know he feels the same way about me. Our marriage is strong and when I find him, it will grow stronger."

"I'm sorry I asked," he said. "I won't ask again."

"That's okay," she smiled warmly. "I thought you and Sandy …"

"No," Levy shook his head. "We're just good friends. I wouldn't be where I am without her though."

"Does *she* know you're just good friends?"

"She's never given any hint that …"

"You'd better open your eyes, Senator," Connie proclaimed. "I see the way she looks at you. You're not seeing the forest for the trees."

"Do you really think so?"

"Women can see things like that. She's an exceptional woman too, you know," Connie smiled.

"I can't argue with that," Levy agreed.

Hurlburt Field, Florida

"You didn't play by the rules last night, Sarge," Roman said to Johnson as he sat down next to him.

Johnson took a sip of his coffee and studied the young man. "Who says combat has rules? I only have *one* rule. Do anything to win. I thought Sun Tzu was required reading for officer weenies?"

"In a real situation, you would have been cut down as soon as you started whistling," Roman said.

"If you guys weren't playing it for real then you deserved to lose, Lieutenant. I *was* prepared for the consequences. Do you think I was kidding when I asked to use live ammo?"

"You *wanted* to get shot?"

"*Hell* no," Johnson shook his head. "That hurts like a motherfucker, but if my getting shot means my unit will be able to overcome an enemy with a more advantageous position than so be it. You clowns just *had* to look at the nut walking down the middle of the street whistling his ass off and you let your guard down. My boys took advantage of that and took you all down. Misdirection, sir, magicians do it all the time."

Roman regarded him for a second. "Maybe we were too cocky to believe that a bunch of bad attitude old geezers could outwit professional soldiers, Sergeant Johnson."

"That hurts," Johnson grabbed his chest. "I don't consider myself a geezer just yet." He smiled. "But I was sorta hoping your cockiness would play to my advantage," he winked at the younger man. Rick rose from his seat. "I've only said this a couple of times in the past, but you're all right for an officer, boy."

"And you're not bad for an old geezer, Sarge."

"Stick with me, kid, and we'll come up smelling like roses."

Langley, Virginia

"Where is he?" Louis Guerin said without preamble when Rice arrived at his office.

"Whom are you asking about, sir?"

"Colonel Holmgren, who else?" The DCI barked.

"I don't know, and I don't want to know," Rice shook his head. "What happened?"

"That miserable Heeb came sniffing around here this morning with a woman who claims her husband was abducted by the Agency," Guerin told him.

"It looks like it is time for damage control," Rice smiled.

"Levy won't learn anything before it's too late," Guerin rationalized. "I've seen to that, but I don't like the idea of Holmgren running around without supervision."

"You should have thought about that before you turned him loose with his crazy plan," the DDO said.

"An adversarial attitude will not help the situation, Mr. Rice," Guerin growled.

"This fiasco was hatched from ambition and a lust for power, sir, yours, and Holmgren's. I do not want to be involved with it."

"If you don't find Holmgren in twenty-four hours, you'll be more involved than you ever dreamed," Guerin warned.

"Yes, sir," Rice said, irritated but pleased at the same time. The best thing that could happen was Holmgren's plan going to shit. He left the DCI's office, not going back to his, but heading over to see Bobby Holt. "Hey, Bob, got a minute?" He said from the door.

"Come in, Dave," Holt motioned to a chair. "What's going on?"

"Lou Guerin is having cold sweats," Rice smiled. "Senator Levy dropped in on him unexpectedly this morning, asking questions about Holmgren."

"I got a call from Manny Green," Holt advised. "Levy was at the Pentagon yesterday, asking the same questions."

"Do you know where Holmgren is?" Rice asked him.

"Probably at Hurlburt in Florida," Holt said. "That's where his team is training." He looked over at Rice. "Now you see why I didn't want this operation on the books. Levy won't figure it out until it's long over, one way or the other. By then we can figure out what kind of spin we have to put on it or whether we can deny it completely."

"What about State?"

"From what I hear, Stanfield got the personal assurance from the North Korean ambassador that they do not have a nuclear weapons program," Holt replied.

"And the President believes this?"

"No, not with the evidence we showed him, but he can't exactly reveal the capabilities of the KH-26 to the U.N. General Assembly. If this operation is successful, he will be able to go to the U.N. with proof and not have to divulge the existence of our new satellite," Holt said.

"So, we're *not* going to abort?"

"Not unless Guerin or the President orders it, Dave. The −26 has to stay secret at all costs and we need that intelligence. The mission's still a go."

Rice smiled and rose from the chair. "I suggest you cover your ass before Levy takes a bite out of it, Bob."

Georgetown, D.C.

"Oh, you're an FBI agent?" The real estate agent said to the tall Latino.

"Yes, ma'am," Estevez nodded. "My wife is going to have a baby," he lied. "And we're in the market for a bigger place."

"Well, you'll like this one," she said as they walked up the drive. "It's priced to sell."

"Why are they selling?" Estevez asked.

"The owner is a widower and it's just too big for him but it's perfect for a family."

"Is there any way I can talk to him? I'd like to hear about the place from the owner," he smiled. "Nothing personal."

"Oh, I understand," she nodded as she slid the key into the front door lock. "But unfortunately, he was transferred out of the area. He won't be back."

"Is there any way I can reach him by phone?" Estevez prodded, giving her his best smile.

"I have a number, but he asked that I not give it out," she shrugged as they stepped inside. "Sorry."

"I understand," he nodded. "You can't be too careful these days."

Chapter Fifty
Arlington, Virginia
Saturday, 18 March 1995

"I thought we'd hear from you last night, Agent Estevez," Levy said when he answered the door.

"I was house shopping," he replied. "Colonel Holmgren put his house in Georgetown up for sale. The real estate agent said he wouldn't be back in town."

"Where did he go?" Connie asked.

"He didn't tell her, but he left a number where he could be reached when she sold the house. I took the liberty of visiting the real estate office after hours last night," he grinned conspiratorially. "And checked his file. The number traces to an extension in the Florida Panhandle, Fort Walton Beach to be exact."

"That's where Ernie Latour comes from," Levy said.

"It gets better," Estevez held up a hand. "The location of the phone is in the Bachelor Officer's Quarters on Hurlburt Field."

"Is that a military base?" Sandy Weitz asked him.

"Ms. Wasserman's husband was stationed there when he was with Air Force Special Operations," the FBI man said. "How much do you want to bet he's there now with the rest of them?"

"Let's go then," Connie said.

"Not so fast," Estevez said. "That's a huge reservation, we can't just show up at the front gate and ask for your husband and the others. I doubt there's any official record of them being there."

"So, what do we do?" Connie was frustrated again.

"We have to be certain they are there, and their exact location," Levy said. "But we should know that soon." And there was another knock on the door. Levy let another man into the apartment.

"Good morning, Senator," Michael Markham said, looking at the others assembled there.

"Hi, Mike, thanks for coming," Levy said. "Ladies and gentlemen, this is Mike Markham. He works for the Central Intelligence Agency in the Intelligence Directorate." Levy introduced the others to Markham.

"I could lose my job for this, Senator," he said.

"Not for doing the right thing," Levy assured him.

Markham was short and his eyes kept darting around the room, never making contact with any others. He seemed overly nervous. "I'm not so sure about that," he mumbled. "This comes from the top."

"The President is aware of this?" Levy was surprised.

"I don't know if there is a *this*," Markham said. "I dug as deeply as I could, just as you asked, sir, but I couldn't find anything official."

"Then what *do* you know, Mr. Markham," Connie said impatiently.

"Just what I hear," he shot back. "There is word that the North Koreans have developed a nuclear missile program. We found out a few weeks back and made plans to mount a reconnaissance operation to verify that intelligence. The South Koreans and Japanese were in a better position to get boots on the ground, so we backstopped them with overhead surveillance of the target area. Unfortunately, their team was ambushed as soon as they hit the ground."

"Someone leaked," Estevez said.

"We think it was either on the South Korean or Japanese end," Markham agreed. "Rumor has it that we're getting ready to put a team of our own in there."

"Rick and his friends," Connie gasped.

"I don't know for certain, ma'am," Markham said. "All I heard was that they were not using Agency personnel."

"Perfect deniability," Levy said disgustedly. "There is no evidence of these men ever being in the military and there is no evidence of this operation either. No wonder Guerin was so belligerent, nothing can be traced to the Agency."

"I have to go," Markham said. "I can't be seen here."

"I understand, Mike, and I appreciate the risk you've taken," Levy said, and Markham departed.

"What do we do now?" Connie asked him when the door was closed. "We're still not sure where they are."

"On Monday, we go back to Langley," Levy said turning to Estevez. "And I'd like you to take a trip to Florida."

The FBI agent smiled, knowing what Levy was thinking. "I'll be on the next plane to Pensacola."

Lubyanka, Moscow, Russia

"You should not work all weekend, Marshal," Popov said when he brought the tray of blini to his boss.

"I do not remember your being appointed my keeper," Kosarev growled.

Popov went to the sideboard and poured Kosarev a water glass half full of vodka. "Your health is a priority, sir."

"To whom, Boris?" Kosarev laughed. "My enemies would surely love to see me die of exhaustion."

"Mother Russia needs you healthy, sir," Popov replied, setting the vodka on Kosarev's desk. "And you have a granddaughter who needs you as well."

"You are a nag, just like my late wife, but do not make the mistake of believing that I share the same affection for you," Kosarev grumbled.

"I have taken the liberty of booking passage on a Japan Air Lines flight from Zurich to Naha tomorrow morning, Marshal," Popov said. "I believe you need to get some rest."

"You *what?*" Kosarev stood. "*I* believe your father will be burying his only son soon."

"Do what you will to me, Marshal," Popov raised his hands in surrender. "But you owe it to those men who unwittingly will do your bidding."

"I owe them *nothing*."

"Then you owe it to Katherine Alexandra," Popov said softly. "Could you live with yourself if she met her end in a nuclear firestorm? Could you live with yourself if Alexa did, knowing you were the one who instigated it?"

"I do know I could live very well without an aide who thinks himself more powerful than he could ever dream to be," Kosarev barked.

"I will prepare your things, Marshal," Popov said.

"You are a willful little bastard."

"I learned from the best, sir."

Chapter Fifty-One
Zurich, Switzerland
Sunday, 19 March 1995

"Would you like anything else, Mr. Osterhaus?" The pretty JAL flight attendant asked Kosarev.

"No, my dear," the man smiled.

"And you, sir?"

"A glass of wine would be splendid," Boris said, drawing a dirty look from Kosarev. "And if you'd have any literature regarding the attractions on Okinawa would be welcome."

"Of course, Mr. Steiner," she said and disappeared into the first-class galley.

"Do not presume for a minute that I would refrain from choking the life from you right here," Kosarev whispered to him.

"Would you risk discovery and arrest, sir?"

"It would be worth it."

"Would it be worth it to Katherine Alexa?"

"Wait until we get back home, Boris."

"Yes, sir," Popov smiled as the flight attendant handed him the wine.

Hurlburt Field, Florida

"Aren't you going to church, Sarge?" Roman asked, wondering why Johnson wasn't in his Class A like the rest of the group.

"Nah," he waved it away. "You need someone to watch the fort."

"Bullshit," Roman smiled. "What's your deal?"

Johnson looked up from his book. "Look, Lieutenant," he said. "God and I made a deal a long time ago. I promised to stay out of his way if he stayed out of mine. It's worked out well for both of us so far."

"You have a very high opinion of yourself."

"Yes indeed," Rick smiled.

"Are you an atheist or something?"

"Nope," Johnson shook his head. "But let's just say that I learned to have faith in myself and my abilities and not to depend on the Good Lord's intervention."

"I don't know about you, Sarge," Roman said as he headed toward the door. "But I'll take all the help I can get, especially His."

Kadena Air Base, Okinawa, Japan

"I'll get it," eleven-year-old Katie Beu said, running to the door. She flung it open and gasped. "*Grandpa!*" And he scooped her up in his arms.

"Who is it, Katie," her mother said as she came around the corner out of the living room. She dropped the water glass she was holding. "Papa?" And she went to him as well.

"Well, I'll be ..." General Nathan Beu said as he came down the stairs.

"Hello, Nathan," Kosarev attempted to shake his hand. "We have much to discuss."

"What is this about, sir?" Beu asked him.

"It will wait," Kosarev boomed. "I want to see my girls first and I am certain there is vodka somewhere in this house."

Fort Walton Beach, Florida

"May I help you, sir?" The security policeman at the main gate said as he looked into the rental car.

Estevez flipped open his credentials. "Special Agent Estevez, FBI," he said. "Can you direct me to the Security Police commander?"

"Straight down this road, Building-3400," the guard said and waved him in.

It was a short drive and he found the correct building easily. Parking out front, he walked up the three steps and entered, showing his credentials to the sergeant at the desk. "I'm here on a fugitive matter," he said. "I need to speak with the commander."

"Sorry, sir," the sergeant shrugged. "He just left for MacDill. He'll be back tomorrow afternoon. Can I arrange quarters for you?"

"That would be fine, Sergeant, thank you," Estevez said. He was pleasantly surprised at the hospitality and thankful he didn't have to drive back into town.

Chapter Fifty-Two
Kadena Air Base, Okinawa, Japan
Monday, 20 March 1995

It was two in the morning by the time they got Katie to bed, the little girl wound up at the prospect of having her beloved grandfather nearby for more than a few hours at a time. Alexa had prepared a snack for the three men and left them alone once her daughter was asleep. "I don't know if this is a good idea, Yevgeniy," Beu said. "While I'm happy for Katie and Alexa they are able to visit with you, your discovery on this base, in my home, will do them no good, you and me even less."

"We have given this much consideration, General Beu," Boris Popov said, drawing a scowl from Kosarev. "And this is the only way this situation might be resolved peacefully."

"I am afraid," Kosarev sighed. "That Boris is correct. My actions have set events in motion that I was not prepared for." And Kosarev went on to explain how he'd learned of the extraordinary abilities of the KH-26 satellite and how he'd arranged for it to get a peek inside the Sung Rocket Complex. He told Beu of the South Koreans' attempt to infiltrate the Communist country and their devastating failure. "There is an American team training for the same mission, Nathan," he said finally. "There is a mole in your Central Intelligence Agency who has been feeding the North Koreans intelligence on American operations and I am afraid they will be more than prepared for the reconnaissance team when they arrive."

"Then you have to inform our government, Yevgeniy," Beu said. "Through *official* channels."

"It is not that simple, General," Popov said. "An internal investigation would probably force the disappearance of your team and the Marshal's admission would cause your government to cut off aid to Russia, either in full or partially. We cannot afford either eventuality, sir. We need the American team to either expose the North Koreans' nuclear program or destroy it, and Russia cannot do without the economic aid from the U.S. The stability of our nation is at stake."

"What do you expect me to do?" Beu shrugged.

"I have someone inside the Sung Complex, and I have arranged to extract him and his family. I believe he could be of help to your team," Kosarev said. "And so can I. So can you, Nathan, if you will take the risk."

Arlington, Virginia

"Oh, this is good," McTavish said inside the third different car he'd rented since he came to Washington. He's changed cars often, knowing the FBI agent who was working with Levy would spot the same car following easily. Levy, Wasserman, and Sandy Weitz left Levy's apartment together this morning and McTavish clicked off several frames before putting the camera away. He followed the old Chevy as it made its way to the Shirley Highway.

***

"Isn't this thing a piece of shit?" Sandy asked Connie as Levy merged into traffic.

"It's a classic," Levy said.

"Isn't this thing a classic piece of shit, Connie?"

"I pointed that out the other day," Connie grinned from the back seat.

"It's getting you around, isn't it?" Levy asked them.

"You can afford a new car," Sandy said.

"It'll ruin the image," he replied. "Case closed."

None noticed the nondescript car following closely, weaving through traffic in an attempt to catch up with Levy's vehicle. The rush hour traffic slowed in Levy's lane and the car caught up quickly, pulling up next to the Chevy as Levy fiddled with the radio, trying to find a traffic report. Something made him look to the left as the man raised a pistol.

"Get down!" he pushed Sandy down in the seat as the man fired.

***

"Son of a bitch," McTavish said as he heard the gunshots. "It's an assassination." He stopped the car and brought the camera up, his finger busily snapping pictures.

***

Levy fell sideways, his upper arm burning in pain. "Get out, get out," he yelled to the women who'd exited on the passenger side. He followed, crawling across the front seat, and falling out the right-side door. Connie and Sandy dragged him the rest of the way to the Jersey barrier and got him over the top as their assailant exited his car, giving chase.

"He's going to kill us," Sandy cried as they peeked over the barrier.

"We have to get away from the road," Connie said, beckoning her to grab Levy by the jacket. He screamed in pain as they dragged him down the embankment, the unknown assassin appearing at the Jersey barrier. Looking down at them, he took aim with his pistol.

Connie cringed when she heard two shots, expecting bullets to smash into her body. Instead, the body of the assassin rolled past them, the back of his head blown open. She looked up to see a D.C. police officer looking down at them.

"Are you all right?" He yelled.

"Senator Levy has been shot," Connie said. "Call an ambulance."

Hurlburt Field, Florida

Estevez drove for about forty-five minutes once he left the more developed section of the base, into an area of marshes and swampland, and hadn't been stopped. He'd driven through several sections where towns that looked like Hollywood sets, but saw no signs of life. Parking near one of the houses, he got out of the car, grabbing a Coke from the small Styrofoam cooler he bought at the Base Exchange.

"Fucking amazing," he muttered as he walked through one of the structures, reminding him of the training area at Quantico. Hearing another vehicle pull up outside, he walked back to the door to see an armored truck next to his rental. The .50 caliber machine gun mounted on a turret swung around and took aim at him.

"Don't move," a voice said over the vehicle's PA. "Or there won't be enough left of you to identify."

Walter Reed Army Medical Center

"He'll be okay," Lt Colonel Jeff Jarrett said to them. "The shot ricocheted through the door before it found him. We got the bullet out of his left bicep and the only permanent damage will be a nasty scar."

"Thank you, Doctor," Sandy said as she brought the sodden handkerchief to her eyes once more.

"Can we see him?" Connie asked hopefully.

"The D.C. Police and the FBI are with him now," Jarrett replied. "You can head in once they're done."

Hurlburt Field, Florida

"You are *not* here on official FBI business, Agent Estevez," the Security Police commander said. "So why don't you begin by telling me exactly *why* you're here?"

"I'm working for Senator Jacob Levy's office under the auspices of a congressional investigation, Colonel," Estevez said.

"And what would you be investigating?"

"I'm not at liberty to say, sir," he said politely.

"You won't be at liberty to do anything if you don't come clean," the top cop warned.

"I suggest you call Senator Levy's office in Washington," Estevez said.

"You don't listen to the news much, do you, boy?"

"Why?"

"Senator Levy was shot a few hours ago," the colonel told him and Estevez' jaw fell.

"No shit?" Estevez asked and the cop shook his head. "Can I make a call?"

"If it will enlighten me on your situation, by all means."

"I need to ask you a question first."

"The answer depends on the question."

"Is there a Special Forces unit training here?"

The colonel laughed. "There are fifteen Special Forces units stationed here."

"A small unit, one not stationed here, a unit trying to keep a low profile?"

"I know of one, but that area has been placed off limits, even to us."

"Can you take me out there?"

"Make that call first, Agent Estevez, or the only place I'll be taking you is to my jail."

Walter Reed AMC

"Oh, Jacob," Sandy ran to his bedside.

"Stop crying," he insisted. "I'm fine, just a flesh would as they say in the movies."

"When can you get out of here?" Connie asked.

"I'm leaving as soon as I can get someone to sign me out," Levy said. "I hate hospitals."

"You're as bad as my husband," Connie smiled.

"You'll stay as long as they tell you to," Sandy declared.

"Yes, mother," Levy smiled. He turned to Connie. "We're close," he said. "Or they wouldn't have tried to kill me."

Hurlburt Field, Florida

"Pack it up," Roman ordered. "We're leaving town."

"Where are we going, Lieutenant?" Reasoner asked.

"We'll know when we get there," Roman replied.

"I love surprises," Johnson quipped.

"Shut up and get going," Roman growled. "We're due on the flightline in five minutes."

***

"Yes, sir," the SP colonel hung up the phone and regarded Estevez. "Okay, you got your ride. Come on."

Estevez got his pistol back and followed the commander out to the white and blue police vehicle. The cop ran lights and sirens on the thirty-minute trip out to Area 1A, locking the brakes in front of the barracks building. They both hopped out and burst in to find the place empty. "Shit," Estevez said. "They're gone."

"They must have just left," the cop observed. "I just spoke to their CO this morning."

"What's his name?"
"A bird colonel, Holmgren I think."
"Let's go see him."

***

"Hey, we're flying first class," Emory said as they all marched into the rear of the MC-130. The trip in the four-engine turbo prop would be anything but, noisy, cold, and uncomfortable on the web seats that ran the length of the fuselage. Rockwood and Reasoner drove the group's vehicles into the belly of the plane and the loadmaster ordered them lashed to the cargo deck. Twenty minutes after they boarded, the –130 began its roll to the taxiway.

***

"Where is Colonel Holmgren, Airman?" The SP commander asked the admin troop at the desk.
"He left a few minutes ago, sir," she said.
"When will he be back?" Estevez asked.
"He won't be," she replied.
"Do you know where he went?"
"No, sir. He was only using the office space temporarily and he didn't say. He signed out and returned his key." They all looked toward the window as a C-130 thundered over.
"How much do you want to bet your people are on that plane, Agent Estevez?" The SP colonel said.
"I'll need a phone," he said dejectedly.

Walter Reed AMC

"Damn it," Levy said as he slammed the phone down. Doctor Jarrett had not consented to his release, so Levy had turned the private room into his personal office.

"What is it?" Connie asked.

"George Estevez from Florida," he replied. "He missed them by minutes."

"Where did they go?" Her eyes became moist.

"He doesn't know, but they left in a C-130. He's trying to get a flight plan from the operations people over there."

"At least they're alive," she said.

Chapter Fifty-Three
Kadena Air Base, Okinawa, Japan
Tuesday, 21 March 1995

"Can we go to the park, grandpa?" Katie Beu asked the Bear.

"In a few minutes, my sweet girl, finish your homework and then we will go," he said as he took her face in his hands and kissed her cheek. "I have to speak with your father first."

"Okay, grandpa," she smiled and ran off to her room.

"If I spend much more time with her, I will never want to leave, Nathan," he said. "What have you found?"

"I can't tell you," Beu replied.

"Do not play this game with me," Kosarev growled. "I cannot help if I do not know what is going on."

"And how do I know you won't use what you learn against the United States?"

"I care about your family too, or have you forgotten that Alexa is my daughter?" Kosarev shot back.

"No," Beu shook his head.

"Please, Nathan," Kosarev stood and walked to the window. "This base could be targeted if the North Koreans decide to launch. Please let me help you so my daughter and your daughter may live long and healthy lives."

Beu looked at him, knowing he was right, yet hating himself for once more ignoring the oath he took so many years ago. It was twelve years ago that Kosarev talked him into essentially stealing a helicopter and spiriting Alexa from Soviet territory. "I've known for a while that a Special Forces unit was on its way here. We've had to vacate space for them. My executive officer informs me they will be here tonight."

"I have to see them," Kosarev said.

Beu laughed. "That'll be the day. I'll talk to them; see what they're planning and what kind of support they'll have. The only time you and your aide will leave this house is to take Katie to the park and back."

"I am not a child, damn you," Kosarev barked.

"No, you're the Chairman of the KGB. Don't you think someone might recognize you?"

"The KGB does not exist anymore," Kosarev corrected him.

"I don't care what you call it now, Yevgeniy. Just keep a low profile while you're here *please*."

"Do not worry, my boy," Kosarev patted his shoulder. "Our dirty little family secret will remain that way. But now I must fulfill my duties as a grandfather." He headed to the base of the stairs. "Katherine Alexandra," he called up to her. "It is time to go for a walk."

Hickam Field, Pearl Harbor, Hawaii

"Man, I always wanted to get to Hawaii, but this is not the way I expected," Johnson said as he marched out of the belly of the –130.

"Enjoy it while you can, Sarge," Roman said. "You've got twenty minutes to stretch your legs. *Don't* make me come looking for you."

"No, sir," Johnson threw up a halfhearted salute. He walked away from the group, to the edge of the flightline where he could get a look at the harbor. The USS *Arizona* memorial was visible, and he fell into thought. *I'd love to spend a week here with Connie.* And he smiled.

God how I miss her, he thought, wondering what she must be going through. *What must she think of me?* He assumed Connie would believe he left her, just ran away from his life, his job, and the woman he loved more than life itself. It was the only conclusion she could come to, according to him, because of the conditions of his sudden departure. *I hope she thinks I'm a better man than that.* And that was what gave him hope, that she would give him the benefit of the doubt until he could get back to her and explain the circumstances. *The million bucks will help,* he laughed at that, for he didn't care about the money, not for the money itself, only caring that he would be able to use it to prove himself. "Please understand," he said aloud as the hot wind took his words away.

Kim Po International Airport, Seoul, South Korea

Holmgren took a deep breath of the polluted air and smiled. He felt safe here, unlike the anxiety that weighed on him while in the States. He was in his element here, though he was Caucasian, he was able to move in this society easily, knowing the language and knowing the customs, blending in was effortless.

Holmgren would be difficult to find, and at this moment, he knew they were looking for him. He looked at it that way now, in his paranoia, which had become all consuming, *they* was an all-encompassing word. *They* meant Levy, the FBI, the CIA, and any other agency of the U.S. Government; he was sure they were all looking for him, especially now since Levy had been shot.

The senator had survived, and that meant Levy's determination was redoubled. *He won't stop until he finds me*, Holmgren thought as he got behind the wheel of the rental and drove into the night. He only needed a few more days and then he would be free of his obligations, to the North Koreans, to Hector Reynaldo, and, most of all, to Roger Hoffman.

"In a few days, you'll be able to rest in peace, my love," he said as he left the city of Seoul behind.

Walter Reed AMC

"I want out of here," Levy growled at Connie and Sandy.

"Just lie there and shut up, Connie said. She'd had enough of his complaining, not about his wound but his confinement to a hospital bed. They turned when the door opened.

"Hi, folks," Jorge Estevez said. "How are you doing, Senator."

"I'll be better when I get out of here. What's new?"

"Maybe some good news," Estevez said. "We got an ID of the shooter. He was a low-level attaché at the North Korean embassy. It was a good move, he had diplomatic immunity so the worst that could have happened to him was expulsion."

"So, the North Koreans are involved with this?" Connie asked him.

"We don't know. They say the man had a history of mental illness and he probably snapped or something. Their only other comment was to demand his body be released by the medical examiner."

"Any word on Rick's team?" She pressed.

"None," Estevez shook his head. "Whatever orders they are operating under, there is no written record of them. No one knows where they went or why."

"You can't hide a C-130," Levy said.

"It's a big world and the plane has good range. They might not even be in the States anymore," Estevez said.

"North Korea," Connie said. "Doesn't that make sense?"

"They'd need a base to stage from," Estevez said. "Somewhere close by."

"That's your next mission, Mr. G-Man," Connie said. "Find out the most likely places in the area that are within flying distance of North Korea by C-130."

"I'm on it," Estevez said. He looked at her for a long second. "I'm sorry I missed them in Florida, Connie."

"You did your best, George," she said, wiping a tear from her eye.

Chapter Fifty-Four
Kadena Air Base, Okinawa, Japan
Wednesday, 22 March 1995

The MC-130 touched down with a squeal, the heavy rain drumming on the fuselage. Johnson peeked out of one of the ports to look around. "Hey, I know where we are," he said. "This is Kadena."

"Japan?" Emory said.

"Yup," Rick nodded. "We're almost there."

The –130 taxied into the hangar built to hold two much larger KC-10s. The plane seemed lost on one side of the structure and the big doors rolled shut once the engines were shut down and the cargo ramp deployed. The men of A-Flight walked out and did their stretches, the flight from Hickam serving to stiffen their joints.

"These are our barracks for the time being," Roman said.

"Here? In the hangar?" Campbell asked him.

"Yes," the lieutenant nodded.

"It just gets better," Gibbs said sarcastically.

"You've slept in worse. The ceiling doesn't leak," Roman replied. "And there's indoor plumbing."

"How long are we staying?" Johnson asked him.

"Until I get word from my CO."

"And who's *that?*"

"You don't need to know that yet, Sarge," Roman told him with a shrug. "Those are my orders."

"It's probably some pencil neck from the Agency," Mason grumbled. "And he knows we'll kill him if he shows his face."

"You can rest assured he is a military officer," Roman told his men. "Now get some rest and keep away from the PCS personnel."

"What about food?" Guthrie asked. "I'm fucking *starving*." Roman pointed to a pallet in the corner of the hanger. "C-rations? You've gotta be fucking kidding me."

"I'm sure you've eaten worse too," Roman laughed. "You guys whine like a bunch of old women."

"Speaking of women," Campbell said.

"Don't even think about it," Roman warned. "I told you, stay inside the hangar and talk to *no* one. There's a squad of SPs surrounding the place and they're under orders not to let anyone in or out."

"So we're stuck in this fucking hangar for God knows how long, eating shit food and inhaling jet fuel?" Johnson said.

"Since you have such a problem, Johnson, *you* can take the first watch," Roman told him.

***

"They got in two hours ago, General," Colonel White said to his boss. "The –130 pulled directly into the hangar and they closed it up tight. The SPs have a perimeter set up."

"Good, let's go have a look," Beu said.

"The SPs are under orders not to let anyone in or out," White said.

"This is *my* base," Beu said. "Let them *try* to keep me out."

***

Johnson readjusted himself on the perch he'd sought out, at a window nearly thirty feet off the ground on a catwalk that ran the perimeter of the hangar. It was an expanded metal structure, and it made his butt sore. The upside was that he could walk the perimeter of the hangar and get an excellent view of what was going on outside. As he gazed out into the foggy morning, he saw movement among the security police personnel as a dark blue Ford approached the checkpoint. They stopped the car and two men got out to speak with the cops. Rick instinctively brought the binoculars to his eyes.

"Well, fuck me," he muttered as he focused in on the taller of the men. "Nah, it couldn't be." He looked again. "Fucking Nate Beu, and a *general* no less; the Air Force must be lowering their standards." And he could see that Beu didn't look happy and was exchanging heated words with the officer in charge of the Sky Cops.

Instinct gripped him once more when Beu tried to walk through the checkpoint and the other officer went for his sidearm. Rick grabbed his M-16 and pushed the window open.

***

"If you proceed toward the hangar, General Beu, I will be forced to fire," the SP captain shouted.

"You aren't man enough," Beu said over his shoulder.

"This is your last warning, General," the cop said as he raised his pistol. He didn't expect the shot into the asphalt between his legs.

"Let him in or the next one goes between your eyes," the voice from the window said. Another shot blew out a tire on one of the police cars. "Put the gun away, Captain, it's *your* last warning." The cop did as he was told. "You may approach and enter, General Beu."

"I know that voice," Beu said as he walked toward the hangar door, wondering what kind of situation he'd just bullied himself into.

***

"What the hell are you shooting at, Johnson? Put that rifle away." Roman called up to him and his eyes went to the door. "Flight, ten-hut!" He rendered a salute as Beu approached him.

"What's going on here, Lieutenant?" Beu demanded, getting in Roman's face.

"I'm sorry, General, but I'm not at liberty to say," Roman said, remaining at attention.

"Keep your shorts on, old man," Johnson yelled to Beu from above. "I'll be right down and tell you all about it."

"It *is* you," Beu smiled as he looked up. "You sorry son of a bitch. When did you get back in?"

"*I'm* sorry? Look at you, a fucking general, I figured they'd run *your* sorry ass out of town by now," Rick replied, jumping the final ten feet to the ground. He came up to Beu and saluted. Beu returned it and the two men embraced. "It's good to see you again, pal."

"Same here," Beu replied.

"Y-you know each other," Roman stammered, not prepared for this reunion at all.

"Rick is my daughter's godfather, Lieutenant," Beu explained. "And now I want to know *exactly* what is going on here."

"Why don't we take a walk, General?" Johnson said to Beu.

"I'm warning you, Johnson," Roman said. "General Beu isn't cleared for this."

"If there is anyone in this world I trust, Lieutenant, it is General Beu." Johnson looked to Beu and laughed. "I can't believe they made you a God damned general." He turned back to Roman. "And *you* can trust him too. He's covered my back in the past, and he's going to cover ours this time too. I'll be back in twenty minutes."

"I'll have you up on charges, Johnson."

"Don't threaten me with that, Lieutenant, because you know my situation," Rick said. "You can't do anything worse than what's already been done," he added as he and Beu walked to one of the doors that opened onto the flightline side of the hangar. He waited until they were outside before turning back to Beu. "So, how is the munchkin?"

"Munchkin?" Beu smiled. "She's *eleven*, Rick. She's turning into a young lady."

"And Alexa?"

"As beautiful as ever," Beu said.

"You're a lucky bastard, my friend," Johnson said.

"What about you?"

"I'm a lucky bastard too," Rick grinned. "I married the most beautiful, intelligent woman in New York City."

"If she's so smart, why did she marry *you*?" Beu kidded.

"She knows greatness when she sees it," Rick replied.

"Still the bullshit artist, I see. Kids?"

"Nope, Connie's doing the career thing," Johnson said. "Maybe in a few years."

"Have you heard from Yung Shu?"

"No," Johnson looked away.

"It still hurts, huh?"

"I've been thinking about her more and more lately since they brought us back. Did you recognize the rest of them?" Johnson asked him as he jerked a thumb back at the hangar.

"Wait a second," Beu stopped. "They brought you *back* into the service?"

"About a week and a half ago, pal, in the most unceremonious manner too. They say they have a job that only we can do."

"Who are *they*?"

"The Agency. None of our families even know where we are," Rick informed him.

"I don't like the sound of this," Beu shook his head.

"Do you think *I* do? We didn't have a choice." Rick looked out at the runway as a flight of F-15s began their takeoff roll. "They say they're gonna pay us a million apiece when it's over."

"When what's over?"

"We're going into North Korea again, Nate," Rick said quietly. "They've got nukes and they want us to get a closer look at them."

"This smells even worse than it sounds," the general offered.

"It smells like shit, pal." Johnson took a pen and paper from the pocket of his BDU shirt and scribbled his home address and phone number on it. "This is my information. When we leave, I want you to call my wife and tell her what happened. She's probably out of her fucking mind by now."

Beu pocketed it. "I will, I promise."

Walter Reed AMC

"It's about time," Levy said to Doctor Jarrett when he announced Levy could go home.

"Quit complaining and get dressed," Connie ordered as she and Sandy left to give him some privacy.

"Good morning, ladies," Jorge Estevez said when he arrived on the floor. "How's the patient."

"They're turning him loose," Connie said.

"They can't stand his *kvetching* anymore," Sandy giggled.

"Have you had any success?" Connie asked Estevez.

"Maybe too much," he replied. "Do you know how many bases we have in the East Asia Theater? The Air Force alone has about ten. Including the Army and Navy brings it up to around twenty-five."

"So, what do we do?" Sandy asked this time.

"We make this investigation official," Levy said as he came out of the room. He turned to Sandy. "I want a meeting with the chairman of the Senate Armed Services Committee *today*."

"Senator Latour?"

"The one and only," Levy hissed. "He's got some explaining to do."

Kadena Air Base, Okinawa

"They will die, Nathan," Kosarev insisted when Beu recounted Rick Johnson's story. "The North Koreans know they are coming."

"I called Washington," Beu said. "No one at the Pentagon knows anything about this deployment, or the circumstances surrounding A-Flight's recall; there are no records, *nothing*. I even called in a favor with the operations office there and ran the aircraft's tail number. According to them, the plane should be attached to the

193rd at Harrisburg IAP in Pennsylvania, on a deployment to Wiesbaden, Germany. Someone has covered themselves well."

"Then you must set this right, Nathan," Kosarev insisted.

"Don't you think I tried?" Beu shook his head. "No one at the Pentagon wants to know about this. They all figure it's a CIA op and don't want to get involved. Now that I think about it, it seemed like everyone I talked to was expecting me to call."

There was a knock on the front door and the men froze. Beu wasn't expecting anyone, Alexa shopping at the Base Exchange and Katie at school. Popov's right hand went inside his jacket, resting on the pistol in his shoulder holster. "That will not be necessary, Captain," Beu rolled his eyes as he went to the door. "Come in, Mark," he said to Colonel White. White stopped when he saw the two men in the living room. "This is my father-in-law, Evan Osterhaus, and my brother-in-law Boris. They're here from Switzerland to visit Alexa and Katie."

"Gentlemen," White said warily as he shook hands with the Russians. He had no doubts that the large gray-haired man was Alexa's father; there was no mistaking the family resemblance. The thing that bothered the former intelligence officer was the fact that he was pretty certain the man's last name was not Osterhaus. "I need to talk to you privately, General." Beu led him into the study.

"What's up, Mark?"

"I was going to ask you the same thing, sir." White said. "I have some information about your A-Flight boys in the phase hangar."

"So, spill it," Beu demanded.

"You first," White said.

"What are you talking about, Mark?"

"Alexa isn't Swiss; is she, Nate?" Beu said nothing. "I want the truth right now, or I start making calls. I *know* who he is," White pointed in the direction of the living room. "Are you fucking *crazy*?"

"I'm not a traitor, Mark, nor am I a spy," Beu said. "He *wasn't* the head of the KGB when I married his daughter."

"Why is he here?"

"It's related to the A-Flight situation. He's here to help save their lives," Beu explained and went on to bring White up to speed on the situation, Kosarev's man inside North Korea and the two Russian helicopter gunships waiting at Vladivostok to extract him, about the failed South Korean raid on the Sung Rocket Complex and the mole at CIA. He recounted Rick Johnson's story as well, how the men of A-Flight had been abducted and pressed into service

"Well then you'd better hurry, General," White said when Beu finished. "Because I got word they're bugging out tomorrow night."

"Colonel White is correct," Kosarev said from the door. "I trust I can depend on you to keep my relationship with General Beu a secret?"

"Do what you have to, Mark," Beu said. "I'm prepared to face the consequences of my actions, *all* of them, past and present."

"I'll decide that when this is over," White said. "For now, we have bigger priorities."

Georgetown, D.C.

"I don't know if I want you in my house, Levy," Ernie Latour said when they were shown into his study.

"It's either here or you'll hear about it on TV when I explain all this to the reporters who've been demanding an interview," Levy shot back. "It's your choice."

"What are you talking about?"

"Your son-in-law and this operation he's arranged," he spat. "The man has broken enough laws to put him in prison for the rest of his life and *you* can be considered an accomplice." He recounted what they'd learned so far.

"I can't believe Alan would do something like that," Latour said. He'd heard from Guerin previously and was expecting Levy to come here.

"Believe it, Mr. Latour," Levy growled. "Alan Holmgren is an agent for the North Korean government, and I am not far from proving it. I'll do *that* on the Senate Floor if I have to. You used your influence with the CIA Director to get Holmgren the job at the Agency, and again when he brought this plan to the Director."

"I have no influence …"

"Maybe you don't have influence *over* the CIA, but there are enough people there who would testify that Holmgren traded on it regularly. What do you think the American public would believe when I explain this to them?"

"Get out of here, all of you," Latour demanded. "You have nothing but speculation and coincidence. If you have any evidence that I was connected to any wrongdoing, it *must* be fabricated. I'll take my chances with the public."

"Yes, you *will*, Senator," Levy said and turned for the door.

Langley, Virginia

"This is going to shit," Louis Guerin barked at Rice. He'd just received a call from Ernie Latour that set him on edge. "Levy feels he can connect the Agency to the assassination attempt."

"*Did* we have anything to do with it?" The Deputy Director (Operations) asked the Director of Central Intelligence.

"Of course not," Guerin barked. "But Levy thinks Holmgren has been doubled by the North Koreans. The senator from New York believes Holmgren arranged the hit because Levy was getting too close."

"So, let's pull the plug," Rice offered.

"It's not that easy," Guerin said. "The President is expecting results."

"Damn it, sir," Rice said. "Holmgren might be the leak we assumed was on the South Korean end. If he is, our team will be slaughtered just as the Japanese and South Koreans were."

"Is that necessarily a bad thing?" Guerin asked him. "Without them, all Levy has is speculation. It gives us complete deniability. Officially, this operation doesn't exist."

"The President knows," Rice suggested.

"No, he *doesn't*. He does not know the particulars, just that we are exploring ways of infiltrating the Sung Complex."

"And he gave authorization for it?"

"I convinced him there were some things he didn't need to know," Guerin said.

"You lied to him," Rice corrected.

"If you want to put it bluntly, yes, I lied to him, but that is irrelevant." The DCI shook his head. "In a few days, the team will either be successful or not. If they fail, there is no way they can be connected to the Agency. If they succeed ..." Guerin looked away.

"You're going to leave them there, aren't you?" Rice said and Guerin did not reply. "Are there plans to extract them or not, Mr. Guerin?"

"No, there never were," Guerin said. "They are going in assuming that they will be able to call for a helicopter to pick them up."

"And they will be slaughtered whether they are successful or not," Rice said.

"That's what deniability is all about, Mr. Rice," Guerin barked. "If you can't live with that, I'll expect your resignation."

"I wouldn't give you the satisfaction, sir," Rice snapped. "I can live with much more than you think." Rice got up and left, heading straight to his office. Once there, he checked the newest sound file on his computer and smiled, hearing that every word of the conversation had been captured clearly. He reached for his phone. "Get me the Justice Department," Rice told his secretary. "I want to speak with the Attorney General."

Hart Senate Office Building, Washington, D.C.

"Senator Levy's office," Connie said when she picked up the phone. Normally one of the staffers would have fielded the call first, but it had come in on the line Levy had dedicated to communications about the A-Flight investigation.

"I would like to speak with Ms. Connie Wasserman," the voice with the southern drawl said. "I got this number from a lady named Maria Johnson."

"This is she," Connie said wondering whom her mother-in-law had given the number to.

"My name is Brigadier General Nathan Beu," the caller said. "I have some information about your husband."

Kadena Air Base

"Hey, Rick," Beu said when he arrived in the hangar.

"What's up, old man?" Johnson said as he cleaned his Colt .45 caliber pistol.

"I just got off the phone with your wife," Beu said. "That's one hell of a woman you have there. She's been looking for you since you disappeared."

"Did you tell her what happened?"

"No, I don't trust the phones," Beu informed him. "They are on their way here."

"They?"

"Your wife has been working with Senator Levy. They're coming here."

"No shit?" Johnson smiled.

"I just hope they're in time, Rick. You're leaving tomorrow night."

"Wrong, General Beu," Lieutenant Roman said as he approached. "We're leaving *now*."

Washington, D.C.

"Japan?" Levy said as they walked out of the office.

"Okinawa to be exact," Connie corrected. "General Beu said they were alive and well, but they wouldn't be staying long. He didn't go into detail because he was afraid the phones were tapped. I took the liberty of booking three seats on the next Singapore Air flight out of Dulles."

***

"Okinawa?" McTavish said to himself as he put the car in gear, following Levy, Wasserman, and Estevez to the airport. "What the hell is going on?" He had some parts of the story, just from overhearing things caught by the parabolic microphone he borrowed from one of the tech heads at the Washington bureau of the *Times*. After purchasing a ticket on the same flight as Levy's entourage, he made a call to New York, informing Al Pritchett of his progress and arranging to be met by someone from the Tokyo bureau on Okinawa. He also had the research department dig up all they could on a General Nathan Beu, United States Air Force.

The Justice Department, Washington, D.C.

"This is indeed a rare occurrence," Attorney General Helene Smith said to David Rice. "This information you have volunteered makes me question your motives, sir. CIA officers generally don't come forward with incriminating evidence against one of their own."

"I am concerned for the President, Ms. Smith," Rice said. "And the effect this will have on the remainder of his term. He was misled, but I doubt the public will see it that way when it comes to light."

"Have you been in contact with Senator Levy's office?"

"No, ma'am," Rice said. "Should I be?"

"It's coincidental that he came to me with the same concerns. The Bureau has been working with him in an unofficial capacity," she smiled. "Until now."

Georgetown, D.C.

"Hello?" Ernie Latour said as he stepped through the open front door of Holmgren's house. Three people came around the corner. "Who are you?"

"I'm the real estate agent," one of the women said. "I'm showing the house to these people, but I can make an appointment for you to see it."

"It's for *sale*?" Latour asked.

"Oh yes," she bubbled. "For over a week now."

"Where is the owner?"

"He was transferred out of town," she told him. "He said he wouldn't be back."

"Are you *sure*?"

"Yes, sir, but ..." She didn't finish for Latour turned and walked to his car.

Kadena Air Base

"Get aboard, Johnson," Roman ordered from the cargo ramp of the –130.

Rick ignored him. "Look, Nate, I don't know if I'll make it out of this," he said to Beu. "When you see Connie, tell her I love her and I'm sorry she had to go through this."

"I did some digging," Beu said, surreptitiously handing him a laminated card. "The more I find out about your mission, the less I like it."

"What's this?"

"Help if you need it," Beu replied. "If it goes to shit, use this radio frequency. Somebody will come for you."

"You?" Johnson asked.

"You don't want to know," Beu said. "Good luck, Rick." He grabbed Johnson and embraced him. "You'd better come back."

"I'll do my best, old man," Johnson said and came to attention, firing off a by the book salute. "Kiss the girls for me, General. I intend to keep the promise I made to Katie."

And Beu smiled as he watched his friend walk into the aircraft, remembering what Johnson had said over eleven years ago. *Your Uncle Rick loves you, Little Katie, and he'll be here whenever you need him.*

Chapter Fifty-Five
Okinawa, Japan
Thursday, 23 March 1995

Naha Airport was located just next door to Kadena Air Base, and it was a short ride for Beu as he headed over there. He'd dismissed his driver for this occasion but left the flag on the government Ford that indicated the car belonged to a general officer. That touch allowed him to park at the curb without the car being towed. He recognized Levy immediately as he stepped out of the Jetway. "Welcome to Okinawa, sir."

"Good morning, General," Levy shook the offered hand. "This is Connie Wasserman and Special Agent George Estevez of the FBI."

"Rick always had an eye for beautiful women," Beu said to Connie. "It's a pleasure to meet the woman who could tame him."

"I'd call it domesticated," Connie smiled. "He mentioned you to me once," she said. "He never spoke much of his Air Force experience."

"I'll fill in some of the gaps for you when we have time," Beu replied.

"We will need lodging," Levy said. "We hadn't the time to make arrangements."

"I have you in the VIP quarters on base. There should be more than enough room for the three of you," the general told them.

"You were very cryptic on the phone, General," Connie said. "How is my husband?"

"First off, call me Nate. They left last night for points unknown," Beu told her. "But they all were fine at that time."

"Do you know the details of their mission," Estevez asked. "We only have bits and pieces and a lot of supposition."

"All will be explained, Senator, but let's get you settled first."

Aboard Air Force 89-688, Twenty thousand feet over the East China Sea

"You were way out of line, Johnson," Roman growled when he found Johnson coming out of the rest station. "That bullshit you pulled with General Beu could have compromised the mission."

"Compromise *what?*" Johnson barked at him. "This mission is going forward regardless, Lieutenant. I'm sure you expected to stay in Japan a lot longer than we did; didn't you?" Roman said nothing. "Yeah," Johnson nodded. "I thought so. While I respect you, sir, your inexperience shows. We're not being moved all over the place to keep our enemies off guard, there are people looking for us in the States and that's whom we're hiding from. There are people back home who are trying to shut this down."

"Did Beu tell you that?"

"Yes, damn it. My wife is working with Senator Levy on an investigation of this damn cluster fuck."

"So Beu told her?"

"He didn't *have* to," Rick snapped at him. "They're putting it together by themselves; there was no way this could have stayed secret to begin with, not when a big shot like Emory is kidnapped. I suggest you make some calls when we land and find out exactly what's going on. It just might save your career."

"My orders are lawful," the young lieutenant said.

"If they were lawful, General Beu would have been aware of our mission, or at least his part in it," Johnson said. He did not tell Roman about the card Beu had given him, which would wait until they actually had to use it. "He wouldn't have had to force his way into one of his own hangars."

"He had no right or need to know," Roman countered.

"Yes, he did, maybe not the intimate details, but we were using his resources. Nobody at the Pentagon knows or cares what we're doing. This operation is off the books, Lieutenant, and so are we. If you ask me, I'll bet nobody expects any of us to come back," Johnson said.

"I *didn't* ask you, Sergeant Johnson. From here on out, until we are inserted, you are confined to quarters."

"And where will that be this time, a hole in the ground somewhere?"

"You'll find out soon enough."

"Dude," Johnson lowered his voice. "Do yourself a favor and call somebody when we land."

"Our CO is already there, Johnson," Roman hissed. "If the mission has been scrubbed, we'll know about it. Until then, we continue as if the mission is a go. If you try to screw this up, I *will* see you in jail."

"Like you said, sir," Johnson shot back. "I've been in worse places."

Kadena Air Base

"Hello, Ms. Wasserman, Senator, Agent Estevez," Beu said when she opened the door of the VIP quarters. Three other men accompanied him. Levy came from the study at the sound of the doorbell.

"What the hell is this?" He said, for he recognized the large gray-haired man with the steel blue eyes. "What is the meaning of this, General Beu?"

"What are you taking about, Jacob?" Connie asked, confused by the sudden mood change.

"So, we meet again, Senator Levy," Kosarev said as he held out a hand. Levy left it there. "It has been several years since you came to Russia." Kosarev turned to the rest of them. "Senator Levy and his political cohorts made a big show of sending us aid when we so desperately needed it," he chuckled.

"This is Marshal Yevgeniy Kosarev, Chairman of the KGB," he said to Connie.

"The KGB no longer exists, Senator," Kosarev said. "But I am indeed the Chairman of the Russian Federal Security Service and this is my aide, Captain Boris Popov. I am pleased to meet you, Ms. Wasserman." He took her hand and kissed it. "General Beu holds your husband in the highest regard."

"General Beu will also be spending some time in jail," Levy declared. "You are a traitor, sir."

"No, I am *not*," Beu spat. "Yevgeniy is my wife's father and the person who made me aware of A-Flight's circumstances. He came here to help us rescue them."

"Yes, Senator," Kosarev nodded. "The North Koreans have an agent within your CIA and they also have nuclear weapons. I believe they intend to use them to extend their influence over the Korean Peninsula and the Pacific Rim. Your team will be the catalyst for them to begin operations. You see, lady and gentlemen, they know A-Flight is on its way and are waiting for them. Their discovery on North Korean soil will give them the excuse they need to cross the border into the South. If we do not work together to rescue them, these men will die as soon as they touch the ground."

"And how am I able to trust you," Levy asked him. "I am certain the General's relationship with you is not public knowledge. How do I know you're not conspiring to drag the United States into a war?"

"You can trust General Beu," Connie said.

"How do you know?"

"Rick trusted him with his life and that's good enough for me until the General proves me wrong."

"Thank you, Ms. Wasserman," Beu smiled.

"Millions could die before you obtain that proof, Connie," Levy said.

"Somehow, I don't think General Beu and Marshal Kosarev are the type of men to put their family in danger, Jacob. If the North

Koreans have nukes, I'm certain the largest American base in the Pacific, this one, is a target. Isn't that right, General?"

"Yes, ma'am," Beu nodded.

"One step out of line, General," Estevez warned. "And I will place you under arrest."

"I understand, Agent Estevez."

"I suggest we get down to business, as you Americans say," Kosarev chuckled. "And try to determine where these men have gone. Every minute we argue is a minute wasted in our cause."

"I want specifics, Marshal," Levy said. "And I want them now."

"That is why I am here," Kosarev smiled.

***

"This gets better and better," McTavish said as he recorded the conversation using the parabolic mike. "The fucking KGB is involved." And he smiled, thinking about how his report would shake up the U.S. military, the Intelligence Community, and the world.

Osan Air Base, Osan, South Korea

Holmgren watched the MC-130 fall out of the clouds and touch down, a wisp of tire smoke curling away as the mains squealed against the tarmac. It would be close, the timing of the operation, for too many people were beginning to ask questions. The mission had inertia of its own, his strict adherence to secrecy had bought him this much time, and that inertia would push it along for a few more days until it was time for the insertion. Orders with the President's signature went a long way also.

The plane rolled, just as it did on Okinawa, into a hangar and the doors slid closed. Holmgren, however, did not go to the hangar and see to his team, he couldn't, not yet, for at least one of them knew his secrets. If Johnson remembered him, the operation would be jeopardized. He would reveal himself to them, but not until they were past the point of no return, and that time was approaching quickly. "You will be fully aware of why you will die," he said aloud as he got into his car.

Kadena Air Base

It was late by the time Kosarev had finished his monologue about the events that led to this point. "Why didn't your government do something about this?" Levy asked him. "If you've known about this guy General Park for so long, why didn't you get rid of him? I thought the KGB was so good at assassinations."

"Money, Senator," Kosarev said. "We needed their money."

"Why aren't you sending a team in?" Levy pressed. "You have a rescue team ready to go to get your agent out. Why not a group of commandos or a few bombers to do the job?"

"Siberia," was all the Russian said.

"Siberia?" Connie asked.

"Siberia contains vast amounts of oil, coal, and natural gas hidden under the frozen tundra," Popov took up for his boss as Kosarev poured himself another glass of vodka. "The Chinese want it badly, very badly, and Marshal Kosarev has spent the better part of twenty years keeping them away from it. Should they learn that we are interfering in the internal affairs of North Korea, they just might use it as an excuse to attack. I need not remind you of the state of our military at this point. I believe your government is absorbing most of the cost of safeguarding our nuclear weapons in that region as it is, Senator Levy, our forces are sorely inadequate to repel a Chinese incursion."

"So, you left it up to *us*?" Levy spat.

"I did not feel your government would be foolish enough to attempt something like this. I assumed it would be handled diplomatically, through your State Department," Kosarev said before turning to Connie. "I am truly sorry your husband and those other innocent men have been brought into this against their will. You must believe me when I say I never meant that to happen."

"I believe you, Marshal," Connie replied. "Or you wouldn't be putting your family at risk by meeting with us and offering to help."

"I gave Rick the radio frequency for your helicopters," Beu said to Kosarev.

"Good," Kosarev said. "My man inside the Sung Complex will call for them when he learns the team has landed. It is up to your team to survive until he can make contact with them, and my people can get everyone out."

"Unless we find them first," Connie said.

"Yes, my dear," Kosarev said.

Georgetown, D.C.

Guerin arrived at LaTour's home in the early afternoon, finding the senator clearly agitated.

"He's gone," Latour said.

"*Who's* gone?" Guerin didn't need to handhold Latour right now. He'd lost patience with the senator after the sixth phone message he'd left in the course of the morning.

"Alan," Latour cried. "My son-in-law, he's gone."

"He's TDY, Ernie," Guerin said. "He'll be back."

"No, he *won't*. He put his house up for sale and all his things are moved out. The real estate agent told me when I went over there."

"Maybe he wanted a smaller place. That house is too big for him after Jessica …"

"It was a wedding present from me, Lou. He would have told me before he sold it, it was *my* old house." Latour looked him over. "There's something very wrong going on here, damn it. I didn't believe that idiot Levy, but this clinches it. He's working with the FBI, you know, this could ruin me," he babbled.

"I'll look into it, Ernie, just relax," Guerin soothed. "Have a drink or something, take a pill, but don't say *anything* to anyone until you hear from me."

"Okay, Lou," Latour said as he wandered into the den. Guerin forgot about Latour as soon as he got in his car, he had his own damage control to begin.

Chapter Fifty-Six
Osan Air Base, Osan, South Korea
Friday, 24 March 1995

"Hey," Campbell said when he walked into Johnson's room. They were quartered in a barracks that was unused. "What's up?"

"Nothing," he shrugged. "Just sitting here playing with myself. Sorry about fucking it up for you guys. If I hadn't opened my big mouth to Nate Beu, we might have at least been allowed to go to the NCO club or something."

"We're at Osan, you know," Campbell offered.

"Yeah, so what."

"I'll bet the Pink Lady is still there," he gave Rick a grin.

"Again, so what." Johnson looked up at him. "Have you forgotten we're confined to quarters?"

"Have *you* forgotten that me and Jake got you out of the hospital when you were confined there?"

"How are we going to get out there? It's fifteen miles from here."

"I still have the touch," Campbell said proudly.

Johnson brightened immediately. "You're a good man, Mr. Campbell. And I figured you'd been kicked in the head too many times by one of those animals you ride. When do we go?"

"Tonight," Campbell whispered. "Jake's checking out the building to see if we can get out unnoticed. I'll be back when I know something."

Johnson waved as Campbell left, allowing himself to fall back on the bed. "Do I really want to go to the Pink Lady?" While the club would be a convenient place to have a little fun, and the last place Roman would look for them, there was the matter of Yung Shu.

She'd dominated his thoughts the closer he came to this place and it scared him now that he was here. He found the feelings he had for her hadn't waned, yet they conflicted with those same feelings he had for his wife. Could he say no to her if she wanted to be with him again? He knew he could, but he didn't want to be in the position to deny her. And then he thought himself foolish. "It's been twelve years, she had to have found someone else." He laughed aloud. "She's probably not even there anymore," he convinced himself.

Kadena Air Base, Okinawa, Japan

"I can't do that," Liz Callahan said. "What, am I just supposed to take you on a tour of the air bases in South Korea?"

"Something like that," Beu said with a smile. "I got you your hangar back."

"And the place was a God-awful mess too," she hissed. "It was *no* favor, let me tell you."

"Come on, Liz, this is important," Beu insisted.

"But you can't tell me?"

"It's better if you don't know, darling," the smile remained.

"I'm sorry, Nate, I can't do it. People will ask questions that I won't have answers for."

"I'll answer them," Beu said. "Tell them I pulled rank on you, tell them I lost my mind or something."

"You *have*." She considered him, and their friendship, for a minute. "Tell me what's going on and I'll think about it."

"Jesus," he threw up his hands.

"He won't help you, General," Callahan shot back.

"The people who took your hangar?" Beu began.

"Yes?"

"They're an old Air Force recon unit brought back into the military by the CIA. I think they're being set up for an ambush and I need your help to save them," Beu spat out quickly.

"And how will this be accomplished with a flying gas station?" Callahan was skeptical.

"I just need you to get us around," Beu said.

"Take the bus," she shot back.

"Would you like to tell that to Senator Levy and the FBI?"

"That loudmouth Jew from New York?"

"He's at the VIP quarters right now with an FBI agent and the wife of one of the men we're trying to find. This is an illegal operation, Liz, and we're the only ones who can stop it. I desperately need your help and I will owe you a big favor, anything you want, when it's over," Beu surrendered.

"You'd do better selling your soul to the Devil, General," she laughed. "Because I'm gonna take a big one."

"So, you'll help me?"

"When have I ever said no to you, handsome?"

"Five times come to mind just off the bat," Beu said with a smile.

"Never mind," she said. "That phase bird my guys have been working on should be done tomorrow. It'll have to go for a check flight first so figure Sunday or Monday at the earliest."

"You're the best, Liz," Beu said as he hustled off to arrange a few other things.

"I know," she said to the empty office.

CIA Headquarters, Langley, Virginia

"I want everything destroyed, right now," Guerin told Rice and Mitchell. "Everything that bastard touched, the game disks, everything. The mission is over."

"So, Holmgren *has* been doubled," Rice said with a smile.

"I don't know, and I don't want to know," Guerin said. "Just get any record of this into the shredder."

"We should contact the FBI," Mitchell said. "If they're working this already, any help we can give them might help track down Holmgren."

"Holmgren was an analyst here, period," Guerin said. "That is *all* the Bureau will get. Is that understood?"

"Yes, sir," they said and departed.

Seoul, South Korea

It was an electronics store on the Choggyechono, the main drag in the city, and Holmgren browsed the latest in cameras. A man came up to him and bowed slightly. "It is a beautiful model, isn't it?" He said.

"German, right?" Holmgren replied.

"Yes, it's better than the Japanese models of comparable price," the shopkeeper said. "Would you like it gift wrapped?"

"No, but do you deliver?" Holmgren asked.

"Yes, but the earliest I can have it to you would be Tuesday."

"That will be fine," Holmgren gave him a nod. And that was all that needed to be said. Holmgren bought the camera and wrote his address on a card before leaving the store. The camera was incidental; it was the shopkeeper he was there to see. He learned that General Park would be ready on Tuesday; the 28th and that would be the day A-Flight died.

Anyone in the store would have thought him just another American soldier buying a camera, as so many did here, and that was what he wanted them all to think. The shopkeeper was a South Korean working for General Park and had done so for over a decade, smuggling agents into the country and information out. While Holmgren now had the final timing of the mission, Park was now aware that Holmgren and his team were in South Korea. "It will be over soon, Roger," he said as he drove away.

Osan Air Base

"Hey," Campbell whispered in the darkness. "Are you ready?"

"Yup," Johnson replied. He followed Campbell out into the hall and then down to the stairwell. Guthrie was there already, doing something to an electrical box near the fire door.

"The alarm shouldn't sound when we go out," Guthrie said.

"What do you mean *shouldn't*, shorty?" Campbell said.

"Fuck you, stick-boy," Guthrie hissed.

"Come on, ladies," Johnson sighed. "Let's do it."

"Right," Guthrie put the box back together and opened the door a crack. The alarm remained quiet. "See, I told you," he whispered to Campbell.

"Yeah, yeah, let's go."

They made it down the two flights with ease, quietly, stealthily, but were stopped by another alarmed door at the ground floor. Guthrie did his magic with that one and they were out on Pershing Street, the Friday night traffic on the base flowing past them. They were in uniform, woodland camouflage BDUs and black berets, a touch Roman thought would give them good unit cohesion, and they blended in with the foot traffic on the sidewalk.

"Do you remember where the motor pool is?" Johnson asked them.

"Shit, we spent a week there after you were shot that time," Campbell said.

"Yeah, I'd remember how to get to that place blindfolded in the dark," Guthrie agreed.

They walked about a mile, detouring off Pershing onto MacArthur a block before the motor pool, Guthrie and Campbell hopping the fence to the parking area and Johnson keeping lookout. Rick was about to question whether Campbell's touch had gotten rusty when he heard a car start behind him. He slid the gate open for them and closed it quickly once the vehicle was liberated, hopping in the back before Campbell pulled out into traffic.

"We're gonna have some fun tonight," Guthrie grinned, rubbing his palms together.

"Yeah," Rick said in a whisper as he thought about the possible meeting with his old love. "Real fun."

Kadena Air Base

"So, we just have to wait around?" Connie was not pleased. "You're a general, can't you just order up a plane?"

"Not without having to explain it," Beu told her. "We have to do this quietly for the safety of Rick and his team. Liz Callahan knows how to keep her mouth shut."

"We would do better trying to determine where to start," Kosarev said. "We have to narrow our search, so we don't waste time unnecessarily."

"I agree with the Marshal," Levy said.

"There is a first time for everything," Kosarev laughed before turning to his son-in-law. "We will need maps of South Korea and Japan, Nathan, with as much detail as you can muster."

"I'll work on it," he said.

Osan, South Korea

"Well, are you going in?" Campbell asked him as they stood outside the Pink Lady.

Johnson stood there, looking up at the marquee that hadn't changed since he was last here. 'Live Nude Girls' it said. "I'm going," he said. "Do you think she's here?"

"Yung Shu?"

"Who else, dickhead?" Johnson growled.

"There's no need to get testy," Guthrie said. "If she's there, you say hi and ask her how the last twelve years have been."

"It's that simple, huh?" Johnson was sarcastic.

"Then stay out here, boy," Campbell told him. "But there are babes and liquor in there and that's where I'm going."

"Me too," Guthrie agreed and began to climb the steps.

"Wait, I'm coming," Johnson said and caught up to them by the time they got to the door.

***

She was just coming down the stairs when she saw them come in and she stopped. She'd heard of them but had never seen one in the flesh. It was the black berets that caught her eye first and then she saw they were Air Force; she could tell by the shape of the stripes on their arms. And then she realized they were a bit older than the usual crowd here, senior enlisted, she saw from the number of stripes, two were master sergeants, the other a senior master sergeant. Most of the guys who hung out here were young, usually on their first enlistment and most no more than twenty-five. Her first thought they were here looking for someone, the way they scanned the room, but then they found an empty table and sat down. She resumed her walk down to the first floor, a bit slower than before, her eyes locked on the Air Force recon troops.

***

"So, do you see her?" Campbell asked.

"Nah," Johnson said. "I don't recognize anyone here anymore."

"What do you want," Guthrie said. "It's been twelve years. Most of the chicks who used to dance here are married with kids now."

"Or dead," Campbell added.

"I don't recognize any of the waitresses either," Rick looked around.

"Service isn't as good as it was when you were living here," Guthrie said, trying to flag down a waitress, but it was Friday night and the joint was hopping.

"That's because I don't live here anymore, Jake," Rick laughed. "You were all spoiled when I had this gig."

***

She picked up the tray and walked toward them, drawn to them for some reason. She knew, but she would not admit it to herself yet; the letdown would be too great.

"Hey, honey," came a voice from one of the tables. "Can you get rid of some of these empties?"

"Sure, GI," she said, grabbing a load of empty beer bottles from the table full of Marines. She set them on the tray and carried the load as if it were second nature, it was for her, and she continued her trek across the floor, oblivious to everything; the loud music, the naked women, and the rowdy GIs were mere background to her. They were close now and she could make out the faces of two of them, one with his back to her. Her heart threatened to beat out of her chest as she came closer and her hands began to shake as the shortest of them made eye contact with her. "Drink, GI?" She asked.

***

"It's about time," Jake Guthrie told the girl who didn't look older than fourteen. In the States, someone would go to jail for letting a girl so young work in a place like this.

Johnson turned around to look up at her. "I'd like a beer and a …"

"Shot of Jack Daniel's," the girl finished for him.

"Yes, how did …" But he never finished, she dropped the tray on him and ran away, up the stairs and disappeared.

"See that, Rick," Campbell said. "I always said you were one *ugly* sucker. You scared the poor thing."

"She was awful young," Johnson said. "I'll bet the Mama-san sold the place. She wouldn't have an underage girl working here."

"How old was Yung Shu?"

"Older than that little girl," Rick replied. And he stopped, feeling eyes upon him from across the crowded room. He stood and turned and there she was, walking toward him.

"Hi, Rick," Yung Shu whispered. "Is it really you?" And the years melted away as they came together.

He took her in his arms, and they kissed. "Yes, it is," he said when they parted.

"I missed you, my love," she said and took his hand, leading him to a relatively quiet corner.

"Tell me I'm not going to wake up in the barracks, Yung Shu. Tell me that this isn't a dream," he said, not wanting to believe she was here, now, and as beautiful as he'd ever seen her.

"I thought it was too," she gave him the smile that he hadn't seen in so many years. "I didn't believe Kim when she told me you were here."

"The little girl who spilled the tray on me?"

"I'm sorry about that," she giggled.

"How does she know about me, about what I drink?" Rick was confused. "She wasn't even born when I was here."

"Because I would tell her about you every chance I had," Yung Shu said. "I still have the picture of us at Inch On. It's still in the same place it was when we were together; Kim would ask me about you all the time. I'd tell her about how strong and handsome and brave you are." She could tell by the look in his eyes that he still didn't understand. "She is my daughter," she brought her hand to his cheek. "She is *our* daughter, Rick."

"How ... when ..." This was too much for him to digest.

"Please don't be angry with me," she said. "But I stopped taking my birth control a few weeks before you left the last time. Do you remember what my mother said?" Yung Shu asked him. "About your destiny?"

Johnson chuckled at that. "The old woman was right," he said. "Where is she?"

"She died a few years ago," she told him, and his face fell.

"God, I'm sorry, Yung Shu."

"It is the cycle of life, Rick, nothing to be sorry about." And she looked past him and smiled as the young girl tugged on his sleeve.

"Are you really my dad?" Kim asked him.

"It seems I am, sweetie," Johnson smiled as his eyes met hers, the same incredible emerald green as her mother's, but the intensity that he'd seen many times when he looked in the mirror. There was no doubt in his mind that she was his child, and the enormity of it hit him, turning his knees to rubber. He sat at the nearby table.

"Are you okay?" Kim asked him.

"Yeah," he replied. "It's just a surprise, that's all."

"Let mommy talk to your father for a few minutes, will you angel?" Yung Shu said to the girl.

"Yes, mother," Kim said before turning back to the man. She leaned over and kissed his cheek. "You're not going away again, are you?"

"We'll see, angel," Yung Shu promised. Kim drifted away, back to her duties that were once her mother's responsibility.

"A lot has changed in a dozen years, Yung Shu," Johnson said when Kim was gone.

She took his left hand in hers and gazed at his wedding ring. "Do you love her, Rick?"

"Very much, darling, as I loved you," he admitted.

"Yes, you would have to, wouldn't you," she smiled, and he saw that she still wore the ring he'd given her. "You are not the man to love frivolously."

"I'm sorry, Yung Shu," he said, wiping a tear away with his sleeve. "I never thought I'd be back here again."

"I had assumed you left the Air Force," she said, a bit hurt.

"I did, ten years ago," he explained. "They brought us all back a couple weeks ago. Remember them?" Johnson pointed to a table where Campbell and Guthrie were offering dollar bills to a dancer.

"Campbell and Guthrie," she smiled. "They are still the same." And then she became thoughtful. "Why did they bring you back?"

"They're sending us back into the North, Yung Shu."

Her face took on a look of worry. "The last time ..."

"I don't know if I'll make it out, darling," he told her honestly. "But if I do, I'll come back for you."

"And how would you explain me to your wife?" She laughed. "No, Rick, my place is here, but you *will* come back for your daughter," she insisted. "This is no place for a young girl to grow up. She needs a life and you're going to give her one. You're going to give her all the opportunities she would never get here."

"I will, Yung Shu," he said. "I promise."

"That is all I need to hear, my love."

All eyes in the club turned to the front door as an officer entered with a squad of Air Force Security Police. They went directly to Guthrie and Campbell, first frisking and then handcuffing them. And then they turned their attention to Johnson.

"Senior Master Sergeant Richard Johnson, I am placing you under arrest," Colonel Alan Holmgren said.

"I know you," was all Johnson said.

"I should hope so," Holmgren replied, turning to the Sky Cops. "Take him away."

"*No!*" Came the shout from across the floor. Kim came running to him, grabbing onto Johnson's waist, and holding tightly as they cuffed him. "You *can't* take him away. *Please* don't take my dad away again," she sobbed.

"*What*," escaped both Guthrie and Campbell's lips.

"He's going away for a *long* time," Holmgren laughed as he pulled her away from Johnson. He released her and she fell to the floor.

"You're going to die for that," Johnson promised Holmgren.

"I seriously doubt it," he said with a laugh. "Take them," he said to the cops.

"I'll be back, Yung Shu," Rick called to her as they marched him out the door. "I promise."

Kadena Air Base

"Oh god," Connie said as she awoke suddenly. "He's in trouble." She sensed it, could feel it with every fiber of her being, the man she loved was in mortal danger. "I'm going to find you, Rick," she promised, hoping he would still be alive when she did.

Chapter Fifty-Seven
Osan Air Base, Osan, South Korea
Saturday, 25 March 1995

"You've really got them snowed, don't you?" Johnson asked Holmgren. Rick was handcuffed to his bed by his left hand. "I figured your queer ass would have been run out of the military years ago."

"Remember, Johnson," he smiled. "Don't ask, don't tell, and I didn't tell anyone."

"So, why us? Are you taking a particular pleasure in screwing up our lives?"

"In fact, I am," Holmgren said. "Just the way you screwed up Roger's."

"I'll tell Lieutenant Roman about you and what you're up to," Rick threatened.

"Go ahead, you moron," Holmgren spat. "Do you think I just picked the names of the active duty people out of a hat? Reasoner is here because he has to die with the rest of you, the rest because their psychological profiles said they would be the most malleable and respectful of authority. Remember, I have the President's signature on the op orders; there is no higher authority. You can tell Roman anything you want to, tell him the truth for all I care, but he will not believe you. He has complained about you in particular from the beginning. Don't you think I know about your contact with General Beu? Roman believes you are trying to sabotage the mission and anything you say will fall on deaf ears."

"I wasn't kidding when I said I was going to kill you," Rick spat.

"You will never be close enough, Sergeant Johnson, and I am certain you will not survive the mission," Holmgren laughed, and Johnson smiled back. "As an added incentive, if you continue to act in a counterproductive manner, I will have your whore and her daughter killed in the most humiliating, painful way possible. Your cooperation will guarantee their survival."

"Fine," Rick said. "But you miscalculated one little detail."

"And what might that be?" Holmgren asked him haughtily.

"I'm close enough right now," Johnson smiled as he vaulted up onto the hand that was cuffed to the bed and threw a kick in Holmgren's direction, connecting with the side of his face. Holmgren was thrown into the wall and then fell to the floor. "What *else* have you miscalculated, queer boy?"

Holmgren got himself up and spit out two teeth dabbing at the blood that oozed from the corner of his mouth. "You son of a bitch." He pulled his sidearm and clocked Johnson in the back of the head. "You'll pay for that."

"Probably," Johnson winced. "But it felt good."

The Pink Lady

"What will happen to him, mother?" Kim asked.

"I don't know, angel," Yung Shu dabbed at a tear. "But he is everything I told you he was. If there is any way for your father to come back, he will. He will come and take you back to the U.S. with him and you will be able to realize your potential."

"But what about you? I will never see you again. You have to come with us."

"I can't leave the bar," her mother said. "And he has a wife who would not be pleased to have me close by. But I will visit you and I am sure your father will bring you here to visit. He is an honorable man, Kim, and you will have a normal family and a normal home. This is no life for a young girl who is as intelligent as you are."

"But what if I don't like his wife?"

"I'm sure she is someone you will like. You have much of your father's personality," Yung Shu smiled.

"You *always* say that," Kim said.

"You will understand eventually."

Kadena Air Base, Okinawa, Japan

"Something's happened, Jacob," Connie said. "I know it."

"Just relax," Levy soothed. "*How* do you know?"

"I feel it, that's all. I felt it last night."

"Don't get yourself crazy until we hear something," Levy declared.

"I just feel so helpless," she sighed. "Rick is out there somewhere, maybe in North Korea already, and we're just *sitting* here."

"They're not there yet," Estevez said as he came into the kitchen. "The full moon was only a few days ago. They won't go in until the new moon when it will be completely dark at night."

"So, you think they are still hiding," Levy asked him.

"Yes," the FBI man nodded. "You can bet Holmgren is in touch with them and he knew Rick made contact with General Beu. That's why they left so quickly."

"What I want to know," Connie said. "Is why this guy Holmgren arranged to have Rick and his friends brought back into the Air Force? He could have done this much more easily if he'd used active duty soldiers."

"He's about your husband's age," Estevez said as he read from the fax he received from FBI Headquarters. The FBI had been given an abridged version of Holmgren's service record. "Maybe they knew each other?"

"Didn't they say he worked at the Asia Desk at CIA?" Levy asked.

"Yes, he was their expert on East Asia," Estevez agreed.

"Maybe they were stationed together," Connie offered. "Rick said he was stationed in Korea for four years. Maybe they met there?"

"Do you know *where* he was stationed?" Estevez said.

"No, he never talked about it much," Connie shook her head. "But I think he met General Beu there too. Maybe he would know."

"Why don't we ask him?" Estevez said as he went for the door.

Osan Air Base

"We gotta end this, John," Johnson said when Reasoner stopped by his room. One hand was still cuffed to the bed. "This isn't some national security thing. We're *supposed* to die here."

"Oh stop it, Rick," Reasoner barked.

"Damn it, do you know who our CO is?"

"Yeah, a bird colonel named Holmgren," Reasoner shrugged.

"He was Roger Hoffman's significant other," Rick said. "He's doing this out of some twisted desire for revenge."

"Revenge? For what?"

"For Roger's death, like it was our fault or something," Johnson shot back.

"Don't be an idiot. You're just trying to get this thing scrubbed so we can all go home."

"Go ask him then," Johnson demanded. "See what he says."

"I'm *not* going to ask a senior officer if he's gay," Reasoner looked at Johnson as if he were crazy. "And I'm sure as hell not going to call him on the legality of this operation. I've seen the orders; the President's signature is on them and direct Holmgren *specifically* to accomplish this mission. That's the end of the story. You'll be released when it's time to go and you will cooperate or, so help me, I'll shoot you myself. I've had enough of your bitching and complaining and it's going to come to a screeching halt. Either that, or I will assist Lieutenant Roman when he brings charges against you. Don't forget, Rick, you're on active duty now and a stay in Leavenworth is *not* out of the question."

"I always said you had a paper asshole," Rick growled. "And now you've just proven it. You're going to march to your death like a happy idiot and be glad to do it. Get out of here, you moron."

"The only way we'll die is if you pull your cowboy bullshit the way you did the last time we were there," Reasoner countered. "Stick to the program, Rick, and you'll be home in a week, a million dollars richer." He turned and walked through the door.

"We'll all come home in body bags," Johnson said to Reasoner's back. "How will Ang and the boys feel about *that*, asshole?"

Kadena Air Base

"I met him at Osan, he was in the base hospital at the time," Beu said as he stared into the middle distance. "I actually met him the day before, pulled him out of a hot LZ after he was shot in the leg. I was too busy flying to see him then, so I visited him in the hospital the next day."

"He said he had some sort of accident, that's what caused the scar on his leg," Connie said.

"No ma'am," Beu shook his head. "That's what got him the Silver Star. I put him up for it myself."

"Can you tell me what happened?"

"It's still classified, I believe," Beu said.

"Damn it, man," Levy barked. "You're married to the daughter of the KGB Chairman, what's the difference if you talk about an operation that's a dozen years old?"

"I told you, I'm not a traitor. I took an oath, Senator, and I intend to live up to it. I did not give secrets to the Soviets, nor did I ever help Marshal Kosarev in a professional manner," Beu declared.

"Then how do you explain your wife?"

"Colonel Kosarev at the time asked me to help his daughter defect from the Soviet Union. He asked me as a personal favor, not on behalf of the Soviets. Our relationship is purely familial. I have no contact with him aside from his once a year visits to see his daughter and granddaughter."

"So you say," Levy said.

"Leave him alone, Jacob," Connie hissed. "Can't you see he's trying to do the right thing?"

"I'll leave him alone when your husband and his men come out of there safely," Levy proclaimed. "I refuse to trust him, or that old Chekist, until then."

"You will cease and desist, Senator," Connie insisted. "Agent Estevez and I are the only ones who are aware of General Beu's relationship with Marshal Kosarev and I will deny it under oath if I have to." She looked to Estevez.

"Same here," he agreed. "You're a principled man, Senator, but General Beu has gone above and beyond and we owe him the benefit of the doubt. You have no fight here, Mr. Levy."

"Thank you both," Beu said.

"Did you know Colonel Holmgren, General?" Connie asked, trying to change the subject. "Or do you know if Rick did?"

"I didn't, he might have," Beu shrugged. "If Holmgren came up through Air Force Intelligence, they might have had contact during the aforementioned operation if he was stationed at Osan then."

"I think we should start there," Connie said.

"I think you have a point, ma'am," Beu smiled. "It *is* the closest base to the North Korean border."

The White House, Washington, D.C.

"Good morning, Mr. President," Attorney General Helene Smith said when she entered the Oval Office with FBI Director Atkins in tow. "I'm afraid we have some bad news."

Osan Air Base

"Jesus Christ," Johnson said as he lay on his bed. "I have a kid." It was something he'd never thought about, he'd thought about it, but it was something far off yet, at least five years. "Not anymore." It was something he wasn't prepared for, something he just couldn't talk away with wisecracks and glib one-liners. He now had what he thought was the most awesome of responsibilities.

"What in Hell am I going to tell Connie?" It was something that hit him like a speeding truck. "Hey, honey, do you remember asking me about the woman I was in love with? Well, I have a daughter with her and she's coming to live with us." He laughed aloud. "Yeah, *that* will work," he said, sarcasm dripping from his words. He tried out another. "Hey, baby, remember when we talked about having kids? Well I got one that's pre-made. It'll cut out all that messy pregnancy bullshit." He laughed again. "Yup, that one's even better." Another thought ran through his head. "Look at the bright side, Connie, we don't have to worry about changing diapers and we don't have to buy a child seat for the car."

"Face it, Rick," he said to the empty room. "She's going to kill me. The poor woman has followed me halfway around the world and this is the reward she gets. Hey, Connie, thanks for everything you did to find me and by the way, I have an eleven year old daughter who can mix drinks and make change."

He thought about choosing the correct words and then something hit him again, as if the truck backed over him after hitting him the first time. "Shit, I probably won't even live through this motherfucker anyway."

The White House, Washington, D.C.

"I don't believe it," the President said. "I've known Lou Guerin for thirty years."

"I can play the recordings for you, Mr. President," Director Atkins said. "I don't like it any more than you do, sir."

"What about these troops?" The President asked. "Where are they?"

"We don't know, sir," AG Smith informed him. "One of the FBI's best field men is with Senator Levy in Japan. We were waiting to hear from them before we made a move on Guerin. We don't want to tip off Colonel Holmgren that we are on to him."

"You have seventy-two hours, Ms. Smith, no longer," the President ordered. "If you don't find Holmgren by then, I want Guerin out regardless."

Chapter Fifty-Eight
Osan Air Base, Osan, South Korea
Sunday, 26 March 1995

"Maybe we should put this off until next month, sir," Lieutenant Roman said as he and Reasoner met with Holmgren. "You have three of my men confined and it is having an effect on the others."

"I agree, sir," Reasoner added. "While I don't condone Johnson's behavior, he does raise one or two valid points."

"Would either of you like to tell the President that you are unable to control your men?" Holmgren hissed. "Our intelligence reports say that the North Koreans are moving more troops south toward the border. We might not have a month; we might not have a week. If they move against the south, and we squandered the opportunity to stop them, millions of lives could be lost. No, gentlemen, the mission goes forward as planned."

"Yes, sir."

Kadena Air Base, Okinawa, Japan

"Thank you for your help, Yevgeniy," Beu said as he embraced the big man once more.

"I should stay until this is over," Kosarev insisted.

"Too many people are aware of you already," his son-in-law said. "We'll take it from here."

"General Beu is correct," Levy agreed. "It is best you head home." He extended a hand to Kosarev. "I apologize for doubting you."

"And my family, Senator Levy?"

"I didn't know you have family in the States, Marshal," Levy smiled. Kosarev grabbed his hand and gave it a squeeze.

"I am in your debt," he said.

"We are in yours, Marshal," Connie said as she hugged him, kissing his cheek before releasing him.

"I would say we are square," Beu declared.

"It was good to meet you all," Boris Popov said. "We must go, Marshal. You have been away from Moscow too long."

Osan Air Base

Roman came into the room and released Johnson from his restraint. "This is your last chance," he said. "If you fuck up again, you're going directly to jail. I want your word that you'll behave."

"I will, Lieutenant," Johnson said. "You have my word." He rubbed his wrist, chafed raw by the metal bracelet.

"Good," he nodded and turned toward the door.

"Tell me something before you go, sir."

"What's that?"

"Did Holmgren say we could be released?"

"No," Roman shook his head. "Chief Reasoner believed I could appeal to your sense of honor and duty."

"I have to thank him."

"Yes, you do," Roman agreed.

"Do me a favor, sir," Rick asked. "When we're in Indian Country, listen to the old guys. Our experience just might save your ass."

Georgetown, D.C.

They were there when he pulled into the drive after the morning's church services, four cars each with two agents waiting nearby. "What's going on, Ernie," his wife asked him.

"Just go in the house," he said. "I'll take care of this." She got out of the car and went into the house, Latour walking to the agent who approached.

"I'm Special Agent Crosier, FBI," the thin black man said.

"What is the meaning of this?"

"We have some questions, Senator Latour," Crosier said. "About your son-in-law, Colonel Alan Holmgren. Would you mind coming along to headquarters? Director Atkins would rather this was done quietly, for all concerned."

Kadena Air Base

"What is going on around here?" Liz Callahan was incensed as she stood on the flightline. Beu had accompanied her but said nothing. This involved her people and her plane. "This thing was supposed to be done *last* night."

"Sorry, ma'am," the maintenance chief said. "We found a broken engine mount on number three and had to change it. It'll be done tonight."

"When," Callahan demanded of the nervous chief. The squadron commander and the base commander, the highest authorities on Kadena, were staring him down.

"About midnight, Colonel," he told her.

"I'm taking this thing out for a check ride at 0600 tomorrow morning and I don't care if your people have to hold that damn engine in place while I do it. Is that *understood*?"

"Yes, ma'am," he said and returned to his troops.

Callahan looked to Beu. "Sorry, Nate, but I won't take it up unless it's right."

"I understand," Beu agreed. "I just hope we're in time."

Osan Air Base

"Come on," Roman said as he stuck his head into Johnson's room.

"Where are we going?"

"You'll see," Roman replied. He had Emory with him.

"Congratulations," Emory said.

"For what?"

"You're a dad now."

"Yeah, and it'll probably be the end of my marriage," Johnson sighed. "How in hell do I tell my wife about this?"

"Worry about that when we get back, Johnson," Roman ordered. "I want your full attention to the mission from here on out." They followed him out of the barracks to the unit's Humvee. He drove them out, past the flightline, to a bunker near the Security Police armory. "Wait here," he said as he got out of the vehicle. He walked inside and two SPs left the building a minute later. They got in their police car and drove away. Roman appeared at the door and beckoned them inside. "This is the explosives bunker; you've got fifteen minutes until they get back." Johnson and Emory just looked at each other and then to Roman in confusion. "Take what you'll need to bring that complex down," the lieutenant explained.

"So, this *is* more than a recon," Johnson asked him.

"It is now."

Georgetown, D.C.

They dropped Latour back at his house and he went directly up to his bedroom. His wife had gone out and he was thankful, she didn't need to see him like this, defeated, humiliated, and betrayed. It was revealed to him that two of the people he considered closest to him were suspected traitors and that suspicion went to him as well. When the CIA Director and Holmgren went on trial, his association with them would surely become public, effectively ending his long and influential political career. Latour retrieved a container from his closet and went back to the garage, sliding behind the wheel of his 1969 Corvette Stingray.

He slid a CD into the deck and Tony Bennett crooned from the speakers, and he smiled. "I never thought it would end this way," he said. It was a short drive to Rock Creek Park, and he pulled into a space, the lot mostly empty on this Sunday morning. He opened the package, a velvet lined box that contained a 9mm pistol, a commemorative piece made by the Hanson Firearms Company of Stamford, Connecticut. Avery Hanson gave it to him personally many years ago, at the time he was elected to his first term in the Senate.

It had never been fired, but he'd kept it in meticulous shape, oiling and exercising the action regularly. It was a symbol of friendship and commitment by one of his staunchest supporters and closest friends. "And none of it matters anymore," he said as he slid the clip into the pistol. The action worked flawlessly as he slid it back and released it, pushing a round into the chamber. He thought of his daughter and grandchild, wondering if they would be waiting for him. "We'll see, won't we," were his last words as he put the barrel in his mouth and pulled the trigger. A woman who was jogging nearby screamed in terror as the rear glass of the Corvette blew out in a spray of shattered glass, followed closely by parts of LaTour's skull and brain.

Chapter Fifty-Nine
Kadena Air Base, Okinawa, Japan
Monday, 27 March 1995

The KC-10 touched own perfectly and Callahan activated the speed brakes, slowing the aircraft drastically. The check ride was uneventful as she knew it would be, the maintenance chief knew she'd be taking it and he did not want to feel her wrath if there was even the smallest glitch, not after being nearly twenty four hours late. Beu was waiting at Base Operations when she walked in after parking the big jet.

"So?" He asked.

"Any time you're ready, General," she smiled.

"I have a couple things to arrange and we'll be back."

"Where are we going first?" Callahan called after him.

"When we're in the air, Colonel," Beu replied and walked directly to his car, ordering his driver to head over to 12th Fighter Squadron HQ. "Hey, Vinny," he said as he walked into Ubriaco's office. "I need a favor."

"You already got one from my old lady, General," Ubriaco said warily. He didn't like the position Beu put Callahan in.

"I need one from you too," Beu barked. "And I'm not taking no for an answer. I'll be the one taking the heat for all this so you can get off your high horse."

"What do you want?"

"I want some of your planes loaded with war shot, Vinny, and I want them on standby for the next forty-eight hours."

"How many?"

"Eight at least, ten if you can spare them from the rotation," Beu explained.

"May I ask why?"

"We might need to break a few things," Beu smiled. "You'll know more once I get where I'm going. I'll have Liz keep in touch."

Ubriaco looked up at him. "You're putting your career at risk, Nate. Do you realize what this looks like? Ten F-15s loaded with bombs and missiles can take out a small city; you're not planning to start a war, are you?"

"I'm trying to stop one, Vinny," he said. "You know I wouldn't be asking if it weren't the only way to do it."

"You've always been levelheaded, General, otherwise I'd have been on the phone to Washington already. This had better be wrapped up in forty-eight hours or I will be."

"I understand, Vin, thanks."

Osan Air Base

"Man, we'll be able to do some serious damage," Campbell said as they loaded the C-130 with their armaments. He and Guthrie had each been given a Dragon III shoulder fired anti-tank missile, Coles and Petersen were packing a 20mm Bofors Squad Automatic Weapon, Gibbs and Rockwood a .50 caliber machine gun, Johnson and Emory with fifty pounds of Semtex plastic explosive each, and Jack George with his .50 caliber Winchester sniper rifle.

"The mission's changed, gents," Roman said. "This is no longer a recon operation. We're going to take their missile base out and I expect you to do a thorough job."

"I just love blowing shit up," Johnson smiled. "And this is gonna make one *big* fucking boom when it goes up. Those rockets are liquid fueled and that shit is flammable as a motherfucker."

"We have to get there first," Roman said.

"I just don't like the way we're going in, sir," Jack George spoke up.

"Ah, get over it, pussy," Johnson said.

"Fuck you, man," George spat back. "If you touch me while we're in the plane, I'll shoot your ass. I thought we were going in by chopper."

"That was changed as well," Roman replied.

"Who changed it, Lieutenant?" Johnson asked him.

"Chief Reasoner and I thought it would be better this way," Roman winked at him.

"I understand," Rick smiled. And he did. While Roman would not scrub the mission, Johnson's information about Holmgren gave him doubts about the Colonel's motives. The HALO jump would take the North Koreans off guard if they were waiting for a helicopter insertion, giving A-Flight an advantage, however small it may be.

Kadena Air Base

"Are you fucking kidding me?" Colonel Margaret Kozlowski, commander of the 961st Airborne Warning and Control Squadron said. "There is no way I'm putting one of my planes in harm's way on *your* say so, general or not."

"Come on, Marge," Beu pleaded. "Liz and Vinny are on board."

"A tanker and a couple F-15s aren't worth what an AWACS is," Kozlowski proclaimed. "Let alone the national security implications if one is shot down and the parts fall into the wrong hands."

"Vinny will detail two of his fighters to escort you," Beu promised. "And you won't even need to get within two hundred and fifty miles of the action. You'll be flying the friendly skies playing lookout for a few hours."

"And you can't tell me why?"

"Not yet, Marge," Beu insisted. "I just need your cooperation for forty-eight hours and then I will explain everything."

"You'll end up in Leavenworth if this all goes wrong," she warned.

"I'll probably end up there if it goes right," Beu said. "But I am comfortable with the fact that I'm doing the right thing."

"I just hope you'll be comfortable in an eight by eight cell."

"So, you're in?"

"Yes, damn it," Kozlowski grumbled.

"Good," Beu grinned. "You'll hear from me through Mark White if I need you."

"Tell your toady that I am the last resort," Kozlowski declared. "If I go up, we'd better be two minutes from going to war."

"If I need you, we *will* be," Beu told her as he departed.

Osan Air Base

"Who gave you permission to change the parameters of the operation?" Holmgren demanded.

"No one, sir," Roman said.

"I want your equipment transferred to the helicopter right now," Holmgren ordered.

"Either we go with a HALO jump or we don't go, sir," Roman insisted. "I've been thinking about what Johnson and some of the others have been saying. This mission has been flaky from the beginning and I'm not walking into an ambush if I can help it."

"I will have you up on charges, Lieutenant," Holmgren promised. "Johnson is just a troublemaker and you'll go down with him."

"You can do it when we get back, sir," Roman insisted. "But for now, it's my way or the highway. If you're so adamant, you can relieve me now and take command of this personally, but when my butt is on the line, I'm taking the best chance for survival."

"If your insubordination leads to failure, your career will be over," Holmgren threatened.

"If we fail, my career is the least of my worries," Roman replied as he left the office.

Aboard Air Force 85-632

"This is no DC-10," Levy said when they were aboard the tanker aircraft. Though the KC-10 resembled its civilian cousin, the interior was vastly different, designed to haul cargo and troops, not commuters and tourists in comfort.

"What did you expect, a first-class seat?" Beu laughed. "This ain't American Airlines."

"Let's just go already," Connie said, anxious to get airborne.

Seoul, South Korea

Holmgren was back in the camera shop on the Choggyechono, a look of desperation in his eyes. "May I help you, sir?" A young woman asked.

"I spoke with a man the other day," Holmgren said, his gaze darting around the store. "Would he be available?"

"I am truly sorry, today is his day off," she said. "But I am his daughter. I am prepared to help you."

"I'd rather speak with him. It is about a camera I bought the other day," Holmgren told her. "Could you have him call me as soon as possible?"

"Oh yes, sir," she nodded.

Holmgren scribbled a phone number on a card and handed it to her. "I will be at this number until this evening."

"Yes, sir," she took the card and bowed slightly.

CIA Headquarters, Langley, Virginia

The door opened and Guerin stood, ready to berate his secretary for the failure to knock, but the two men in business suits surprised him. "Mr. Guerin, I am Special Agent Crosier of the FBI. I am placing you under arrest for the crime of espionage, among other things."

"What?" Guerin screeched. "You have no evidence …"

"The Attorney General has enough evidence to put you away for a long time, sir," Crosier cut him off. "Will you come along peacefully, or will I be able to have some fun first?"

Aboard Air Force 85-632

"We're landing," Connie said as her ears popped from the change in pressure. "That was quick."

"It isn't far," Beu said with a smile as the tanker touched down and taxied to the Transient Aircraft Area. The hatch was opened, and a mobile staircase extended up to it allowing them all to exit the craft. The ground crew was surprised to see a general officer and three civilians step onto the tarmac. Not far away, an MC-130 Combat Talon began its taxi to the runway.

"Isn't that a C-130?" Connie asked Beu.

"Yes," he replied sadly. "I fear we might be too late."

Aboard Air Force 76-471

"You're enjoying yourself, aren't you?" Jack George asked Johnson as night fell over East Asia.

"I love HALO jumps," he said. "It's a hell of a ride." HALO stood for High Altitude Low Opening and that's exactly what it was. They would dive out the back of the –130 at fifteen thousand feet, on oxygen due to the thin atmosphere, and free fall to a thousand feet before opening their chutes. They would jump on the South Korean side of the border and would end up twenty miles inside North Korea by the time they landed. "Would you rather ride in a chopper that the North Koreans are probably waiting for with anti-air missiles?"

"I'd rather die than do this," George admitted.

"Just don't puke in your oxygen mask," Johnson warned as Lieutenant Roman stood.

"Check your gear, boys," he said. "We're ten minutes from our destination."

Osan Air Base

"I'm Major Greenlee," the officer who greeted them at Base Ops said. "I'm General O'Brien's executive officer."

"We'll need a place to work, Major, several phones, at least one with AUTOVON capability, and a car for Special Agent Estevez," Beu said.

"I'll need an explanation, General Beu," Greenlee said. "General O'Brien is in Washington and I can't just …"

"When you get me what I need," Beu ignored his complaints. "I will have to establish a direct line to the White House. I have to speak with the President immediately."

"But General …" Greenlee tried to continue.

"Do you know who I am, Major?" Levy asked him.

"No, sir."

"This is Senator Jacob Levy, Major Greenlee," Beu said. "Now, any career advancement on your part depends on how quickly you fulfill my requests. Am I getting through to you?"

"But I just need to know one thing, sir," Greenlee said.

"And what might that be?" Levy asked him.

"*Why*, sir?"

"Because," Beu said, "in a few hours, we might just be at war with the North Koreans and Chinese."

***

Holmgren's anxiety and paranoia were getting the best of him. After weeks of everything going right, things were starting to go wrong. Roman's unexpected stand against him and the camera store owner's absence served to set him on edge. Levy's arrival from Kadena along with the others was his cue to leave. They were close, not close enough to save A-Flight, but close enough to find him. He collected his things and packed his suitcase, giving one last look around the room when he saw the Air Force blue Chevrolet Caprice pull up in front of the BOQ. He hurried out the back when the FBI agent working with Levy walked to the front door of the building.

Aboard Air Force 76-471

"Stand up," Roman ordered as the cargo door opened. The cold wind blew into the plane, whipping the men with its ferocity. "Thirty seconds," he said and checked his watch.

"Me first," Johnson said as he made his way to the edge of the ramp. He looked out into the blackness and smiled. Much as he knew he might be jumping to his death, he relished the thought of going into combat once again against the enemies of his nation. Adrenaline flooded his system, his heart threatening to thump out of his chest, and he reveled in it, embraced the rush, and had to hold himself back until the word was given. He wanted to go now.

"In the door," he heard Roman's voice in his earpiece, and he tensed. "*Go!*" And he leapt into the night.

Yong Hung, North Korea

"Is everything prepared?" Soon Yat Oh asked his wife. She nodded and went to see about the children. He'd followed the directions he'd received from the Russians explicitly, going to work today as usual, the children going to school as well, but their bags had been packed with the necessities and waited in the small closet. They followed their normal routine until night fell, the parents putting their children to bed at the normal time and they too turned in a little after ten. The house was dark but Soon and his wife did not sleep. The Americans would be here just after midnight and they would have to be ready.

It angered Soon that Kosarev would place this last demand upon him before he was able to defect, but he'd been paid well, and his family would live comfortably once they were in the United States. This would be the most dangerous time for them when the Americans attacked and the NKPA troops engaging them. It would be easier for him to slip his family out in the confusion, but the chance of being caught in the crossfire between the Americans and North Koreans was great. At 11:15, he rose from the bed and began moving their things near the door. At midnight, his wife went to wake the girls.

"We are ready," his wife said as their children followed her.

"Now we wait," Soon Yat Oh said to them as they all took their places on the floor.

Chapter Sixty
Osan Air Base, Osan, South Korea
Tuesday, 28 March 1995

"I just missed him," Estevez said when he got back to Base Ops. "But he's here. I have the locals keeping an eye on the airports just in case he tries to leave the country. The Air Police are looking for him on base too."

"Damn it," Levy said. "We keep coming up short." They all looked up as the door to the conference room they were using swung open and security policemen showed two officers in.

"Are you the pilot of –471?" Beu asked the lieutenant colonel wearing the insignia of 7th Special Operations Squadron.

"Yes, sir," he replied.

"What was your mission?"

"I'm sorry, General, but I can't say," the pilot said, still annoyed at being dragged out of his plane so unceremoniously. "It's classified." Beu handed him the phone. After listening for a minute, the pilot said "yes, Mr. President" and handed the phone back to the general.

"I ask you again; what was your mission?"

"We took a twelve-man commando team up for a HALO insertion into North Korea, sir."

"What's HALO, Nate?" Connie asked him.

"High Altitude Low Opening," Beu shook his head and looked at his watch. "They parachuted in from fifteen thousand feet. They're on the ground by now."

The Sung Rocket Complex, Yong Hung, North Korea

General Kim Sun Park summoned his aide. "Have the radar people spotted the helicopter yet?"

"No, sir," Cho replied.

"They should have been here by now," Park fidgeted.

"Maybe they aborted?" Cho offered.

"I would have heard from my man in Seoul if they did," Park said. "Double the patrols. If they used some sort of stealthy helicopter, I do not want them taking us by surprise."

"Yes, sir."

***

"Look at *that*," Johnson whispered to Roman. "Look how they're moving; they know we're here. That rat bastard sold us out." They were on a low hill watching a squad of North Korean soldiers searching through the trees.

"You can't be sure," the lieutenant replied.

"What did I tell you about listening to us?" Johnson asked him. "We were chased out of here once upon a time; I know how they operate. They're looking for something and that's us."

"Do you want to abort?"

"You ask me this *now*?"

"I'm sorry, Johnson, but I didn't believe you."

"Give the chopper a call," Rick said. "See what they say."

Roman motioned to Reasoner who came up with the satellite set. Roman tried to raise Osan several times but all he came up with was static. "I can't raise them," he said to Johnson.

"I guess that clinches it," he said to them. "We're on our own."

"What now, sir?" Reasoner asked Roman, refusing to meet Johnson's 'I told you so' stare.

"If we stay here, they will find us," Campbell offered. "I say we do what we came here to do and get the hell out in the confusion. If they're worried about saving their shit, they'll give finding us a lower priority."

"I'm with Chuck," Johnson agreed. "If we're going to die here, we might as well do some serious damage first. Take as many of them with us as we can."

"What about the rest of you?" Roman asked the team and got nods from all of them.

"As long as we don't have to jump out of a plane again," Jack George said.

Osan Air Base

"I'm sorry, General," the communications tech from the 51st Comm Squadron said as he worked the satellite set found in Holmgren's quarters. "I can't raise them, no one can unless we have a set programmed with the correct encryption code. Without knowing the code, we're SOL."

"We have to find Holmgren then," Levy said. "He's the only one who'd have it."

"What does that mean, Nate?" Connie asked him.

"It means there's no way to communicate with Rick and the team," he explained. "They're on their own."

"Can't we do *anything*?"

"Not until we find Holmgren," Beu replied.

"I doubt he'll cooperate when we do," Estevez said.

"He'll cooperate," Beu said. "I'll take him up in a chopper and hang him out the door by his ankles until he talks."

"Find him, George," Connie insisted. "I don't care what it takes, just find him."

"I'm working on it," he said. "Believe me, I want him as badly as you do."

"General Beu," an officer from 303rd Intelligence Squadron burst into the room. "We have reports that several NKPA armor and infantry units are on the move toward the border. We're talking division strength. There is also an indication that several North Korean air bases have gone on alert. If I didn't know better …"

"You *don't*," Beu insisted. "Thank you for your report." He turned to Greenlee who'd been put to work for the group. He wasn't going to leave them alone, so they gave him a job monitoring the phones. "Get me Colonel White at 18th Operations at Kadena."

Yong Hung, North Korea

Johnson stepped out from behind the tree, his arm going around the neck of the Korean infantryman. His larynx crushed; the man struggled for his life, but Rick snapped his neck in one easy motion before disappearing back into the scrub. He looked over to see Emory removing his survival knife from the throat of another man. They moved on, the two dead soldiers bringing the kill count to forty. They approached the barbed wire fence carefully. "We're at the perimeter fence," Johnson said into the microphone mounted on his headset.

"Good work guys," Roman said. He'd taken advantage of the hilly terrain and set up his two heavy weapon crews as high as possible. Gibbs and Rockwood were on the southern flank, Petersen and Coles on the northern, and Jack George was in position with his long rifle on another hill, able to cover Johnson and Emory's approach to the facility with Mason acting as spotter. Reasoner, Campbell, and Guthrie remained with Roman at the command post below George and Mason's position.

"Yeah, tell me that when I send you the bill for my shrink," Johnson said. He'd killed over twenty men in the past hour with his bare hands and he felt something change in him. A religious person would call it possession, the Devil taking over, for he had the bloodlust now, all his hatred toward Holmgren, and the situation he'd put them in, was coming to the surface. Johnson relished the feeling, not just looking to get in to the complex unnoticed but taking absolute pleasure in killing as many as possible in the process. He thought himself the beast, a rogue wolf or lion, not just killing to feed itself but for the thrill of it.

"Are you all right, Rick?" Emory asked as he came up next to him.

"I'm fine," he replied, both of them covered with the blood of their victims. His breath came in pants, as a wild animal would after so much exertion. "Let's go."

He crept along the fence, up behind one of the perimeter guards who'd been scanning the horizon, looking for a helicopter. The kid was young, but he wore a uniform and Johnson didn't much care whether he lived or died. Rick reached up and grabbed him, dragging him back down into the scrub, punching him in the side of the head several times to disorient him. "Do you speak English?" Johnson whispered in his ear. The young soldier nodded. "Good, how do I get into the missile complex?"

"I do not tell you," he said with a heavy accent. Johnson reached down and grabbed his little finger, breaking it with a snap. His other hand went over the soldier's mouth to muffle his screams of pain.

"Tell me or I break another one," he growled.

"*Anyo*," he replied in his native tongue.

"*Yes*," Johnson hissed and reached into the man's pants grabbing his testicles, holding one between his thumb and forefinger, he squeezed until he felt it crush. The soldier went limp, passed out from the excruciating pain. Rick slapped him awake. "How do I get in the fucking complex?"

"Door in small hut," the man pointed, very cooperative now.

"How many guards are inside the complex?" The man shook his head again and Johnson applied pressure on his scrotum once more, which was now filling with blood from the ruptured organ. "How many?"

"*I'ship*," the man replied in his delirium. Rick had to remember the little Korean he knew to realize there were twenty men inside the complex buildings.

"*Kamsa hamnida,*" Johnson thanked him in Korean before smashing his palm into the man's nose, driving it up into his brain. He rose, leaving the dead man in the bushes and sprinted across the road, up behind the guard shack on the other side. For the first time, he removed his silenced .45 caliber Colt automatic from its holster. Chambering a round, he brought the pistol up and threw the door open. The two soldiers within were surprised and he dispatched them each with a bullet between the eyes. "Come on, Jerry," he said into the mike. He rigged the door with several ounces of plastic explosive before they slipped through the gate. Anyone checking the guardhouse would get a nasty surprise when the door was opened.

Osan Air Base

"I have commenced a combat air patrol with the F-15s from the 12th and there is an AWACS on station also, sir," Beu told the President on the phone. "I also arranged for tanker support for the fighters. I know I took some initiative, sir, but I thought it prudent once I heard from Senator Levy." Beu winked at Connie. "Yes, sir," he put the phone down. "The White House is faxing over authorization," he told Greenlee. "Is that good enough for you?"

"Yes, sir, I feel much better now," he replied.

Another phone rang and Connie answered it. "Base Ops," she said and then listened for a minute before hanging up. "Holmgren was spotted at Kim Po Airport, but he evaded the police. They think he's heading back here."

"We'll get him," Levy said confidently.

***

McTavish inched along the wall of the Ops building, looking for a way in. He'd taken a flight to Kim Po when he'd learned Levy et al were on their way to Osan and had gained access to the base using his press credentials and a bullshit story. Air Force Security Police guarded the entrances to Ops, and he was certain they wouldn't allow him into the building regardless of what he said. As he crawled through the shrubs planted to beautify the place, he heard the sound of a toilet flush on the other side of the wall. Looking up he saw a small window that was left partially open. "Yes," he said quietly.

***

Holmgren ditched the car in the parking lot of a large shopping mall and set out on foot, doing his best to keep to the shadows. Vehicle traffic was sparse and only one or two pedestrians were on the street; he would be spotted easily if he were not careful. He'd almost been caught at the airport and Johnson's words came back to him. *What else have you miscalculated, queer boy?*

He rationalized that it wasn't a miscalculation but Fate's hand exercising its option. He couldn't have known that Levy would get involved or that Johnson's wife would be so determined. He didn't count on General Beu's involvement either, an old friend of Johnson's that Fate had put in the right place at the wrong time. *I have to get to the coast*, he thought as he ducked into an alley, changing from his uniform into jeans, a shirt, and a winter jacket. A navy watch cap covered his head, allowing him to blend in more easily with the locals. He would try to book passage aboard a cargo ship to Singapore, where he would be untouchable, safe in the enclave he'd built for himself.

Yong Hung, North Korea

"There are a lot of them out here," Reasoner said to Roman. The North Korean patrols were becoming more frequent and it was just a matter of time until they came upon one of the bodies Johnson and Emory left in their wake.

"I know, Chief," he replied and then keyed his mike. "Twelve, one," he said.

"Twelve," Nick Mason answered.

"Where are our boys?"

"Almost to the entrance, Lieutenant," Mason replied after checking with his spotting scope.

"If they're discovered, we're all dead," Guthrie said.

"We're dead anyway, Jake," Campbell told him. "Like Rick said, it's just a matter of how many we take with us."

"Regardless, we're not leaving until the complex is destroyed," Roman said. "How are you doing, three?"

***

"Leave me alone, Lieutenant, I'm busy," Rick hissed as he approached the building, Emory covering his back. He came to the steel door and applied pressure to the handle surprised it was unlocked. Johnson was fully prepared to blow the door open using explosives. "We're in, one," he said before ducking inside, Emory following closely. A guard came around the corner and Johnson felled him with one shot. "Come on, Jer."

"Right." The building was small, only a hallway and a few offices on this level and Johnson wired the doors, just as he had the guard shack, before they headed down the stairs. "We have to find another way out then," Emory said.

"Do you think we are getting out anyway?" Rick asked him as they continued lower. They came out of another door into a tunnel. "Drop a pound here," he said. "And time it for twenty minutes. We might as well distract them." As Emory bent to his task, Johnson listened for the telltale sounds that would advise which direction to go.

"Done," Emory said.

"One, three," Rick keyed his mike but received only static. "Too much metal," he said. "I can't raise the Lieutenant."

"They'll know what we're up to in …" Emory checked his watch. "Eighteen minutes and thirty seconds."

"Let's go then," Rick ordered, and they hurried off down the long tunnel.

***

"I can't raise them," Roman said.

"They're probably too deep and who knows what kind of metals are in the ground over here," Reasoner said. "This is a big mining area."

"Great," Roman sighed. And then they heard voices from below. "Get ready, boys," he said. "We're about to have company."

***

"What?" Park was livid.

"There are thirty confirmed dead and we can't raise the perimeter guard," Cho told him.

"Are any Americans among the dead?"

"We have yet to find any, sir."

"Where *are* they?"

***

"Stop, raise your hands," they heard from behind. As Johnson and Emory turned, they saw two soldiers running up the tunnel toward them. Rick went to bring his hands up but grabbed his pistol instead, firing twice. He dove as one of them got a shot off before he died.

"I got them, Jer," he said but heard nothing. "Jer?" He looked up to see Emory flat on his back. "Oh fuck," he cried as he ran over to his friend. Pink foam was bubbling out of his chest.

"I guess you were right," Emory gasped. "We're not getting out of here, are we?"

"I was just kidding, Jer," Johnson said as he wiped away a tear. He reached into his med kit and pulled out a morphine syrette.

"Don't bother, Rick," Emory said. "I don't feel a thing." His eyes closed and a final breath escaped his lips.

"Fuck," Rick hissed and then did something he never thought he could do. He slid a six-ounce block of Semtex under Emory's body and wired it to a pressure detonator. If someone rolled the body over, they would be blown to bits along with it. He pressed on.

***

"That's one," Jack George said as he fired his first silenced shot and one of the Koreans approaching Roman's command post fell. He chambered another and took aim at the next man, dropping him just as easily.

"Like fish in a barrel," Mason said as he watched the soldiers fall one by one.

***

"Well, fuck me," Rick said aloud as he peeked through the crack he'd opened in the doorway. Inside was his destination, twenty-four missile launchers arrayed as they were in one of the U.S. nuclear submarines. There was activity in the chamber soldiers standing guard and technicians servicing the missiles, but it didn't give him pause. He only had to make it about a hundred feet across the open floor before he would be in relative safety among the missile tubes. Checking his watch, he saw he had less than ten minutes to plant his explosives and get out before package in the tunnel exploded. "I can do this."

He slid through the doorway, opening the door only as much as necessary. There was no stealth involved now and he stood up and walked across the floor as if he owned the place. "Well I'll be damned," he said when he was about ten feet from the tubes, and none had challenged him. A second later, he felt a rifle being jabbed into the small of his back. He turned to see the largest Korean he'd ever laid eyes on.

"Yes, American, you *will* be," Cho said.

Rick just smiled. "Didn't I see you in a James bond movie?" He asked before grabbing the barrel of the rifle and shoving the butt back into Cho's midsection. The man doubled over, and Johnson gave him a kick to the side of his knee. It broke with an audible crack and Cho fell to the floor. Rick then smashed he sole of his boot into the Korean's face, rendering him unconscious. "The bigger they are . . ." he said as he removed Cho's belt and tied his wrists together. Grabbing the unconscious man by the collar, he dragged him in among the missile tubes.

***

George capped the last man in the patrol without Roman's group having to fire a shot and he searched for more targets. He dropped another lone sentry that was scanning the area with NVGs and that's when the hills erupted with fire. Someone had seen his muzzle flash and had sighted in on him. "Let's get the fuck out," he said to Mason and they evacuated their perch.

"One, twelve," Mason called. "We're on our way to your position. Hold your fire."

Osan Air Base

"Right, thanks, Marge," Beu said and put the microphone down before turning to the group. "That was our AWACS commander. She's reporting muzzle flashes on the ground at Yong Hung."

"How can they see that?" Levy asked. The AWACS was circling over South Korean territory.

Beu pointed skyward. "They're getting the satellite feed from the National Reconnaissance Office at Fort Meade, Maryland," he smiled. "Forget I said that."

"So, we have support from Washington now?" Connie asked him.

"The CIA Director has been taken into custody," Beu told her. "The President was duped and he's committing resources to make this right. On a sad note, Senator Latour committed suicide Sunday morning."

"His career would have been over when Holmgren's part in this was made public," Levy said.

"I can't help feeling that we drove him to it," Connie said her eyes moist.

"No one can help him now," Beu said throwing his arm around her. "Our only concern is the men on the ground in hostile territory, and it looks as if it's getting more hostile by the minute."

Yong Hung, North Korea

Johnson finished setting the charges and then turned his attention back to Cho, slapping him awake. "Where's the commander?" Cho spat at him in reply, the bloody sputum hitting Johnson in the face. He slit the side of Cho's pants open with his survival knife and tore them away, exposing him from the waist down. He held the knife near Cho's sexual organs. "I swear I'll cut them off," he said. "Where's your CO?" Cho said nothing, just looked up toward the ceiling. Two floors above was a glass enclosure, an office in which a diminutive man paced back and forth impatiently. "*That* little bastard?" Again, Cho said nothing, but Johnson could see the man in the office wore a uniform that belied his high rank. Rick took Cho's underpants and stuffed them in his mouth as a gag. "You've been a *big* help," Rick said sarcastically. He jammed the knife into Cho's belly and slit upward, to the sternum. The Korean's eyes went wide as his intestines spilled out onto his lap. He screamed in sheer terror, but the sound died in the gag. "Die slowly, asshole."

Osan Air Base

McTavish waited in the bathroom for a half hour before screwing up the courage to step out into the hall. He worked his way toward the conference room, slowly, ducking into doorways when someone would pass. He was almost to his destination when he heard a low growl from behind. Turning slowly to see a large SP with an equally large Belgian Malinois on a short leash, he debated his options.

"Stand where you are and don't move," the cop ordered as he and the dog approached. McTavish ran for the door and the SP released the dog. The Malinois covered the distance easily and McTavish could feel it gaining on him. He reached into his camera bag for the only weapon he carried, a can of mace. The dog took a bite of his calf and spun him around. McTavish bounced off the wall but kept his footing, bringing the mace vial up to spray the dog. The cop knew not what was in the reporter's hand, only that his partner was in danger. He pulled his sidearm and fired once, catching McTavish just under the chin with the nine-millimeter projectile, killing him instantly. His body flew backward, through the double doors of the conference room.

***

"Oh my god," Connie said as she rushed to the man's aid. She felt for a pulse, but his heart had stopped when the bullet tore through his brain, the control area for the autonomic nervous system being the first destroyed. She looked up to come eye to eye with the snarling Malinois. "Easy, puppy," she said soothingly to the dog.

"Hold, Spike." The SP was there a second later and leashed the animal. "He was gonna shoot the dog," the cop said.

"With mace," Connie sighed, picking up the vial, and the cop looked away.

"Who is he?" Levy asked.

Beu rummaged through McTavish's pockets and found his press credentials. "Damn, he's a reporter."

Sung Rocket Complex

"They know where we are," Roman said. Someone had radioed their position to the other NKPA troops, and they were streaming out of the gate by the hundreds. "We have to move." One of the North Koreans decided to check the guard shack, flinging the door wide. Johnson's booby trap exploded, killing twenty.

It seemed as time stopped for a second, the NKPA troops looking back to see the carnage and Reasoner saw their chance. "Eight and twelve, *fire*," and both heavy weapons opened up, Gibbs and Coles playing their withering fire over the men in the valley below, and a hundred fell like dominoes in the first few seconds. The chief turned to Roman. "Let's move *now*."

"But Johnson and Emory will expect …"

"Damn it, Lieutenant," Reasoner shouted at him. "They were dead when they went inside. We have to go; this might be our only chance."

***

Johnson checked his watch. "Seven minutes," he said aloud as he sprinted up the stairs. There were shouts from the floor below and he looked over the side to see someone had dragged Cho's body out from between the tubes, his bloody entrails making a sticky, greasy mess for twenty feet as they unfolded. And then someone pointed in his direction.

Shots began to rig off the metal structure and he ran faster, emptying a clip of .45 caliber from his pistol. He ejected it and replaced it with a full one, aiming up the stairs as guards appeared from his destination. He fired into them and they fell, several over the side to their deaths twenty feet below, others down the stairs toward him. At the landing, he pulled a fragmentation grenade from his web gear, yanked the pin, and dropped it into the group firing up at him. Rick dove through the door as it went off.

***

"What is happening?" General Park said as he looked through the window as soon as he heard the shots. He'd received word that the Americans had been engaged on the perimeter, but it seemed some had made it inside. And then the grenade went off, shattering the window and throwing shards into his office, two of them embedding themselves in his back. And then the door was thrown open. And there was a man there, an American soldier, bloody, sweaty, with the look of a wild animal in his eyes. "You will never get out of here alive," Park said to him.

***

"I don't plan to," Rick replied as he looked over the little man. "And neither will you." Park's eyes gave him away as he looked to his desk drawer, telegraphing his move for the pistol. Johnson shot him in the elbow, and he wailed in pain. Rick retrieved another grenade and went to Park, pulled the pin, and jammed it down the front of his pants. "Later, asshole," he said and ran from the room, yanking the door shut behind him. Three seconds later, he was thrown to the floor as the room was blown apart. "Shit," he looked at his arm to see a six-inch wooden splinter jammed in it. He grabbed it and pulled it free. "That's gonna leave a mark," he said through gritted teeth. Duct tape from his bag served to stop the flow of blood and he pressed on, looking once more at his watch. "Two minutes, *shit*."

Hustling up three flights of stairs, Johnson found the emergency exit door and beyond it, freedom. It was locked. "Fuck, shit, God *damn* it," he cursed as he took three ounces of explosive from his bag, split it in half, and stuck it to the hinges. A remote detonator was wired in, just as he came under fire once more. Diving for cover, he pressed the arm button on his remote and the red LED glowed. He delayed, waiting for his pursuers to approach, and they did in a hurry. "Bye, boys," he smiled as he pressed the button.

The door blew apart, metal shrapnel whizzing by Johnson's position sounded like jet engines, hitting the NKPA troops like supersonic daggers, cutting them to pieces. Johnson administered the coup de grace to any that survived and then ran out into the chilly air.

***

"Hey," Guthrie poked Campbell. "Who's that?" Campbell swung around to check.

"It's fucking Johnson," he said. "Three, five, do you read?"

"Go, five," Rick replied.

"Keep running straight ahead, we're fifty yards off," Campbell replied. "Where's Jerry?" There was no reply.

***

He ran, and he thought his lungs would explode, but he picked up the speed when bullets struck the dirt at his feet. "Shit," he muttered as he pulled the M-16 from his shoulder, emptying a clip into the approaching Korean line. Several fell and he resumed the race toward the tree line. "One, three," he said.

"One," Roman replied. "Good to see you, Rick."

"This place is gonna blow in about thirty seconds," Johnson replied. "One big fucking boom, just like I promised." And he laughed as he entered the trees, branches whipping his face. His timing was off, for fifteen seconds later it began.

It started as a low rumbling, almost as an earthquake, and then turned into a roar. The entry building blew first, upward for the pound of Semtex in the tunnel below threw everything skyward, and then, one by one, the missile doors blew, fountains of flame accompanying them, twenty-four roman candles burning in the Korean night.

Johnson practically flew through the woods, oblivious to the branches, twigs, and briars that stung and ripped at him. He felt something grab his leg and he fell to the ground.

"Hey, boy," Chuck Campbell grinned, releasing his ankle. "You're coming to my next Fourth of July party." He keyed his mike. "One, five," he said. "Three is at our position."

"Rog, five."

"Holy shit," Guthrie said. "What's that?"

They followed his arm to where he pointed, and it looked as if the side of one of the hills was opening. It was a large door behind which stood several trucks, troop carriers that were rapidly filling with infantry. "Take them out, guys," Johnson said.

Campbell and Guthrie raised the Dragon anti-tank missiles to their shoulders and activated the seekers. It took twelve seconds to lock on and, in that time, Johnson watched part of the valley floor collapse, the heat from the liquid fuel fires melting the metal support structure beneath. Campbell got the lock on tone first and fired, the Dragon leaving the launcher a second before Guthrie heard his tone. Both missiles were in the air for what seemed an interminably long time as they raced to their targets. Campbell's missed the lead truck, flying past and exploding in the rear of the large bay, but Guthrie's found its mark, the truck exploding, rising upward in the blast as a butterfly riding an air current, it looked almost elegant. Two hundred Korean troops were incinerated within the structure.

Osan, Air Base

"We're getting massive explosions from Yong Hung," the Intel officer said excitedly. "AWACS reports a flight of Chinese J-8 fighters on their way south. They'll cross into North Korean territory in seven minutes."

"Damn it," Beu spat. "This is what we were trying to prevent." He picked up the phone that was the open line to Kadena. "Mark, it's Nate. Tell Vinny to expect some company. If the Chinese enter South Korean air space, they are to be engaged." He put that phone down and picked up the one that connected him to the White House. It took a minute before the President came on the line. "Mr. President," Beu said. "We need your help."

Yong Hung

They were in a cave, one of many formed in the surrounding hills by Mother Nature over the past hundred million years, Soon Yat Oh keeping his family in the very back as he peeked out from the mouth of the natural shelter. They left their home when they heard the first of the explosions and now the night sky was colored a dull orange from the fires that burned only a half-mile away. He had made the call to the Russians and did not receive good news. There was Chinese air activity over North Korea and would have to delay the extraction until the following night. Soon looked to the six women in the back of the cave, all wore a mask of terror. "It will be all right," he told them, doing his best to show he believed it.

***

"RPG," Johnson yelled and dove for cover behind a rock as the rocket propelled grenade burned its way toward them. It exploded a foot from where he last stood, showering him with dirt and debris. "Chuck, Jake?" He called into the darkness. He keyed his mike. "Five, six, do you read?" No reply. "Shit, fuck," he cursed and crawled through the undergrowth. "Ah, *damn* it," he said as he found Guthrie's dismembered corpse. And then he heard moaning a few feet away.

"Did anybody get the tag number of that truck," Campbell said weakly when Rick came upon him.

"Oh *man*," Rick cried. Campbell's legs had been blown off and one of his arms was twisted up behind his neck. He jammed the morphine syrette into the arm that didn't look like hamburger and applied tourniquets around the severed limbs. "I'll get you out of here, pal," he promised.

"No …" Campbell replied. "You know I won't make it." His eyes met Johnson's. "Wire me," he demanded.

"I can't …"

"Remember what you said, Rick?" Campbell said through dry lips. "We'll take as many with us as we can before we go down. *Wire* me, God *damn* it."

And Rick did, placing a half pound block of plastic on Campbell's lap and then wiring it to a detonator. "Here," he put the detonator in Campbell's hand.

"Set it for five minutes," Campbell said.

"No," Rick shook his head as the tears ran down his cheeks. "I'm not going to kill you. You'll have to do it yourself."

"Pussy," Campbell spat. Their eyes met once more. "Get going, Rick. I'll slow them down for you."

"See you in Hell, buddy," Rick smiled.

"I'll be waiting for ya," Campbell replied as Johnson disappeared into the night. A minute later, a squad of NKPA came upon him. "Hey, boys, you like to party?" And he flipped the switch.

***

Rick heard the explosion behind him and knew what happened. As the sound echoed away through the valley, he heard the moans of the dying that weren't killed instantly by Campbell's body coming apart with the force of the explosive. "One, three," Johnson said.

"Go, three."

"Five and six are gone. I'm a minute from you."

"Rog, three," Roman replied. "I'll be waiting."

Washington, D.C.

"Thank you for coming so quickly, Ambassador Xing," the President said.

"I am at your service, sir," the Chinese ambassador to the United States said with a bow before taking a seat in front of the leader of the free world.

"As I am sure you know, there is a situation in North Korea," the President began. "It is part of a rogue operation conducted by members of our CIA that are now in federal custody. There are American troops on the ground near Yong Hung and we are doing our best to extract them. We … *I* ask that the People's Republic of China show restraint in their reaction to this event. I assure you that we have no intention of invading North Korea and our forces in South Korea will stand down as soon as our people have left the country. We, however, will not permit an incursion into South Korean territory by North Korean *or* Chinese forces."

"I see, Mr. President," Xing became thoughtful.

"Let us not resurrect the Korean War, Mr. Xing. This will be over in a few hours and it can be put to rest," the President added.

"I will speak to my superiors," Xing said as he rose. "I appreciate your honesty, Mr. President. Be assured that we do not want war either."

Yong Hung

"We have to head toward the shore," Roman said. "We can swim for it, maybe we can signal a ship."

"We can't swim that far, Lieutenant," Johnson said. "I have another option." He removed the card from his pocket that Beu had given him. "General Beu gave me this. He said if we call, someone will come for us."

"Who?" Reasoner asked.

"He said I didn't want to know."

"Call them, Ch …" Roman never finished. There was a crack of rifle fire and the young lieutenant was thrown off his feet, backward into the dirt.

"Sniper," Johnson yelled and all dove for cover. There was the sound of heavy weapons, Gibbs with his .50 caliber, and the forest was silent once again.

"Let's get out of here," Reasoner ordered as Johnson punched up the frequency on the sat set.

"This is A-Flight, does anyone read?" Johnson said as the men packed up their gear.

"We were expecting you, American," a Russian accented voice replied.

"We need a ride, my friend," Johnson said.

"We will arrive in eighteen hours," the voice said. "There is a North Korean civilian family hiding in the caves east of the Sung Complex. You are to make contact with them, and we will extract you."

"Do you have a better fix on their location?" Johnson asked.

The Russian laughed. "From what I hear, you are supposed to be the best. Find them and we will take you home." The line went dead.

"Come *on*, Rick," Reasoner ordered. "We gotta go."

Johnson looked at Roman's body once more, a hole the size of a quarter in his temple, his dead eyes staring off into the distance. "Right," he said as he packed the sat set away. "We're headed east."

Osan Air Base

"The Chinese are still coming," the Intel officer said as one of the monitors flashed to life. They managed to access the sat feed from the AWACS. Red blips signified the Chinese fighters, blue ones, the F-15s from 12th Fighter Squadron and Beu knew Vinny Ubriaco was flying lead.

All eyes turned to the monitor as the blips came ever closer to one another. "What's happening?" Connie asked Beu.

"They're about thirty seconds from a dogfight," he replied. Everyone in the room held their collective breath as the red and blue blips merged. "They should be able to see each other now." And the red blips made a hard-right turn.

"The Chinese are breaking off," Levy said. "Son of a *bitch*," he exhaled deeply.

Yong Hung

They moved slowly, for the woods were still thick with North Korean infantry, picking their way carefully, Johnson on point as they headed east. He figured they were outnumbered ten to one at this point, better odds than when they arrived, but still depressingly hopeless. He scrabbled up a ridge to get his bearings, searching out the enemy with his NVGs, when he spotted a patrol fifty yards from his men. "Two, three," he said. "There's a patrol just off to your ..." And the woods exploded once again.

Bullets sped past him with a whine and a zing, then a slap as they hit the trees; he jumped to the side, behind a boulder, laying down automatic fire into the Korean patrol. He could see muzzle flashes from his own men when they returned fire as his rifle clicked empty.

Rick tossed grenade into the enemy line before reloading the M-16, again emptying a clip before the forest became quiet. "Two, three," he called. "Two, *three*," he said again.

"Two," Reasoner replied, breathing heavily. "It's just me, George, and Rockwood." There was silence for a minute. "They're all dead, Rick. They're all *dead*."

"Keep it together, John," Johnson demanded. "It's just a couple more miles. I'll hold position until you get here."

"Rog, three," Reasoner replied.

"Shit," Johnson said as he sat down on the ground. Eight of them were gone now and he knew that reaching the Russian contact, let alone surviving this, was next to impossible. "As many as I can before I go," he proclaimed. "I'll kill them *all* if I can."

PVO Vladivostok, Russia

"Why are you still here?" Kosarev asked Colonel Petr Lovenko, the son of one of his closest friends.

"The Chinese have fighters up," Lovenko replied. "We can't go in ..."

"I do not care if your mother is flying over the coordinates. You can and you *will*," Kosarev growled. "Or you and your crews will be taken out to the parade ground immediately and shot."

"But we will ..."

"You will die if you do *not* go, Petr," Kosarev bellowed.

"Yes, Marshal," Lovenko said and gathered his crew.

Yong Hung, North Korea

"Not in here, either," Johnson said as he emerged from the cave. "Shit."

Reasoner scanned the hillside, farther on up the slope. "There's another one about a hundred feet up and to the left," he said.

"I'll head up there," Rick volunteered. "Keep me covered." He turned away and then looked back. "I'm sorry, John," he said. "I'm sorry we never were closer friends."

"Maybe if we get out of this, we can work on it," Reasoner said.

"You bet," Rick replied as he started up the slope.

Osan Air Base

"General," the Intel officer said. "There are two choppers entering North Korean airspace from the northeast and they're big."

Beu came over and looked at the monitor. "Russians," he whispered and looked to Connie and Levy.

***

Holmgren pulled the stolen car into the alley and got out, walking back to the corner. The local police had roadblocks up and Air Force Security Police accompanied them.

"They're looking for me," he said aloud. He realized now that he could not get out of Osan by car, any vehicle approaching the roadblock was stopped and searched. Checking his watch, he saw that it would be dawn in three hours. "It's over," he said. "I'm finished."

When the sun came up, they would find him, his white skin standing out prominently among the population, not to mention he stood a head taller than most of them. It might take the police a few hours, but once they put his description out over the public airwaves, it was just a matter of time before one of the locals turned him in. "They won't take me alive." And then he remembered another promise he made to Johnson.

Yong Hung

Johnson heard a soft footfall and froze. He waited as it came closer, stopping just on the other side of the tree. Tensing in anticipation of the kill, he held when he heard the person relieve himself. Listening closely, he heard the other finish and stand, adjusting his clothing. Johnson got to his feet and approached. Reaching out from behind the tree, he grabbed the other with his left arm and was about to plunge his knife through his chest when he felt something soft and fleshy, and he let go.

The girl could have been no more than sixteen and her hands went to the breast that Rick had inadvertently manhandled. Her face was contorted with fear. "American," she whispered.

"Yes," Rick whispered. "Shhh."

"We ... we are waiting for you," she said. "My father says so. We going to America tonight too."

And he allowed himself to relax just a bit. "Two, three," Rick said into the mike. "I found them."

"Rog, three," Reasoner replied. "We're on our way."

At that moment, Rick caught movement from the corner of his eye. He threw the girl to the ground and opened up with his M-16, cutting the soldier down. Down below, he heard more automatic weapons fire.

Hustling the girl behind a boulder, he took aim at the Korean patrol that had engaged the remaining three and loosed a barrage down upon them, followed by two grenades. When the horrible noise died away, he keyed his mike. "Two, three," he said as he checked on the terrified girl. "Seven, three," he tried Rockwood. "Four, three," he tried George as he got the girl up and they ran up the path. "Two, three," he tried again. "Fuck."

The girl pointed toward the cave. "In there," she said, and they ran for it.

Once inside, Rick felt something very sharp at his back. "Do not move," a male voice said.

"I'm a friend," Rick said, releasing the girl and putting his hands up. "I'm an American."

"I was told there would be more of you," Soon Yat Oh said.

"They didn't make it." He relaxed when the knife was withdrawn and turned to face the man. "Do you have any other weapons?"

"No," Soon said. "Just the knife."

"I'll keep watch," Rick said tiredly and unlimbered his M-16. "Keep to the rear of the cave. If I think we're about to be overrun, I'll lead them away from here."

"Why?" Soon asked him.

"Because they deserve to have a life," he pointed to the children. "And you have to give it to them. Too many children have lost their fathers this night."

Osan Air Base

"I don't get it," Greenlee said. "What are the Russians doing?"

"Maybe they want to see what the fuss is all about," Beu offered. "I'm sure their satellites picked something up." He smiled at Connie, knowing that this would be A-Flight's chance to get out of hostile territory. They both prayed the team made contact with the Russian agent. Beu walked over to her. "It'll be finished soon, darling."

"When will we know?" She asked softly.

"It might take hours," he said. "Maybe even a day or two. It all depends on the Russians and whether Yevgeniy got to Vladivostok before the helicopters left."

Yong Hung

The radio came to life, startling Johnson as he waited at the mouth of the cave. He looked to the rear and heard Soon speaking. The Korean came forward to his position. "The Russians are three minutes out."

"I thought they were waiting until tonight?" Johnson asked him.

"They said there was a change in plans."

Rick looked back to the six women. "Get them up here," he ordered. "This place will get hot again when the chopper comes in. I'll cover you when you go for it. Tell them to run like they've never run before. You and your wife have to carry the two little ones, or they'll slow you down."

"What about you?"

"They haven't killed me yet, sir," Johnson smiled and checked his watch. He scanned the hills with his NVGs and then looked up at the sky to the northeast. "There they are," Rick whispered. "Two Hind gunships. At least they brought some big guns." And then he saw an NKPA patrol. He looked back up to see one helicopter assume a covering position as the other dove for the ground. "It's coming down now," he said to Soon. "Get ready."

An anti-air missile emerged from behind a nearby hill, burning toward the flaring chopper, the pilot jinking left to avoid it. It struck the hill above Johnson's position and exploded. "Get out, get *out*," Johnson insisted as debris started raining down upon them.

The second Hind launched a rocket in the direction of the launcher and there was another explosion in the distance. Johnson and his band were spotted immediately by the patrol and they engaged. "Go, go, *go*," he yelled to Soon and his family as he stopped, his M-16 spitting death at the Korean troops. They ran for the helicopter that hovered five feet off the ground. Rick looked back to check they were aboard before throwing two grenades, turning and sprinting for the helo. He stopped once more, firing at the Koreans who were in the process of setting up a heavy machine gun. Running out of ammo, he dropped the rifle and ran as bullets zipped by him.

The Russian Hind opened up with 40mm covering fire as Johnson ran for the open hatch, shredding trees and soldiers alike. He was just about to climb in when he was thrown the rest of the way into the chopper, a burning in his left shoulder.

"Welcome, *tavarich*," the Russian Special Forces troop said when Rick landed at his feet. "You almost didn't make it."

"Let me see that," a Russian medic said as he cut Johnson's shirt away. The bullet dug a trench in Rick's back from the shoulder blade up to nearly his neck. "I will have to sew it shut."

Rick pushed him away and stood, looking to the scared civilians, "Are you all okay?" He asked Soon.

"Thanks to you, yes," he smiled.

Rick turned back to the medic. "Do your worst," he sat on the bench. The Russian tried to give him a morphine shot, which he refused. "I need my wits about me, this isn't over."

"This will hurt," the medic warned as he threaded the needle.

"I'll live," Rick shrugged.

"Yes, you will, Sergeant," the Russian laughed as he began to suture the wound closed.

Aboard USS *Nassau* (LHA-4), the Sea of Japan

Navy Captain Paul Wallace watched the night launches from the bridge wing. Though a blue water sailor through and through, he enjoyed aircraft as well. Nate Beu had taken him for rides in his Air Force chopper many times and Wallace never turned down a ride. It was Beu who was on Wallace's mind just then. He still had no idea what Beu's cryptic message meant, but it was nearing the time frame Beu had indicated. "Crazy, Aggie," Wallace muttered as two AV-8B Marine Corps Harrier Jump Jets began their takeoff roll.

Captain Wallace to the CIC, the PA overhead blared.

"This is it," he said as he made his way down several decks to the Combat Information Center.

"Sir," the comm officer said. "We are getting a Mayday from two Russian helicopters. They're asking to speak with you."

"Give me that thing," Wallace growled, picking up the mike. "This is Captain Paul Wallace of the USS *Nassau*. Please state the nature of the emergency."

"Greetings, Captain Wallace, I am Colonel Petr Lovenko of the Russian Air Defense unit at PVO Vladivostok. We are seriously low on fuel and request permission to land on your ship."

"Are they fucking crazy?" Wallace asked the comm officer who just shrugged. "We're not *that* friendly yet."

"They *are* declaring an emergency, sir," Wallace's XO pointed out. "We're the closest, friendliest place they can land."

"Fucking Nate," Wallace muttered, finally getting the meaning of Beu's message.

"Sir?"

"Nothing," Wallace growled. "Clear the flight deck of all non-essential personnel. I just want the fuelers and two plane captains out there. Tell those two Harriers that just took off to shadow the Russians at *all* times. One hostile move and I want those helicopters in the water."

"Aye, sir."

"Colonel Lovenko," Wallace said. "You are cleared to land. I suggest you turn your weapons radar off before you approach my ship. If you paint us, it will be the *last* thing you do."

"I understand, Captain, thank you," Lovenko replied.

Wallace looked to the Sergeant at Arms. "I want Marines everywhere they will fit on the superstructure. If those Russians do anything funny …"

"Aye, aye, sir."

"They're coming in now, sir," the radar officer said.

"I'll be on the flight deck," Wallace said, pointing to another armed Marine. "You're with me." He stuck his head back in the comm shack. "And get me Brigadier General Beu at Kadena. I want to talk to that boy."

The flight deck was empty by the time the two Russian gunships appeared out of the night. Wallace thought this a first, Russian helicopters landing on an American ship and he walked toward them as they touched down. If he was surprised when the Russians asked permission to land, he was even doubly surprised when the hatch on the lead helicopter opened and the faces of five young girls peeked out at him. The plane captain helped them down, and then two civilian adults. An American soldier jumped out after them and scanned the deck. "What the fuck happened to him?" Wallace said as he made eye contact with the man who was covered in blood, sweat, and gore, the left side of his uniform shirt torn away.

He marched over and saluted. "I am Senior Master Sergeant Richard Johnson, sir, and I need a ride to Osan Air Base in South Korea. I have a mission to complete."

"You have a date with the ship's doctor, Sergeant," Wallace said.

"With all due respect, sir, I don't have the time," Johnson said.

"Who are they?" Wallace asked as the family joined him.

"They are North Korean defectors, sir. Those nice Russians gave us a lift out." Johnson grinned.

"And what were *you* doing there, Sarge?"

"Killing Communists, sir," Rick replied. "And now I'm after a traitor."

Osan Air Base

"Connie?" Beu nudged her. She'd fallen asleep on the couch, the emotional roller coaster and the adrenaline hangover serving to knock her out. "Connie?"

"Shit, I fell asleep," she said drowsily.

"I got word from the *Nassau*," he smiled. "Rick is alive and aboard."

"They got out?" She still thought she was dreaming. "They got *out*!" Connie reached up and hugged him to her, kissing his cheeks. "How are they? When can I see him?"

Beu looked at her sadly. "Rick was the only one who made it."

"What?" Her tears came freely. "They're *all* dead?"

"All I know is Rick was the only one the Russians picked up."

And then it dawned on her that he might be hurt. "How is he? Is he hurt?"

"They said he was a bit dinged, but he'll be fine," Beu told her.

"What does that mean, Nate? What macho bullshit is 'a bit dinged'? Don't try to spare my feelings, damn it. Was he hurt badly?"

"I honestly don't know, Connie. All they said was he was walking under his own power. We'll just have to wait and see."

"How long?"

"Captain Wallace wants to debrief him first. A few hours, maybe less."

Aboard *Nassau*

"Thanks for the coffee, Captain," Johnson said as he sat heavily.

"Does that hurt?" Wallace pointed to his shoulder.

"Like a son of a bitch, sir." Rick smiled.

"I talked to General Beu, Sarge. He says to give you whatever you want."

"That's nice of him, sir."

"I'm not that nice," Wallace barked. "You said you're going after a traitor. Tell me about it."

"Begging the Captain's pardon, but I don't have the time. This guy could have split by now. I appreciate the coffee and all but ..."

"The only ride you'll get, Sergeant, is on the toe of my boot directly into my brig. Spill it or you get shit." Rick did, over the course of twenty minutes and three cups of coffee. By the time he finished, Wallace's jaw was agape. "What are going to do when you find this Holmgren fella?" Wallace asked.

"I'm going to kill him, sir," Rick said flatly. "If he hurts my daughter, I'm going to kill him very *slowly*."

There was a knock on the door. "Enter," Wallace said, and a black Marine major entered the cabin, dressed in a flight suit, carrying another on his arm.

"I'm ready, Captain," Major Edward Hoskins, commander of the Marine Air Wing aboard *Nassau* said. His eyes went wide when he got a look at Johnson.

"Hi," Rick waved at him.

"Ed," Wallace said. "This is Sergeant Johnson. He needs a ride to Osan Air Base as fast as possible."

"Aye, sir," Hoskins said, taking another look at Johnson. "May I ask why?"

"I'll explain it when you get back," Wallace replied.

"You were going to fly me out of here anyway, even if I didn't tell you," Johnson said to Wallace as he changed into the flight suit Hoskins brought for him.

"Oh yeah," the Captain said. "Nate Beu is an old friend and he says he's known you longer. I would have done it either way."

"So, why break my balls?"

"I want to know how big a favor he owes me," Wallace grinned.

"One *big* motherfucker, Captain. I'd go for a new car," Rick smiled back. "And thanks for your help." He set the cup down and offered a hand, which Wallace shook.

"You sure you don't want to wash up?"

"No time, sir. Lead on, Major, I still have work to do," he said to Hoskins as they made their way to the flight deck.

"You ever fly back seat?" Hoskins asked.

"I took a cat shot off Eisenhower in a Tomcat about ten years ago. I know the drill," Rick said as he accepted a flight helmet from the Marine. "Let's do it."

Osan Air Base

"He'll be landing shortly," Beu told them. "He caught a ride with a Marine Corps jet."

"It's finally over, Connie," Levy said.

"Not quite," Estevez said. "We still need Holmgren."

"What do the locals say?"

"They're still looking," the FBI man replied.

The Pink Lady

There was an incessant knocking at the door and Kim put the broom down to answer it. She pulled it open a crack. "We're not open yet," she said. "Come back …" And she was cut off by a slap in the face, knocking her to the floor.

Holmgren picked her up by the hair and dragged her over to a chair. "Sit there and shut up," he ordered, waving a pistol around. "Where's your mother?"

"At the market," Kim sobbed. "She'll be back soon."

"Good," he smiled and poured himself a drink.

Osan AB

"We're here," Hoskins said as he pulled the plane to a stop. "I'm putting the canopies up."

"Thanks for the ride, Major," Johnson said as he fed a fresh clip into his forty-five. He climbed out of the rear seat, ran across the wing, and hopped down to the tarmac, running for the maintenance van. The startled airman at the wheel went sheet white when Johnson stuck the pistol in his face. "Do you know where the Pink Lady is?"

"The tit bar?"

"*Yes*," Rick growled.

"Sure do, Sarge," the kid stammered.

"Go there," Rick ordered. "And don't stop for anyone or I *will* kill you."

"You got it." And the young man threw the van in gear.

***

"I'm looking for General Beu," Major Hoskins said from the door of the conference room.

"Yes, Major?" Beu turned form the small knot of people.

"Your boy just hijacked a flightline truck and took off," Hoskins said. "He's going someplace called the Pink Lady."

"What's that, Nate?" Connie asked him.

"It's a topless bar in Osan," Beu said.

"Why in Hell would he go there?"

"It's a long story, but I think we'll find Holmgren there," Beu replied. He signaled to Estevez. "Get as many SPs as you can. Rick's going after Holmgren and he's probably at the Pink Lady."

"How can you be sure," Connie pressed.

"Rick was in love with the owner's daughter when we were stationed here," he explained. "They were going to be married but that never came to be. Maybe Rick thinks she is in danger from Holmgren. Maybe Holmgren knows of his feelings for her."

"I ... I never knew," she said, feeling as if she'd been punched. "I'm going with you."

"It could be dangerous," he countered.

"There was a man killed right outside this fucking door, General," she spat. "How much more dangerous can it get?"

"Fine," Beu surrendered. "But stay out of the way. Rick's frame of mind might not be ... he just saw eleven of his friends killed, Connie."

"Let's go before *I* kill someone," she said and marched off after Estevez.

The Pink Lady

"Go back to the base and send the cops," Johnson said when the van came to a stop. "Thanks for the lift." He stepped out and flipped the safety off his pistol. Looking up, he could see the sky brightening to the east. "What a fucking night," he muttered as he climbed the steps, looking for Yung Shu's van and remembering she always went to the market first thing in the morning. He put the safety back on and holstered the pistol.

"Good morning, Johnson," greeted him as he walked through the doors. Rick turned to see Holmgren holding his daughter like a shield. His first instinct was to go for his pistol, but Holmgren knew that. "I'll kill her if you go for it," he warned.

"D-dad," Kim said in a tiny voice. "Is that you?"

"Yeah, sweetie," he said, his hand twitching near the holster, just waiting for the chance.

"Where are the others?" Holmgren asked.

"Dead," Rick snarled. "I stayed alive just to come back and kill *you*."

"I thought you would be the one to survive, if any of you did. You survived twelve years ago when you shouldn't have," Holmgren spat.

"Well, Colonel, you can end it now," Rick offered. "Let her go and you can kill me here and now."

"Oh no," Holmgren shook his head. "You're going to see me kill your daughter and her mother before I kill you."

"The APs know I'm here," Rick replied. "You don't have time if you want to get away."

"They have the roads blocked leaving town, there is no escape, Johnson. We will all die here today."

And the back door of the club swung open. "Rick?" Yung Shu said as she appeared. And she saw her daughter. "*No!*" And she lunged at Holmgren.

"Yung Shu," Rick gasped. "*Don't* ..." And he saw Holmgren change his aim. Seeing an opening, Johnson drew and fired, too late. Holmgren flew backward as Johnson's shot hit him between the eyes but not before he got off two shots in Yung Shu's direction. He looked over to see her crash over a table.

"*Mother!*" Kim wailed and ran to her, Rick getting there the same time.

"Yung Shu," Rick cradled her in his arms. Blood poured from her shattered chest and her eyes fluttered.

"Remember, Rick, you promised," she said.

"No, mother, you *can't* die," Kim sobbed.

"I love you, angel," was said with her last breath.

"*No!*" Kim shouted.

Johnson set her gently on the floor and took his daughter in his arms, sobbing along with her. Startled when the front doors crashed open, he pushed Kim down, drawing his pistol and taking aim at the four SPs who were pointing M-16s at him.

"Drop it, Sarge," one of them warned.

Connie pushed past them, followed by Beu and Levy, her stomach turning at the carnage around her. She pushed it back down and ran to her husband. "Oh God, Rick," she said as she looked at him.

"Connie?" He said as he lowered the pistol, setting it on the floor. "What the fuck are you doing here?" And Kim peeked out from behind him.

"Who's this?" Connie asked.

"This is my daughter, Connie." And their eyes met, and she knew her questions would be answered later. "That was her mother," he pointed to Yung Shu.

"Come here, honey," Connie said to Kim as she took the girl in her arms. "Let's wait for your dad outside."

Levy went to Holmgren's body, its eyes wide open in surprise. "Holmgren?" He pointed at the corpse.

"Yeah," Johnson said as he rose. "I was too late to save Yung Shu."

"Come on, pal," Beu said as he put an arm around his friend. "Let's get you to a doctor."

"Is it over?" Johnson asked him.

"Yes," Beu said. "It is. It's all over." And they walked out of the club to the waiting car.

Epilogue
Arlington National Cemetery, Arlington, Virginia
Sunday, 1 April 1995

The April rain drummed on the hundred or so umbrellas deployed around the eleven coffins. All eyes were turned toward the President. Rick listened to the man speak of honor, duty, and country. He spoke of madmen and treachery, and the crimes committed in the pursuit of false glory and Rick heard none of it. What Rick Johnson remembered for the rest of his life were the eyes, the eyes of the families, the accusing eyes, directed at him.

Every one of the mourners looked at him at least once, their eyes asking one question: "Why you?" Rick had asked himself that same thing a thousand times over the past few days. Why me?

The only answer that satisfied him was that he was lucky. He was lucky to have Connie, he was lucky to have found Kim so many years after the fact, and most of all, he was lucky to be alive.

He wished he could tell them. Angie Reasoner, with her two teenage sons, standing with stoic grace. Ron Gibbs' blind mother, staring blankly into the rain as the President spoke of her son's valor. Jake Guthrie's son, Jason, a toddler when Rick last saw him, was now a handsome young man. Rick wanted to go to all of them and say, 'I was just lucky'. He couldn't. He just stood there, his arm around Kim, Connie at his side.

The President finished his eulogy. Eleven Air Force Honor Guard teams folded the flags draped upon the coffins. A rifle team rendered the salute. A lone bugler played *Taps*. Rick watched it all as if in a fog.

The sound of rotor blades in the distance made his head turn. A flight of four MH-53J Pave Lows from the 20th Special Operations Squadron flew over in tight formation. Rick felt a chill run up his spine. The four black choppers looked like ghosts as they cut through the overcast.

Rick felt his knees go weak for an instant when four F-16's began their flyby. When they were directly over the graves, the number two aircraft broke formation and shot skyward; the Missing Man formation, an aviator's final tribute to his fallen comrades.

Suddenly, it was over. The President was ushered to his limousine by his Secret Service entourage and the other dignitaries present made their departures as well. Johnson and Beu walked to the coffins to pay their respects, leaving Connie, Alexa, and their daughters standing a respectful distance away.

"Hello, Rick." Angie Reasoner didn't look at him as she passed with her sons.

"I'm sorry, Angie." She turned as if to say something, then changed her mind. She pushed the boys ahead of her as they walked to her car. The other mourners just acknowledged him with their accusing eyes. When they were out of earshot, Rick turned to his friend.

"They despise me, don't they?" Rick asked.

"They will for a while. They are angry that you made it while their loved ones didn't. Subconsciously, they blame you."

"What do I do?"

"You say goodbye to *them*," Beu gestured to the coffins. "And carry on with your life. You know in your heart, as well as I do, that you performed your duty with honor. So did they. You were lucky to get out alive. They weren't. They don't blame you for *anything* and that's what counts, Rick. Just remember that, okay?"

"Thanks, Nate." Rick turned to face the coffins. "Goodbye, gentlemen. It was an honor to serve with you." Rick snapped to attention and saluted. He faced his friend, a tear forming in his eye.

Beu slung an arm over his friend's shoulder and led him to where their wives waited. "Come on, pal. I'll buy you a drink."

***

The two men watched from the hill, a quarter mile away, their umbrellas twitching in the breeze. It was impossible for them to pay their respects during the service, but they could do it from afar.

"It's a shame, isn't it, Boris?" Kosarev turned to his aide.

"What, Marshal?"

"Those young men. All dead. For *what?*"

"They achieved their objective, sir. They died with honor."

"They died unnecessarily, Boris." Kosarev wiped a tear from his eye. "They died because the fools of my generation built those missiles, and the fools of this generation sold them to a madman. That is why they died, Boris."

"You're right, sir. It is a shame."

They turned and walked toward the waiting car.

***

"Are you all right, baby?" Connie asked. They had come to the Sheraton with Nate and Alexa after the funeral. After drinks in the lounge, Rick and Connie retired to their room. They made love passionately, with sleep following shortly after. Both of them were emotionally drained. When Connie awoke, she found him, stark naked and staring at himself in the mirror. "Can I do anything?" She asked him.

"No."

"Do you want a robe? It's chilly in here."

"No."

Standing behind him, Connie looked at the reflection of his face. She knew the look; she'd seen it several times before, always after his nightmares. The 'thousand-yard stare' they call it. She gazed at the angry wound on his shoulder. *That's going to scar,* she thought, and wondered what kind of scars would be left on his psyche.

Connie appraised him objectively. His body had firmed, and he had the look of a warrior in his eyes and suddenly it dawned on her.

"You're staying in, aren't you?"

"If they let me."

"Have you talked to them yet?"

"No."

"I don't have much of a say in this, do I?"

"No, not really."

"I know that you wouldn't be happy as a civilian again. I realize that this is something that you have to do. I love you, Rick, and I'll support you in whatever you decide. I just want you to know that."

"I love you too, Connie. Thanks, that means a lot."

"Why did you go to her?" Connie didn't want to ask Rick that question, but it was out before she knew it. She had to know.

"Because I loved Yung Shu very much. I had the chance to make sure she was all right and I took it. I guess I had to settle with my conscience. I regret that by going there, I probably got her killed."

"But you found Kim. I know that we never wanted children Rick; but she is your daughter and we can't change that. I promise you, that I will love her as my own ... as *our* own. One day, when she has dealt with the loss of her mother, she'll need a mom again. I'll be there for her when she does."

"I love you, Connie." Connie put her arms around him and kissed his cheek. He turned to face her. They embraced, squeezing each other tightly. Nothing more was left to say.

"You're a good man, Rick Johnson," she said, leading him back to bed.

The White House, Washington, D.C., a week later

"Sir, Senior Master Sergeant Richard Johnson reports as ordered," Rick said as he came to a stop in front of the President's desk.

"You're a hero, Johnson," the President said.

"No, sir, just doing the job my country needed me to do."

"Whatever," the President waved it away. "I wanted to personally release you from military service with my thanks. You will be compensated as promised."

"And the families of the other guys, Mr. President?"

"They will be taken care of, Rick," the President assured him.

"Good," Johnson said. "As for my money, you can shove it up your ass."

"What?" The President rose in surprise.

"I don't want it," he said. "While the methods used to secure my cooperation were questionable, the job *needed* to be done. The North Koreans couldn't be allowed to have nukes. I'm no mercenary and I don't want your blood money."

"So, what *do* you want, a medal?"

"I don't collect medals, sir," Rick grinned. "I want a job."

"A job?"

"Yeah, a job. I hear General Beu is going to work over at Langley."

"Yes, I appointed him Deputy Director (Operations) when Mr. Rice was named Director."

"I want to work for the General," Johnson said. "*That's* my payment."

"That's all?" The President asked and Johnson nodded. "What would you do there?"

"Kill the enemies of the United States of course, sir," Rick smiled, and the President saw something in Johnson's eyes that shook him to the core.

The End